Gran and Mr Muckey is the first volume in a quartet entitled *Memory and Imagination.* Through Sajit Contractor, an Anglo-Indian (and the author's literary clone, or alter ego), it covers the experiences of a young boy throughout the late thirties and early forties. It starts in Edgware where he lived in the midst of the Jewish immigrant population, and then progresses through bizarre and hilarious incidents to end Volume One with idyllic schooldays on Exmoor. On the way, Sajit introduces a succession of fascinating characters, foremost among them being his Indian Grandmother and his family's arthritic gardener, Mr Muckey. Sajit throws a completely new light on the wartime 'home front' and his experiences of early racism and his blatant political incorrectness gives one the comforting feeling that maybe all is not yet lost after all.

Also by John Hollands

The Dead, The Dying and The Damned
Able Company (USA Only)
The Gospel According to Uncle Jimmy
Never Marry a Cricketer
Never Marry a Rugby Player
Not Shame The Day
The Exposed

MEMORY AND IMAGINATION
Volume I

Gran and Mr Muckey

The fictionalised memoirs of
SAJIT CONTRACTOR,
an Anglo Indian

John Hollands

EDWARD GASKELL *publishers*

EDWARD GASKELL *publishers*
Cranford House
6 Grenville Street
Bideford
Devon
EX39 2EA

First published 2002

© John Hollands

Illustrations © René Cochlin

isbn 1-898546-52-5

GRAN AND MR MUCKEY

Printed and bound by
Lazarus Press
Unit 7
Caddsdown Business Park
Bideford
Devon
EX39 3DX
www.lazaruspress.com

Dedicated to the memory of
Michael Lamb.
One of the best.

AUTHOR'S NOTE

Gran and Mr Muckey is the first of four volumes, embraced by the title *Memory and Imagination*. This volume covers the period from 1933 to 1944. All four volumes are based on my experiences, aided and abetted by touches of imagination, with locations and timings sometimes altered or transposed, purely to assist the narrative. All characters are fictitious with the exception of Sajit. He is my literary clone, or – if you prefer – my alter ego.

ACKNOWLEDGEMENTS

I am indebted to Lesley Pyne and Paul Willey for their help. I have also gleaned much confirmation of details from: Sir Winston Churchill's War Memoirs; *London A to Z; Finest Hour* by Tim Clayton and Phil Craig; *Spitfire Summer* by Malcolm Brown; and *Children of the Blitz* by Robert Westall.

Introduction

An early memory—My fight against Alzheimer's disease—The use of the ancient art of regression—An assurance of good intent.

My first memory in life is of an act of appalling vandalism. Such wanton destruction was beyond my comprehension. Why was Dad doing it? Why was he destroying our pictures of Sir Oswald Mosley and Herr Adolf Hitler?

Unlike the rest of the family, who were urging him on, I watched in dismay as Mum held the frames over the dustbin and Dad smashed them to smithereens with a claw hammer. Then Dad ripped out the photographs and put a Swan Vesta match to them until they curled into ash and disintegrated, just to make sure the police didn't discover any fragments and piece them together.

I felt a sense of deep betrayal. How could we be so disloyal? Hadn't Dad always said that the partnership between these two great men would be the salvation of civilisation and secure Britain its rightful place at the pinnacle of world power? Their pictures had always held pride of place in the hall, so why were we suddenly ashamed of them? Weren't we prepared to stick to our principles?

Every detail of that incident is crystal clear. It made me realise that everything in the world is far from simple and straightforward, that with adults there are always complications.

In retrospect the memory acts as a catalyst, a trigger mechanism which forces other incidents to the surface, giving me a broader perspective on what shaped my early life. Yet now, sixty years later, when I am at last ready to record these events, my doctor suddenly tells me that I am a clear case of Alzheimer's disease. At least, I think that's what she said. However, there are consolations. She added that Alzheimer's won't inhibit my long-term memories. Only death – which she implied was pretty imminent – will do that. On the other hand, the loss of short-term memories could be a major problem: I might even forget that I'm writing my memoirs, thus adding years to their completion, indeed jeopardising them altogether.

Fortunately, I am an experienced practitioner in the art of regression, so if, at any stage, my memory falters all will not be lost. Not that I will follow the modern trend and use regression to condemn wicked parents for molesting or abusing me, thereby excusing my own deplorable behaviour. I will use it to ensure accuracy. These memoirs are as things were; and if, at times, I appear to perceive events with an all-seeing eye, enabling me to pass oracular judgements, this is attributable to my exhaustive research. Mind you, in some of the less literary publishing houses, where they specialise in politicians' memoirs, such perspicacity is known as 'Old Fart's Prerogative'.

1

A clash of nationalities—Our Jewish neighbours—
Gender domination—Dad's business obsessions—
Mum's Welsh pride.

One of the highlights of my life was studying sociology. My tutor defined it as 'the study of how man's behaviour is moulded by his early environment and the conduct and expectations of those around him'. So that's how I'll start: with my early environment and those around me.

If you were able to zoom in on my life from way up in the sky, as they so often do at the start of epic films, you would think that my situation was ordinary to the point of tedium. First you would see England, then London, then Edgware, then Glendale Avenue and a semi-detached house, Number 49, one among hundreds in a long, long road with identical houses strung out along both sides; all the same design, all the same size, all the same colour, and with the same pint-sized gardens.

At that stage, as you zoom in through a conveniently open window, you would think, 'Oh, God! *Mrs Dale's Diary* all over again. Another every day story of the average boring English family'.

Nothing could be further from the truth. Glendale Avenue was completely untypical of Britain. It was a foreign oasis and provided a foretaste of the cocktail of ethnic culture and racial tensions that would beset the country in future years and contribute to the evolution of the new Britishness of which we try to feel so proud, yet of which we are still so uncertain.

The Contractor family led the way. We were a microcosm of racial friction. Sticking with the film metaphor, if you intruded even further into our house, and you were granted the short-lived miracle of Todd AO Smell-O-Vision, you would be assailed by the odour of vindaloo curry and you'd see a vast, steaming pot of it sitting on a low gas on our cooker. On going into the lounge you'd notice that all the ornaments and pictures betrayed split loyalties between Wales and India. Cobras ready to strike and elephants rearing their trunks stood next to Welsh dolls playing harps; pictures of the Taj Mahal and wood-carved monkeys nestled below cheap prints of Rhosllanerchrugog; small brass temples and statuettes of Bengal Lancers competed with gaudy, hand-painted plates depicting scenes of the Gower coast.

On one end of the mantelpiece was the first lump of coal Grandpa (my maternal Welsh grandfather) extracted from the Maerdy pit, and at the other end was a bottle of Holy Water Gran (my paternal Indian grandmother) had scooped from the Ganges. Gran cursed the coal, saying it symbolised evil Welsh ways, the rape of the land and the pollution of the air. In retaliation, Mum said that to call the water from the Ganges holy was downright blasphemous. Instead, she called it 'international water' on account of all the foreign bodies floating about in it.

The houses clumped around us in Glendale Avenue were in stark contrast. Individually, within the confines of their four walls, the residents were united, but collectively they were as diverse as us, the most polyglot gathering of Jews imaginable – Ashkanazims and Sepharins, Orthodox and Reformists; even atheists, Jews by race only. They all dressed differently, had different sized chips on their shoulders, ate different food, smelt differently, and clung tenaciously to different national traditions from all over Europe. They had moved into Glendale Avenue en masse when it was constructed in the early thirties, the first of a tidal wave of asylum seekers who established an instant Jewish enclave in Edgware, making it more like Judea than a suburb at the heart of the British Empire. How Dad came to buy a house slap-bang in the middle of them, I'll never know.

Apart from the Wales/India divide, the fundamental conflict within our household was gender domination. Mum and Dad both thought they'd been ordained by God to be the head of the household. Because Dad was born and brought up as a native Indian, he was only aware of women having three functions in life: to do as they were told, to comfort and gratify their men folk, and to bear and raise children, preferably male children. On the other hand, Mum was from a mining community in the Rhondda Valley where women ruled supreme. From the very first week of her parents' marriage, her father (Grandpa) had handed over his weekly wage packet to Grandma every Friday night and thereby abdicated all marital power. So to Mum, that's how all married men were expected to behave.

Thankfully, there was one point on which my parents were in accord and it was probably the only thing that kept our family together: our turbulent relationship with our neighbours. Their weird behaviour was something that could be discussed and mulled over with unanimity and amusement, without crossing swords. The fact that Mum and Dad adopted different tactics towards the Jews didn't matter.

Dad had fascist sympathies, born out of admiration for the way Germany and Italy had revitalised their economies. However, he kept a very open mind about other aspects of their activities, notably the fights the blackshirts got into in the East End and their anti-Semitic attitude. He accepted that the Jews were part of an international financial conspiracy, but he never extended his disapproval of this to a personal level. He regarded those among whom we lived as mere pawns and something of a joke, and whilst he was happy to ridicule them he wished them no harm. He was a peaceable man who wanted to live in harmony with everyone. He saw the fascists more as nationalists than Nazis and racist fanatics, and with the Jews in Glendale Avenue his main aim was to demonstrate to them just how much more 'English' he was compared with them, or anyone else in the vicinity, including genuine Englishmen.

He had the considerable advantage of being relatively affluent, thanks to a thriving tyre and battery factory he ran at Lomond Grove, Camberwell Green. Money was never a problem to him and his main avenue for emphasising his Englishness, and his loyalty to king and country, was by championing British industry. He supported any organisation he thought would enhance this cause, be it the British Union of Fascists, the Masons, the CBI, the Institute of British Industry, the Institute of Directors, Moral Rearmament (a big mistake, this one), the Camberwell Chamber of Trade, the Rotary, and even the obscure Buy British Society, of which he was deputy to the assistant publicity director.

As part of their drive to boost Britain, members of the Buy British Society were expected to purchase outstanding British products and inventions and then show them off to their friends, relatives, neighbours and business associates. Dad worked all hours to accomplish this and he spent a small fortune on all manner of things, ranging from fantastic developments to gadgets of no practical use. At one stage he bought a share of a business producing door chimes which played a sizeable part of Elgar's *Pomp and Circumstance March No 1*, an enterprise that collapsed when the London Philharmonic threatened to sue for breach of copyright.

Gran and Mr Muckey

His best domestic purchase was a television set. It was the only one in Glendale Avenue. Indeed, he had it from the very first day of transmission and I well remember a remarkable assortment of people piling into our lounge to watch one of the early programmes. Due to a series of technical hitches our guests weren't impressed. After we'd stared at the blank screen for half an hour, the best the BBC could offer was a Mickey Mouse cartoon which had featured at the Odeon the week before, and even this came to an abrupt halt halfway through, leaving a close-up of torn film and the sound of loud groaning.

When Dad bought a new car his efforts to impress our neighbours were far more successful. He drove his shining new Wolseley 12 saloon up and down the avenue God knows how many times and there was no doubt that it was easily the best car for miles around. He also acquired a gleaming gas-operated refrigerator and this entailed inviting guests around every night for a fortnight and serving them drinks clinking with enough ice to sink the *Titanic*. The only time Dad's efforts to publicise his purchases were thwarted was when he bought the latest automatic washing machine with an electrically operated mangle. Once it was safely installed, Mum made it quite plain that there was no way she was going to give demonstrations and thereby have people think she was setting up shop as a washerwoman.

Sometimes, Dad's determination to impress everyone with his latest British purchases backfired on him. The best example of this was the Frank Whittle Self-Igniting, Smokeless Garden Incinerator.*

* Sir Frank Whittle, the famous aviation pioneer and inventor of the jet engine, had nothing whatever to do with this incinerator. Its name was all part of a Japanese ploy to secure an unfair advantage in international trade. Everyone knew that anything made in Japan was junk, so the crafty swine resorted to naming towns and villages in Japan 'England', or 'Birmingham', or 'London', and then prefixing their shoddy goods with 'Made in....'. This duplicity reached the height of bad taste when the owner of an engineering company in Osaka named his third child (a girl!) 'Frank Whittle' to enhance the sales of his potentially lethal incinerator. All this came to light when Dad finally condescended to read the instructions. Immediately, the author betrayed the origins of the incinerator by his inability to handle his 'L's and his 'R's, the instructions referring to '...keeping the blacket ligid and the lubber tubing flee of obstluctions with the crips and frints plovided...'

The incinerator was based on the latest petrol injection technology which made it especially good at burning off damp refuse. It involved the use of a two-gallon can of petrol and a long length of rubber tubing. This had various kinks, clips, and valves along its length and, at the very end, two enormous flints which, when crashed together, produced a spark big enough to kick-start a London double-decker bus.

Dad made sure that as many neighbours as possible saw this ingenious device by giving Carter Patterson an incomplete address, forcing the driver to make several enquiries along the avenue, and in the course of being helpful the Jews made sure they discovered what the Contractors were now up to. They needn't have taken the trouble for later that evening Dad strolled up and down the avenue explaining to everyone he met, or who happened to be tending their gardens and were within hailing distance, that thanks to the brilliance of Frank Whittle's new British invention, the incessant bonfires that polluted the avenue every weekend would soon be a thing of the past.

"Just watch my new Frank Whittle and you'll see what I mean..."

Politely, they all promised to keep an eye out.

The instruction manual warned against impatience, but Dad was far too keen to get on with things to worry about reading the instructions. He only ever read instructions when all else failed. He soon had the petrol flowing and he kept pumping away until the whole contraption was flooded. Even though my brothers and I pointed this out, Dad couldn't see the likelihood of a major disaster. All he could see – and with great delight – were the long lines of Jewish faces peering over the fences on either side of the garden. He waved to them cheerfully and called out: "Watch the birdie!"

However, it wasn't the birdie they needed to watch. It was the incinerator lid. When Dad operated the two flints there was an almighty explosion and the lid soared thirty feet into the air. It was then caught by the wind and zoomed off like a flying saucer, eventually crashing into a garden five houses along. Whilst this would have served as a dire warning to most – and it certainly scared the shit out of the Jews, all of whom disappeared in a trice – it merely encouraged Dad. Always a young boy at heart, he had no comprehension of danger. Danger, to him, was an experience; and experience was the essence of life – a philosophy he considered to be the hallmark of all true Englishmen. It was therefore quite consistent that Dad looked upon a flying incinerator lid as a bit of a lark and he just couldn't wait to have another go. In fact, we ended up having numerous goes. He seemed to think that he'd discovered some new kind of propulsion and he was determined to establish the optimum flight potential of the lid. He even bent the small chimney over flat to close the hole and thereby enhance the thrust and reduce the wind resistance while in flight.

These thoroughly irresponsible experiments continued for an hour or more and, by the time Mum discovered what was going on and put a stop to it, it was established that the optimum flight was seven gardens. The only snag was that after each flight it fell to me, as the youngest, to retrieve the lid. I wouldn't have minded asking for my ball back, but asking for my incinerator lid back, which I was obliged to mention might still be very hot, took some gall. Yet the Jews, bless them, always gave it back.

They weren't in the least impressed by Dad's new British invention but they were prepared to humour him, even though several expressed their concern with remarks such as: "Sonny, please be asking your Papa to be vatching out for mine greening haus."

I think they regarded the Frank Whittle Incinerator as just another British quirk they would have to put up with, something on a par with body-line bowling, in which cricketers threw rock-hard balls at each other's heads, and Rugby Union, in which the elite of the nation's manhood gathered together in small clusters throughout the country every Saturday afternoon and proceeded to knock seven bells out of each other in thick mud.

No doubt they reasoned that since they'd opted to live in England they were obliged to endure the natives' foibles, in the same way as foreigners living in Spain could hardly complain if, when doing their weekly shopping, they were confronted by a herd of bulls charging down the high street. After all, flying incinerator lids and charging bulls were small beer compared with concentration camps.

Whilst Dad was concerned with proving his Englishness, Mum had no such hang-ups. Her Welshness was never in question and to her the superiority of the Welsh was so self-evident that it didn't even have to be mentioned, let alone flaunted. She just stuck to everything the way it was in Wales, especially when it came to discipline within her house. I used the words 'her house' advisedly for in Wales wives ruled supreme in the house. To them, their houses were an end in themselves, the manifestation of a family's character and standing in the world, certainly something far beyond a utilitarian object designed and furnished for the convenience and comfort of the inhabitants.

At Edgware I was never woken by a gentle shake, or a kiss from a loving parent, but by the sound of Mum commencing her daily chores, cleaning and polishing the front door and the knocker, a task which entailed slamming the former and crashing the latter, a deliberate attempt to rouse the entire neighbourhood, based in the philosophy: 'I'm up, everyone should be up'.

From dawn until bedtime she strove after a dust and germ-free environment. "Sanitization is what we need," she'd shrill, as she paced about the house: "Sanitization!"

Every morning at eleven o'clock precisely, she went around the house readjusting the wicks on the ten Air Freshners that were strategically sited throughout the house, the epicentre of these evil devices being in the kitchen where no less than three of them fought a losing battle against the cauldron of curry. Once every wick had been extended by exactly half an inch, Mum would do another grand tour of the house, sniffing the air appreciatively, but to the rest of us it was like living in a public lavatory.

I doubt if any other children in the entire world were forced to wash as frequently as we were, and on countless occasions I recall being banished to the bathroom to wash my hands, with Mum yelling up the stairs after me: "And don't forget to wash the soap when you've finished."

Likewise, whenever my two brothers and I ventured out of the house we exuded a healthy aroma of carbolic, and when we went off to school, Mum would still be brushing our blazers as we went down the avenue.

What surprised our neighbours most of all was that every day, without fail, Mum washed the house down with a hose pipe, as though it was a car. In the Rhondda the terraced houses lay in the path of the prevailing sou'wester, which meant that unless they were hosed down every day they became black with coal dust off the adjacent tips. It was pointless to tell Mum, as Dad frequently did, that there was no coal dust in Edgware.

Mum's iron discipline and her success in keeping the house in pristine condition was achieved by a plethora of rules. She was a great one for rules just so long as she devised them and others obeyed them. These rules came in three categories: basic rules, principle rules, and personal rules.

The first were verbal and seemingly endless, being added to on a minute-by-minute basis as circumstances demanded.

Principle rules were clearly established and constant. They were written out in capital letters in red crayon and stuck on the side of the refrigerator. They specified which domestic articles were not to be used or touched, which rooms must remain undisturbed, and other antisocial activities which were strictly forbidden, including placing hot cups on polished surfaces; entering the house without removing shoes; sitting or leaning on cushions; stepping on the deep-pile hearth rug in the drawing room; and – worst crime of all – tracing pictures on windows covered in condensation and drawing match-stick men on the lavatory wallpaper.

Personal rules concerned hygiene, everything from washing one's neck to not wetting the bed. They included keeping one's hands away from one's private parts and not splashing pee over the toilet seat. Dozens of other off-putting childish habits were included but since everyone the world over knows about these from personal experience, I'll say no more.

As far as punishments went, the flouting of basic rules was dealt with summarily, usually with a smart clip around the ear. Transgressing principle rules met with something far more telling: starvation by the withdrawal of at least one meal. The breaking of personal rules resulted in a cruel punishment which I can only conclude was inspired by some kind of deep-seated sexual vendetta on Mum's part. The culprit was stripped naked and banished to the empty box room at the front of the house. This had a window which reached down to within a foot or two of the floor and was about the same size as the bamboo cages in which the Japanese incarcerated prisoners-of-war serving solitary confinement. The box room had no curtains and in hours of darkness Mum insisted that the light was kept on, thus creating the sort of affect more often seen in the red-light area of Amsterdam, albeit with more decorative occupants.

James (my 'middle' brother) and I coped with this punishment easily enough: he merely sat with his back to the window and read a book, whereas I put on displays of Charles Atlas exercises for the benefit of the two young Jewish girls who lived opposite. With the eldest of us – Brother Nothing – it was different. He was very sensitive about nudity at the best of times and at his age (approaching puberty) it was a particularly vindictive punishment that scarred him for life. However, these punishments did not go unchallenged. Dad was always on our side and they sent him into frequent rages. If he returned home to see the light on in the box room, or found one of us missing, he'd yell: "Christ! He's not in the Black Hole of Ferndale again, surely?"

He would then leap up the stairs three at a time and release the unfortunate victim. If we were all present and correct when Dad returned, the first thing he did was go into the kitchen, rip the list of rules off the fridge, and consign it to the dust bin. Just as regularly, Mum reinstated a new list as soon as he left for work at Camberwell Green. At weekends lists went up and down like yo-yos.

2

Brother Nothing and the Wolseley 12—Brother James, the scholar—Gran and the call of India—Meeting the milkman and dear old Wally—Rows about Dad's nationality.

As the eldest son, Brother Nothing had instinctive arrogance. He assumed total ownership and automatic authority, traits he retained throughout his life. Although he rose to considerable eminence as a barrister, no one ever understood him, least of all his three wives, none of whom had the slightest difficulty in convincing divorce judges that they were the victims (respectively) of unreasonable behaviour, mental cruelty, and physical abhorrence. The rest of us were equally victims of these shortcomings but as blood-relatives we had no alternative but to grin and bear them.

Everyone said that as a child Brother Nothing was mousy-looking, but this wasn't a reference to his colouring, which was strictly of the tar brush. It was because of his pointed chin, his twitching nose, his protruding, chisel-like teeth, and his elongated and flapping ears which were of an odd, near-transparent texture. At birth Brother Nothing was the apple of Dad's eye, the offspring through whom the Contractor family would make their mark in the world. Whilst he was still at the stage where he could only defecate, urinate, gurgle, and waggle his arms and legs, Dad fantasised over him to such an extent that he was convinced he would eventually become The Rt Hon Sir Charles Contractor KG, the first coloured Prime Minister of Great Britain. However, as soon as he started to talk, such optimism swiftly evaporated and by the time I was born, Dad was looking to his second son, James, to fulfil his ambitions, now somewhat reduced in grandeur, his sights on Chancellor of the Exchequer.

Brother Nothing wasn't his real name, of course. Strictly speaking he was Charles, a moniker bestowed upon him for its ring of class. I coined the name Brother Nothing. It came spontaneously, a classic case of 'out of the mouths of babes'. The reason was simple enough: everything about him was totally negative. If I asked him a question I was guaranteed to get one of the following answers: "No", "Never", "Nothing", "Not likely", "Don't know", "Nowhere", and, "Couldn't care less!" It was only when he lost his temper that he abandoned these monosyllabic negatives and reverted to shouts of "Shut up, squirt!" or, "I'll knock your block off!"

Another thing about him was that if anyone ever contradicted him by saying, "Not at all", he would retort, "Yes at all."

This always left me nonplussed, which was his intention, of course. It was all bound up with the fact that he was a bully and loved to dominate people, or – as he put it – squash them; and having squashed them he would crow: "KCYS!" (Kindly Consider Yourself Squashed).

My parents found him just as negative as I did but for a long time they refused to admit it, and even when they bowed to the inevitable they excused his behaviour by saying he would grow out of it. However, by the time he was a teenager they'd got so fed up with his 'Nothings' and 'Nowheres' that they threatened him with a good tanning if he didn't pull himself together. Even when Dad proved this to be no idle threat and gave him a dose of his leather belt, it had no effect on Brother Nothing and I could never decide whether this stubbornness was guts or plain stupidity.

Brother Nothing was several years older than me and the thing that surprised me most about him was his lack of normal interests. He didn't model with Plasticine, he declined to play with Dad's fantastic Hornby railway set, or his Meccano collection. He didn't even have any lead soldiers. However, he did have a passion: our car. It was hardly a normal interest because he never enthused over cars generally, or played with toy cars, or even collected number plate numbers as did other kids of a moronic bent. It was purely an unhealthy love affair with our Wolseley 12.

As a family status symbol the Wolseley was supreme. After the fiasco with the Mickey Mouse cartoon, our television was seen as a toy that would never catch on, whereas the Wolseley had real class. Even Mum, who knew nothing about cars except that they took you from A to B and back again, boasted about it all the time. For some reason she picked on the most obscure items to brag about. She always emphasised that it had four doors and how the tyres were pure Dunlop, as though tyres had pedigrees like dogs. Even when she tried to curb her swanking she only made thing worse by revealing her ignorance.

"Mind you," she'd say, pretending to be modest, "the Wolseley's sun roof isn't too clever. It's operated manually... by hand. . . I'm surprised a company that makes such lovely socks can't do better than that."

Fortunately, the Wolseley didn't have much competition in Glendale Avenue. According to Dad, the Jews were far too busy investing their money in industrial consortiums designed to undermine the financial fabric of Europe to splash out on decent cars. There were a few who'd had a rush of blood and allowed their greed to take precedence over their master-plan of subversion, but this avarice was tempered by discretion and they never aspired to anything better than Austin 7s, and – as everyone knew – Austin 7s were only made late on Friday afternoons. What's more, they only had two doors, mongrel tyres, and no sun roof. They were such bad starters that extensive use of the starter handle was necessary. Often, as Dad ate his breakfast, he would glance out of the window and remark: "Mr Cohen is winding up his toy car again." Then he'd go outside, start the Wolseley with one touch of the button, and call out to Mr Cohen: "Morning Izzy! Careful you don't break the rubber band."

The Wolseley was seldom kept in the garage. When not in use it stood at the curb-side in front of the house, a display of pure ostentation on Dad's part which cried out: "Beat this, you buggers!"

It was also parked there to placate Brother Nothing. His greatest pleasure in life was pretending to drive the Wolseley. If Dad put it in the garage, Nothing threw a tantrum. Only once did Dad refuse to give in to him and he soon regretted it. It was raining so hard that he garaged the car and told Nothing he could just as easily play his games inside. Nothing retreated to the garage in tears and since it was dark inside he switched the Wolseley's lights on, full beam. Of course, when called in for dinner he forgot to turn them off and the battery ran down.

When Dad couldn't start the Wolseley the next morning it put him in a really black mood, and when Mr Cohen called out: "Vot's the mattering, Mr Contractor? Your vagon busting its rubber orchestra?", he turned puce with anger.

Worse followed: as he stormed indoors he shouted: "The bloody battery is flat..."

"Oh dear," sympathised Mum. "What shape should it be?"

The Wolseley was black, a bad colour for keeping clean, and since it was a showpiece on the curb-side, my brothers and I were responsible for keeping it in pristine condition. Brother Nothing was the self-appointed supervisor, James was responsible for the inside, and as the youngest I got the dirty work, cleaning and polishing the outside, one of the few things I wasn't too young for.

It was whilst supervising James and me that Brother Nothing did most of his driving. Being a short-arse, he couldn't see over the steering wheel but that never deterred him. With his lower jaw stuck out he would make all sorts of disgusting noises and spit and dribble copiously as he imitated an internal combustion engine, all the time tugging at the steering wheel and crashing the gears. If he glanced in the rear-view mirror and saw one of our Jewish neighbours approaching in an Austin 7 he would wait until it was right on top of him and then shoot his right arm out of the window, the perfect signal for 'I'm pulling out'. There would be a horrendous squealing of tyres followed by a flow of Yiddish which we were very fortunate not to understand.

As always, Brother Nothing was very secretive about his driving. He would never tell anyone where he imagined he was going or where he imagined he had been. Any normal kid would have admitted to racing around Brooklands, or winning Le Mans, but Nothing simply stuck to, "Nowhere" and then added menacingly, "MYOB!"

However, he wasn't just sitting there making rude noises. Occasionally, he would jump out, pull the bonnet side-panel open, and make a few fine adjustments to the engine, like ripping off the plug leads. At other times he would leap out, dash into the garage and re-emerge with Dad's spare can of petrol. He would pour the entire contents into the tank, throw the empty can aside, and jump back in: a refuelling stop accomplished in record time.

It was all innocent enough and wouldn't have mattered except that it added to the friction with Mr Cohen. Brother Nothing rarely, if ever, replaced the plug leads in the right order so that when Dad started the engine in the morning it coughed and backfired alarmingly, giving Mr Cohen the satisfaction of saying: "Your vagon having zer vapours again, Mr Contractor...?"

On the other hand, Dad was one of those proud owners who kept a meticulous record of the Wolseley's miles-per-gallon performance, and when, to his delight, he discovered that he was doing 40 miles to the gallon instead of the specified 25, he showed his evidence to Mr Cohen and gloated triumphantly.

"What about that then, Izzy?" he kept saying. "What about that?"

Mr Cohen went green with envy. His Austin 7 only did 22 miles to the gallon and that included being towed back to garages.

What Brother Nothing loved most about the Wolseley was that the police used them. Indeed, the Metropolitan Police used nothing else and it was such a distinctive car that, apart from Inspector Lockhart's Central Division, they didn't even bother to attach police signs. However, as every crook knew only too well, the distinguishing mark of Wolseleys was their illuminated signs at the top of their smart, chrome radiators. When their lights were on, 'Wolseley' shone forth like a beacon, which meant that wherever Dad went in the dark he was mistaken for the police. That really tickled Brother Nothing.

James was four years older than me and he possessed uncanny intelligence. No one was ever surprised by this due to the incredible size of his head. His features were normal and reasonably attractive, but his cranium was vast. It had a great bulge at the back, and there was no doubt that the brain inside was in direct proportion. What made people nervous of him (or, more accurately, anxious for him) was that his oversized head waggled about as though enjoying a life of its own. It lolled backwards and forwards, and from side to side, on the end of a thin, stalky neck, and it put everyone in mind of a spinning top in the throes of exhaustion. It was so alarming that I never once heard Brother Nothing threaten him with, "I'll knock your block off!" because it could so easily have worked.

As brothers, Nothing and James were very close and the only time I can recall them falling out was over the car. James was far too adult to indulge in imaginary driving, but he had his heart set on being allowed, if only once in a while, to sit in the front seat on our Sunday drives into the country – marvellous trips which included cream teas in the garden of an ex-colonial administrator supplementing his pension. However, for James such a privilege was out of the question. Brother Nothing monopolised the front seat as though by divine right. Even Mum had to give way to him. One Sunday, an hour before we set off, James put a notice on the front seat: "Bagged by James. By order."

This sent Nothing into the biggest wobbly I've ever witnessed. There were tears, screams, stamping feet, and threats to kick James's backside down the Edgware Road to Marble Arch and back again, the whole performance culminating with Brother Nothing declaring that if he was consigned to the back seat he would be sick over everyone else. This was recognised as no idle threat. It was just the kind of thing he would do. So he got his way. This rankled with James for years. It probably still does.

By the age of eight James was well into foreign languages with good French, some German, and a smattering of his latest interest, Swahili. He was fascinated by physics and chemistry, to say nothing of obscure subjects such as why the German Zeppelins had been a failure during the Great War. In his thirst for knowledge he would often interrupt television programmes and confront Dad with questions such as: "Dad, what do you really think of Albert Einstein?"

James read copiously and liked to commandeer Brother Nothing's school text books. The authors I adored, like Richmal Crompton and Arthur Ransome, he'd discarded years before but when he was in a good mood I got him (against Mum's orders) to read me stories of William, Ginger and the others and excerpts from *Swallows and Amazons*: sheer bliss.

As for myself, I will not bore you with a synopsis of my character. You must make up your mind about me as you read these memoirs. I will, however, make brief mention of

Lucky, my dog, who I considered to be an integral part of me, a feeling that was entirely mutual. He was a stray who had attached himself to us when we first moved into Glendale Avenue. He'd tried just about everyone else in the avenue first, but they'd all booted him out. When he came to us he was so desperate that he just stuck and refused to take no for an answer.

He was as black as pitch and a genuine Heinz 57. He was of indeterminate age and during an obviously eventful life he'd been involved in numerous fights, to say nothing of altercations with cars and motor cycles, all of which he hated and attacked in the grand manner of cavalry by means of a frontal assault. He'd come off worst in all these fracas and was the most beaten-up and handicapped dog you were ever likely to come across. His long tail had been driven over so many times that the end section was limp and hung straight down. His rear, left leg had been broken and was so misshapen that he was never able to use it, for all intents and purposes making him a three-legged dog. He was blind in his left eye, deaf in his right ear, and had several bald patches about his body through fighting his principal enemy, a bulldog from Ashcombe Gardens. The only thing in his favour was that he'd never been castrated. That's why Dad christened him 'Lucky', and he certainly made the most of his luck, being a father fifty or sixty times over.   Dogs of his ilk popped up all over Edgware, their parenthood betrayed not only by their looks but also by their keenness for a good fight.

The luminary in our household was Gran. She and I were great pals. Maybe it was because I was named Sajit as a favour to her. Also, she knew that I was an unplanned and unwanted addition to the family and that Mum – having resigned herself to bearing me – would much rather have had a girl. Gran, with her Indian background, appreciated the value of boys and this, linked to her general animosity towards Mum, gave us an inexorable link – one which inevitably made us the odd ones out.

Gran made Dad's claim to be a thoroughbred Englishman look pretty ridiculous. All of us – apart from Mum – were clearly coloured even though, in the manner of a paint-colour sample card, we got a shade lighter as we went down the scale. Gran was at the top of the card: mahogany-brown, as wrinkled as a walnut, with gums bright red from chewing betel nuts. She always dressed in a multicoloured sari with no midriff, showing off a large jewel in her belly button which matched the coloured spots on her forehead and nose. She was in her early sixties but to me she looked more like eighty-five, and all this added to her sinister mystique as far as our neighbours were concerned. Had it not been for her presence I think the Jews would have been happy to excuse the colour of the Contractors as a mere blip in our genetic engineering, but Gran certainly put the kibosh on that. She made things worse by refusing to make any concessions. She went out of her way to emphasis her heathen links by making salaams to anyone she met and refusing to speak English to anyone outside the family, bar visiting tradesmen.

The final affront to the Jews was that she wasn't even a member of an interesting species. If she'd been a Red Indian, or an Aztec Indian, or even a West Indian, then that would have sparked some interest; but she was no more than a common or garden Indian Indian, and although the Jews had only been in England a year or two, they considered the presence of a colonial Indian to be the thin edge of the wedge, something that lowered the general tone of an otherwise salubrious district and played havoc with the property prices.

In particular, Jewish children didn't know what to make of her. The younger ones ran screaming as soon as they saw her, convinced they'd happened upon the dreaded Bogey Woman; while the older and braver boys, members of a gang aspiring to be hooligans, would creep up on our house from the open ground at the rear and prowl around, seeking her out, only to run in terror when she stuck her head out of an upstairs window and cursed them in shrill Hindi.

The net result of all this was that malicious rumours about Gran and what went on in our household were legion. These rumours irritated Dad no end, particularly the nonsense they spread about us keeping a pet mongoose in the garden shed to stop our cobra escaping from the bathroom. Also, their snide remarks about the smell of curry, and their speculation about our other eating habits (which I'll touch on shortly), soon drove him to retaliate.

Every Saturday morning he would lie in wait for the visiting tradesmen and then harangue them with stories of how the Jews were squeezing the lifeblood out of Europe. First the postman, then the 'Stop-me-and-buy-one' ice-cream man, and finally the Betterware salesman, would have to listen patiently as Dad quoted great chunks out of *Mein Kampf*. He even had slips of paper inserted in the relevant pages for easy reference and I could see by the expressions on their faces that they were completely convinced, just as I was.

Gran egged him on without being too obvious, but her speciality was to stir up trouble among the younger trades-men. She told the paper boy that Jewish men wore skull caps to prevent the hot air they talked escaping from the top of their heads, and she persuaded the butcher's boy that the Jewish men with long beards were members of a secret nudist camp in Golders Green. The young fellow who rode on the back of the Advance Laundry van, and who delighted the local girls by swinging about like a chimpanzee on the rope hanging from the back of the van's roof, was warned by Gran that if he got too friendly with a Jewish girl and ended up marrying her, the elders of her synagogue would insist that he was castrated. The lad was pretty sure that she meant circumcised but either way he was determined not to be deprived of anything – big, small, vital or disposable. What he had, he intended to hold on to, and eventually he disappeared, never to be seen again.

In all things, Gran was utterly convincing. She was such a good storyteller that I believed every word she uttered and I suppose this was what made her such a great influence on my early life. Her stories were always about India and they created within me a bond with her other world. I saw tears of pleasure welling in her eyes as she spoke of the heat and the dust; the beggars and the stoic acceptance of hunger and poverty; the colourful markets and the teeming mass of humanity struggling to exist; and above all the man-eating tigers that roamed the remote villages and the holy cows which were allowed to wander at will. As she imitated characters from her past and broke back into her native Hindi, she sparked off in my unformed mind a picture of romance and adventure and danger, a combination which made me determined one day to sample the diversity of such a vast and struggling country.

I came to regard India as my spiritual home. I always put it down to an inborn instinct but now, with hindsight, I realise that Gran was manipulating me. She impressed upon me that I could never deny or discard my true origins and her crowning and convincing argument was to tell me to listen to Dad as he hummed or whistled to himself, and to note that it was always Indian music, never European.

"In his heart he never stops thinking about India," she would whisper to me. "And it will always be the same with you, Sajit."

Then she would smile with satisfaction, convinced I was soaking in every word, and that India would forever draw me like a magnet. In short, Gran was as crafty as the monkeys she described frolicking in the blue-blossomed Jacaranda trees that formed a sun-leaking parasol over the avenues of Simla.

Gran never mentioned that in India she was an Untouchable and therefore suffered far more than most. Sometimes, I think I should be writing her story, not mine, and perhaps one day I will, but for now I will gloss over her early days. Suffice to say that she seized the chance to come to England, knowing that however hard the transition might prove, it was her only chance of spending her final years in physical comfort.

It was a year or two before I was born that Gran arrived in England and things were obviously hectic enough for Mum without the additional burden of someone of a different religion, race, and culture. For example, Mum not unnaturally expected her to partake of her Welsh home cooking, of which Welsh cakes, Welsh rarebit, and leek soup were her specialities; but whenever Gran tried these delicacies they brought on sustained bouts of chronic diarrhoea, and with two young children in the house her need to monopolise the toilet was out of the question. So Gran got her way and a cauldron of curry stood permanently on our cooker. It was kept on a very low gas as though, for some reason, Gran might need instant access to it. All day long it bubbled and plopped and spat and rumbled like a mud spring at Rotorua.

When Mum got really browned off with Gran she would stand over the cauldron, stare into it, and chant: "Double, double, toil and trouble, fire burn and curry bubble, warts sprout and hair to stubble..."

She would then cackle with glee, imitating Shakespeare's witches, and this somehow calmed her: a sort of Welsh equivalent to holding one's breath and counting to ten.

Mutual irritation between the two women peaked early on. In the evenings, once Brother Nothing and James were in bed, Dad, Mum and Gran would follow the British routine of sitting around the radio to listen uncritically to anything that was dished up. Gran adapted to this easily enough, but what she couldn't stand was Mum's custom (ingrained into her since early girlhood) of knitting. To Mum, knitting was second nature. She would never dream of sitting down without using her hands, and there was always an embryonic garment on her lap, stretching towards her knees. She was a beautiful knitter, her stitches as smooth as any machine knitting, and she was so fast that her needles clashed like foils in an Errol Flynn duel: clickety-click, clickety-click … on and on it went with the rhythmical certainty of a speeding train.

The noise sent Gran ballistic. To her it was like the high-pitched buzz that tinnitus sufferers find so tormenting. She would make frequent appeals for a little respite, but the more she objected the faster and louder Mum clashed her needles. Eventually, Gran would opt out from the family circle, retire to a corner of the room, and seek solace from yoga exercises, during the course of which she went into a meditational trance which banished all the clickety-clicking. First, she would adopt the headstand position, then the arm and leg stretch position, and finally she would relax in the plough position which, although designed to improve the elasticity of the spine, looked (to Mum especially) alarmingly like the missionary position.

On numerous occasions Mum suggested to Gran that she should limber up somewhere else, her bedroom perhaps; to which Gran suggested that an even better idea would be for Mum to do her knitting elsewhere, in *her* bedroom, perhaps. After such exchanges, Mum swivelled her chair around so that she couldn't see what Gran was up to, but she could never dispel the suspicion that her antics were all part of a heathen ritual to call-up the spirit of one of her ancestors. Such a prospect sent Mum pale and made her shiver and lose concentration. The radio jokes of Arthur Askey and Stinker Murdoch went in one ear and out the other and her knitting became jerky and uneven. She sought Dad's support by showing him what was happening, but he retained his neutrality by observing: "Never mind, it'll look better when it's pressed."

Eventually, this became a family joke. Whenever any of us made a complete mess of something, there would be a chorus of, "Never mind, it'll look better when it's pressed."

*****

Gran and Mr Muckey

Gran rarely went out of the house. She said she had no desire to but we all knew that Dad had told her to stay indoors as much as possible to minimise our Indian background. On the occasions when she did sally forth she and I were always alone in the house. Normally, I would never have been an accessory to defying Dad's instruction, but Gran bribed me. She knew my weaknesses only too well: chocolate buttons and laziness. The chocolate buttons were taken care of at the corner shop and my laziness was indulged by promising me a ride in my old push chair. Really, this push chair should have been thrown away for I was too old and big for it; but the truth was that Mum was the fertile type of female prone to spasms of broodiness, hence her refusal to discard the accoutrements of childbirth. So although my old push chair still cluttered up the porch, and gave Mum great comfort, one of her principles rules was: 'Sajit will not ride in his push chair. He will walk like all other able-bodied people.'

Consequently, when Gran promised me a long ride in it she found me a willing accomplice. The trips were supposed to be to the local recreation ground so that I could play football, but this goal was never achieved. Instead, the trips were always very short and ended with a wild dash back home, the recreation ground forgotten.

First I was strapped into the push chair and then off we went to the corner shop for two quarter-pound bags of chocolate buttons. Riding in the push chair, without the fag of walking, and with nothing to do but look around, I had no trouble in spotting how the lace curtains of the houses we approached were pulled aside and our progress monitored. Then, as we left houses behind us, how the women would come out to their drives to stare after us, discussing us quite openly, not only with their immediate neighbours but with those across the other side of the road who were observing us in exactly the same way. Houses which I could have sworn were empty, with everyone at work, sprang to life.

This great interest in us wasn't inspired by racial prejudice but by a very natural curiosity to see what happened when we came across Mr Harper, the Express Dairy Milkman. Mr Harper made his deliveries from a horse-drawn milk float stacked high with perspiring gold and silver-topped bottles. His horse, Wally, was a lovely old fellow, a chestnut with the most becoming brown eyes, yellow teeth, grey whiskers, and withering halitosis. As soon as Gran spotted Wally coming down the avenue the push chair surged forward. Wally was always pleased to see us and as he lowered his head to get a good look at me, I would stroke his muzzle. Then Gran prompted me to feed him one of the bags of chocolate buttons and she chipped in with a full tin of Mum's Welsh cakes.

This combination worked as a laxative on Wally and within a few more deliveries down the avenue, he would raise his luxurious tail, fart a little, and then drop a colossal dollop. At least, to me it was colossal, although I dare say that to Gran, with her experience of elephants, Wally's efforts were pretty feeble.

Feeble or colossal, Gran never failed to hotfoot it back to the scene of the steaming action. She'd whip out a coal scuttle shovel secured to the side of the push chair, and with one deft motion she'd scoop the dollop into her shopping bag. Thank heavens, she never actually did any shopping, but the neighbours weren't to know that. Judging by the looks they gave us as we sped back home, and the way they scurried back indoors as we approached them, they were convinced the Indians in Number 49 supplemented their diet with horse shit. They knew it wasn't for fuel because all the houses had gas heating, nor could it be for manuring the garden because we had no real garden. That had long since been concreted over back and front, not only to prevent any further incinerator incidents, but because washing it down with a hose at the same time as the house was a lot less messy than weeding flower beds and cutting grass.

Gran and Mr Muckey

So what else could the neighbours think it was for?

What they didn't know was that Gran was a very keen gardener who kept magnificent window boxes on the ledge of her bedroom window, at the rear of the house. She specialised in Sweet Williams and such was their splendour that they could have been easy winners at the annual Edgware Flower Show. Gran once put an artistic display of them on the dining room table and so keen was I to give credit where credit was due that I asked Dad: "What do you think of Gran's Sweet Wally's?"

My brothers, who were well aware of how such spectacular results were achieved, burst into giggles and when Dad demanded to know what was going on, Brother Nothing for once had our full support and my undying gratitude by responding with his usual: "Nothing."

"Nothing?" exploded Dad. "You're laughing at nothing? Are you an idiot?"

"MYOB," replied Brother Nothing, never one to be intimidated.

That got him a good tanning with Dad's leather belt and there was much piping of the eye; but at least Dad's anger had been diverted from the real issue. Had he discovered what Gran had been up to he would have died of shame.

I loved Gran dearly, but the others didn't and they responded to her in diverse ways. Dad tolerated her because she was, after all, his mother, and it did him credit that even though there was no great love between them he couldn't stand the thought of her being left to rot in India as an Untouchable.

Brother Nothing simply ignored her and James regarded her condescendingly. He usually addressed her in his newly acquired smattering of Swahili, the quality of his geography failing to match his linguistics. Gran was the stubborn type who wasn't going to be patronised by anyone, so she replied in Hindi, thus creating an interesting situation in which they had quite lengthy conversations with neither of them having the slightest idea of what the other was talking about. James would eventually conclude matters by reverting to English: "How very interesting. Thank you, Grandmother."

Gran thought he was too clever by half and kept suggesting to Mum that she should have him examined. She never specified by whom, since the only word, or term, she knew to cover the situation was 'head shrinker' and even she had enough sensitivity to avoid suggesting that.

However, the real trouble came with Mum. That's when sparks flew like fireworks. Mum loathed Gran on four counts. First, her crass ignorance in claiming that India was superior to Wales; secondly, because she reported her to Dad every time she broke something or did something wrong; thirdly, her habit of disappearing into the toilet with a tin can of water and how she urged her grandsons to do likewise; and fourthly because she would keep dragging up the question of Dad's nationality.

Normally, one would assume that the nationality of the head of the family would be beyond dispute, and I'll wager that no other household in the realm came precious near to female fisticuffs at least once a month over such an issue. Every time it happened, the two women squared up to each other, toe-to-toe like boxers, jabbing each other with their forefingers instead of trading blows. Gran was brief and straight to the point. She claimed that Dad was pure Indian. He was born in India. He had Indian parents, and any fool could see that he was Indian. She was his mother, so she should know.

Mum would bide her time, trying to control herself, but as Gran went on and on repeating herself she'd suddenly explode with typical Welsh fervour. With her voice rising several decibels she would claim that Dad was brimming over with Welsh blood from his father. Then, for some obscure reason, she would start her real tirade with the least convincing of all her arguments: that when Dad grew a moustache it came out ginger. This was a well-known

Welsh characteristic. Welshmen with black hair and ginger moustaches were as common as muck. Yet whoever heard of an Indian with a ginger moustache?

Next she would harp on about Dad's war service, how he'd served in Wales' most prestigious regiment, the Royal Welch Fusiliers, a regiment that would never tolerate an Englishman in its ranks, let alone an Indian. Furthermore, anyone with ears could spot Dad's Welsh accent a mile off; and when she'd first known him, and before the daft bugger changed his name to Contractor, he was known to everyone as 'Jones 176' or, among his friends, as 'Suntan Jones'. When she met him he was stationed in the regimental depot in Porth and she still had his pay book (hidden in the bottom of her wardrobe, as I very well knew) to prove all this. Her final rejoinder always referred back to Gran's original claim that he was Indian simply because he'd been born in India.

"For God's sake," she would yell. "Jesus Christ was born in a stable. But that didn't make him a bloody horse."

On the rare occasions when Dad was present and became embroiled in the argument, he made it a tripartite dispute by insisting that he was English.

All this confusion was caused by one fundamental problem: Dad didn't have a birth certificate. This was normal in India. Birth certificates were never issued.* However, Dad did have a passport. It lacked any evidence of his father but it nevertheless declared him to be British/English. He carried it with him wherever he went and he would invariably conclude these family arguments by whipping it out and demanding: "So how do you think I got this?" And, as if this wasn't proof enough, he'd rip open his jacket, point to the medal ribbons stitched to his waistcoat, and cry: "What about my Oak Leaf?"

His Oak Leaf was perfectly genuine but the challenge about his passport was strictly rhetorical. He didn't expect

*Even Lord Wavell, who was born in India and later became Viceroy, never had one and when he applied for a British passport he was told by Somerset House that he was an alien.

an answer and he certainly wasn't going to give one, so the mystery remained. It wasn't until he died that I discovered that one of his army comrades had bequeathed it to him whilst dying of wounds, which meant that a ham-fisted barrack room lawyer then had to amend as much of it as he could with a stick and paste job. The name Contractor* was genuine enough, but Dad's photograph showed clear evidence of being a replacement and other items, such as colour of eyes and height, were equally as suspicious. The most curious thing of all came with 'Distinguishing Mark' which had been altered to read: 'Only one testicle'.

On a family holiday to Switzerland immediately before the war, his passport was examined with the utmost suspicion at every customs post we drove through. In fact, when we arrived back at Dover, the immigration authorities (who were convinced that German spies were flooding into the country) grilled Dad for two hours; and even when he flashed his medals, told them he'd shared a shell hole on the Somme with Robert Graves, and had every intention of joining the ARP the following morning, they were unmoved. It was only when they ushered him into a private room and discovered that he did indeed only have one testicle that they were satisfied and he was allowed back into the country.**

---

* The forger's inability to change 'Contractor' to 'Jones' is how we came by our family name. That might seem odd, but it's something you'll have to get used to with Dad. In all, he had three names, ending up in fine style as Lord Lomond of the Grove, a title of foreign authenticity which in the end did at least gain him admission into the East Devon Home for Impoverished Gentlefolk.

**Why the authorities thought this made him *bona fide* I've no idea. After all, the popular song of the day (to the tune of Colonel Bogey) stated:
>'Hitler, he's only got one ball,
>Goering has two but rather small.
>Himmler has something similar
>But Goebbels has no balls at all',

all of which would suggest *complicity* with the Third Reich, not *innocence*.

3

Doubts about my parentage—A trip to the Rhondda—
I meet Kyber Morgan at the Old Comrades Club—
Up and under!—Grandpa acquires a new name.

I watched and listened to these rows about Dad's
origins with the glee of a mischievous small boy. At the
time it didn't matter to me who or what Dad was: just
being Dad was quite sufficient. Likewise, I was far too young
to entertain suspicions that his army service had enabled
him to enter the country as an illegal immigrant on a false
passport. I just took pleasure in watching adults arguing
among themselves. It made them more human and
approachable.

It wasn't until years later, when I was well into my teens,
that several racist incidents at school made me appreciate
the importance of knowing and understanding one's roots.
Suddenly, I realised that the family closet was rattling with
God knows how many skeletons and I became convinced
that I had to discover the truth about my ancestry if I was
ever to succeed in the prejudiced world I was about to enter.
The key to the whole mystery was Dad's father. Somehow or
other, I had to find out who he was.

My first step was to discuss the matter with my brothers.
When I asked Brother Nothing if the ambiguities in our
family and our colour worried him, he answered: "No."

When I put the same thing to James he replied: "It did at first. But I've since given it careful consideration and come to the conclusion that I am what I am. Everyone else will have to accept that. 'Shikata nago', as they say in Japan."

I envied them their indifference, but it was not something I could settle for. I knew I'd have no peace until I discovered the truth.

I never did produce absolute proof, but I came as close as made no difference. It happened when I was seventeen, during one of my long summer holidays. I was the proud owner of a 250cc Panther motor cycle so I decided to visit Mum's parents, Grandma and Grandpa, at 445 Tip View Terrace, Ferndale, in the Rhondda Valley. It was the first time I'd made the effort to visit them and I'm sure Grandma, being the suspicious type, realised there was an ulterior motive behind it. She certainly knew I hadn't gone there through love. On the odd occasions when we had met over the years, Dad and I had always made it abundantly clear that we couldn't stand the way she had reduced Grandpa to cringing subjugation. For forty years he'd been one of the miners who handed over their unopened weekly pay packets to his wife and, even now, in retirement, he was still only allowed half-a-crown pocket money each week. She wouldn't even give him a chance to answer for himself. If anyone asked him if he wanted another cup of tea, she would cut in: "No. One is all his bladder can stand." If he was offered a cake, before his eager hand could stretch forth, she snapped: "He doesn't eat cake. Only bread and dripping."

During the first two days of my visit I encouraged Grandpa to speak up for himself but it was quite useless and I soon resigned myself to watching a man being treated as a cabbage. Even when I tried to get him on his own I was foiled. Grandma insisted on going everywhere with us. Once, when she'd gone upstairs, I invited Grandpa to have a pint with me at the local, but she heard every word through the ceiling and shouted down: "He doesn't go to evil places like that."

Eventually, I summoned up the courage to make a direct approach to Grandma concerning our family history. I reasoned that if I could get her to tell me about Mum it would then open the way for information about Dad, which Grandma had gained in turn from Mum. It was a long shot and it didn't work. She made it perfectly clear that as far as she was concerned the less I knew about my parents the better. When I persisted I was cut down to size.

"We're not going to go into all that business about your mother," she declared, thereby betraying the existence of a dark secret. "All I can say is that your mother has never been the same since she married that bloody Indian, or whatever he is..."

I made no reply but thought what a crying need there was for some kind of Race Relations Board to which one could report people like Grandma. I was so angry I would have shopped her with alacrity. Grandpa obviously agreed with me. I could tell by the way he squirmed about on his stool that he was highly embarrassed by her attitude. Either that or he was having terrible trouble with his piles. Whichever it was, the following morning (a Sunday) he rebelled and spoke up for himself. He suggested he should take me to the Old Comrades Club in Porth to hear the Treorchy Male Voice Choir's final rehearsal for the coming performance of *The Messiah* in Cardiff (Llandaff) Cathedral.

It was a masterstroke by Grandpa. In those days, the Treorchy Choir was the glory of the valleys. It stood for everything fine and traditional about Wales. Mentioning them was like playing a trump card and eventually, after a display of enthusiasm for Welsh culture on my part, Grandma granted her approval. Her only proviso was that I should wear a suit and borrow one of Grandpa's black ties. The Chapel ruled supreme in the valleys and there were severe restrictions on Sunday activities, but in practical terms one could do virtually anything one pleased – from drunkenness to fornication – just so long as one did it in a suit and black tie. *

*In Wales, the expression 'born in a black tie' means having been conceived on a Sunday.

43

Our trip to the Old Comrades Club was most productive. It cleared up all my anxieties regarding my family history. It also did Grandpa a power of good, indeed it changed his life for ever. As soon as we stepped inside the Old Comrades Club I realised Grandpa had lied through his dentures about the Treorchy Choir. They weren't anywhere near the place. They were on tour in Oslo and the only singing came from a bunch of old reprobates who were warbling their way through an endless repertoire of disgusting army songs.

Grandpa wasn't a member of the club but we gained entry easily enough by saying that I was a visitor from London. People from London (the big smoke) were always welcome in the Rhondda. They were so rare they were regarded as celebrities and granted the sort of reverence solicitors and doctors were accorded in those days by the working class. As the words 'from London' were repeated in hushed tones, the visitors' book was produced for us to sign. Of course, Grandpa only had his usual half-a-crown pocket money on him, so I made our contribution towards the evening's drinks kitty.

As a seventeen year-old who'd been on numerous away matches with school teams, I thought I'd learnt to sink a few pints in English pubs, but the Old Comrades Club was something quite different, in another league altogether. Here, we were down to straight, hard drinking. No one ever placed orders. Men on the far side of a small hatch at the end of the room simply pulled in empty glasses and pushed out full ones, everyone drinking like the clappers in order to get their fair share from the kitty. The only places I've ever known to equal this were the Sydney Plonk Shops on pensions day and the Six o'clock Swill at Melbourne.*

At first it was difficult to see much detail because of the smoke drifting about like a fog bank, but as my eyes adjusted to the atmosphere I saw that there was hardly a man there who wasn't maimed in some way. Every other chair had a crutch propped up against it and dozens of empty

*Both now long since gone, alas!

trouser legs were doubled back and pinned to backsides. Empty sleeves were even more common.

We found a place at a table and pints of mild and bitter were thrust before us and I soon discovered that I was sitting among the remnants of several battalions of Royal Welch Fusiliers, men who had served in the Great War. These were Dad's old comrades: veterans of the Somme, Passchendaele, and Gallipoli. These poor, tormented souls, so bravely making the most of all that was left for them, were the men who had volunteered and risked their lives on the promise of a better, more equal and just world if they survived. They should have been the elite of the Rhondda, but instead they were physical wrecks who'd been shuffled to one side and left with nothing to do but drown their memories with cheap beer.

Grandpa soon abandoned me in order to join those singing and as I sat there, bewildered by my strange surroundings, I became aware of men gathering around me, staring at me in a disconcerting manner. Then one of them said: "You must be Suntan Jones's boy."

Another grinned at me and declared: "Jones 176! Written all over your face, Boyo."

A third chipped in with: "And he must be Megan Jones' son. That's why he came in with Under-the-Thumb Jones."

I didn't bother to explain that I was Sajit Contractor. I was quite happy to assume the mantle of 'Suntan'. I suspected that it could well lead to the information I was seeking.

I didn't see Grandpa again until the kitty ran out and it was time to leave, but during that period the details I'd been seeking about my background were revealed to me. This was thanks to Kyber Morgan, a legendary figure in the Fusiliers. He was the ex-RSM of the 3rd battalion and the guardian of all regimental gossip back to the turn of the century. Serving with the Fusiliers since 1899, he'd got his nickname after going up and down the Kyber pass more often than anyone. Like Dad, he'd served in Flanders and then Gallipoli and his second DCM was awarded to him after he'd cleared a Turkish trench single handed.

Kyber Morgan was a true raconteur and for nearly three hours he kept everyone enthralled with regimental stories. Interwoven among these was a detailed account of Dad and my grandfather; and as though that wasn't enough, he gave us a hilarious account of my mother's early downfall and the circumstances which led to her marrying Dad.

Kyber Morgan was one of Britain's great unsung heroes and I will always be grateful to him for resolving my doubt and queries about my parents and especially for the final, generous remark he made about Dad.

"Your old man was a bloody mixture all right, Boyo. But he was a bloody fine Fusilier. Fearless, look you. Fearless. He'll always be one of us."

When we finally left the Old Comrades Club we were all drunk.

To be honest, we were stinking drunk. I was worst of all. It was my first time and there's nothing more drunk than a first-timer. I don't remember a thing about our trek back to Ferndale until we turned off the main road and started to climb up Tip View Terrace. Then, there were three of us. God only knows who the other one was. Another interminable Jones, I assumed. At one point he complained: "Christ, this bloody hill. For every step forward, I'm slipping back two."

"Turn round and go up backwards," advised Grandpa.

This made us laugh so much that we collapsed in a drunken heap. As we sorted out our tangled arms and legs I discovered that one of the legs was wooden, the old-fashioned type as sported by Long John Silver. I also saw that our companion was clutching a rugby ball. When I commented on it, he told me that he'd played centre three-quarter for Penarth for ten years and only gave up when the opposition complained of getting splinters when they tackled him. He also claimed that he would have got a Welsh cap in 1938 had it not been for an incompetent referee. He'd scored under the posts after beating Haydn Tanner and Vivian Jenkins with perfect dummies, only for the referee to blow up and yell: "You can't fool me, Jones. Forward pass."

As we began to wend our way up the Terrace this one-legged veteran (Dummy Jones) became so inspired by his own stories of past rugby triumphs that he began to re-enact some of them by way of the famous Garry Owen, or 'Up and Under!' I can't remember if he kicked the ball with his wooden leg or his good one, but as soon as it soared into the sky the three of us charged after it, yelling, 'Up and Under!' As often as not, the ball bounced on the roof of a house and seconds later a window would fly open and the head of an irate resident would appear. They would curse and swear at us but then suddenly go silent. They wondered if they'd gone mad, or if they were hallucinating. Either explanation seemed more credible than what their eyes told them: that Under-the-Thumb Jones was as pissed as a newt and playing rugby in the Terrace in the middle of the night – Sunday night! Even in a suit and black tie that spelt trouble, and other people's troubles were something they loved. Some of them called down, demanding to know what was going on, but all they got by way of reply were discordant cries of: "Up and Under!"

Once they'd got over the shock of it, their attitude changed abruptly. They cheered us on, laughing at our clumsy attempts to catch the ball, and most of them couldn't get downstairs and out on to the street quick enough, intrigued as to what the outcome of such outrageous behaviour would be. It wasn't long before practically every household in the Terrace was aware of what was happening. By the time we were on the last stretch, approaching Number 445, those who hadn't been aroused by the ball bouncing on their roofs had been tipped off by others and were so frightened of missing something that they made up for lost time by cutting through the houses in the road above them. Then across the gardens, through the next row of houses, and finally on to the last stretch of the Terrace – the old escape route when fleeing from the Dorset police during the pit strike of 1926.

Our very last Gary Owen was an enormously high kick and although the three of us charged after it with our now familiar cry of, 'Up and Under!', we all missed it. It bounced high and went backwards, over our heads. I turned to chase it down the hill and it was only then that I became fully aware of what was going on. I pulled up abruptly. I was confronted by a solid wall of silent, statuary people. They filled the road, house to house. They were in their night clothes, some in dressing gowns, others in pyjamas or night shirts. The women were all in curlers and I have never seen such a large collection of people without teeth. Their collapsed faces were clamped in concentration, their eyes riveted on the front door of Number 445.

I forgot about the ball and followed their gaze. Grandpa was now nearly up to his front door. He couldn't make out what the delay was and yelled out: "Come on, Sajit. What the hell are you doing, Boyo? Let's have another Gary Owen."

Then, among the crowd around me, there was a perceptible murmur, inwards gasps of air and mutterings of fear, all in Welsh for in the Rhondda they revert to their native tongue in moments of crisis. I glanced around them and I'll swear, even though it was pretty dark, that they'd all gone deathly pale. They were certain blood was about to be spilt.

As Grandpa approached Number 445 he turned and stared out across the valley. He seemed to gain confidence from such grandeur. The voices of his forefathers were calling him, reverberating across the hills, urging him to assert himself. There was a new glint in his eyes, a hint of reckless courage as can only be inspired by a deal too much beer. We watched, mesmerised, willing him on, praying that we were about to witness a moment of rare human drama, an emasculated wimp rediscovering his male dignity.

Gran and Mr Muckey

Then, just as swiftly, our hopes plummeted. The front door of 445 was flung open and Grandma strode forth, as dramatic and awe-inspiring as Genghis Khan emerging from the gates of Kabul. There she was, five foot damn all of invincible Welsh womanhood, the personification of supreme authority. She was festooned with curlers and toothless, a harrowing sight. There was a frozen, protracted moment of silence as they glared at each other. They knew – we all knew – that this was the final reckoning, the moment of truth, Ferndale's OK Corral. Lawrence's blood-thirsty cry of 'No prisoners!' echoed around the hills.

Grandma made the first move. Her nostrils flared as though about to belch fire and brimstone. She sucked in air and expanded like an indignant bullfrog. Then she advanced with the resolution of a squad of Nazi storm troopers. Jackboots rang out as she strode up to him. Her lower jaw took on a life of its own, flying up and down with the speed of a two-stroke piston. No doubt she let out a stream of foul invective but we heard not a word of it. Opposite her, Grandpa had exposed his tonsils and from the depths of his larynx came a roar that would have done credit to the full Treorchy ensemble climaxing with 'Sospan Fach'. Considering his condition, every word was beautifully artic-ulated. To my untrained ear it sounded like: "Taffyn llanandwi caradden cwm myfann!" (which, being loosely translated, means: "Get back indoors, you ugly old bat!").

He then grabbed her by the shoulders and gave her a shove, making her reel backwards. She recovered and flew at him like a terrier after a rat, but he gave her another shove and she staggered back again and shrank to normal proportions. Her leather jackboots reverted to Co-op bedroom slippers with pink pom-poms and for the first time in living memory she looked frail and pathetic. Grandpa capitalised on his advantage and kept pushing her and shouting at her until she stumbled back indoors. Then he turned, his right arm aloft as though he'd just

49

drawn Excalibur, and with the inventiveness of a drunk he substituted his cry of, 'Up and Under!' with, "Up and at 'er!"

The last thing we saw before the front door slammed was Grandpa signalling to us with typical male chauvinist triumphalism: a clenched fist and an extended forearm jerking up and down.

I stayed the night with Dummy Jones. In the morning there was a new spirit in Tip View Terrace. It was like the relief of Mafeking, Rorke's Drift, and V-E Day all rolled into one. Once again a righteous cause had prevailed.

From there on Grandpa made up his own mind as to whether or not he wanted another cup of tea and he ate as many cakes as he damn well liked. He became the only person in the valleys ever to have his nickname changed. From that day forth he was 'Transformation Jones'.

4

Gran's murky past—Death over the Kyber—
Dad's native cunning—Taking the King's shilling—
An accident at Anzac Cove—Dad's fate sealed—
Mum's early promise—A slip of the tongue—Back in favour
with another prize—Expelled from school—Shop girl par
excellence—A meeting with Dad.

When all this happened, and I learnt of my parents'
early circumstances, I was approaching adulthood. My early years had passed happily enough
even though there had been tragedies and tricky undercur-
rents within our family. I had reacted to things instinctively, just as a child should. However, before I proceed with my
story in correct sequence, I feel it only right and proper that
you – my readers – should have a couple of flashbacks to
inform you of my family background. In this way you
will, hopefully, understand far better than I ever did the
psychological influences that moulded my life. This chapter
is therefore devoted to what I discovered about my parents.

Dad was born in Simla, northern India, in 1898. Gran was,
of course, his mother. He was undoubtedly Anglo/Indian
but it is impossible to be categoric about the identity of his
father due to the lack of any blood-tests or DNA and the
varied love-lives of British Tommies in India during that era.
One has only to read Kipling to realise that life for a

John Hollands

red-blooded ranker was not easy. The senior officers had their memsahibs in tow, single officers were kept more than happy by the regular arrival from the UK of nubile, upper-crust British girls seeking husbands, but somewhat typically the army made no provisions at all for the unrequited lust of that most frustrated of all creatures, Tommy Atkins. So serious was this problem that in the latter part of the 19th century army medics referred to the matter as LSI (Lack of Sexual Intercourse) and frequently quoted it in reports on men who'd suddenly gone berserk for no apparent reason. It wasn't until World War II, when the forces enjoyed an influx of ATS, WRENS, and WAAFS, that the abbreviation LSI became obsolete and was superseded by ESI, this being applicable to females suffering from cystitis (Excessive Sexual Intercourse).

Of course, some of the Tommies had sufficient initiative to make their own arrangements. Rather than suffer the indignity of being classified LSI, they turned to the indigenous population, even though fraternisation of a sexual nature was strictly forbidden and carried the dual risk of 28 days confined to barracks and contracting syphilis, then a virulent and incurable disease.

During the course of my research into these matters, several unpalatable facts emerged, things I would normally sweep under the carpet. However, memoirs are nothing without honesty so I have to record that Gran was hardly a young lady of impeccable character. In fact, she was one of the local girls to whom Fusiliers turned in order to escape the ranks of LSI sufferers. Naturally, her motivation was money, yet there was a side to the picture which reflected credit on her. Of all the local girls on the game, she was renowned for the great care she exercised in selecting men. She could afford to be particular since she was the most beautiful and desirable of them all. Kyber Morgan, who knew her well, explained to me that within the Fusiliers there was a group of rankers who'd formed a masonic-style elite; the original gentlemen songsters out on a spree. These men had taken a solemn oath to help each other in war and peace and to share all things, and this included suitable women. That might sound sordid, but who are we, members of the permissive society, to pass moral judgements?

The crux of the matter was that a prime instigator and founder-member of this rankers' elite was my paternal grandfather: Private Kelvin Jones. Kelvin was a citizen of Chepstow where the English/Welsh divide is, and always has been, confusing. He signed on as a band boy with the Fusiliers and served for twenty-five years, boasting medals for both the Boer War and Kitchener's expedition to the Sudan. Apart from these campaigns, most of his service was in India, either on the north-west frontier, Poona, or Simla, the last being his favourite on account of the climate and the presence of Gran. Although their relationship was, of necessity, a very on and off affair, it lasted several years. It was doomed from the start. For one thing, neither of them had any worthwhile money. Also, Gran was an Untouchable and Kelvin was a Tommy, which amounted to much the same thing. This meant that any marriage, or even a meaningful relationship (today's politically correct term for people having it off with impunity), was out of the question.

Nor did luck help them. Shortly after Dad had been conceived, the Fusiliers were despatched with all haste to the north-west frontier where there was trouble with the dreaded Pathan tribesmen. From all accounts, Kelvin Jones volunteered for a recce patrol which had the misfortune to be ambushed. Two of the patrol were killed outright. Another shot himself rather than be captured, but poor Kelvin was taken alive. His torture and death are therefore best glossed over. Suffice to say that when his body was recovered it lacked certain treasured organs due to the handiwork of the Pathan women, whose pleasure it was to take care of the prisoners.

With his father dead and his mother an Untouchable, Dad's prospects of acquiring an education and then a decent job with the railways or the post office – as were often given to Anglo/Indians – were nil. As a child, even his chances of being a camp follower with the Fusiliers disappeared. Had his father lived to acknowledge him, the regiment would have rallied around, not in an official or grand way, but with gestures, like Christmas parties for the ORs children, or sports days and coaching, and a few odd jobs when he was old enough to run errands and whitewash stationary objects.

Gran certainly made vigorous remonstrations on Dad's behalf, standing for weeks outside the guardroom with her infant cradled in her arms, first of all pleading for help and then heaping abuse upon the British when they ignored her; but, of course, if the regiment had listened to the claims of an Untouchable woman proffering a child in their direction, they would very soon have been inundated. As a result, Dad was dragged up in the most poverty-stricken circumstances imaginable. He was lucky not to have been mutilated and used for begging purposes, and although he grew into a strong lad he remained a low-caste Anglo/Indian and was cursed and kicked up the backside by everyone. There was no place for him on either side of the racial equation. He was the lowest of the low.

As the years passed he tramped northern India forlornly denying his mixed blood and trying to establish an acceptable identity in order to earn a crust and escape starvation. He had the advantage of a light complexion so he kept well out of the sun, knowing that his destiny lay on his British side, not his Indian. Although he had no schooling of any description, he mastered English. He was also lucky to learn it with a Welsh accent, known locally as 'chi-chi'. Although Mum would never accept that such a duplicated Welsh accent existed, it nevertheless did and it helped Dad enormously in giving credence to his claim that – like his father – he was Welsh. Even his colour was something he managed to explain away. Whenever he referred to Wales as 'home', he explained that he meant Tiger Bay, the melting pot of Cardiff where things had been molten for so long that mixed blood and dusky complexions had been openly accepted for many years.

When the Great War broke out Dad was fifteen and as luck would have it he again met up with his father's old regiment in Poona. He lost no time in making himself known around the guardroom, chatting away to any squaddy who chanced by about the valleys and the hillsides. He soon had the more gullible Fusiliers calling him Emrys and wishing him luck when he returned to Tiger Bay, and from these witless idiots he picked up as much battalion gossip and inside information as he could. When he heard they were looking for recruits, being keen to get back to full strength and thereby enhance their chances of active service in France, he volunteered. If the regiment hadn't been so desperate he would never have got away with it, but since he spoke good English with a Welsh accent, swore on the Bible that he was seventeen, and (thanks to a discarded letter he'd found lying around) was able to provide evidence of a seemingly authentic address in Tip View Terrace, Ferndale, they signed him on.

It was only after he'd been kitted out and had settled into barracks that they discovered he couldn't sing a note and became suspicious, but by then it was too late. They'd given him the King's shilling and he was on the battalion strength as 'Jones 176'. He'd even acquired a nickname, 'Suntan Jones' and to clinch matters he was doing a great job looking after the regimental mascot, a white-bearded billy goat name 'Bleater Jones', the only Jones in the battalion without a number after his name.

Fortuitously, there were 62 other Joneses in the battalion which enabled Dad to get lost in a crowd. His only concern came some weeks later. When they were already on the high seas, bound for France, he discovered that four other Joneses (238, 402, 679, and 813) lived in Tip View Terrace, the home address he'd purloined. Fortunately, he'd taken the precaution of changing the number of the house (from 45 to 445) but even so he went through his service

John Hollands

more concerned that one of his comrades would expose him as a fraud than of avoiding whizbangs and bullets.

The Royal Welch Fusiliers was one of the finest regiments in the British army and in Flanders they established a war record second to none. However, it was when they sent Dad's battalion to Gallipoli that he was overtaken by the most significant moment in his life. He was sunbathing on the beach at Anzac Cove* when an Australian accidentally shot him through the foot. Since the bullet entered through his sole, and the Aussie admitted having done it ('Good on yer, mate! A dinkum Blighty touch'), no one on the spot doubted that it was an accident; but when Dad was evacuated to the regimental depot in Porth, someone walking around with a limp, and who was permanently 'excused boots', excited dark rumours. The word flashed around the Rhondda that one of the Fusiliers had worked his ticket, a slur which sent Dad wild with rage and created within him a pathological hatred of all Australians.

*Apart from the Charge of the Light Brigade, Dad's presence at Anzac Cove, together with 35 other Welch Fusiliers, was the British Army's greatest-ever cock-up. Anzac Cove was the most dangerous place on earth and Dad and the others should never have been sent there on 14 days leave. They should have been sent to the official British Leave Centre at Anzio Cove, Italy.

When they didn't turn up in Italy they were listed as AWOL (absent without leave). Since Dad was the only one among the Fusiliers to survive Anzac Cove, one might think that this didn't matter too much; but not a bit of it. When they still hadn't appeared at Anzio after seven days (they were dead at Anzac within four) charges of 'Desertion in the face of the enemy' were laid against them. Then, when 35 shell-torn corpses were returned to General Headquarters in Lemnos (with a note from the Australian Beach Master at Anzac Cove demanding: 'Who were these jokers? All they did was swim and arse about.'), a whitewash was ordered to avert trouble with the next of kin.

The 35 Fusiliers were therefore declared to be heroes rather than deserters. A report was concocted to the effect that they had deliberately forsaken their leave in order to help their valiant colonial comrades. Each man received a posthumous award for gallantry, making Anzac Cove, pro-rata to units involved, the most decorated engagement in British Army history. However, Dad left General Hamilton's staff with a tricky dilemma, and it was about the only one the incompetent swine ever dealt with successfully. They certainly weren't going to give a worthwhile medal to a dubious-looking Taffy who'd escaped with a foot wound, but they had to give him something in order to keep him quiet. So they awarded him the lowest honour of all, a Mention in Dispatches (Oak Leaf). Dad was happy to settle for this and his life.

Despite this, Dad faced the future with confidence. After all, he'd done well with the Fusiliers. He'd risen to the rank of acting, unpaid lance corporal and been mentioned in dispatches, and – most vital of all – he'd acquired a British passport.

What he hadn't reckoned on was meeting Mum. His duties at Porth were virtually non-existent so he spent his time traipsing the Rhondda trying to get rid of his limp and amusing himself by pretending that the pathetic little coal tips rearing up around him were the peaks of his beloved Himalayan foothills. Inevitably, one day he found himself in Tip View Terrace, so he decided to see if there really was a house numbered 445. There was, and he found it easily enough. He just followed the road and there it was, the last-but-two in a long row of identical terraced houses stacked in shelves on the steep hillside.

To his surprise he saw a pretty girl sitting on the newly scrubbed door step. He guessed correctly that she was seventeen and he was surprised when she flashed him a dazzling smile. More than that, she spoke to him, and for a young Welsh girl to take the social initiative with a complete stranger in the Rhondda Valley in those days was daring, to say the least. Dad's fate was sealed.

The story of Mum's early life is one of unfulfilled promise. Whilst most things turned out well for Dad, everything went wrong for Mum. She was an only child and her father was a timber man down the Maerdy pit, just as his father had been before him. Normally she would have married a Boyo from the same pit and their sons would have disappeared down the same hole in the ground for the best part of their lives. That was the pattern of life in the Rhondda and very few escaped from it. Yet Mum had it within her to break the mould and achieve significance in the outside world. She was a plump, cheerful girl and an incurable romantic, forever memorising the poems of Keats and Shelley and famous passages of Shakespeare; and perhaps her greatest joy came from writing fairy stories. A measure of her inventive mind was that she excelled at the traditional Welsh art of inventing amusing nicknames for relatives and local residents. Her best one was for her Uncle Dai. When he emerged from the dentist, unaccountably divested of all his front teeth, bar a beauty in the middle of his upper gum, she immediately christened him 'Dai Central Eating'.

It was therefore a surprise to everyone when Mum came horribly unstuck at school. One minutes she was the star pupil and the next she was in dire trouble, and it was typical of her that the latter eventually prevailed and she was expelled. If she'd had a good teacher things might have been different, but all she had was the unimaginative ministering of an elderly and traditional headmistress, Miss Blodwyn Wynford-Barclay. She should have groomed Mum for a scholarship to Oxford or Cambridge, but after 35 years of having her hopes dashed by so-called bright pupils she was not easily impressed. With her, outstanding pupils had to be impeccably behaved as well as clever, and Mum was what Miss Wynford-Barclay termed: "Far too uppity."

Specifically, Mum's downfall was because of a language impediment. Not a speech impediment, but a language impediment, which is rare and entirely different. She was a victim of Spoonerisms before such things had ever been heard of. Indeed, it wasn't until the Reverend William Archibald Spooner was well into his spell as Warden of New College Oxford, in the early 1920s, that he became famous for slips of the tongue such as, 'He hissed his mistory lecture.'

For several years before these gems became the talk of Oxford, Mum was saying, 'It's not far as the fly crows'; and the first time she ever rode in a car – at her Grandpa's funeral – she screamed at the young driver: 'There, look you! Now you've gone and pissed the marking space.' When the 5th battalion of the Royal Welch Fusiliers marched off to war through Porth, she said to her mother: 'It's nothing, Mam. They're only flowing the shag'.

Her impediment could, perhaps, best be described as verbal dyslexia and whilst the intellectuals at Oxford saw this as amusing when perpetrated by a brilliant academic and one of their own, the working-class Welsh regarded it as plain bloody daft, a sure sign of someone who was loopy-loo. Another difference was that whilst the Reverend Spooner knew exactly what he was up to, and even rehearsed and repeat his slips, Mum was always blissfully unaware that she'd said anything untoward.

Two incidents were particularly disastrous for Mum. Both occurred on school Speech Days. The first wasn't a true Spoonerism, merely an unconscious slip of the tongue. She'd won the school prize for poetry and this carried with it the obligation to recite a famous piece of literature to the assembled parents, relatives, school governors, and local dignitaries, Speech Days being by far the most prestigious social event in the Ferndale calendar. Mum chose to recite Shakespeare's 'The Death of Falstaff'.

Unfortunately, instead of announcing the piece by its correct title, she said: "The Death of Flagstaff!"

The titter that went round the audience so infuriated Miss Wynford-Barclay that she leapt to her feet and ordered Mum to start again; and Mum, being unaware of her slip, thought she was being rebuked for being too timid in her delivery. She therefore strove for greater dramatic affect, putting far more emphasis on each word. There was more laughter and Miss Wynford-Barclay was straight back on her feet, shouting at Mum to begin again. This little pantomime was repeated four times with Mum still not realising what she was doing wrong and getting more and more theatrical, eventually crying out in a sobbing voice and with waving arms: "THE DEATH OF FLAGSTAFF!"

It all ended with the audience rocking with laughter, Miss Wynford-Barclay shouting: "How dare you be so silly?", and Mum running off the stage in a flood of tears and wetting her knickers in shame.

Three years later Mum won the Senior English Composition Prize, which entailed another Speech Day performance. The Falstaff/Flagstaff incident wasn't forgotten, of course, but since Mum was now a big girl and the school's star pupil, there was no question of her not reading her prize-winning entry. Indeed, Mum's composition was so brilliant that Miss Wynford-Barclay made a point of introducing it with great pride. She told the audience: "Megan Jones has written a truly wonderful fairy story. I can assure you that we have a budding Hans Christian Anderson on our hands and this particular story will shortly be published in the magazine, 'Welsh Mothers and Toddlers'. I am especially proud of this fairy story because Megan tells how a dear little fairy helps a small girl's aunty Blodwyn – my own name as you'll be aware (titter, titter) – to triumph over wicked Englishmen by utilising a very original stunt... I'm sure you'll all love it...Megan!"

Mum stepped forward, full of confidence after such a glowing introduction. "A fairy story," she announced tweely. "Entitled: 'Aunty Blodwyn's Stunning Cunt'."

There was an audible gasp: incredulous disbelief that Miss Wynford-Barclay's star pupil had done it again. Her audacity in uttering such a vulgar and taboo word in front of the elite of the Rhondda – to say nothing of the personal connection with Miss Wynford-Barclay – momentarily struck them dumb. Then there was uproar. The fathers and male dignitaries were unable to contain guffaws and their wives, red-faced with shame and embarrassment, shrieked and screamed hysterically. Three spinster ladies fainted. Miss Wynford-Barclay chased Mum off the stage, beating her over the head with her rolled-up notes. By the time she returned to the stage to apologise, the Mayor and Corporation had been led out by their wives. Speech Day was over.

As always, Mum had no idea of what she'd said wrong. She didn't even know there was such a word, let alone what it referred to.

*****

Gran and Mr Muckey

Because of Mum's expulsion and disgrace it was several months before she got a job. Then she struck lucky. She was taken on as a trainee sales girl at Alternative Jones's General Emporium in Porth, the biggest shop outside Cardiff, Swansea and Newport, which attracted customers from all over Wales. Mr Jones was known as Alternative Jones because of the sign outside his shop. It read: 'We sell everything. If don't have it, we *guarantee* an alternative'.

There was sound logic behind this policy since Alternative Jones's range of goods was so vast that he could only afford to stock a few items of each line. Thus he was forever running out of things and he spent most of his working hours dashing around his various departments urging his sales girls: "Sell Madam an alternative. What's the matter with you, girl? Think alternatives, look you."

Usually, this worked admirably. Who cared if they ended up with a fork instead of a spade, or a hammer instead of a mallet. Mum was among the best sales girls and she sold alternatives galore. She even dreamed up alternatives of her own, her favourite being pipe cleaners instead of hair curlers.

Then dawned the day when Mum found herself serving Miss Wynford-Barclay, and her desire for revenge got the better of her. "And two rolls of toilet paper you say, Miss Wynford-Barclay? Well now there's a pity, look you. It's a ridiculous situation but we're clean out of toilet paper. But we do have some beautiful emery paper... Or perhaps, in your case, a few sheets of Grade 10 sandpaper would be more suitable..."

Shortly afterwards, Mum found herself sitting on her front doorstep, feeling sorry for herself. She had no job, hostile parents, and she was a figure of fun throughout the valleys. Worst of all, she had no prospects of a husband. The few young men who would eventually return from France would soon hear about her stupidity and only those missing an arm or a leg, or quivering and twitching with shell shock, would deign to have anything to do with her. She was an outcast, desperate for something or someone to lift her gloom and give her hope for the future.

As she watched Dad strolling up the hill she saw only a tall, dark, reasonably handsome, and complete young man.

The following evening they started their short courtship. Every evening they walked to the head of the valley and then back again. They stopped at Fryer Williams's shop for chish and fips and once these had been devoured and they'd licked their greasy fingers clean, they tarried in various shop doorways along Ferndale High Street, selecting their amorous havens according to the vagaries of the wind for it was autumn and getting mighty cold. Once Mum realised she was pregnant she swiftly concluded the formalities of courtship. Dad had no chance. In those days a man did what he was obliged to do and they got married before the Reverend Edwards – who steadfastly refused to marry pregnant girls – had any hint of her condition. *

The only hitch on the great day came when Mum repeated her vows after the Reverend Edwards. Instead of giving her names, she said: "I, Jegan Mones..."

Dad never forgot that. He must have told the story a thousand times, but always for sympathy, never a laugh. His punch line was, "Talk about a Freudian slip!"

*The female child conceived in the doorway of Dai Davies's Pet and Reptile Exchange Mart in Ferndale was miscarried two months later. It was several years before Mum conceived again and gave birth to Charles (Brother Nothing)

5

*Narrative reconstruction – The University of Life –
Camberwell Green – The Works in Lomond Grove –
The Mystery of Dad and Brother Nothing – Nothing is grilled
– Good-bye to Sir Oswald and Herr Adolf.*

The flashbacks are over and I now return to my childhood, to a highly significant incident. I had very little part in what occurred and in order to give a rounded picture of what happened I find it necessary to repeat family tales handed down over the years, knowing that this can lead to distortions. However, this fault – if it is one – is more than adequately excused by dressing it up in the term beloved of the media: 'narrative reconstruction'.

The incident took place on the night of Friday August 13th 1937. On such a doom-threatened date we were lucky to escape a major disaster. As it was, Dad very nearly ended up in jail and Brother Nothing, during the course of a third-degree interrogation by Inspector Hackett of Scotland Yard, was warned in explicit terms that he might well be destined for a new school, a boarding establishment noted for its strict discipline and physical punishments, namely Borstal. If Dad had ended up in jail it would have been catastrophic, but with Brother Nothing I'm not so sure. Although he attained the temporary status of hero, I still think Borstal would been an eminently suitable place for him.

To appreciate how this Friday 13th incident came about it is necessary to explain the general pattern emerging in the Contractor family. For some time Dad had been obsessed by the education of his three sons. By education he didn't mean sitting in classrooms acquiring academic knowledge, for in this respect Brother Nothing was doing well and James was way, way ahead of his age group. As for me, I was in kindergarten under the watchful eye of Miss Deeping, a young, liberal-minded teacher pioneering the modern theory of self-expression. Since Mum had so far brought me up on lines of repression and intimidation, I welcomed Miss Deeping's new approach and became her star pupil. She'd never known a kid so adept at banging nails into the furniture and smothering every inch of blank wall with match-stick men murals. Furthermore, she was amazed by the skilful way I used my spoon as a catapult at lunch time. She said the accuracy with which I pinged mashed potatoes into the faces of those opposite me was quite uncanny and she was constantly urging the others to rid themselves of their inhibitions and follow my example.

Although these activities were difficult to evaluate in educational terms, and best not itemised in written reports, I was nevertheless earmarked as a pupil with a bright future, just as my brothers were. However, this kind of conventional assessment left Dad unimpressed. He visualised far greater horizons for his three sons and after much careful thought he concluded that what we needed was to graduate in the 'University of Life'. As far as he was concerned, the 'University of Life' was no mere catch phrase. Nor was it lip service to a vague theory. Least of all was it a smart riposte by those who lacked a formal education. To Dad, it was something very real. It amounted to developing initiative: doing new, active things as opposed to being taught old, passive things. It was seeking out challenges and dangers; witnessing major events; and never shirking the difficult or avoidable.

Gran and Mr Muckey

As a first step in this new approach, Dad sought to open our eyes to the realities of life. Whilst he had no intention of disrupting our pleasant, cosseted lower-middle-class existence, and least of all of imposing on us the harrowing poverty he had experienced as a boy, he was nevertheless determined that we should realise that we were members of a privileged minority. Significantly, he didn't see our colour as a problem. To him, colour prejudice was rarely vented on those who had something positive to offer.

His initial plan was to introduce us to the hurly-burly of London commercial life through visits to his factory at Lomond Grove. He drove us there by various routes, taking us through the plush areas of the West End and the City, and then across various bridges and so into the grot of south London, terminating in the soot-encrusted greyness of Camberwell. As we progressed from one extreme to another, he lectured us on how one was dependent on the other, emphasising that to create affluence the efforts, co-operation, and sacrifices of the working class were essential, which meant we must never despise or underestimate such people.

He kept referring to 'muck and graft' and whenever we arrived in Camberwell we were never in any doubt as to what he meant. Tucked away behind the main shopping streets, the living conditions were positively Dickensian, with narrow, cobbled streets, rat-infested and broken down stables which still stank of the long-departed horse, and row upon row of jerry-built hovels with walled lanes behind them, all dotted with dog shit. It was a land of labourers, grafters, costermongers, wide-boys, and petty crooks, all forever on the make out of sheer necessity.

The men were dressed in double-breasted jackets, flat caps, and with long white scarves which fell down to their waists with still enough to spare to tuck into their trousers to keep their vitals warm: a local uniform that was instantly available at the Thirty-Nine Shillings Tailor for fifty-nine bob. The women talked interminably on doorsteps but were more individual, especially with colours, their badges of uniformity being hair nets and voluminous aprons girded around them.

These south Londoners were cheerful and loud, full of cries of 'Wotcher Guv!' and "Ello my old cock sparrer!' Here, the spirit of old London lingered on – in its death-throes, but still there. Alongside the new Odeon and Regal cinemas stood century-old spittoon and sawdust pubs and music halls where gilt paint had all but peeled away and on whose creaking boards Stanley Holloway and Max Miller followed in the steps of Marie Lloyd and Charlie Chaplin, making their audiences bay for more with comic songs and risqué jokes.

Dad also drove us around the area after dark, even though it was one of the most notorious red-light areas of London. Occasionally, he would turn to Brother Nothing to ask him if he understood certain sordid aspects of life and Nothing would go as red as a beet root and claim to know everything, far too embarrassed to admit his ignorance and thereby risk having to listen to Dad stammering his way through explanations. Thus when Dad told us of brothels in dark, towering houses with long-legged girls especially imported from Paris, I lacked an elder-brother's guidance and was left to conjure up my own scenarios, all based on sloppy adult kissing and rude undressing.

What we saw quite openly were street prostitutes who, as soon as it was dark enough to mask their imperfections, issued forth from basement bed-sits. In their tight jumpers, split-sided skirts, and high-heeled shoes, they tottered over to the Green and then sheltered beneath lamp posts. For long hours they stood there like sentries, statuesque in their provocative poses apart from when stray mongrels sallied forth on demarcation patrols and tried to lay claims to lamp posts already spoken for. Then, with splendid athleticism, but with a total lack of feminine decorum, the ladies of the night despatched the said mongrels with well directed kicks up their backsides.

Gran and Mr Muckey

All these ladies were grotesquely painted and decorated, crusty with powder, rouge, and mascara, but there was a delightful naiveté about them. They were eternal optimists and had enormous faith in their allure, with never a hint of the modern tendency towards early retirement. They had pride in their notoriety and boasted that it was their predecessors who had inspired 'Gloriously Obscene/On Camberwell Green' the famous poem by Britain's foremost erotic poet, Roy Middleton, of Eskimo Nell fame. I only mention it here because some years later, when I was in the army, I earned many a pint of beer by being able to recite all 36 verses. Unfortunately, only the first few lines are printable:

'Forty whores in purple drawers
Went gambolling on The Green
And ne'er in all old Bony's wars
Was greater mayhem seen.
With gleeful cries and open flies
Lads could scarce believe their luck...'

Dad also gloried in The Green's reputation as the stamping ground of West End toffs, the place where Hooray Henrys rounded off good nights at the Cafe Royal and the Ace of Spades Road House by treating their scantily-clad flappers to a spot of slumming. This entailed a visit to a pub vibrating with raucous singing, giving outrageous donations to the Salvation Army lassies who haunted them, and then patronising street stalls where they gathered around glowing, red-hot, braziers and swallowed whelks and jellied eels at a tanner a time.

Adjacent to all this, just one street behind the brown, brown, grass of The Green, belching out toxic fumes of burning rubber and molten lead, which cut local life expectancy by ten years, was Dad's factory, what he lovingly called, 'The Works', officially registered as The Camberwell Tyre and Battery Factory. Here, in a row of converted stables, Dad suddenly became 'Guv!', a man of

status. He was liked and respected by everyone. We didn't
know it at the time but he was an artist in rubber, the finest
retreader of bald tyres London had ever known. He had a
technique all his own. By sprinkling powdered chalk on the
smooth rubber he could depict the old tread pattern and
then, with his gouging tool at just the right temperature,
and with the blade as sharp as a razor, he could recreate a
perfect tread without ever cutting into the canvas. He had
the touch of a surgeon and his skill was so coveted that
wherever he went in Camberwell he was lauded; there were
cheery greetings from shops, witty quips from behind fruit
and veg barrows, and caps were doffed by scrap merchants
as they thundered past on their horse-drawn carts. I loved
to bask in his glory and I have never felt more at home than
in Camberwell Green.

Gran and Mr Muckey

Youngster though I was, it always fell to me to go to the shops for fresh supplies of sweets and cigars (Dad rarely smoked at home, but always had a Havana on the go at work) and, no doubt partly because of my colour, I was instantly recognised by the natives and fussed over, the sweet shop lady never bothering to weigh out my chocolate buttons, merely filling the paper bag until it overflowed.

Sometimes I tarried in Lomond Grove. It abounded with noisy, shouting kids, all having a wonderful time. The boys concentrated on football with an old ball that had no air in it, but it was the girls who fascinated me. Most of them had their dresses tucked up into their knickers and they looked every bit as tough as the boys. Their main preoccupation was skipping and hopscotch but lamp posts were another great attraction to them. From each one a rope hung from the top and they grabbed these and swirled round in wide circles. Once or twice I joined in the football, but each time, within minutes, Brother Nothing appeared in the entrance of the main yard and called me back in.

We became known to Dad's workers as 'the Nippers' and we were encouraged to try our hand at some of the simpler tasks but never – unfortunately – the riskier ones like casting molten lead. As we scampered around the place and watched Dad's men handling giant tyres from London Transport, Carter Patterson, Pickfords, and other huge haulage contractors, we also discovered that Dad had come by the business in a curious manner. During his days with the Welch Fusiliers he'd had a spell in the Motor Transport Section where he and a mate had been responsible for the inflation and repair of tyres. Like Dad, his mate had been invalided out of the army. He had then achieved great commercial success and was soon known in the City as the Fusilier Financier. One of the companies he acquired, as a part-payment of a bad debt, was the Camberwell Tyre and Battery Factory, and the only person he knew with any knowledge of tyres was Dad, so he offered him a 75% share in the company if he ran it.

John Hollands

On the day Dad went there to take over, he found the place deserted apart from six men sitting around a packing case with mugs of beer at their sides, gambling on the outcome of a game of 'Snap!'. His initial impulse was to sack them all and start from scratch, but wisely he decided not to be rash. He needed the support of locals so he stood and watched the game and he was so impressed by the sharp, eagle-eye craftiness of the winner, known to everyone as 'Old Percy', that he appointed him foreman, a judgement he never regretted.

This introduction to the tyre and battery business was just one part of our 'University of Life' syllabus. There were also trips to the Tower of London; the Imperial War Museum; the Natural History Museum; a mass meeting of striking dockers at Tilbury; a rally of latter day suffragettes in Hyde Park; a performance of Tchaikovsky's 1812 Overture at the Albert Hall; the Crazy Gang at the Stoll Theatre; Wembley; the White City; Henley; Epsom; Wimbledon and Twickenham.

Dad was so enthusiastic that sometimes he would spot events advertised in the Evening Standard and off we'd dash at a moment's notice. The most spectacular event we attended was the Coronation of King George VI and that filled Dad with enormous pride. Mum refused to go, fearing that the toilet facilities would be inadequate,* but the rest of us were there at the crack of dawn, standing three rows back from the curb near the Abbey. Dad hardly saw a thing of the procession. He was so determined that I should see every last detail that he had me on his shoulders for over four hours. When we got home and told Mum about it, she asked me: "And what was the best thing, Sajit? The very best thing?"

I replied: "Oh, that's easy. Gran's curry sandwiches."

Dad was none too pleased.

*****

*She was right. They were non-existent.

70

Gran and Mr Muckey

The highly significant incident to which I've already referred, and which I'm leading up to, is best described as an extra curricular activity. It was confined to Brother Nothing, both James and I being ruled too young to take part. Nothing was even sworn to secrecy, something he crowed about continuously.

Every Friday evening Dad and Brother Nothing disappeared in the Wolseley, with never a hint of where they were going or what they were up to. Naturally enough, this caused ructions. Mum was already near the end of her tether with Dad's 'University of Life'. Once she realised that domestic science had no part in it, and basic essentials like disinfecting toilets and starching sheets were ignored, she declared the whole concept a load of utter rubbish and refused to have any part in it. She wouldn't even join us in any of our outings and this resulted in her being frozen out of her own family. She had no one to turn to for sympathy, no receptive ear in which to pour her woes. Gran was as implacably opposed to her as ever and although Mum tried to make an ally out of me, she had no chance of success. With so much sport on offer, and all the fascinations of Camberwell Green, I was Dad's greatest fan.

When Dad and Nothing started their disappearing act, Mum became convinced Dad was having an affair with his secretary. Dad countered this by asking why he would take his son on a romantic liaison. Also, why his secretary? She was forty-five years old, racked with pain from her varicose veins, had six kids, and a jealous husband with three convictions for GBH. Confronted by this argument, Mum changed tact and said it was her constitutional and statutory right as a mother to be kept informed of her son's whereabouts. This bogus claim of civil rights was dismissed out of hand and Mum eventually accepted that her protests were a waste of time. When Friday evenings came round she would sit at the kitchen table and slurp gin and puff Craven 'A's. Only once did her plight excite anything that passed for sympathy. Then Gran observed: "Men have to go off on their own occasionally..."

"But they haven't even eaten yet," protested Mum.

"Perhaps that's what they're doing," said James, applying his usual logic to the situation. "Going out for something decent to eat for a change..."

"A good curry perhaps," smiled Gran.

"Yes," agreed James. "And naturally they don't like to tell you. I wish Dad would take me as well..."

Mum gave James's thigh a stinging slap. Then, when our meal was served, she gave him a double helping of spinach and stood over him until he'd finished every last shred of it. I thanked Hare Krishna I'd kept quiet. A double helping of Mum's spinach, which always reminded me of a mass of tangled green string floating bottom up amid algae, was something I could well do without.

It was nearing the witching hour when trouble struck.

James and I were in bed, supposedly asleep but in reality under his sheets with a torch, James reading me a Just William story. We never went to sleep until Dad and Nothing returned.

As soon as we heard a loud knock on the door William was forgotten. We emerged from our cocoon and strained our ears. When we heard a deep, male voice ask: "Is this your son, Madam?", we leapt out of bed and crept stealthily to the top of the stairs where we could peek through the banister railings and see what was going on in the lounge without being observed.

In all my life I've never been so terrified as when I saw those two enormous policemen standing in the lounge. They still had their boots on. I knew then that they were doomed, no matter why they'd come. They still had their helmets on too, which made them giants, reaching to within an inch or two of the ceiling. One of them was holding Brother Nothing by an ear, twisting it so hard that Nothing had his head to one side and kept squealing like a piglet. My fears increased when the other policeman took out a small notebook, extracted an indelible pencil from behind his ear, and then licked it copiously in preparation for recording everything that was said, obviously to be used in evidence against us at a later date.

"So what's your son been up to, Madam?" asked the policeman holding Brother Nothing.

"You tell me," responded Mum. "And where's his father?"

"I've no idea, Madam. What I need to know is what your son has been doing?"

"Well don't ask me, Boyo," yelled Mum, coming over all Welsh in her excitement. "How the hell should I know? He went out with his father. And now you bring him home alone. So what have you done with his father? And let go of his ear."

The policeman obeyed meekly and when Brother Nothing scurried to Mum's side nursing his ear, seeking comfort after such brutal treatment, she grabbed his other one and gyrated it so viciously that Nothing squealed even louder, no doubt wishing that he'd stayed in police custody.

Mum – emboldened by half a bottle of Holland's gin – was now capable of demolishing a brick wall. The interviewing policeman sensed this and tried to reinforce his authority by pulling out his notebook. This time we didn't have to wait for an indelible pencil to be lubricated. He cleared his throat, bent his knees, and proceeded to read out the contents of his notebook so falteringly that it was difficult to credit that he'd written it himself under an hour before.

"We... er... found the suspect... er... acting very suspiciously in suspicious circumstances... um... proceeding suspiciously in an east/south/easterly direction at a suspiciously brisk walking pace... er... down the Old Kent Road..."

"The Old Rent Koad!" screamed Mum.

The policeman's mouth fell open. His colleague stopped writing. "Beg pardon, Madam?"

"The Old Rent Koad..."

"Rent code?"

"Rent code?" repeated Mum in astonishment. "What are you talking about? You said you found him down the Old Kent Road."

"I did indeed, Madam."

"Then why suddenly bring up rent codes? We don't pay rent. Do I look like a rent-payer?"

"No, Madam... But you said..."

"What is a rent code, anyhow?"

"I've no idea, Madam."

"Then what the hell are you talking about?"

"Madam, it was you who said..."

"Never mind what I said... Are you soft in the head, or something?"

The policemen exchanged despairing glances, both hopelessly befuddled. "Not soft in the head, Madam," said the interviewer with commendable patience. "Just trying to do our duty." Then he referred again to his notebook and resumed quoting. "During the course of our... er... motorised patrol duties we... er... had occasion to apprehend the suspect..."

"Don't bloody well talk to me as though we're in court," interrupted Mum. "My son isn't a criminal. Nor is he a suspect. Just tell me what he was doing."

"Basically, as of now, at this moment in time, that's something we're still trying to establish..."

"Well have you asked him?"

"Christ, I'll say we've bloody asked him," responded the policeman, reverting to the vernacular, his training forgotten.

"And what did he say?"

The policeman regained his composure, having received an admonitory glance from his colleague. "At the end of the day, Madam, he said 'nothing'. And by 'nothing' I mean literally 'nothing'... Not that he didn't just say anything. He just wouldn't say anything but 'Nothing'. Nothing, meaning not anything..." His voice trailed away lamely, aware that he had failed to clarify matters.

"And did you ask him where his father was?"

"Repeatedly, Madam."

"Well what did he say?"

"Nowhere."

"So your enquiries so far have established that he was doing nothing in the Old Kent Road and his father, who took him there, is now nowhere..."

The expression on the policeman's face confirmed that, all things considered, that was a pretty accurate summary, but he certainly wasn't going to admit it. He consulted his notebook for guidance and added: "Not nowhere, Madam. We prefer to use the expression, 'Whereabouts unknown'."

"Well you're a right bloody Sherlock Holmes, I must say. Now clear off out of here and go and find my husband." Mum was now really underway. This was the tearaway we all feared. "And if you can't sort things out," she yelled, jabbing the policeman's chest with her index finger, "you tell your bloody superintendent that I want him down here quick-bloody-sharp to do it for you. Understand? And if you ever come back in my house again, which I certainly wouldn't advise, take your great clod-hopping boots off..."

"Yes, Madam." The policeman made haste towards the door, only to find that his colleague had beaten him to it with some ease. Their Wolseley sped off with squealing tyres. What happened next was inevitable. Brother Nothing caved in. Mum sat him on a high-back chair, pointed a finger straight between his eyes, and said in a voice similar to the final warning of a striking rattle snake: "Right, Boyo! Every last bloody detail, look you!"

A clear, concise account of things was never one of Brother Nothing's strong points but the gist of the matter was that every Friday evening Dad drove him into Golders Green where they bought a large, ready-mixed tin of whitewash and four giant paint brushes from the local hardware store.

They then drove to points in Hendon, Neasden, Cricklewood, and Park Royal, picking up members of the British Union of Fascists at each stop. Once dark, they would set off for south east London. Their route varied but they were systematically making their way, week by week, towards Chatham, the idea being that they would then link up with other fascists working their way up from Margate. The reason for the time spent on the journey was because en route they painted large fascist signs (a circle with a zigzag line through it) on blank walls, the arches of bridges being highly favoured since they afforded good cover whilst painting.

Brother Nothing's role was as the DLM – Destination Lookout Man. In other words, having spotted a suitable piece of wall or bridge to deface, Dad (as the driver) parked the Wolseley as inconspicuously as possible and then acted as the ALM – Approach Lookout Man. Brother Nothing would hare off down the road for at least a hundred yards or until he was around any bend in the road, and then keep KV. As soon as he, or Dad, spotted anyone, especially a police car or a couple of bobbies on their beat, they raised the alarm. The blackshirts would then abandon their task and pile back into the car. If Brother Nothing hadn't raised the alarm and gone back to the car, they would pick him up as they proceeded on their way towards Chatham.

So far they'd only been disturbed twice in four weeks and on both occasions their escape had gone smoothly.

As the weeks slipped by, fascist signs were spreading like a plague across London. This caused a public outcry and the London evening papers, headed by *The Star*, were vociferous in their demands for action. No one really expected anything to happen, but then it wasn't generally known that hidden in the bowels of Scotland Yard the spread of these fascist signs was being plotted on a giant map board.

The clearest signal flashed out by this map was that the fascists heading for the Medway ports were about to enter the Old Kent Road. The metropolitan police saw this as a heaven-sent opportunity to spring an ambush and eliminate at least one cankerous cell in the Union of British Fascists. Their confidence was based on two things: they knew the fascists would wait until late at night, when traffic was virtually non-existent, and that the proliferation of blank walls and bridges around the area would make their progress slow and stuttering, which would make it easy to monitor their progress towards the ambush site.

The site was to be the best known of all railways arches in London, the original home ground of Flanagan and Allen: the bridge that crossed the Old Kent Road between the Thomas A'Beckett public house and New Cross. A squad of specially trained constables was lying in wait for the fascist daubers with instructions to apprehend them and charge them under the Parliamentary Act of 1798 which made it illegal to pollute or deface public property, with a statutory minimum sentence of five years in jail or deportation to Botany Bay. The fact that this Act of 1789 was designed to stop people urinating and defecating in public places was deemed to be immaterial. The Department of Prosecution was adamant that this piece of legislation was the best way to secure a conviction and the stiff jail sentence public opinion demanded. If the magistrates opted for Botany Bay – as they were quite entitled to – then so much the better and bloody bad luck on the Aussies.

On Scotland Yard's map the chosen bridge looked perfectly normal but in reality it was very unusual. It was so high that locals often referred to it (quite erroneously) as a viaduct. The plan relied on surprise and to ensure that the fascists had no chance of being pre-warned, a squad of constables was concealed behind the retaining wall on the top of the bridge. There, they were to wait until the fascists were actually underneath the arch and busy painting, whereupon they would lower ropes down both sides of the bridge support columns. The constables would then slide down the ropes and surprise their prey. They would also have them very neatly sandwiched, ensuring an easy roundup.

The plan went wrong due to one vital factor. When the ropes issued by Scotland Yard were thrown over the side of the bridge, the constables who slid down them soon discovered that they were at least thirty feet too short, which left them dangling precariously in mid-air. At that height even the most conscientious among them were unwilling to indulge in a spot of free-falling. Those organising things on the top of the bridge were full of good advice, but the only practical result of their hollering was to tip off the fascists. They broke away from their painting duties to see dozens of policemen swinging about above them, for all the world looking like overzealous apprentice campanologists who'd made the classic error of grabbing their sallies and then forgotten to let go.

The fascists sprinted back to the Wolseley. Dad had seen the police spilling over the top of the bridge so he had the engine running and as soon as his colleagues were in the car he did a three-point turn and drove off at high speed. They couldn't have gone forward to collect Brother Nothing even if they'd tried. By this time the road was scattered by recumbent policemen who'd failed to climb back up their ropes and had, instead, fallen to the ground with bone-breaking consequences.

Like any good KV man, Brother Nothing stuck to his post. He didn't exactly ignore all the shouting and moaning and groaning going on behind him, in fact he rather enjoyed the spectacle of them writhing about in agony, but he kept his distance, with no intention of becoming involved. It wasn't until an hour later, after the ambulances had cleared away the human debris and the bloodstained road had been hosed down, that Brother Nothing decided to wander about for a bit, simply to keep warm. Then a police car on a routine patrol from Sidcup saw him and apprehended him. After parrying a barrage of questions, Brother Nothing had the gall to say: "Would you mind taking me home now, please."

*****

Gran and Mr Muckey

Once Brother Nothing had confessed everything, Mum had a horrific thought. The two policeman who'd returned him must surely have seen the pictures of Sir Oswald and Herr Adolf in the hall and drawn the inevitable conclusion. "Jesus wept!" she cried. "Those pictures..."

"Don't worry," replied Gran. "As soon as I saw who they were, I took them down. They're in the kitchen Easiwork."

That was the first and only time I ever saw a spark of kinship between Mum and Gran. Mum actually smiled at her and touched her arm in appreciation. This esprit de corps was short-lived, however. The full significance of Gran's remark soon dawned on Mum. "You knew all along what they were up to," she snarled. "You knew but never said a word."

"At least I've saved the situation," said Gran.

"Have you hell! I've told them to bring their inspector back here..."

"And what happens if Dad turns up whilst he's here?" asked Brother Nothing in a trembling voice.

"Especially if your father brings his blackshirts back with him," added Mum.

This intriguing possibility failed to materialise. Dad still hadn't returned by the time the two policemen reappeared with Inspector Hackett of the Yard, a high-flyer who, with the advantage of the Yard's greater overall picture, had had no difficulty in piecing together what had happened. He was so appalled by the way his junior officers had been fobbed off by a young, half-caste Indian boy and his neurotic, gin-soaked Welsh mother that he was determined to demonstrate the art of real interrogation. He met his first setback when Mum refused him entry until he produced a search warrant or unless he removed his shoes. When he reluctantly agreed to the latter, large potatoes were revealed in the heel of each sock and the big toe of his right foot was sticking clean out of another hole. These defects in his otherwise impeccable appearance stripped him of all dignity and made one shudder to think of what other horrors might be exposed if he was ever run over by a bus.

Even when Inspector Hackett commandeered Dad's angle-poise lamp and embarked upon third-degree tactics by shining it directly in Brother Nothing's eyes, he failed to regain the initiative. Not that he didn't try all the tricks of his trade. He bullied Nothing, laid cunning traps, put words into his mouth, tried trick questions, offered him an honourable let-out, fired a whole series of leading questions at him, and finally threatened him with a long spell in Borstal unless he confessed to his involvement in the Old Kent Road fiasco. None of this got him one iota further forward. In desperation, he said: "Sonny, I'm going to give you one final chance. Have you anything further to say?"

"KCYS," said Brother Nothing.

"KCYS?"

From my usual position, peering through the banister railings, I heard my own voice squawking out. Whatever possessed me to betray my presence I'll never know. Maybe the sudden enquiry about something as simple as 'KCYS' was too much for my vanity to resist.

"Kindly consider yourself squashed."

Everyone stared up at me in surprise and there was no doubt at all from the expression on Inspector Hackett's face that 'squashed' was exactly how he felt.

The upshot of it all was that Inspector Hackett ordered his two subordinates to sit outside in their police car and wait until Dad returned, as we all knew he would have to eventually. The two policemen didn't take kindly to their new instructions. They'd started off at 8 p.m. from sleepy old Sidcup anticipating nothing more involved than telling a few drunks to behave themselves, consuming numerous cups of tea and a free nosh-up at Annie's Transport Cafe in Catford, and discussing the prospect of the Hammers beating the Gunners at Highbury the following afternoon. After all, that's what experience had taught them constituted a hard day's work. Now, some eight hours later, they were camped outside a house in Edgware, by the look of it until dawn. One of them was particularly irate, repeatedly telling Inspector Hackett that his wife was expecting a baby and could be rushed to hospital at any moment. This did receive a modicum of sympathy and the Inspector said he would do his best to get a patrol car to relieve them, but he couldn't promise anything definite.

By the time Inspector Hackett left, and his two patrolmen had taken up their position in their car, it was five o'clock in the morning.

James and I slept soundly for a few hours. When we scampered downstairs for breakfast we were staggered to see Dad sitting there as large as life, scoffing his usual full house of eggs, bacon, chipolatas, mushrooms, and tomatoes, with black coffee and soldiers of toast oozing with butter to help things on their way. Somehow, without hindrance to stuffing his face, he told us what had happened.

The two policemen outside the house had got so browned off with their vigil that when they spotted a telltale illuminated Wolseley emblem coming down the avenue they were so delighted by the prospect of relief that they simply drove off, confident that the fresh policemen would have been fully briefed by Inspector Hackett and would be able to sort things out for themselves when Dad returned.

Ironically, it wasn't a police car at all. The Wolseley they saw approaching was Dad's. He arrived back so exhausted after hours of combing the streets for Brother Nothing that when he saw the police car parked outside the house he resigned himself to a fair cop and was prepared to confess everything in order to secure their co-operation in finding his son. When they drove off before he could make his confession he was amazed, but not nearly so amazed as when he discovered that Brother Nothing was already home and safely tucked up in bed, asleep. Seizing his opportunity,

Dad removed all the incriminating evidence from the Wolseley.

When he got back indoors he had a tremendous row with Mum. On being told about it, I couldn't see what all the fuss was about. What was wrong with painting blank walls? I was given Bulls Eyes for doing it at kindergarten, and Guinness, Austin, Morris and hundreds of other businesses had pictures on walls all over the place; and what about the public benefactors who wrote witticisms on the walls of the Gents toilets? No one ever complained about them: on the contrary, Dad and others lapped them up.

Anyhow, even if it was wrong, we'd all come out of it pretty well. Brother Nothing had covered himself in glory, Gran had saved us with her quick thinking, and Mum could take comfort from the way Dad had done a U-turn against the fascists. In fact, he was so disgusted by the four black-shirts telling him to look for the young wog by himself that he forthwith severed all connections with the saviours of the world. He took his claw hammer to the frames of Sir Oswald and Herr Adolf and then burnt their pictures and consigned their ashes to the dustbin.

If anyone had grounds for concern, it was me. When Dad heard of my cheek towards Inspector Hackett, he said that in the traditions of Scotland Yard the Inspector would have marked me down. Mum and Gran nodded grimly and for years I quaked in my boots, convinced that Hackett of the Yard would spend the rest of his life gunning for me, in the same way as Slipper of the Yard did with Ronald Biggs.

So ended Dad's flirtation with the blackshirts. The police returned later in the morning but they'd had their chance and blown it. When they asked Dad to explain his all-night absence, he told them – in absolute confidence – that he'd been with his secretary. He'd taken his son with him as 'cover' but the lad had become so embarrassed that he'd wandered off. With the panache of a veteran liar, Dad concluded: "The kid only refused to answer your questions in the interests of family unity... And we must preserve family unity at all costs..."

"Oh, absolutely," agreed the police. "Mum's the word."

Later on it came to light that Scotland Yard did further checks on Dad but drew another blank. Luckily, he'd never been enrolled as a member of the British Union of Fascists. When you consider his colour, it's obvious that they wouldn't have been seen dead with him as a proper member. They'd just used him as a sucker with a suitable car. The result was that in 1940, when members of the British Union of Fascists were interned for the duration of the war under Section 18B of the Defence of the Realm Act, Dad was not among them.

6

*Television – Among the first to watch – Dispute over which
set to buy – Mum nearly beats Mary Whitehouse to it –
First television addicts – Hooked on cricket –
Dad and the cunning bastards.*

D ad was enormously proud that we were about to
be among the first people in the world to watch a
proper television service.

As he was continually telling us, television was
pioneered by Logie Baird, a Scotsman, even though the first
regular television service was actually in Germany.
However, Dad told us to forget about that. Having been so
thoroughly disillusioned by the British Union of Fascists he
reckoned that television in the Third Reich would be
confined to pictures of the Gestapo making house arrests,
distant shots of Adolf strutting around Berchtesgaden, and
maybe a thrice-weekly serial of Hermann Goering's batman
polishing the Reich Marshall's medals. One thing he
guaranteed was that there would be no repeats of Jesse
Owens winning his four gold medals at the Berlin Olympics.

So he told us to forget Kraut television, that the first
proper television was going to come from Alexandra Palace
in north London, only a stone's throw away from Edgware.
The only problem in all this was which television set to
purchase. There were only two worthy of consideration, the

Baird and the Marconi, so Dad opted without hesitation for
the former on the grounds of it being 100% British.
However, when he showed the Baird brochure to Mum she
was highly indignant. She said it looked really cheap-jack
and refused to have it in her house. When Dad retaliated by
saying it was that or nothing, she called his bluff and went
to the local electrical shop and got a brochure on the
Marconi. When the two brochures were laid side by side
there was no comparison. Regardless of technical merit, the
Marconi was a magnificent piece of furniture, something
she would be proud to polish every two or three hours. It
was shapely and huge, almost twice the size of the Baird,
and it was finished in the most exquisite walnut veneers,
with a natty lid that closed down over the screen when it
wasn't in use.

In the ensuing row, James didn't help matters by saying:
"What you must remember, Dad, is that the Marconi does
scan the picture elements at least twenty-five times a
second and is far more efficient in the way the electrons are
accelerated and focused by the anode..."

"You pipe down," snarled Dad, sensing that he was
losing the argument.

Eventually, Dad came over all democratic, knowing that
Gran and I were on his side. He declared that we would put
it to a family vote. This went as follows:

Dad: Baird.
Mum: Marconi.
Brother Nothing: Neither.
James: Marconi.
Sajit: Baird (sucking up to Dad)
Gran: Baird (opposing Mum on principle).

On the face of it, a 3 to 2 majority in favour of the Baird,
but when Gran cast the deciding vote, Mum demanded:
"Who the hell asked your opinion? You don't have the
franchise in this house."

"Oh, and why not?"

"Because you're not proper family."

"What am I then?" screamed Gran. "A lodger?"

"You said it!" retaliated Mum.

Dad restored order by making a great concession. He abandoned his principle of never going shopping and suggested that on Saturday afternoon we should all go to Gamages to see the two sets demonstrated. When we got to the radio department the two televisions were standing side by side and the Marconi definitely had the edge. To clinch the deal, the salesman assured Dad that the Marconi Telegraph Company was, in fact, fully incorporated in London. So Dad bought the Marconi.

The set wasn't delivered until the first day of transmission and Dad made sure he was at home when it arrived. To his delight, it was too big to get in through the front door. The lounge bay window had to be removed, which in turn assured maximum exposure to the neighbours. The Gamages men installing it did a great job and the moment of final glory came when they produced an enormously long extending ladder and fixed the aerial to the chimney stack, a moment that can only be compared to the famous occasion, a few years later, when the American Marines hoisted the Stars and Stripes to hail the conquest of Iwo Jima.

The Marconi turned out to be highly temperamental, but the Gamages men nursed it along until they produced an excellent picture of the transmission signal. By this time there was only an hour or so left before the service opened, and there we were, drinks on laps, all set to witness a truly historic moment. Until, that is, Dad decided the picture needed to be darker. We all shouted at him to leave it alone but he wouldn't listen and within seconds the screen went blank. Dad told us not to worry, that he'd simply reverse what he'd done, but it seemed there was no reverse on the Marconi and whatever Dad did he was unable to restore the picture.

As with the incinerator, he eventually condescended to consult the instruction manual. It was an enormous tome, so technical that only James could understand it. 'Turning on' covered nine pages and other things, which these days don't warrant a mention, such as contrast, brightness, horizontal hold, vertical hold, focus and sound/picture synchronisation, took up 6,4,7,5,6 and 8 pages respectively. Even how to turn off took a page and a half.

"What's the matter with these Eyeties?" demanded Dad. "I told you we should have brought a Baird."

"But, Dad," I said. "What about Mussolini? I thought..."

"Never mind Mussolini... And you know what Thought did..."*

Eventually, James succeeded in restoring the picture. We then witnessed the very first *proper* television. There were several inaugural speeches, some super variety acts, and a long line of high-kicking chorus girls in what must have been the inspiration of Bermuda Shorts. This was succeeded by the peace and tranquillity of 'Interlude', an appropriate pause which gave us the chance to absorb the implications of this new phenomenon. Dad predicted that it would sweep the world like a bush fire and weld humanity into a single, superior entity. Documentary programmes and the freely available knowledge of experts would guide us to a new age of enlightenment, tolerance and understanding. Our political leaders would be able to talk to us and be questioned in our living rooms, thus enabling democracy to flourish as never before. We would see all the major sporting events, and the example of our heroes would inspire the younger generation to new heights of sportsmanship, manners, and integrity. Most of all, with family audiences to please, the high tone of future entertainment would be assured throughout the world.

As usual, Dad only saw the positive side of things. He never dreamt that television would degenerate into explicit sex and titillating nudity, documentaries based on propaganda, and sport corrupted by vast fees, drugs, cheating, and bribery. It was beyond his comprehension

*Dad often said 'You know what Thought did...' but he would never tell us.

that politicians would turn out to be such greedy, self-seeking liars, and if he'd ever suspected that the most common scene in our dramas and adverts would be men using urinals, he would have thrown a brick through the screen without hesitation.

'Interlude' soon became the most frequent programme. Gran thought it was also the best. It consisted of a beautiful old water wheel going round and round, accompanied by Ralph Vaughan Williams's arrangement of Greensleeves. Other than that, there were lots of cartoons and we were soon familiar with Walt Disney's wonderful array of animal characters: Mickey, Minnie, Goofy, Pluto, Donald Duck, Clara Cluck, and others. Popeye films were also popular and were highly approved of by Mum because of the way they demonstrated the value of spinach. The BBC considered cartoons to be adult viewing and they were shown so long after our bedtime that Mum refused to let us stay up for them. However, we put our faith in Dad. We'd lie awake until eventually he'd call up to us: "Come on, boys! Mickey Mouse," and we'd stampede down the stairs, pulling our dressing gowns on as we went.

Most programmes revolved around television's first personalities, Jasmine Bligh and Leslie Mitchell. They spoke perfect King's English, the sort of dulcet tones that now makes BBC producers reach for their sick bags. Their appearance was likewise immaculate, Jasmine in long dresses, cool and serene, with never a hair out of place, and Leslie in a dinner jacket, a natty bow tie, and sporting an Anthony Eden moustache. In the very early days, whenever Leslie Mitchell read the news, the screen went blank apart from a black surround, as though the items about to be mentioned were so disastrous that a period of mourning was called for; and certainly he dug up some pretty horrendous events. Once, he read: "China has suffered an earthquake reading 12 on the Richter Scale. So far, quite a few people are dead."

Gran and Mr Muckey

There were frequent plays and two stand out in my mind: *The Monkey's Paw* and *Death on the Second Floor*. Both caused great consternation in the Contractor household. With the former Gran was emphatic that there was nothing sinister or unlucky about a monkey's paw and only Europeans would ever carry one around, let alone pass it on to others as a curse. With the latter, Mum got in a real tizzy about its morality, and when the villain tip-toed into a young lady's hotel bedroom, clearly full of evil intent, she vowed to write in protest to Charles Reith. It was only when she discovered that the villain had merely murdered the girl, and not ravished her, that she changed her mind, thereby forsaking the chance to precede Mary Whitehouse by twenty years as Britain's foremost puritan.

One snag we didn't appreciate about the Marconi until it was too late was that the picture was located down a long tunnel, right at the back of the set, making it essential to sit straight in front of it. If one veered to either side even a fraction, a slice of it disappeared. Similarly, if one watched it either standing up or sitting on the floor, one only saw part of the picture. This meant that when we were all watching it we had to sit in a long line in front of it. As a family we managed okay but when friends and business associates of Dad's came round to watch major events, or when Dad invited all and sundry in to impress them, we had to watch in what can only be described as a gradientised queue. Even so, several people missed out on the full picture. James and I came off worst. We squatted on the floor in the front and saw nothing but talking heads and the roofs of the football stands. Then, according to age and fitness, others knelt, sat on low chairs, sat on our high, dining room chairs, stood according to height, and finally, situated right in the back in the bay window, Brother Nothing perched himself on the top rung of Mum's kitchen steps, rather in the fashion of a Wimbledon umpire. For him, the picture disappeared altogether, but what he saw was the picture on the bottom of the tunnel, from whence it was somehow bounced to the back of the set to form the proper picture. The snag in that was that everything Nothing saw was upside down and back-to-front. He said he preferred it that way, and it's perfectly true that he often laughed uproariously at things which weren't in the least funny to the rest of us.

Brother Nothing and I were very probably the world's first TV addicts. We both developed a passion for an aspect of television and we would allow nothing – but nothing! – to stand in its way. With me it was sport. With Brother Nothing it was fainters.

Fainters wasn't a programme, of course. It was people passing out. It happened frequently, maybe four or five times a day, and Nothing enjoyed the spectacle so much that he sat in front of the Marconi throughout all transmissions, waiting for the next one. The reason for so many fainters was quite simple. To get a decent picture the lighting in the studio had to be brilliant, so the BBC engineers developed arc lamps which were the forerunners to those now used at floodlit football grounds. Not only were they dazzling but they sent the temperature in the studio soaring, which meant that anyone not accustomed to such conditions soon began to wilt. Nut-brown colonial officers from Burma, Borneo, and Bengal, took it in their stride, but pasty-faced locals from Bermondsey, Battersea, and Burnt Oak, who had never been anywhere hotter than Hayling Island, were prime victims.

What fascinated Brother Nothing most was that one could spot those about to succumb. They cracked up and then collapsed in well defined stages, almost by numbers. First they shielded their eyes, then they perspired in torrents, then they mopped themselves down with their handkerchiefs, then they forgot their lines (or, if being questioned, gave answers of utter gibberish), and finally they keeled over, usually crashing into the surrounding equipment, causing a 'technical hitch'.

Gran and Mr Muckey

There was, indeed, a certain fascination in watching this happen, but the rest of us never stooped to the level of Brother Nothing by bouncing up and down on our chairs yelling: "There he goes!" in the manner of Captain Ahab sighting Moby Dick.

I'm glad to say that my obsession was more salutary. Also, whereas fainters was a passing phase and has long since disappeared, the coverage of sport on TV has increased and improved out of all recognition. Yet even in the very early days, the sport on offer was excellent. Football had pride of place and Arsenal, being a local side, soon had my undying support. One of my great regrets in life is the way this marvellous British game has degenerated into an avaricious shambles with vicious yobbishness on the field and terraces. Pre-war it was an orderly, family sport, devoid of anger, spite, greed, professional fouls and extreme partisanship. There wasn't even any racing around the pitch in ecstatic, celebratory circles when a goal was scored. Such antics and wild excesses were still the prerogative of decapitated chickens.

Quite often amateur football was shown and these games were superb: British sportsmanship at its very best. One team, the Corinthians, still practiced the tradition of refusing to score from the penalty spot. When awarded a penalty they shot wide on the grounds that their opponents would never have fouled them deliberately.

The best game I saw on television was the Wembley Cup Final of 1939 when Portsmouth ran riot and beat Wolves 4-1. Another highlight of the sporting world was Don Budge dominating everything at Wimbledon in 1937 and '38. Then there was boxing with Tommy Farr coming back from America where he'd out-boxed Joe Louis over fifteen rounds, only to be robbed of the world heavyweight crown by biased judges.

However, what really captured my interest was cricket. It was so leisurely and gentlemanly, yet spiced with split second drama. It was an ideal game for early television due to the fact that there was only one camera available for outside broadcasts, and whilst this was totally inadequate in other sports, it had no difficulty in keeping up with cricket. Much the same applied to the main commentator, the legendary Howard Marshal. Actually, he was no great shakes as a commentator and made more mistakes than David Coleman ever did, but since there were rarely any close-ups, and for the most part the ball was invisible, and the players mere dots on the screen, his plethora of errors went largely unnoticed. Mind you, I spotted them. I recall seeing the Australian fast bowler, McCormick, send Wally Hammond's leg stump cart-wheeling (but only after he'd scored 240) and Howard Marshal waking up in time to say: "Hello! Hammond's been run out. What a sad way to go." On another occasion, when Bill Edrich failed yet again, the great commentator said: "Edrich is out. Same old trouble... Clean bowled playing forward to a ball he should have left well alone."

Wally Hammond's innings of 240 at Lord's in 1938 is still the greatest innings I've ever seen, but the best Test Match came shortly afterwards at the Oval. The series against Australia was 1-0 in their favour which meant there was a sour atmosphere in the Contractor household. Dad wasn't interested in cricket as a game, but he was praying that the Australians wouldn't win the series, that they would be thrashed in the final game. He even took time off work in the hope of seeing it happen. This hatred of Australians dated back to when he was shot through the foot by a Digger at Anzac Cove. As the years slipped by he forgot that it had saved his life and instead he became convinced that the Digger had done it on purpose. It got to the stage where every time anyone noticed his limp, his loathing of all Australians grew deeper and more bitter. He followed their cricket tours simply in the hope of seeing them humiliated and the years 1926, 1928/9, and 1932/3, when England won the Ashes, were his golden years. His greatest regret was that during the Body-line tour of Australia Harold

Gran and Mr Muckey

Larwood had so narrowly failed to kill Bill Woodfull and Bertie Oldfield with his dreaded bouncers.

Just before the Oval Test started, the Australians went out on the field for a team photograph. Dad muttered two fateful words: "**THE BASTARDS!!**"

I resort to bold, capital letters, two exclamations marks, and underlining, simply because there is no other way to convey the depth of loathing and contempt in Dad's voice. I was puzzled. I was familiar with 'buggers', 'poofters', 'Wogs', 'Yids', and 'Indibums' (which other kids called me), but 'bastards' was a new one on me. I waited until the game had settled down and then asked: "Dad, what are bastards?"

"Australians. That's what bastards are."

That struck me as a straight answer to a straight question so I thought no more of it. Every time I pointed to a tiny figure on the screen and said: "Look at that bastard, Dad," he rewarded me with an affectionate smile.

Nothing much happened until just before lunch. Then Dad suddenly went bright red in the face and exclaimed: "Oh no! They're putting on that bastard O'Reilly."

I sat forward in alarm and stared down the tunnel. Now, instead of two bastards flinging the ball down as fast as they could, there were two rather odd-looking bastards tossing the ball into the air in what looked like a very friendly manner. One of the bastards was so slow that the ball had actually become visible. Then Mum came in with our lunch on trays. "Which side is throwing the fall birst?" she asked.

"The bastards are," I volunteered.

Mum snorted critically and gave Dad a really nasty look. I ignored her. She'd brought the lunch in, that was the main thing. When she'd gone, Dad said: "Don't take any notice of her. Bastards are bastards. And believe me, Sajit, all Australians are bastards. And some are bigger bastards than others. Like these two bowling now. Fleetwood-Smith and O'Reilly."

"Why are they bigger bastards, Dad?"

"Because they're leg-spin bowlers. And being leg-spinners, they're not just bastards, they're cunning bastards. They'll soon get young Hutton out. He won't have to hurry over his lunch."

For reasons I've never understood, and despite Hutton staying at the crease for three days instead of enjoying his meals with his feet up, I made up my mind there and then to become a leg-spinner and a cunning bastard, albeit it an English one. It became a major obsession in my life and I've never regretted it, even though it cost me my first marriage and earned me the first of several canings at school.

7

*An isolated family – Christmas 1935 – the influences
of our bicycles – Brother Nothing comes a cropper –
Mr Greenbaum takes us to the magistrates court.*

I t never occurred to me at the time, but as a family we
were very isolated. Dad certainly had business
colleagues, clients, and associates, but none of them
were drinking pals. Likewise, Mum had no woman-friend
with whom to go shopping or attend matinees, and Gran
was little more than a hermit. As for Brother Nothing,
James, and myself, we never got invitation to parties of our
classmates, even though there were plenty of them floating
around. Christmas holidays were just as lonesome, apart
from 1935. Then, a great gang of Mum's relatives came up
from the Rhondda.

Things got off to a lively start when Uncle Dai Central
Eating declared that the house needed fumigating on
account of the curry. On Christmas Eve there were even
more serious contretemps when they all got so blotto that
they developed a fixation about the need to sally forth down
the avenue to sing their favourite carols, oblivious to Dad's
repeated warnings that their efforts would not be appreciated. They gave several beautiful renderings of "Hail Jesus,
King of the Jews" but on receiving no response to their
warbling they banged on the front doors in high dudgeon.

John Hollands

When doors were grudgingly opened to them and they flour-
ished collection tins in aid of the Welsh Miners' Benevolent
Fund, they were amazed to have door after door slammed in
their faces.

They soon came home in disgust, making such highly
derogatory remarks about the English that (as Dad later
pointed out) it was easy to see that the cause of Plaid Cymru
had taken a huge step forward.

The final breakdown in the festive spirit came when Dad
refused point blank to finance a trip to watch the
London/Welsh play rugby at Richmond on Boxing Day.
They left early the following morning and never returned.

It would be easy to blame our isolation on racism, but the
fault lay within the family. Mum and Dad had both been
loners as children and this inevitably rubbed off on my
brothers and me and confined our horizons. If we'd had an
elder sister (as we so nearly did) our social activities would
no doubt have been broadened, but as three Anglo/Indian
brothers we remained a tight, self-contained entity.

The absence of a sister also meant that we lacked certain
social niceties. We viewed girls with curiosity and suspicion
and I've no doubt this retarded our sexual awareness and
development. Whereas other kids were forever playing
doctors and nurses and either removing or peering into each
other's underwear, thus working out for themselves why
some had one and others didn't, I remained blissfully
ignorant of such things and assumed that everyone had
one. Maybe Brother Nothing and James were better
informed than I was but I can't be sure since we never
discussed sex. We knew that if we did, and Mum overheard
us, we'd all get another long spell in the Black Hole of
Ferndale. Hence my confusion over Camberwell brothels
and why I had no hesitation in showing off my physique to
the Jewish girls opposite when incarcerated in the Black
Hole. I really thought they were watching so intently
because they admired my Charles Atlas poses, not because

96

Gran and Mr Muckey

I had one and they didn't. When I eventually discovered the truth, and how I'd betrayed the entire male sex, I felt positively ill.

In the spring of 1938 Dad suddenly realised he was getting a paunch. Anxious to keep it in check, he went into Edgware and bought himself a Raleigh. It was a racing bike, a fantastic model with drop handlebars and no less than three gears. In his inimitable way he added several accessories: a Union Jack on a chrome rod fixed to the rear mudguard, a massive rubber-bulge horn on the crossbar that played two rude-sounding notes when he operated it with his knee, and on the handlebars the most important thing of all, the speedometer. When the bike was delivered one Saturday morning, Mum was horrified. "You'll break your neck," she declared. "You've never ridden one in your life."

"So what?" responded Dad. "It's only a matter of confidence. The faster you go, the easier it is."

He then stuffed the bottoms of his trouser legs into his socks and sprinted, as best he could, down Glendale Avenue for some fifteen yards with the Raleigh at his side before leaping on to the saddle. He was off and away, pedalling like hell. Half an hour later he returned, flushed with success, and it was only a matter of time before we were all equipped with bikes bristling with the same accessories. Brother Nothing had another Raleigh, James had a BSA, and – very much to my chagrin – I was fobbed off with a Triang tricycle.

For a month or two our lives revolved around these bikes. Brother Nothing and James went far and wide and came back with fascinating stories of hitherto unexplored parts. Once, they went all the way to Marble Arch. When Mum realised they'd gone on the road, instead of the pavement as she insisted, she was furious. Dad only laughed. He said that riding on the pavement was for kids and that there was no better way of learning anything than jumping in the deep end. "A pity you didn't carry on and have a go at getting around Hyde Park Corner," he told them.

He was just as relaxed when it came to instructing them on the rules of the road, such as hand signals, stopping at halt signs, taking care on the brow of hills, and who had the right of way at junctions and roundabouts. His attitude was typical of the times. Everyone worked these things out for themselves. There were no driving tests and the only Highway Code was a skimpy, botched-up job which few people were even aware of, let alone read. You parked anywhere you liked (yellow lines being unheard of) and although a speed limit had recently been introduced in towns, the AA and RAC patrolmen tipped off motorists when the police were in the area by not saluting them.

What obsessed Dad about cycling was speed. He taught Brother Nothing and James to duck their heads well down on their handlebars and keep their elbows tucked into their sides in order to minimise wind resistance. He also explained that if they kept really close to the back of cars, buses and trolley buses, they could ride in their wake and this would enable them to go faster and with less effort. In order to convince them, he conducted speed trials along the avenue and made them practice riding behind the Wolseley with their eyes fixed on the brake lights.

The Jews watched all this with grave misgivings. They had good cause to: they knew the Contractor family well enough by now to realise that their latest craving for speed could only lead to disaster.

The first incident could best be described as a self-inflicted wound. Although my brothers' bikes worked perfectly, they were forever searching for ways of making improvements. Their favourite practice was to turn them upside down so that they rested on their saddles and handlebars and then whirl the pedals round and listen for suspicious noises. Whilst doing this, Brother Nothing detected a weakness in his brakes. His theory was that the rubber blocks had become shiny due to the great speeds he achieved and were therefore inefficient. So he removed them and roughened them up with sandpaper for greater purchase. When he had everything reassembled he announced that he would test them by getting up a good turn of speed along the avenue and then turn into our short drive and come to a screeching halt by slamming on his new, high-powered brakes. He duly got up to around twenty miles an hour but when he turned into the drive and applied his brakes, the roughened-up rubber blocks flew straight out of their metal housing which he'd replaced back to front. The bike smashed into the garage and Nothing went straight over the handlebars, face first into the doors.

I had seen similar things happen in Tom and Jerry cartoons so at first I enjoyed the spectacle and had a good laugh. After all, in the cartoons Tom was never more than temporarily stunned and he never bled, never broke any bones, and a good shake soon restored him to his normal shape. For some reason none of this worked for Brother Nothing. He remained flattened against the garage doors for what seemed like several seconds, his arms out to his sides, his heels together, as though crucified back to front. When he did eventually drop he remained prone on the drive and was bleeding like a stuck pig. Worse still, his nose was a terrible sight. Normally, it was a long, thin protuberance, but now it was as flat and as broad as trampled chewing gum, splattered across his face from ear to ear.

Mum heard the crash and was soon on the scene. She wrapped his head in a towel and rushed him to the nearby hospital. When he reappeared he was heavily bandaged, with his nose in a splint. For a month or two he went around looking like a half-finished Egyptian Mummy, but when the bandages were removed a splendid Roman nose was revealed. Everyone agreed that it was a vast improvement on his previous little snout.

*****

John Hollands

Brother Nothing was going through one of those phases in life where everything goes wrong the whole time. We all have them, but he had far more than his fair share of them. It was typical of him, and his bike riding, that no sooner had he become accustomed to his new nose than he had an even more catastrophic pile up. This time, instead of ending up in hospital, he was summoned to the Edgware Magistrates Court to face a civil case for compensation. It was brought against him by Mr Greenbaum, one of our Jewish neighbours.

The incident occurred on a Saturday afternoon. Dad and I were watching football on the television. Mum had sent Brother Nothing off on his bike to get a fresh bottle of Green Label Chutney for Gran's curry supper. He went willingly enough, there being no possibility of fainters during an outside broadcast. Sam Bartram had just made a spectacular save from Ted Drake when there was frantic knocking on the front door. It was Mr Greenbaum from halfway along the avenue. He was well known for his appalling English and his highly excitable nature.

"Your crazy son," he stormed. "He been making zer terrible crash-bank! He crazy... Head down and crash-bank..."

He was so agitated that we all assumed Brother Nothing had at least fallen under the wheels of a trolley bus. Then, as Mr Greenbaum continued to splutter in his broken English, we heard Nothing putting his bike back in the garage; and sure enough,a moment later, he appeared from the kitchen as right as rain.

"There he beink!" yelled Mr Greenbaum. "Zat boy crash-bank mine Austin. I vant compensation..."

Although it was natural to assume that Brother Nothing was in the wrong (because he so often was), Dad resisted the temptation. He knew that however bad his son was as a cyclist, Mr Greenbaum was a much worse motorist. Everyone in the avenue had seen and heard his efforts. Dad said he was the type of uncoordinated, head-in-the-clouds intellectual who should never have been allowed in control of a wheelbarrow, let alone a car. He couldn't even negotiate bends properly. Instead of turning the steering wheel the required amount, he merely edged it in the right direction and then, together with his family, leaned heavily to that side as though their weight would make up the difference. When they came to hills they were in even greater trouble. His gears lacked synchromesh which meant that when changing down he had to double-declutch. The timing and co-ordination needed for this was so beyond Mr Greenbaum that he had long since given up trying. Instead, he remained in top gear and he and his family would sit on the edge of their seats and jerk backwards and forward in unison, urging the Austin 7 on. About the only thing they didn't do was take a whip to it. When the car eventually stalled, Mr Greenbaum started again from scratch and went up the hill in first gear.

Another of Mr Greenbaum's weaknesses came after dark. He was then totally confused by the close proximity of the clutch pedal to the dip switch (both located on the floor, by the left foot). Every time he tried to dip his lights he went into free-wheel and when he attempted to change gear his lights went on to full beam. To Mr Greenbaum the whole thing suddenly became like Spanish plumbing, with whatever he did being rewarded by something totally unexpected: either the sound of tearing metal, or being totally blinded by the full beams of retaliating oncoming traffic. Eventually, on a moonless night in Watford, he became so confused and distraught that he abandoned his car and completed his journey by bus. He never went out in the dark again.

Mr Greenbaum's greatest dread was having to do three-point turns. Reverse gear was his bête noir. He only ever engaged it before the engine was running, and once he'd located it and got into it, he liked to stay in it and make the most of it. In this he was encouraged by his wife who was convinced that going backwards reduced their petrol consumption.

I mention all this for a good reason. It explains why the Greenbaums, when visiting their friends the Goldsmiths at the far end of the avenue, went all the way there in first gear and then all the way back in reverse gear, a classic exercise in the art of minimum effort. He didn't even turn round, cross the road, or change gear on the move; and – since they went as far backwards as they did forwards – Mrs Greenbaum reckoned that the journey cost them nothing and furthermore included a free tea at the Goldsmiths.

On the Saturday afternoon in question, as Brother Nothing sped along the avenue, doing his damnedest to notch up the golden figure of 25 mph, and struggling to stop the bottle of Green Label Chutney from slipping out from beneath his pullover, Mr Greenbaum's Austin 7 was reversing towards him on the same side of the road, galloping and zigzagging in a most erratic manner, with his family swaying this way and that with each change of direction.

When the inevitable crash occurred, Brother Nothing – as was rapidly becoming his wont – sailed over his handle-bars. He landed on the roof of Mr Greenbaum's car, slid across it and then dropped on to the bonnet. His weight caused numerous dents and the broken bottle of Green Label Chutney inflicted multiple scratches.

When Dad refused to meet Mr Greenbaum's claim for compensation, and counter-claimed for a fresh bottle of Green Label Chutney, the police were informed but very wisely declined to get involved. Hence, one bright Thursday morning, the Contractor family attended the Edgware Magistrates Court where Dad (as the responsible parent involved) was required to face Mr Greenbaum's claim for £50 10s 7d. It soon transpired that Mr Greenbaum was a solicitor by profession and when the case got underway he had enough files and documents spread out in front of him to see him through a ten day murder trial. However, amongst all the trappings of his profession was a copy of the Highway Code, and it was on the information gleaned from this that Mr Greenbaum so confidently based his exorbitant claim.

Quoting from the Code, he established that the law granted him the right to reverse down the road in the wrong direction for thirty yards. Therefore, although he might appear to have been going in the wrong direction, and should have been on the other side of the road, he was, in law, going in the right direction on the correct side of the road. He didn't dispute that the Indian boy was also going in the right direction, on the correct side of the road, even though he was doing exactly the opposite to Mr Greenbaum.

Unfortunately, in the said circumstances, the Highway Code didn't specify as to who had the right of way. Mr Greenbaum therefore claimed that the reason for the accident was that the Indian boy was travelling at an excessive speed with his head down over his handlebars, not looking where he was going. He had ten Jewish witnesses of impeccable character waiting outside in the corridor, listed in Old Testament order, prepared to testify that the Indian boy did this all the time, encouraged by his father.

Dad's counter to this was that if his son hadn't been looking where he was going he wouldn't have pulled over to the right, the same as Mr Greenbaum had during the course of his frenzied, out of control, zigzagging.

A lady magistrate had the honesty to admit that she was confused. So too were all the others, but as male motorists they were never going to admit it. The lady magistrate asserted that if both parties were, in the eyes of the law, on the correct side of the road, proceeding in the correct direction, surely the manoeuvre was, by definition, overtaking, which was covered in the Highway Code in the sub-section headed: 'Overtaking'. This stated that the slower vehicle should hold a steady course and the faster vehicle should pass the slower vehicle on the right-hand side. It was therefore a clear case of which party was going the faster.

The logic of this view would have helped but, as everyone else conceded, both parties had already claimed that the other was going at an excessive speed and, without an independent witness, who could tell who was going faster? With each confusing and nonsensical twist, Mr Greenbaum's excitability and frustration increased, and when the Clerk of the Court managed to bring a modicum of sense back to the proceedings by recommending that the distance from the Goldsmiths' home to the site of the accident should be measured, to make sure it wasn't over thirty yards, Mr Greenbaum (who knew it was at least a hundred yards) took refuge in an outburst of righteous indignation and demanded the right to call Mr Abraham, his first witness. When this was refused, Mr Greenbaum over-played his hand with a touch of Teutonic arrogance, a trait the magistrates did not admire.

"Wots the matter wiv you Englanders?" bellowed Mr Greenbaum. "You fink I know damn nothink. But you are wronk. I know damn all!"

Amid general laughter the magistrates ruled in favour of Contractor. Dad got a new bottle of Green Label Chutney and a report in the *Edgware Gazette* carried the headline: "*Reversing Motorist Laughed Out of Court.*"

8

*War looms – The nation makes ready – I have trouble with
my gas mask – Mum and the bureaucrats –
A pervert calls from the town hall.*

I t soon became obvious that the Second World War was
about to break out. Neville Chamberlain had flown back
from Munich with an assurance of peace in our time but
everyone soon realised he'd been hoodwinked by Herr Adolf.
People started to talk of 'when' rather than 'if'. I had little or
no conception of what the war would entail, only that it
would certainly liven things up a bit. I knew there would be
death and destruction but I visualised it as being as remote
and impersonal as it was in feature films like *The Iron Duke*
and *The Four Feathers.*

Naturally enough, Dad was my main source of information. After all, he had fought in the previous war and he took
a keen interest in politics, so all my knowledge had his
slant, and probably still does. According to him, the whole
thing was going to be a disaster and we might even end up
fighting the wrong people. As for the Poles, even if they were
our allies, what could we possibly do to help them? They
were hundreds of miles away and completely inaccessible.
What we needed to do, he said, was to hope like hell that
Adolf continued to advance eastwards, away from us, which
meant that he'd end up having a go at Russia, not France.

The communists were our real enemies so the best thing would be for the Krauts and the Ruskies to fight each other to a standstill in the barren wastelands of Siberia and leave the rest of us in peace. Like everything Dad said, it made good sense to me.

Anyhow, war was soon such a foregone conclusion that everyone began to prepare for it. The first thing we had to do was report to the local school hall to be fitted with gas masks. I was confronted by an old dear with a pheasant's feather in her hat and a dead fox draped around her neck, and instead of giving me a proper gas mask she took me for some kind of moronic infant who was hankering after a Mickey Mouse gas mask.

"I'm sure you'd like to join Mickey and all his little friends," cooed the silly woman.

"No I bloody wouldn't," I retorted, swearing knowingly for the first time in my life. "I want a proper one."

Mum gave me a vicious whack around the ear. "How dare you swear at the nice lady like that? And where did you get that language from? You'll have what you're bloody given. God, how I wish you'd been a girl."

Then, in the vindictive way Mum had, she grabbed a pink Minnie Mouse gas mask and made me have that. It not only had a picture of Minnie on the cardboard box, but the mask itself sported two large black ears. I screamed blue murder, but it did me no good. As I carried it home, trying to hide it behind my back, I vowed that I would never wear it. I'd rather be gassed to death. With the first German raid I'd be a goner, but at least I'd die with dignity.

Another thing about the approaching war that made me sore was that halfway through the summer the West Indian Cricket Tour was cancelled. By this time I was a well informed cricket fanatic and I'd been longing to see Learie Constantine in action. I was also looking forward to study-ing their leg-spinner, Bertie Clark. Nor was I alone in my disappointment. The BBC even sent Leslie Mitchell to

Lord's to interview the assistant groundsman. He was a splendidly outspoken fellow who was dead against the cancellation. He reckoned that even if there was all-out war, cricket should continue to be played at all levels. When Leslie Mitchell raised the question of possible bomb damage to Lord's, particularly the sacred square, the groundsman was most scathing. "Bombs," he laughed. "No need to worry about bombs, Guvner. Jerry won't dare to come over here in daylight. And the last thing we do every evening is rope the square off."

One of the most curious things about war-fever was that council workers suddenly started digging ditches all over the place. We were told that these were to stop German planes landing. For the life of me I couldn't understand why we should try to do that. Wouldn't it be better to let them land and then capture or destroy them when they were sitting ducks, rather than to encourage them to keep flying around the place, dropping bombs on us, with a good chance of getting back to Germany? According to my cigarette cards, none of their planes could carry more than 20 men so even if a dozen of them landed in Hyde Park, what good would that do them? If they tried to off-load a brigade of men, they'd need to land around 200 planes and there just wasn't room for that many, not even at Croydon Airport; and if the Krauts dropped parachutists the trenches would simply provide them with somewhere to fight from. The whole thing seemed pretty daft to me.

When I put these points to Dad – thinking I must have missed a vital factor – he agreed, but said that it was no good making a fuss about it. The authorities were just trying to be positive. If they waited for the planes to land they'd be accused of doing nothing, whereas if they did something, no matter how ill-conceived, everyone would think they were on the ball.

"Sajit, old chap," he said patiently, smiling at my innocence, "war is just as much about propaganda and morale as anything else."

John Hollands

Anyhow, however misguided the authorities were, these ditches were soon established in fields, the middle of football grounds, in parks, and in children's playgrounds. There were even some in our local recreation ground and these caused a nasty accident. On the far side of the ground was a small wood, known to locals as The Nest on account of it being where young lovers went for a bit of nooky after being turned out of the cinemas and pubs. Returning from The Nest late one night, a couple fell into one of the trenches and the fellow broke a leg. Nowadays he'd get a million quid compensation, but in 1939 everyone except Dad thought it served him damn well right. Dad saw the girl's picture in the Edgware Gazette and he said a broken leg was a small price to pay for what the bloke had got.

Another thing that was common practice was building sandbag walls outside the windows of council and local government buildings, and the newspapers were full of advice on how to build Anderson Shelters in your garden and then how to drain off all the water they filled up with. Also, we were introduced to stirrup pumps with which to put out incendiary bombs. These stirrup pumps didn't look up to much and Dad dismissed them contemptuously, saying they had about as much chance of putting out an incendiary as piddling on them.

It soon got to the stage where there was so much preparation going on for the war that it was obvious we'd have to have one simply to justify all the expense in preparing for it. Also, the more people dressed it up in euphemisms such as 'hostilities' and 'when the balloon goes up', the less terrible it seemed. Indeed, war soon assumed a weird fascination. Most people saw it as a welcome relief to boring jobs, or standing for endless hours in dole queues, or wearing out boots on hunger marches to the indifferent sods in London. For the masses, it would be a form of release, a chance of adventure and an opportunity to prove themselves; to be wanted and valued.

Gran and Mr Muckey

In my life I've been heavily involved in two wars and whilst, like any sane person, I would never wish a war on anyone, my knowledge indicates that those involved in them come to regard their experiences as the highlight of their lives. Clearly there are those who have good wars and those who have bad ones. The latter usually end up dead, so their side of things is never heard, whereas those who survive only ever recall the good times, especially as they grow nostalgic in old age.

(This was brought home to me many years later when I was drinking in the Sidmouth cricket pavilion with a very quiet, retiring member named Ben Williams. Beside him was his wife, a great dragon of a woman aptly named Bertha. Ben and Bertha had been married for a fortnight in 1939 when Ben, as a 2nd Lt in the Territorial Army, was called up and sent to Gibraltar within 24 hours. He told us that he'd spent the next six years there, indenting for fresh supplies of food and ammunition in the safety of an underground bunker, surrounded by lovely young WRENS and local girls. For a time he looked into his beer, obviously recalling all the beach parties, moonlight walks, mess booze-ups, and the host of girlfriends he'd obliged. Then, with a blissful sigh, he said: "Ah yes! Six years in Gibraltar. The best six years of my life." For that careless moment of honesty he received the biggest handbagging I've ever had the misfortune to witness.)

Some of the preconceived ideas about the war were not only strange but laughable. The obsession with German spies was typical. Overnight everyone became convinced that Britain was crawling with traitors. Posters, pamphlets, and hoardings, warned us that spies came in all shapes and sizes and were to be found not only in suspicious circumstances (hiding under bridges and living rough on the moors) but also in normal, every-day situations. We were urged to be on our guard against those next to us in trains, or anyone scoffing food in a pig-like manner in cafeterias, and most of all to tread warily in the Gents urinals. Those glancing furtively from side to side, and taking an inordinate time to complete their mission, weren't necessarily after what you'd always imagined, but were spies seeking useful information. (Sorting out the Jews from the Gentiles, perhaps?)

People took all this so literally that in Edgware, with its horde of Germanic refugees, the police were inundated with denunciations. These spies apparently used a wide variety of ingenious communicating techniques in order to contact their masters in Germany. Hand torches flashed in an easterly direction seemed to be favourite, but there was also a large number of more subtle spies who flashed out signals by lowering and raising the blinds in their bathrooms. One Saturday morning the *Edgware Gazette* carried a story about two old ladies travelling together on a bus. Some worthy do-gooder reported them for exchanging secret messages of a highly technical nature, a code no less; but after they'd been questioned for half an hour at the local police station it transpired that they'd been swapping knitting patterns.

The saddest thing about this mass hysteria was that the government was so taken in by its own propaganda that whole sections of the community who didn't fit in with their conception of true-blue Brits were rounded up and incarcerated for the duration. Among the first to go were members of the British Union of Fascists, followed by recent immigrants from Germany and Austria. Conscientious objectors fared a little better. They were given the option of driving ambulances on active service. Jehovah Witnesses went inside in the interest of peace and quiet and they were soon joined by known and highly suspected homosexuals (none of whom could believe their luck at being kept in close proximity to so many lovely new friends). At the time, all this seemed natural enough, but the truth was that whilst we talked about our devotion to fighting for freedom, we had no choice but to live in what was no more than a police state.

To win what we were fighting for, we had to endure what we were fighting against.

If ever there was a heaven-sent gift to bureaucrats it was the war. It might have taken Adolf Hitler to start it, but once it was underway Little Hitlers emerged out of the woodwork by the thousands, streaming out of government offices, military headquarters, county halls, town halls, schools, and even parish councils.

Mum and Dad went along with the general anti-German hysteria the same as everyone else, but I'm proud to say that when confronted by bureaucrats they stood their ground and told them what they could do with their petty regulations. Dad came across them at work, so I only know what happened to him from the stories he related; but every time a bureaucrat approached Mum I was right beside her and saw her reaction for myself, and she certainly gave them a hard time.

What infuriated the Edgware bureaucrats was that our garden was covered by six inches of solid concrete. There had been no regulation against such a measure at the time, but the bureaucrats were now so omnipotent that they demanded the removal of it on the grounds of national interest, something to which they said there was no argument or appeal. How, they wanted to know, could we build an Anderson Shelter under six inches of concrete? Also, how could we *Dig For Victory*?

When Mum told them unequivocally that she had no intention of doing either, and to bugger off and mind their own business, they retired in disarray but with a promise to return. True to their word they soon did, backed up by senior reinforcements. When Mum still wouldn't budge they wanted to know why she wasn't at work, contributing to the *Work Through to Victory* campaign? They even tried to enrol her as a cleaner at the local Church of England Primary School and then, when she demanded to know just who the hell they thought they were dealing with, they offered her a job at the Adult Further Education classes, lecturing on *Your Housework in Four Hours a Week*. Mum told them what to do with their lectures, pointing out that any self-respecting housewife would devote herself to her housework twelve hours a day, seven days a week.

To Mum, the final insult came when her chief persecutor turned up in the company of a very tarty-looking young female and told her that in accordance with Article 7, para 4, sub section C, of the Fuel Economy Act, he was instructed by the Home Office to demonstrate to all householders within his jurisdiction how two people could bath together adequately once a week in five inches of tepid water.

At that, Mum screamed: "You bloody pervert!" and slammed the door on him. We saw and heard no more of him until two years later. Then, whilst shopping in Allders in Croydon, we saw a notice directing everyone to the fifth floor where, *How to Bath in Five Inches of Water*, was being demonstrated. I made a beeline for the lifts but Mum grabbed me by the scruff of the neck and we went to Bentalls in Kingston instead.

9

A holiday in Switzerland – A missing French toilet –
Flippy-Floppy the ghost – The glory of Wengen –
Life among the Krauts – The Charge of the Dark Brigade –
The Devil's Ledge – Back in the nick of time.

At the beginning of August 1939, Dad announced that despite the political furore we were going on holiday to Switzerland. What's more, we would go by car. He already had the necessary carnet for the Wolseley and a brand new passport for Mum with our names on it.

"But what about the war?" demanded Mum.

"That won't start until we get back," said Dad.

"You've arranged that with your friend Hitler, have you?" Dad ignored her.

"But why go abroad?" persisted Mum.

"Because that's where the Alps are."

"But think of all the complications... Quite apart from the war, what about food? And the language problem? And the water? And driving on the right? And lavatory paper..."

"Lavatory paper?" we echoed.

"Oh, yes! They don't have lavatory paper in France, you know. When Uncle Dai came back from the Somme he never said a word about half the Rhondda being wiped out all around him. The only thing he said was, 'Thank God I'm back to civilisation and bog paper'..."

"Well I'm not cancelling because of loo paper," said Dad.
"Then we'll take our own," declared Mum.

So we did: five rolls of Bronco. One roll each with every-one responsible for their own.

On the first night of our trip we stopped at a small village hotel and we soon discovered that Uncle Dai was dead right. The Frogs didn't use lavatory paper. All they had was old newspapers torn up into squares. Worse still, they didn't even have proper toilets. Certainly not as we understood them. Their norm was a hole in the floor with two oblong blocks to stand on. When you flushed it a feeble trickle of water came out at floor level to wash the surrounds of the hole clean, if you were lucky.

As I say, that was the norm, but in our hotel the upstairs 'Hommes' had what must have been a 'Super' or 'Deluxe' model. When one flushed it there was a dramatic pause and whilst one waited in vain for the usual jet of water to wash the hole clean, water suddenly cascaded down from a show-er-head in the ceiling. We never did discover whether this was the Frog's idea of a high-powered flush or an all-in-one toilet and shower. Maybe the Frogs enjoyed a cold shower after a crap, or a crap after a cold shower, or even a crap and a shower simultaneously ... who knows? About the only merit I could see in the system was that it would have saved the likes of Gran the inconvenience of carrying around a tin can.

I went in first and duly got soaked. I warned the others and although Dad coped admirably, Brother Nothing suffered a major calamity. He was so worried by the sound of a head of water building up in the cistern above him, and the drips still descending from Dad's flush, that he stood the wrong way round, neglected to bend, and didn't even take proper aim, with the result that he might just as well have left his trousers where they were in the first place. When his predicament became known, Dad made James and me howl with laughter by saying: "Now you know what Thought did ..."

Gran and Mr Muckey

Mum didn't fare much better. She used the 'Dames' further down the corridor and she was so thrown by the paucity of appropriate furniture that she came storming out and reported to the owner that some thieving Frog had nicked his lavatory pan. With shrugs and grunts, this worthy denied any theft and tried to explain what was expected of her. In the end, things became so indelicate that he summoned his wife to give Mum a demonstration, but all to no avail. By this time Mum was so traumatised that, right at the vital moment, she dropped her roll of Bronco down the hole. Rather than brand herself with the inky headlines of La Monde, she yelled for fresh supplies. At first, since she was the one who insisted we were all responsible for our own rolls, we refused to help, but she hollered so loudly that Dad soon caved in.

Only James took things in his stride. He found the French bog paper highly informative. When he came out after about half an hour he was full of interesting facts and figures out of the previous week's Ce Soir. When he told Dad that the Maginot Line had enough shells in stock to last five years, and that all German movements were monitored by spotter planes, Dad was so fascinated that he told him to go back for the bog paper and read out what else the Frogs were up to.

We then sat on Dad's bedside and James went through the squares, picking out items of interest. We soon discovered that on the western front the French had more men under arms than the Germans, and 15% more tanks. We were so encouraged by this that we failed to hear an argument going on in the corridor. Then there was a knock on the door and the owner barged in. Without a word, he grabbed the squares of paper from James and handed them over to the man he'd been arguing with. He then apologised to the man, speaking so loudly, with so many references to "L'Anglaise', that his remarks were obviously intended for our ears. When he finished, Dad asked James: "What was all that about?"

"He said that only their gallant English allies could be so mean as to get their news by translating other people's lavatory paper. And God help them if they ever had to rely on the Roast Beefs in a tight corner."

I had a bedroom to myself. It was so damp and dismal, and I was so scared of being on my own in a foreign country, that I burst into tears. Instead of appreciating my sensitivity, and realising that I hadn't got Lucky to comfort me, Mum told me not to be so silly and to go to sleep. Eventually Dad made a major concession and agreed to tell me a bedtime story. That made me feel a lot better. Of all the things I'd yearned for, but never had, it was bedtime stories. Dad was a greater story teller, but he had no idea of the vulnerability of youngsters and he proceeded to tell me a ghost story. The ghost's name was Flippy-Floppy and Flippy-Floppy was so flippy-floppy that he couldn't stand up straight. Nor could he stand still. Instead, he wobbled about like a jelly straight out of its mould. People he tried to haunt just laughed at him as he flipped and flopped and wobbled about the place. Eventually, he became so fed up with it that he went to several doctors, seeking a cure. One by one they told him there was nothing to be done. He'd been born flippy-floppy so that was the way he'd have to stay. As Dad related this he dangled his arms and waggled them around. Then he bent his knees and stumbled around the bedroom. He was so realistic that – although I believed in ghosts and dreaded encountering one – his antics made me giggle happily.

"Then a miracle happened," related Dad. "Flippy-Floppy found a doctor who said he could cure him. He got out a huge syringe and injected Flippy-Floppy. Wondrously, Flippy-Floppy began to stiffen up and become normal. Then, as the doctor forced in the last of the magic potion, he became huge and muscular and able to walk upright like a proper ghost. And he immediately began to make plans to haunt and terrify as many human beings as he possibly could.

" 'But will the injection last?' Flippy-Floppy asked the doctor.

" 'Last!' laughed the doctor. 'I'll say it will last. I've just injected you with top quality Portland cement.'

" 'But what will happen when it sets?' asked Flippy-Floppy.

And even as Flippy-Floppy asked," whispered Dad dramatically, "the cement began to set. As it got harder and harder, Flippy-Floppy got stronger and stronger. Then he felt himself get stiffer and stiffer. Soon, he was totally rigid. His arms were stuck out in front of him, his head wouldn't turn, and the only way he could move was to jerk his legs forward like Frankenstein's monster."

Dad got off his chair and imitated this new form of ghost. He jerked himself around so realistically that the joke was suddenly over. I watched in abject terror. My eyes popped. I clutched the top of my sheets, ready to dive under at any moment. When Dad got to the door and opened it with out-stretched arms, he said in a peculiar, deep voice: "And that's how Flippy-Floppy changed from a ghost who frightened no one to the dreaded monster, Rigor Mortis. A monster who spends all his time making his victims as stiff as ramrods. Even if you can't see him, he's there, lurking round the corner, ready to pounce when you least expect it... Especially on little boys who won't go to sleep."

If Dad thought that was going to send me into a peaceful slumber he must have been off his rocker; but he obviously did because before I could say a word or move a muscle he'd closed the door on me. I damn nearly died of fright. If I'd had Lucky with me it would have been all right. He would soon have seen off any ghost, but without him I was defenceless and I spent the rest of the night under the sheets, continually testing my arms and legs and neck to see if they were getting stiff.

*****

The following day we drove for endless miles through the boring French countryside. I remained slumped in the middle of the back seat, never saying a word, still thoroughly scared. I just couldn't forget the monster Rigor Mortis. I kept stretching my arms and legs out to make sure they weren't going stiff, and swivelling my neck around as far as I could, as though checking to see if we were being followed. Each time I moved Mum whacked me and yelled: "Sit still!" but sitting still was the last thing I intended to do.

That night we stayed at a hotel in Mulhouse and I disgraced myself at dinner by continually kicking Brother Nothing under the table as I stretched my legs out. Then, when I knocked over a jug of water while testing my right arm, and Dad's glass of red wine while checking my left arm, I was sent to bed in disgrace. That was a big mistake. I managed to get to sleep but then, whilst everyone else was still up, I had a screaming nightmare that brought my family, the management, and all the other residents, sprinting up the stairs to see what foul crime had been committed.

This time, Mum forced me to explain what was wrong. She went straight into a rage. "How dare you treat your own flesh and blood like that?" she screamed at Dad. "How dare you fill his head with horror stories... Have you no sense at all?"

Then she demanded that we should turn round and go back home. "If we have to see mountains, we'll see the bloody Welsh mountains." At this, Brother Nothing and James protested and as everyone argued hammer and tongs, I shrank further into a shell of misery and disgrace. My childhood was in crisis. If Rigor Mortis didn't get me, here in France, then the Krauts would get me in England with their first gas attack. Either way, I was doomed.

What brought me back to normality was that Dad had no intention of allowing my sensitivity to wreck his chances of seeing the Alps. After breakfast he put an arm around my shoulders and walked me around the hotel gardens. He apologised for having scared me with his bedtime story and assured me that he had meant it to be funny. He spoke to me man-to-man, as I'd often heard him speak to James, and he soon restored my confidence, telling me that as a six year-old I was far too big a boy to believe in ghosts. He emphasised the futility of fear and how, as a young boy, he'd often been scared stiff, only to discover that it was always unfounded. He even described the ultimate fear of the soldiers he had served with: their dread of going over the top. Yet he assured me that even with those who did die, what showed in their eyes in the final split second was peace, not fear.

"So President Roosevelt is right," he said. "All we have to fear is fear itself."

Since I hadn't the faintest idea who President Roosevelt was I didn't feel inclined to argue. However, I did ask: "Dad, aren't you ever frightened of anything?"

"Only your mother getting her way...That's why I'm relying on you, Sajit..."

"Dad, do you wish I'd been a girl?"

"You, a girl? Good God, no! I love you exactly the way you are, Sajit."

Instinctively, I sensed that the time was ripe for some crafty bargaining. "Dad, when we get back home, can I have a proper gas mask?"

"Haven't you got one already?"

"Only a Minnie Mouse one."

"Well we can't have that. Throw that rubbish away and have my old army one. It's adjustable...It should fit..."

"The one with the two eye pieces and the tube like an elephant's trunk?"

"That's it."

"Wow! Thanks, Dad."

That made all the difference. My crisis was over. With death from gassing now out of the question, and with the prospect of being able to swank around the place with a

Great War army gas mask instead of a Minnie Mouse one, everything took on a fresh perspective. The monster Rigor Mortis became a joke, just as Dad had intended, and by the time we entered Switzerland I'd forgotten all about him.

Switzerland was like discovering Shangri-La. Within a few miles of crossing the border I knew I'd stumbled upon a phenomenon of nature that would open my eyes to the unlimited potential of the world. Light rain overnight had cleansed the countryside and given it a glorious freshness and sheen. The sky was blindingly blue, the sun bearing down warmly, and now, instead of flat fields and poplar trees flanking the road, rugged mountain peaks reared in the background and meadows rose steeply on either side. Late harvesting was in full flow and peasant families in shirt sleeves or long, colourful dresses were arranging hundreds of small, triangular sheaves of wheat, each pile a measured quantity in an orderly line. As we passed by, they paused in their labour to wave, as though a car was rare enough to deserve a response. As we went deeper and higher into the mountains, snaking about tortuous passes and grinding around hairpin bends in second gear, arable farming gave way to dairy herds, and we heard the steady clonking of cow bells as these sandy-coloured beasts munched their way about the steep slopes. Eventually, we entered the Bernese Oberland. As they say of the Bay of Naples, it should be seen before dying.

I have never had such a marvellous holiday as we enjoyed in Wengen. We all felt the same way and for a fortnight we went from being a family given to silly squabbles and arguments to a family in harmony. Even old Nothing cast aside most of his negative vibes and enjoyed himself, and Mum joined us in all our activities for the first time that I could remember.

We stayed at the Alpenhorn Hotel. We didn't know it at the time, but it was a very select hotel and we were very lucky to have been selected. To look at, it was the supreme example of a giant Swiss chalet. It was high on a slope, facing south, looking down the Lauterbrunnen valley, and from the gardens there were equally good views towards the Eiger and the Jungfrau.

It was the kind of hotel which had the same clientele year after year, a hotel which had become legendary for its impeccable personal service and old-fashioned standards. It was relatively small but that didn't stop it being on a par with Raffles, Reids, Mount Lavinia, and the Dome. The only difference was that whilst all the aforementioned hotels were the domain of the wealthy, well-connected and globe-trotting upper-crust British, the Alpenhorn was the preserve of their German counterparts.

As we parked, our dust-covered Wolseley looked shabby against the sparkling Mercedes and Rolls Royces of the other residents, but because it was a bulky car it wasn't entirely out of place, just well travelled. Directly in front of the hotel, on what we soon came to know as the 'Cafe und Kuchen Terrace', a brass band was playing and all the male guests were in leder hosen. In short, it was not the kind of place a suburban Anglo/Indian family would normally have chosen for their first holiday abroad. Initially, Mum was so over-awed that she wanted to turn tail and go in search of a Zimmer. This infuriated Dad and he would have none of it. He summed up the situation in a flash and became determined not to kowtow to anyone. He may have lacked breeding, but he certainly didn't lack audacity. Acting with the instinct of a born con man, he adjusted himself in fine style; and in retrospect the interesting thing is that we had very little difficulty, or hesitancy, in following his example. Subconsciously we were already immersed in his fantasy world, as eager as he was to inculcate our importance and standing on others.

The first thing Dad did was issue us with plenty of small change. He then told us that if any waiters, porters, or maids, helped us, or spoke to us, or even if we merely heard them coughing, we were to press coins into their hands, one of which we'd find dangling in the area of their backsides with fingers pointing outwards, the universal pose of all hotel servants. The next thing he told us was to leave our luggage exactly where it was and not even to bother to shut the car doors. Two things genuine ladies and gentlemen never did was carry their own luggage and lock their cars. Finally, he told us to march forward confidently and nod courteously to anyone who happened to be sitting about the foyer, as though we were accustomed to being recognised and acknowledged.

Obeying our instructions to the letter, we made a fine entrance. The only hiccup came when the manager appeared from his office to welcome us. He clicked his heels, bowed, and wished us all a very comfortable stay, and then, when he chucked Brother Nothing playfully under the chin, he found two francs being pressed into his hand, and when he ruffled James's hair he got another. He was so embarrassed that he left me well alone. I still managed a generous contribution, however. I tipped the lift boy three francs on entering and another one on departing.

Our rooms were decked out with fresh flowers and there was a box of Swiss chocolates each. The views were breath-taking and each room had a balcony bathed in sunshine. News of our tipping habits had obviously spread like the scent of a beautiful woman and a platoon of porters came up with our luggage. So much discreet coughing took place that once my brothers and I had sorted out our cases we trooped around to Dad's room to have our tipping money replenished. According to Mum, we'd only been in the hotel five minutes and it had already cost us £9.2s.5d., and this meant that unless we started to behave properly, and ignored Dad's highfalutin and silly ideas, the holiday would cost us over £300.0s.0d. in tips alone.

"Never mind," urged Dad. "If we want to enjoy ourselves among these people, we've got to be on a par with them."

"But they're Germans," protested Mum.

That didn't worry Dad at all. He said there was nothing wrong with Germans. They were perfectly normal human beings like the rest of us. Of course, he was right. As individuals they were splendid people. They were aristocrats, way above the baseness of politics, so lousy rich they could afford to be above everything. They were counts, barons, and princes, the creme-de-la-creme of Germany who lived only for culture, blood sports, and gracious living; people to whom manners, courtesy, formality, and duelling scars were the essence of life. To us they couldn't have been nicer. By the surreptitious way they watched us, we knew they were intrigued by our colour, bearing, and conduct, and it was soon pretty obvious that they assumed Dad to be some kind of Maharajah, at the very least a man of great wealth. After all, who but someone with more money than sense would allow his children to dispense such enormous tips? How they accounted for Mum, I'm not sure. They probably thought she was Dad's Number Three or Four Wife, a cold, wet-weather standby in Europe who was expected to look after his children by his Number One Wife whose responsibilities towards his harem in India precluded the luxury of foreign travel.

We'd only been in the hotel a few hours when the Prince of Prussia, the senior German present, was delegated to find out more about us. As we soon discovered, there is nothing rich people find more impressive than people they fear might be richer than themselves. The Prince approached us as Dad was ordering char on the Cafe und Kuchen Terrace. He sprang to attention, clicked his heels, and then, removing his monocle as was his habit when addressing people, he asked Dad in impeccable English: "And how are things in Poona, old boy?"

This was the defining moment. Was Dad going to come clean and admit we were from Edgware, the haven of all traitorous Deutsche Juden, or carry on with the pretence he'd started as soon as we'd stepped out of the Wolseley? There may have been doubts in our minds, but there were none in Dad's; and the clever thing about his deceit was that he never lied or made false claims. He just let them draw their own erroneous conclusions.

"Came from north of there, old chap," he replied. "Devilish hot there at the moment. August in India is the time for altitude. I've always favoured Simla, but there are too many flies in Simla. India is full of damn flies. I thought there might be fewer flies here."

A family that travelled the world to avoid flies confirmed our status forthwith and indubitably. The Prince of Prussia was so impressed that the story soon spread throughout the hotel. The management immediately sent forth junior porters with metal fly sprays boasting enormous metal drums to disinfect everywhere, and as an additional precaution they hung fly papers at strategic spots along the corridors leading to our bedrooms. They even hung one directly above our table in the dining room. On the Cafe und Kuchen Terrace flies were more difficult to control and whenever one appeared the Krauts became terribly apologetic. If a fly was careless enough to settle, there was a stampede towards it and a great ham fist crashed down, squashing it flat. There would be cheers and loud guffaws and what was left of the creature would be held aloft for general inspection.

What I particularly liked about the Germans was that they made a big fuss of my brothers and me, probably because we were the only children in the hotel. Also, they fully approved of the way we'd been taught to behave in the dining room. We sat up straight, kept our elbows off the table, and spoke only in modulated tones. We ate all our food and never ran off before the adults had concluded their meals. Another thing in our favour was that we were very quick to adapt to the German dinner ritual. Every time a couple entered the dining room in the evening, they would pause before the tables already occupied and pay their respects by snapping their heels together. Those males already seated would leap up to return the compliment, these formalities being a mere prelude to an exchange of detailed information about what they'd been doing during the day.

Fortunately, the Alpenhorn was a small hotel, otherwise dinner would have dragged on until breakfast. As it was, during the first hour of the meal the room resounded to the sound of clicking heels and Dad, and my brothers and I, spent most of our time jumping up and down, trying in vain to get some noise out of our rubber-heeled shoes. Much to the delight of the Krauts, James was able to respond to their enquiries about our activities in their own tongue. He also made a point of assuring them: "Hardly any flies about today, thank you, Count."

We would then bash our silent heels together once more, resume our seats, and try to get a quick bite or two in before the next guest came in and the ritual was repeated.

The Swiss management and staff were especially attentive towards us, and with the tips they were still receiving, small wonder. They were full of helpful advice and supplied us with endless maps of the area giving us the best walks. Even when there was a complaint against me they uttered not a word of criticism. They merely had a discreet word with Dad, confident that a gentleman of his standing would take the appropriate action. The complaint came from Count von Bisternmark. He said that during his afternoon siestas he kept hearing a loud banging at the rear of the hotel followed by even louder juvenile shouting. The manager investigated immediately and discovered that I'd had used a lump of chalk to draw three lines on the wood cladding of the rear wall of the hotel and that I was 'throwing' a hard, leather ball at them. Being Swiss, he had no idea that I was playing cricket. The lines were my stumps and the shouts were my imitation of Tom Goddard's famous appeal: "How was that, then?"

Dad explained all this away as a mere idiosyncrasy of the British Raj, something to be indulged rather than punished.

Consequently, although my stumps were scrubbed off, the next time I went to practice one of the hotels maids greeted me. She took me by the hand, led me to a sparsely wooded area at the rear of the hotel, and suggested that I threw my ball at one of the trees. It was an invitation I was happy to accede to, especially since the maid, on being slipped a tip, agreed to stay with me to act as wicket-keeper, thus saving me much wasted time and energy retrieving the ball.

As one might suspect, Brother Nothing soon found out about this and teased me. At first he referred to the maid as, 'Sajit's little Swiss miss' but then, when he discovered that I called her George, after George Duckworth the ex-England wicket-keeper, his teasing became so intense that Dad intervened and stopped it.

When we went on outings, my interest in cricket continued. So keen was I to become another cunning bastard like O'Reilly that wherever we went I practised my bowling action. In the middle of Wengen, or Interlaken, or Andermatt, or Murren, locals and tourists alike would suddenly be confronted by me sprinting down the middle of the road and then going into a flurry of arms and legs before coming to a halt, at which point I would stare intently at some invisible object about twenty yards ahead of me, point an accusing finger at it, and shout at the top of my voice: "How's that, then?" In Wengen, this became such a regular occurrence that once the Contractor family was seen entering the town the shops emptied and curtains were drawn aside as people watched to see if the Indian boy would repeat his ritual. The others became so embarrassed that Dad tried to put a stop to it. Eventually, we compromised. I continued with my bowling action but cut out the appeals.

The novelty of an Indian family at the Alpenhorn meant that anything we did aroused interest. A good example was the incident Brother Nothing sparked off. Within the family, we referred to it as: 'The Charge of the Dark Brigade,' or 'My Horse Won't go'.

Gran and Mr Muckey

Having studied the hotel literature about the amuse-
ments open to us, we decided on our first full day to explore
the surrounding countryside on horse back. The pamphlet
assured us that the horses and ponies supplied were so
docile and well-trained that no horse-riding experience or
guide were necessary. We therefore ordered four horses and
a pony (for me) to be brought round to the hotel after lunch.
We mounted in front of the hotel terrace, so there was a
good audience watching us. It was pure chance that Brother
Nothing was allocated the biggest and oldest horse. When
the time came to move off, we went forward at a slow walk,
except for Brother Nothing. He remained stock still. This
caused the other horses to stop and we all looked back.

"Dad, my horse won't go," bleated Brother Nothing.

Dad went back and prodded the old horse into action,
but Nothing soon dropped behind again. When we came to
another halt, Nothing let out another plaintive cry of, "Dad,
my horse won't go."

When this happened for a third time there was general
amusement among the Germans. They knew, from years of
experience, that the riding stables was the biggest tourist
catch in town, and that Nothing's horse was the Father of
the stable, from whom the other hacks took their lead. They
also knew that he was a lazy, cantankerous old beast who
needed a rider of character to exert his authority.

What they didn't know was that Dad was a horseman of
great experience, gained in very trying conditions in
Flanders. To him, horses were beasts of burden and they
did as they were told, or else! He lost no time in changing
horses with Brother Nothing and the very manner in which
he mounted left the old nag in no doubt as to who was in
command. Dad looked across at the grinning, enthralled
spectators and then turned back to us with an expression
of grim determination. "Grab the pommels of your saddles,"
he ordered. "And then hold tight. For all you're worth."

Finally, he gave his mount such an almighty boot in the
guts, and let out such a harrowing cowboy yell of "Yahoo!",

that the old horse went straight into a gallop. The others galloped after him with us hanging on like grim death, just as Dad had advised. It was like a cavalry charge, all of us in extended line, thundering down a slight incline, neck to neck, all of us screaming, as much in exhilaration as fear. All the Kraut spectators saw of us was dust.

Dad didn't call a halt to the gallop until we reached some trees about two hundred yards away, out of sight of the hotel. Then, when our excitement had subsided, we settled down to the usual routine, the horses just mooching along the tourist track. It was all so familiar to them that they did it without reference to us. Because of our speedy start we got back half an hour before our time was up and, as a matter of principle, Dad made sure that as soon as we came into sight of the hotel, we broke into a well-controlled trot in line abreast, as disciplined as a patrol of Bengal Lancers. News of our return brought the Krauts rushing to the edge of the terrace and, in their usual desire to underline their presence and become part of the event, they laughed and applauded.

Dad was ecstatic, knowing he had enhanced the reputation of the empire.

One of the strangest things about that extraordinary ride was the change that overcame Mum. As we paused in the trees after our initial gallop, she suddenly looked happy and younger. Her usual frown of disapproval had disappeared. At first I thought little of it, but as the days slipped by the change became more obvious. She was laughing and carefree and on many occasions I saw her either clinging to Dad's arm or holding his hand, intimacies between them which I'd never seen before.

It was also the first time I'd known Mum go more than five minutes without cleaning or polishing something. She was totally relaxed and at length I realised the reason for it: the Alpenhorn was such a superb hotel that even Mum could find no fault. Its perfection liberated her.

*****

Gran and Mr Muckey

Riding was only one of many activities. We went boating on Lake Thun, played tennis on the hotel courts, swam in the local pool, and enjoyed enormously long walks, all of us equipped with metal-tipped sticks on which we attached colourful badges from the surrounding resorts. Dad never ceased to wonder at the engineering expertise of the Swiss. There were mountain railways and funiculars everywhere, some of them reaching into the most inaccessible spots. We used them all, whether starting from Interlaken, Wengenalp, or Murren. I well remember going to a spot called Harder Kulm where we had a magnificent view of the entire Bernese Oberland. We also went to Wilderswill where everyone kept telling us that no less an authority than Ruskin had claimed it to be the best view in Europe. Byron was also mentioned and at least three villages we visited claimed to be the inspiration for *Manfred*.

Our most memorable trips were on the Wengenalp railway by way of Kleine Scheidegg to the Junfraujock and then, on a second visit, to the Jungfrau. We got well above the snow line and even though it was August and really hot we were able to pelt each other with snow balls and then have our first experience of skiing and tobogganing. Back in Wengen, Dad claimed that the best time of day was sunset. He insisted that we all sat on the Cafe und Kuchen Terrace to watch the sun go down below the mountains, leaving behind a fascinating orange glow which I've never seen repeated in any other part of the world.

The evenings in the hotel were also great fun. There was a games room where we played table tennis and skittles and no one ever objected if we roamed the entire hotel playing hide-and-seek. James, having already gained a reputation as a linguist, often sat and talked with a German family who were delighted to put him right on correct grammar. Dad spent his time in the billiards room, one of several ghostly figures stalking around beneath low-slung green shades and drifting cigar smoke. Between sips of brandy from enormous balloon glasses he proved unbeatable at snooker and then went on to teach the Krauts a raucous Indian Army game at which they dashed around the table, taking it in turns to fling balls against the cushions. The object of the game was never clear to me, but judged by the way they stripped to their shirt sleeves, and by the laughter and shouts it evoked, it beat snooker and billiards to a frazzle.

Mum, in her new serenity, was content to converse in the lounge with other ladies who spoke excellent English. Having become an adjunct to Dad's new persona she discarded her Welsh accent and assumed a timbre more appropriate, what at home we called her 'Lady Muck telephone accent'. On the rare occasions when I listened in, she was exaggerating and boasting outrageously, alluding to our London retreat, Edgware having apparently slipped several degrees south east to the Belgravia and Sloane Square area, very handy for the Cafe Royal, The Waldorf, and the Savoy Grill Room.

Everyone dressed for dinner and one of Mum's greatest thrills came when Dad took her to the leading Ladies Outfitters and made several purchases, thus saving her the indignity of appearing in the same gown twice. Dad was resplendent in a white tuxedo but he hardly compared with his German counterparts who had decorations on their chests, special hereditary orders hanging around their necks, and sashes denoting aristocratic rank and social affiliations. Attempting to compete, Dad transferred his medal ribbons from his waistcoat to his tuxedo and although his Oak Leaf attracted the usual attention he still fell well short of matching the Krauts. My brothers and I were in ordinary boys' suits (me in short trousers) but Mum made a great effort to upgrade our appearance. She crafted beautiful black bow ties for us which I thought were very swanky and helped a lot. Mum wasn't so easily satisfied.

"If only I'd known," she sighed. "I could have fitted you all out in tow ties and bails."

During the daytime we also made a suitable impression. Our mode of dress was hardly alpine, but it did at least have a touch of character. I don't think Wengen had ever seen three Indian boys before and I'm even more certain they'd never encountered a father who dressed his sons in identical outfits as himself, which happened to be loud check plus-fours, yellow socks, porkpie hats, and stout walking boots. At first I felt a proper Charlie in this gear, but at least I was in semi-long trousers and we did attract a lot of favourable comment, even though most people thought we were golfers, not walkers.

Every morning, directly after breakfast, we assembled in the lounge for what Dad called our daily Orders Group. We pored over maps, pamphlets, tourist books, and hand-written suggestions from the manager's secretary, trying to decide how best to spend our day. More often than not, several of our new German friends would join us and give us the benefit of their experience. Most of their contributions were invaluable but there were occasions when they became a trifle sardonic, with remarks such as, "But there is no cafe on that track. What will you do for your cup of char?"

We accepted such leg-pulling in good part, but we also took due note when they warned us of mountain tracks that were too steep, or routes that were too long to complete before dark. In particular, we were warned off 'The Devil's Ledge'. It was a notoriously dangerous track much favoured by ibex which the inexperienced were sometimes tempted to take as a shortcut back to Wengen. We were told that over the past ten years it had claimed five lives.

On our last full day, four Germans joined us at our Orders Groups to help us plan a walk which was to be a fitting climax. They were keen for us to take a well-known circular route which would take us towards Klein Scheidegg, veer round in the direction of Mannlichen, and come back through the rear of Wengen. The only difference to our usual preparations was that Mum opted out in order to start packing. Everything went normally until late afternoon when we were on the return leg of our walk. Then, after a fortnight of uninterrupted blue skies, hideously dark clouds began to form. At first we ignored them as they hovered over the distant peaks, but all of us, unbeknown to the others, watched them with the growing conviction that we were about to be caught in a thunderstorm, the like of which we had never seen.

Soon, these grotesque, rolling cannonball black clouds had massed ranks to such an extent that they totally obscured the Jungfrau massive, getting closer all the time. As they closed in on us they became more like aerial avalanches, so laden with moisture that it was only a matter of seconds before they burst. The wind changed direction every few seconds and before long the clouds were racing down various valleys in battalions, making a series of major collisions inevitable. When they crashed together in bitter, head-on combat they made enough noise to awaken the dead. Brilliant shards of lightning forked off in all directions, terrifyingly close. Finally, rain cascaded down on us with the force of mountain waterfalls. We were in the eye of the storm, soaked to the skin within seconds, thunder and lightning booming and flashing all around us, so scary that we kept ducking and flinching.

In desperation we ran forward, looking for somewhere to shelter. Eventually, with the lack of anything better, we squatted beneath some overhanging rocks. Dad pulled out his maps and pored over them but they were already so wet that most of them were unreadable. The only one of any use was a hard-backed travel book with only a small-scale map of the area. However, on this Dad spotted a dotted line going down the side of the mountain on which we were stranded. Although quite lengthy, it eventually led into the rear of Wengen, quite handy for the hotel. Dad estimated that it would save us about two hours and enable us to get back before total darkness closed in. When he asked us if we were game to try it, he didn't get any arguments.

Dad led the way, consulting the map as he went. After half a mile or so he let out a cry of triumph. He had found the track. Ahead of us was an outcrop of rock and twisting to one side was a barely discernible pathway. We hurried down it and were soon losing height. As the track descended so it narrowed and became no more than a footpath clinging to the side of the mountain, with the valley on the other side falling away steeply. We were just beginning to have our doubts about the wisdom of this route when Dad came across a wooden notice wedged into a crevice between two rocks. He was delighted.

"Just look at this, boys," he shouted over the noise of the rain and thunder. "Typical Swiss efficiency. They even put road names on their mountain tracks. Der Felsvorsprung der Teufel. I'll bet you anything you like there's another tea room in a few hundred yards. We'll all have hot chocolate with cream topping. And a dash of brandy..."

"Dad!" James shouted back. "Der Felsvorsprung der Teufel means 'The Devil's Ledge'."

None of us said a word. We all knew what that meant. We'd been told many times: whatever you do, keep off The Devil's Ledge. Five lives in ten years. Or was it ten lives in five years? Which ever it was, there was no question of us continuing. None of us had any desire to add to these grisly statistics.

"Back to the original route, boys," declared Dad. "Come on, waste no time..."

He turned and we all turned. Then he stopped dead and we all stopped dead. Ahead of us, staring at us with shining, beady eyes, were four ibex. They were as surprised to see us as we were them. They were thickset brutes with massive, backward-curved, ridged horns. We knew nothing about the general disposition of ibex, whether they were timid or aggressive creatures: we only knew that they were wild animals and they were looking at us as though they were going to defend their ledge with the same determination and ferocity as Horatio held his bridge.

"Shout at them," said Dad, and we all shouted: "Shoo!". It had no effect. With the din of thunder going on around us they probably never even heard. Next, Dad tossed small stones at them. These were likewise ignored. He tried bigger stones and they didn't like that at all. They pawed the ground and edged towards us. Simultaneously, we edged away from them, all of us aware that we were in a situation commonly known as a tricky dilemma: snookered which ever way we turned. When the ibex began to make odd noises, Dad decided on the lesser of two evils. Rather than be tossed off the track, we carried on down The Devil's Ledge.

Soon, the track became perilously narrow, no more than four or five feet wide, and there was now a sheer drop of some 2,000 feet into the valley on one side and a solid rock face rising vertically on the other. Behind us, the ibex followed at a respectful distance. Although it hardly seemed

possible, The Devil's Ledge got worse. In many places the surface was smooth and shiny and as slippery as ice, nothing but a slab of wet granite. Elsewhere, it was loose gravel on which we skidded about. The gradient varied considerably, from steep to damn nearly perpendicular. At an early stage Dad decided that the only way we could cope was to slide down on our backsides, our hands on the track behind us, acting as stabilisers. He led the way, with Brother Nothing at the rear, and all of us within touching distance of the one in front. That way, we minimised the risk of slipping over the edge and our closeness to each other gave us comfort, if not confidence.

About the only real comfort was that the ibex lost interest in us, but by that time the ledge was already too narrow to turn round on. As airline pilots love to say in disaster films, we'd reached the point of no return. The thunderstorm carried on as ever, but we were concentrating so hard on not falling over the edge that we ignored it. Being cold and wet with the possibility of being struck by lightning were the least of our worries. One of the advantages of the visibility being so restricted was that even if we gave way to the temptation to look over the side of the ledge, all we could see were swirling clouds, not a straight fall into the valley below.

We slid along on our backsides for what seemed like miles. Then, quite suddenly, the ledge broadened out, the track melded into a broad meadow, and we were out of danger. We got back on our feet and hurried down the hillside and were soon in sight of Wengen. We stopped to regain our composure. We were laughing and chattering, in shock. Dad calmed us down and tried to smarten us up. It was a lost cause, of course. Our plus-fours were dripping wet, covered in mud, and had holes in the backsides due to the way we'd anchored our butts so closely to the ground. Dad suggested that it would be best to slip in through the rear entrance of the hotel, have a bath, change into our evening clothes, and not even mention the Devil's Ledge, just admit to having been caught in the storm. Being unable to boast about our adventure would be a small price to pay compared with facing the wrath of Mum.

It's amazing how much better one feels after a hot bath. When Dad came into my room to make sure I was getting on okay, and to gather up all my wet clothes, I slipped into my dressing gown and went on to the balcony to see how the thunder storm was progressing. It had calmed down a lot. It had even stopped raining and I noticed that on the hotel terrace people were milling about, radiating a sense of drama. Mum was amongst them, the only person with an umbrella still up, as always terrified that her hair might get wet. Then several people pointed towards the town in excitement. Coming along the road was a group of men. They had climbing picks and stretchers, with coils of rope over their shoulders, just like a mountain rescue team I'd seen illustrated in my comics.

"Hi, Mum!" I called out. "What's going on?"

She lowered her umbrella and turned around. At first she showed no surprise. "It's a rescue team. They're going to..."

She stopped abruptly and demanded: "What are you doing up there?"

"We've just got back." Then, unable to contain my natural boastfulness, I did exactly what Dad had told me not to and let the cat out of the bag. "We took a short cut down the Devil's Ledge..."

It was then that Mum let the side down. She went berserk or hysterical – I'm not sure which because I've never understood the difference between the two. Most likely, she managed both simultaneously. Either way, she raised her hands to heaven and ploughed through the people packed on the terrace, screaming: "My boys! My boys! My darling boys!"

As Dad said later, it was a pretty poor performance. Amongst a whole lot of foreigners she completely demolished the British reputation for stiff upper lips.

Gran and Mr Muckey

The search party was called off, of course. No harm was done. No expenses had been incurred. Only a few men had been inconvenienced and when Dad rewarded them with Gluwein in the hotel bar they couldn't have given a damn. Indeed, by the time they rolled back to their Swiss chalets, having listened to Dad's account of how he'd deliberately opted for the Devil's Ledge with three young kids in tow, rather than face the thunder storm and pursuing ibex, Mum's lack of a stiff upper lip was forgotten.

The following morning we set off back for England. The Alpenhorn stocked us up with the most marvellous pack lunches and to a man and woman the Krauts assembled on the Cafe und Kuchen Terrace to wave and cheer us off. Two days later we were at war with them. Dad had already explained that it was due to politics, but I still didn't understand what politics were. What power was so great and dreadful that it could turn friends into enemies?

10

Back home in the nick of time – War is declared –
Panic of the first air raid – The ARP and the phoney war –
We're evacuated – An eventful journey – Humiliation and
rejection – Lucky saves the day.

We arrived back in England in the small hours of Sunday morning, September 3rd 1939. We'd had a long, hard journey through France, dodging in and out of military convoys. The ferry crossing was beautifully smooth but then we had trouble over Dad's passport, as I've already explained. That upset Mum more than it did Dad and by the time we got back to Edgware she was still nagging him, demanding to know how, by stripping him naked, the immigration authorities arrived at the conclusion that he was bona fide after all. As we staggered into the house we were all so tired that we went straight to bed.

Just before 11 a.m. Dad woke us up. "You'd better come and listen to this. History is about to be made."

It was Neville Chamberlain's declaration of war. It didn't strike me as very historic. He sounded like Uncle Mac announcing the cancellation of Children's Hour. There was no animation, no clarion call, only a sense of embarking upon a doomed enterprise. When he'd said his piece we all went back to bed. A few minutes later the air raid siren sounded, not only in London but over most of the country.

Gran and Mr Muckey

So many accounts have been written, broadcast, and retold of the nation-wide panic caused by this 'raid' that I'm happy to relate that at least Dad took it in his stride. While Mum rushed around like a maniac, and pushed us into the cupboard under the stairs (decorated with flock wallpaper and wall-to-wall Axminster for just such an eventuality), Dad went into the lounge to read his Sunday Express.

"Take cover," yelled Mum.

"Bollocks," retorted Dad. He looked at her as though she was mad and as she slammed shut the small, angled door, he added: "We only declared war five minutes ago. So how the hell do you expect the Luftwaffe to suddenly appear overhead? Even if they were sitting on the tarmac with their engines running, it would still take them two or three hours to get here. It's a false alarm."

Dad was right, of course. Apart from half the population metaphorically shitting themselves, nothing happened.

The months that followed became known as The Phoney War. Dad said it was a very useful breathing space. Certainly he was kept very busy with his War Office contracts in Camberwell, but he still found time to do his 'bit' and enrolled as an ARP warden. He was issued with an armband and a tin hat with a big **W** on it and he had to report to a temporary headquarters at the local school every other evening. According to his account of things, the Chief Warden would read out new instructions and guide lines which spewed out from the Home Office and then they all had cups of tea and played cards until it was dark, where-upon they went on patrols, making sure everyone was complying with the blackout regulations.

Dad said it was the most boring job imaginable. Everyone was so scared of air raids that their blackout precautions were absolutely spot on. No one dared to show even a speck of light for fear of a Stuka dive bomber immediately scream-ing down on them and releasing a stick of bombs. Torches were forbidden, there was no street lighting, and heaven help anyone who tried to light-up a fag in the open.* Dad swore that Glendale Avenue had become the darkest spot on earth, with the Jews so terrified of letting the war effort down that they sat in their lounges, listening to the radio, with their lights out.

The main task of the ARP soon became helping with road accidents. The biggest single type of accident was people walking into lamp posts and knocking themselves out cold. After some time, a bright spark in the Home Office decreed that all lamp posts should have three white rings painted around them, but since these were put at ankle-to-knee height, only children and dwarfs benefited, others continued to knock themselves out.

The most ridiculous aspect of the whole thing was that traffic lights were kept going. Any half-trained, semi-inebriated Luftwaffe pilot could have gone straight up the A2, from Dover to Piccadilly, on traffic lights alone. When this anomaly was highlighted by letters to the press (by the actor David Niven among others), the British sense of humour was demonstrated by 'Bored of Piddlehinton'. In a letter to the Times, he expressed (in the formal prose of the day) that he and his fellow residents in the Piddle Valley were pissed off with all these petty regulations and he pleaded for the retention of traffic lights on the grounds that going into Dorchester to watch them change colour was the only free entertainment still available to them.

The most serious accidents occurred because all cars, lorries, and buses, were fitted with slotted hoods over their headlights which made it impossible for drivers to see more than two yards directly in front of them and, if there was one thing vehicles in those days could not do, it was stop dead within two yards. Thus, despite no enemy activity, the emergency services were kept at full stretch and the truth was – even though no one liked to admit it – that every time police cars or ambulances were called out to deal with these

* As Churchill reveals in his memoirs, one man was fined for 'Smoking too brightly'.

accidents all they did was cause more. It was like unwinding a ball of string: there seemed to be no end to it.

It fell to Dad and his ARP colleagues on their foot patrols to sort out the chaos. During the first few months of the war, Dad's unit was responsible for removing no less than 47 people off the roads and into the hospitals. Dogs and cats suffered even more disastrously and were that much more difficult to dispose of, and hedgehogs were virtually wiped out and so difficult to scrape off the roads that they were left where they were. Just to walk down Glendale Avenue was enough to give a member of the RSPCA the screaming abdabs.

Sometimes, Dad would take me out on patrol with him, although never further than down Glendale Avenue. By this time I had a toy tin hat and Dad gave me the unofficial title of 'ARP Runner' which, he explained, meant that if there was a proper raid, I ran like hell back home again. To stave off boredom during our patrols, and to satisfy his mischievous streak, Dad would suddenly shout out at the top of his voice, through the total darkness: "PUT THAT LIGHT OUT!"

Instantly, chinks of light would appear in the lounges of all the houses in the vicinity and then spread rapidly throughout the houses. "Just look at the stupid devils," Dad would say. "Every time they hear me shout that, they all put their lights on to go to see if they've left a light on elsewhere in the house."

Dad would then let out another mighty shout. This time: "PUT ALL THOSE LIGHTS OUT!" and just as suddenly everything would plunge back into total darkness.

Throughout the war Dad was either an ARP Warden, a Private in the Home Guard, or a fire-watcher at the Works in Camberwell, and it wasn't until he died that I discovered that he had tried to write a book about his experiences. He never got it published but his research was first class and enabled me to make some interesting discoveries about the blackout. For example, official government figures were released which revealed that the percentage increase in road accidents during the Phoney War was over 210%, which meant in turn that the blackout restrictions caused an estimated 458 extra deaths, compared with nil by enemy action.

Nor was there any evidence to suggest that when German aircraft did start bombing they ever had any difficulty in locating their targets for the want of lights showing on the ground. Of course, plenty of them did miss their targets and the reason for this was explained with brilliant clarity in Sir Winston Churchill's book, *Their Finest Hour*. In this, he explains that the Germans did not navigate by conventional means (by the stars as our airmen did) but by a variety of methods devised by their boffins based on the convergence of radio beams. The first and best known of these was code-named 'Knickebein', and more sophisticated later developments were known as X-Apparatus and Y-Apparatus. Hermann Goering declared these developments to be infallible; and so they were until the British Air Defence found ways to bend their radio beams. This could divert German planes hundreds of miles out of their way. From intercepted radio messages it is known that many German pilots were totally confused by what was going on. They kept finding themselves in the most unlikely places, but Krauts being Krauts, and with their Reich Marshall's orders still ringing in their ears, they followed their orders, abided by 'Knickebein' and dropped their bombs accordingly. Even if Piccadilly Circus and Leicester Square had been ablaze with lights it wouldn't have made the slightest difference.

One poor Kraut on a special, solo mission had his beam so bent that he landed on the Torquay Cricket Ground, thinking he was back in the France. Indeed, there were numerous cases of entire raiding parties dropping tens of thousands of tons of bombs on open farmland, and in *Their Finest Hour* Churchill estimates that bent beams meant that only one fifth of German bombs fell anywhere near their targets. Perhaps the greatest triumph of British Air Defence came on May 30th 1941 when they diverted a large German raiding party to Dublin. The Micks, who were playing Britain against Germany shamelessly, soon found out that it was the Krauts who'd bombed them, but they had no idea that it was the British who sent them there.

Dad revealed all this in a chapter of his unpublished book. His conclusion (which may give a clue as to why it wasn't published) was: 'A great mystery of the war (on which Churchill sheds no light) is why we didn't get the Krauts to bomb the buggers more often'. (No comment.)

Despite the lack of enemy activity in The Phoney War, the Home Office remained as keen as ever for all children under sixteen living in major conurbations to be evacuated to country areas. In Edgware this evacuation euphoria caught on in a big way. Most of the Jews had long since accepted that their lives would be a continuous process of westerly evacuation. A lot of them had visions of eventually settling on the Canadian prairies, so they regarded their children being sent to Dorset, Devon, and Cornwall, as no more than another step in the inevitable direction.

As the great exodus got underway, Mum decided that we should be part of it – anything to get a break from us. I refused to go unless Lucky came with me. We all thought this would put the kibosh on the idea, but one thing we soon learnt about the bureaucrats was that they loved to confound you, to make you feel as though you had no idea of what was good for you. Mum's favourite bureaucrat suddenly took the line: "Of course he can take his little doggy with him. Kiddies are encouraged to take pets with them. Just so long as they aren't reptiles or rodents."

So it came about that on October 19th my brothers and I made towards Paddington Station, taking all manner of junk with us, not least of which were our gas masks, our newly issued ration books, my cricket bat and ball, James's chess set, numerous books, and umpteen changes of under-wear. Even Lucky, who sat on my lap, had to conform. He wore a brand new collar and about half a hundred weight of Bob Martin's flea powder. Since we were among the first batch of evacuees we had no idea that we would be expected to have labels tied to us. Even as a youngster, I was most indignant. The labels were written centrally in the town hall and then a squad of bureaucrats visited the homes of evacuees to attach the labels personally, explaining that they had been specifically designed to meet all eventualities, even though (as you'll see) no specific arrangements had been made for us to stay anywhere. Brother Nothing's label read:

Charles Contractor (Major of 3),
Late of 49 Glendale Avenue,
Edgware. Destination, South West.
Via Paddington, Taunton and points west.
Ration Book around neck.
Next of kin, mother, as above.

James's label was the same, except that after his name the brackets housed the words (Minor of 3). Mine read, (Minimus of 3). Lucky's label read:

Dog.
Allegedly answers to 'Lucky'.
Property of Contractor Minimus.
Disposable, according to behaviour.
No rations. Good ratter.

The sight that greeted us at Paddington was unusual. Normally, a major railway terminus is an amalgam of the nation. Now, it was the kindergarten. The entire concourse was packed with crying and screaming kids and their mothers.

This mass hysteria had been sparked off by a Daily Herald photographer taking a large group photograph of the children. It was one of those major efforts, as taken at boarding schools, with a time-exposure camera panning from one end of the group to another, thus enabling bolder spirits to run from end to end and appear on the photograph twice.

Naturally, all the Mums had pushed their kids forward to be included and then gathered around to watch. When everything was set up, with the group in three tiers extending from platform 1 to platform 11, the photographer's reporter tried to raise a big smile among the children by calling out: "Come on, kiddies! Smile. You might never see your Mummies and Daddies again."

The following day the Herald published the picture as a middle page spread and a brilliantly emotive one it was. The reporter's callous 'joke' just had time to sink in with the kids before the camera started to pan. Consequently, it caught them in various degrees of shock and panic, with expressions covering the full gamut from perplexity to terror. Some darling, innocent, little faces were puckered up, others had teardrops spilling from their eyes, and towards the far end of the photograph, opposite platforms 9, 10, and 11, it was all systems go with faces like waterfalls and all manner of pathetic gestures and appeals for help, with one little bloke in the back row actually leaping into thin air in his haste to get back to his mummy.

No other picture has ever caught such human misery. The final touch came when a sub-editor, striving after alliteration, added the headline: '*Hitler's Heartless Havoc*' and it became one of the war's great propaganda pictures. It was syndicated in the United States and inspired thousands of tons of food parcels.

We spent seven hours on that evacuee train. Laughingly, it was called the Cornish Riviera Express. It stopped at every station en route. Sometimes people got off, sometimes people got on, once people got on and off; but more often than not, nothing happened. Along the way, we had glimpses into the chaos which lay ahead of us. At Shaftesbury, a lady in a tweed suit, shoes that clomped, and a walking stick which she used as a weapon rather than an aid to mobility, held the train up for half an hour. She was demanding to know if the Bloggs twins were on the train. When the guard said, "How the hell should I know?", she raised her stick over her head as though about to belabour him and retorted: "Well ask, you silly little man... Go down the train and ask..."

So the guard went the length of the train calling out: "Any Bloggs aboard? Any Bloggs abroad?"

Typically, Brother Nothing stuck his head out of the window and said: "Yes, but you're not allowed to use them while we're in the station."

The guard gave him a clip round the ear for being cheeky and then turned back to the lady in the tweed suit. "Are you sure they should be on this train, Madam?"

"Of course I'm not sure, you silly little man. They should have been here two days ago. But I've met every train since and they still haven't arrived."

"Then they must have gone back home," said the guard.

"No they haven't. Do you think I haven't rung up and asked, you silly little man? They've disappeared..."

The guard was anxious to be off and tired of being called 'a silly little man', especially since he was six foot three tall and the lady insulting him only reached four foot ten with the aid of the feather in her hat. When she pointed her stick at him as though about to run him through, he decided he'd had enough and parried her impending lunge by waving his green flag. The train jerked off and her parting insults were drowned out as she vanished like a panto demon king amid a cloud of steam which belched up from beneath the train.

The next insight into our possible fate came at Taunton. There, during an hour's delay, we had the misfortune to overhear a discussion between two porters.

"I'm telling you, Alf, this little bloke has been in Left Luggage for two days. And since I'm in charge of Left Luggage I have to take him home to feed him... But I can't go on doing that for ever..."

Gran and Mr Muckey

"Well you can't release him without a receipt."

"But there is no receipt. Someone dumped him while I was having my tea break. And the poor little devil has lost all his labels... So he's not Left Luggage at all... He's Lost Property... He's the responsibility of Bob Daniels. Let him feed him every night."

Late in the afternoon we detrained at a Halt outside a Cornish fishing village. Other children had been getting off at various points along the route. I never discovered how they knew when to get off and I think a lot of them just guessed, or because they were feeling sick or hungry, or because they thought they were already far enough from home. We got off because it was the end of the line. With Brother Nothing in charge that was as positive as we were likely to get.

About thirty other kids had stuck it out to the end and we were driven to the local village hall in horse buggies. There, Lady Violet Hammish introduced herself. She was in WVS uniform but it was so splendid, with her own touches of gold braid, and several medals on her enormous bosom, that she looked as though she was determined to convert the WVS into a military unit with herself as C-in-C. She was a born do-gooder. She knew exactly what was best for everyone and the remarkable thing about this universal benefactor was that no matter what sacrifices were necessary none of them were ever required of her, and even the greatest upheavals were never to her detriment or inconvenience. We later discovered that her husband was a naval commander and she was the chief busybody in the village by token of her title, her ruthless control over the estate she'd inherited from her father, her education (Roedean), and the fact that she was the only person within a radius of fifty miles who could speak King's English, which enabled her to intimidate the rustic bureaucrats from Truro.

She told us to sit on the floor around the hall and then gave us a lecture on the kindness of the villagers about to

offer us safe homes. As she spoke she strode about the hall,
her trunk bent forward as though the weight of her bosom
and her medals was too much for her, her hands clasped
behind her back as a counter-balance. She then branched
off on to the ways of the country, namely that cows had
horns whereas horses didn't, pigs were short and fat with
curly tails, and sheep were woolly and cuddly at the front
and dirty and smelly at the back. She warned us to watch
out where we were treading, how we mustn't be alarmed if
we saw animals jumping on each other's backs, and how we
must respect the ways of the country by shutting gates after
us. Finally, she told us that the villagers would be calling in
during the next hour in order to choose those they wished
to offer homes to. As soon as I heard that, I knew we were
in trouble, serious trouble.

The people who came to inspect us were very strange. They
were shabbily dressed and wandered about in slow motion,
as though in a daze. On the rare occasions when they spoke
it was in a strange dialect. The men wore boots instead of
shoes and the women wore woollen stockings which
wrinkled up around their ankles like the skin of ageing
bloodhounds. It seemed to me as though they'd strayed into
the village hall by accident, or to shelter from the rain, or to
avail themselves of the cups of tea a young maid from Lady
Hammish's household was handing out. A few of them
wanted to know if there were any biscuits and when told
that there weren't, they wandered off muttering mutinously
as though the whole thing was a swindle, just as they'd
suspected. Those who stayed showed no real interest in us
but, prompted by Lady Hamilton, they wandered around in
a circle as though being forced to view exhibits in a
museum. Deciding who were the least obnoxious among us
was clearly not an easy task. Some of them, more as an
afterthought that anything else, scrutinised my brothers
and me in the manner of Roman citizens appraising young
slaves freshly arrived from some barbaric, recently

conquered part of the world. One old hag prodded us with her umbrella and muttered: "Proper dog's dinner... Need fattening up. Just come down here for proper victuals."

Yet gradually our numbers dwindled. They had to: if any of the villagers circled the hall too often Lady Hamilton took them to one side, told them they couldn't take all night, and then added: "There is a war on, you know." This statement was recognised as a final warning and rather than evoke the wrath of her ladyship the offenders grabbed an evacuee and disappeared.

Brother Nothing, James and I exchanged frequent glances. By this time it was perfectly obvious that we were going to be passed over by everyone. It was nearly dark when the last of our fellow-evacuees was taken away. He was a right little ruffian who'd wet himself twice and had snot running out of his nose, over his lips, and down his chin. To be passed over in favour of him was about as humiliated as you could get.

So the four of us just sat there. Even Lucky kept looking at me, wanting to know what was happening. Lady Hammish didn't make things any easier for us. She talked out loud to herself. "So what am I supposed to do now? They've no right to send people from the colonies...No one is going to bomb Delhi or Calcutta... I told them we wanted Cockneys... That's what the villagers here expect from London...Cockneys saying 'Cor blimey, mate' and 'Watcha cock!'. Not little Lord Fauntleroys from the Raj..."

After this outburst, James said: "Shall we go home?"

"Don't be ridiculous," scoffed her ladyship. "This is a matter of duty. There is a war on, you know..."

Darkness closed in and Lady Hammish drew the black-out curtains before lighting the oil lamps. Then the village constable came in. He had the keys with him, ready to lock up for the night. He was a fat, jolly fellow and when Lady Hamilton explained her difficulties and railed against the villagers for their indifference, he was forced to take an interest in us. He realised he would be very lucky to get out of the hall empty handed, so he was looking for an excuse or an easy way out. He walked up and down in front of us several times. Then he stopped and was thoughtful for a moment. "Tell 'em what, Ma'm. I'll take the black 'un."

Lady Hamilton sighed with contempt. "Constable, in case you hadn't noticed, they're all black...That's the whole trouble..."

"No they bain't be, Ma'm," he replied. "With respect, them three there be khaki. This 'un be a black 'un." He pointed at Lucky. "And a right good little mongrel 'e be... Ain't 'um my beauty."

Lucky growled, curled back his quivering top lip, and exposed his gleaming teeth.

"Ah, and a spirited little bugger too, ain't 'um, my beauty." The policeman then read Lucky's label. "And a good ratter too. Danged if I won't have 'im, Ma'm."

That's how they came to steal Lucky off me. I protested and cried, but it was no good. As Lady Hammish continually asserted, she knew what was best for me and Lucky; and Brother Nothing (God rot his smelly socks) piped up with: "There is a war on, you know."

Predictably, we ended up staying on Lady Hammish's estate, but not in her house. That was the local Manor, a mini stately home with about thirty unoccupied bedrooms. Most of the rooms downstairs were unused as well but two of them – one at the back and one at the front – were gun rooms, and it was through their open windows that Lady Hammish shot any rabbits or squirrels she saw frolicking on the lawns. It was the head gardener's task to gather up the dead bodies, the rabbits being passed on the cook for serving 'downstairs' as rabbit pies and the squirrels to an unknown person in the village for unknown purposes best left uninvestigated. Her ladyship lived alone in the Manor House – her husband was at sea – and this was the reason the locals were so reluctant to volunteer their hospitality. They felt, not unreasonably, that the whole bang lot of the

Gran and Mr Muckey

London kids could easily have been put up in the west wing and nobody would have known the difference; but they equally knew that this would never happen. Her ladyship and the commander were of the old school. They adhered to the strict naval social code in which 'like' only mixed with 'like' and we were told that every year, when the commander organised the annual Western Approaches Ball at the United Services Club, he sent invitations to, 'Officers and their Ladies', 'Non-commissioned officers and their wives', and 'Ratings and their women'.

My brothers and I were classified on a similar basis. We were billeted with the servants, but since we were coloured, and thought to be foreign, we became servants to the servants. Although they gave us a wretched time, and made us do everything bar sweep the chimneys, it was impossible not to feel sorry for them. They worked around the clock and were paid a pittance. Yet instead of this making them sympathetic towards us, it had exactly the opposite result. They delighted in making us suffer. I've since discovered that this is a well-documented quirk of human behaviour and is best exemplified by a notorious speech Stanley Baldwin made to a delegation of striking Welsh coal miners in 1926. He said: "There are many people in the country who are far worse off than you are. And so long as I'm prime minister, the Tory Party will make sure this state of affair continues."

Two incidents lightened our gloom. The first was a simple little story which arose when a second batch of London evacuees was ear-marked for Cornwall just before Christmas. Lady Hammish took command again but this time she decided to allocate accommodation before the children arrived. So a couple of days prior to their appearance she visited likely foster parents. When the first door she knocked on was opened, she said breezily: "Good morning, Mrs Trescothick. How would you like an evacuee for Christmas?"

"Oh, no thank you, Madam," replied Mrs Trescothick. "I've already bought a chicken."

The second incident provided me with one of the great laughs and pleasures of my life. It revolved around Lucky. After he'd been stolen off me I saw very little of him. A couple of times I spotted him walking with the constable as he trod his beat and once I spied him running alongside the constable's bicycle, attached to the handlebars by a piece of string. I gave him my usual, shrill whistle, and Lucky – recognising it immediately – turned and tried to dash towards me, causing the constable to take a real purler. I cleared off quickly, knowing that if I was seen, I would be accused of doing it deliberately, which I did, of course. The real incident occurred not long afterwards. Lucky and the constable often went for walks on the nearby moor which had been used as a training ground by the territorial army shortly before war was declared.

The constable was in the habit of throwing things for Lucky to chase, one of Lucky's greatest pleasures. However, he wasn't always too clever with returning with the original object. If there was something else around with human scent on it he was just as liable to take that back, his sense of smell being superior to his eyesight on account of his blind eye. On this occasion, instead of taking back half a broken chair leg, he took back a live and very rusty hand grenade which had been left lying around by the TA.

Gran and Mr Muckey

When the constable saw what Lucky had in his mouth, he panicked. Only the day before he'd received a thousand pamphlets from the bureaucrats in Truro warning that cleverly disguised German booby traps had been spread around the countryside. Furthermore, these booby traps were either on delayed fuses or triggered by vibrations, so the fact that the grenade Lucky was carrying still had its pin in place wasn't of any great comfort. Steeling his nerve, the constable eased the grenade out of Lucky's mouth and threw it away with all his might. Then he ran back to the village to contact the army. When he reached the pub at the start of the village he was so out of breath that he slowed to a brisk walk. The Village Idiot (or mentally disadvantaged local resident) hailed him cheerfully from his seat outside the pub. "Morning, Constable..."

"Sorry, lad... Can't stop now... Emergency..."

"Oh, ah! I can see that, Constable. Better hurry and tell someone about that grenade..."

"What grenade?"

"The one your new dog's bringing on down the road. Way 'es got his teeth around that ring, looks like the pin's about to come out. If it do, won't it go off?"

The constable swivelled around. Lucky was now right behind him, his tail wagging with pride, the grenade hanging from his mouth. The constable started to run again, but as soon as he did so, Lucky ran with him. So the constable stopped and eased the grenade out of Lucky's mouth for the second time. Then he threw it as far as he could down the street, well clear of the houses. As soon as it left his hand he made a grab for Lucky, but he was too slow. Lucky was up and away, going split-arse after the grenade. The constable yelled after him: "Come back, you silly bugger. Heel! Heel!", but there was no stopping Lucky. After all, one of his 57 Varieties was Retriever.

They watched Lucky carefully as he sniffed around. When his head bobbed up again and they saw that he'd found the grenade and was bounding back with it, both the constable and the village idiot (who wasn't all that mentally disadvantaged) sprinted off towards the police station, yelling: "Take cover! Take cover!"

Lucky was a lot quicker than either of them and by the time they got to the police station and the constable had found the keys and unlocked the door, Lucky was beside them again. Dutifully, he dropped the grenade at their feet. The force of its fall caused the rusty housing around the pin to give way. The detonator clip sprang out. The grenade was active. They had seven seconds. The constable grabbed the grenade, opened the station door, and flung it in. Then he slammed the door and they ran for it. One of the Dirty Dozen couldn't have done it better.

They were about ten yards down the road when the grenade exploded. No one was hurt, but the interior of the police station was rendered a complete shambles.

The following day Lucky was returned to the Manor House on the direct orders of the chief constable of Devon and Cornwall. Lady Hammish said there was no way she was going to provide accommodation and food for a dog with no financial allowance, no ration book, and a propensity for picking up dangerous objects. The do-gooder, having done no good at all, washed her hands of the whole thing. We were told to get the next train to Paddington and to take Lucky with us. As the butler put it in his parting remark: "Back to the jungle, lads."

I thought he meant the concrete jungle, but of course he didn't.

11

*Back to a hiatus – Action at last, but chaos soon takes over
– We're bombed out and I'm wounded – Dad drops a brick
and it's time for us to leave Edgware.*

We were certainly glad to be back home even though everything did seem very peaceful and tame. Dad thought Lucky's efforts in blowing up the police station were hilarious and made a great fuss of him. He wanted to rename him 'Bomber' but I wouldn't let him. Mum wasn't so easily amused and was furious at the way we'd been treated, her main complaint being that whilst there had been a big hoo-ha about festooning us with labels to get there, we came back without a single one between us and with unwashed laundry to boot. Lady Hammish's cook had even pinched our ration coupons for the rest of the week.

For what seemed like months I was bored and restless. Everything was so negative. Barrage balloons were bobbing about in the sky like great toads; all the trenches they'd spent so much time digging were now full of water; and everywhere you went there were half-finished Anderson Shelters sticking out of the ground with owners as often as not poring over plans and diagrams, wondering what to do with misshapen sheets of corrugated iron.

Christmas 1939 was equally dismal. After the way I'd reacted to Dad's story of Flippy-Floppy, Mum told me the truth about Father Christmas which meant that Christmas was never the same again until I had kids of my own, many years later. My Christmas was also spoilt by the knowledge that at the beginning of the next term I was to start at a proper school. I'd attended a few classes in Cornwall but all I'd done there was sit in the back row and ignore everyone, the same as they were happy to ignore me. I was all in favour of doing the same thing at my new school, but I knew I'd never get away with it for long.

Dad and I spent this time preparing war maps, not only of the western front but the naval war in the Atlantic, with sea routes and shipping lanes in dotted lines. I was just beginning to think we'd never get beyond making maps when the Germans moved against Denmark and Norway, and things began to happen with a vengeance. I was beside myself with excitement. Every morning I woke early and dashed down stairs to study the latest maps in the Daily Express. The only trouble was that within a few days all the arrows were going the wrong way. Disaster followed disaster. Holland folded up, Belgium tried without success to cling on to their neutrality, and the Frogs, quite contrary to the propaganda on their lavatory paper, keeled over as though they were outnumbered 100 to 1. Worse still, they were soon co-operating with the Krauts. About the only good thing was that we got rid of Neville Chamberlain and put Winston Churchill in command. He at least exuded confidence and made it clear that even though everyone else had surrendered, we certainly wouldn't.

When I asked Dad: "What happens now?" he replied: "God knows. War is ninety per cent boredom and ten per cent chaos. And the chaos has just started."

"But what will happen, Dad?"

"Sajit, when there's chaos, no one knows. That's why they call it chaos."

Gran and Mr Muckey

Very soon all the arrows on my maps either ended on the English Channel or the nether land of Vichy France beyond Paris. It was fini. As far as western Europe was concerned, the Krauts had won hands down. All that was left on the continent were small, rapidly diminishing enclaves.

Dunkirk and the spirit it engendered is all part of history, of course. I remember it well, especially the Pathe News and Gaumont News shots at the local cinema in which defeated Tommies, still wet through from standing in the sea at Dunkirk, swore to get their revenge on Hitler. Inspired by the broadcasts of Churchill, we all swore along with them.

During the course of all this activity, there were one or two minor air raids over southern England. In one of them a Heinkel got lost (or had its Knickebein bent) and jettisoned its remaining bomb on the outskirts of Greater London. This caused little comment and no response, even though when a similar thing happened in central London in August, Churchill was so infuriated that he ordered a reprisal raid on Berlin, which in turn escalated the Battle of Britain into the London Blitz.

However, it was the first bomb – the one everyone ignored – which formed one of the major events of my life. The bomb scored a direct hit on the house opposite us. The house was demolished and a lot of the blast came straight across the road and into our front rooms. Upstairs, Mum and Dad were in one bedroom and I was in the other with Lucky curled up at my feet. I was blown clean out of bed and Lucky fared even worse. He was flung across the room and got a splinter of shrapnel in his gammy leg. Fortunately, the blackout curtains and the patterned brocades Mum had in all the bedrooms kept flying glass to a minimum, otherwise Mum, Dad, Lucky and I would have been torn to pieces. Instead, I was the only one to get cut and even that was a minor nick on my forehead.

Being blown out of bed is not a pleasant experience. In the initial moments I had no idea of what had happened, and there is no greater terror than the unknown. Those moments have haunted me all my life. As I was to learn years later in Korea, when the blast of high explosives hits you and hot metal is in flight, the mind is temporarily void: one reacts instinctively, sometimes well, sometimes badly, sometimes not at all: it's all down to character.

At Edgware, it wasn't until well after the raid was over (and due mainly to recurring nightmares) that I was able to reconstruct events. When I first found myself spread-eagled on the floor, my mind was dominated by the fear of either dying alone or surviving alone. Whatever happened, I wanted to be with the others. I also recall scanning myself, a lightning check up to see if I was still complete, half-fearing that I'd be armless or legless. At first I seemed okay, but then I became aware of blood pouring down my face. I wiped it away and when it reappeared I started to scream, convinced I was bleeding to death. Then, for reasons unknown, I staggered to my feet and went over to the window. A trail of blood was later found across the floor and I have recollections of blackout curtains hanging in shreds, and shards of glass crunching under my feet. Window frames were reduced to jagged splinters, pointing inwards like great spears; smoke and smell engulfed me; the house across the road had gone, reduced to a pile of rubble, roof timbers sticking up in the air at odd angles and a wash basin perched among them like a grotesque nest. Flames were spurting, dying, only to roar again as gas leaks took hold.

Finally, Dad rushed into the room. He grabbed me off the broken glass and carried me into the bathroom. He bathed my head and washed away the blood. He laughed with relief when he discovered that it was only a small cut. Then came the stinging sensation as he poured iodine on it and covered it with a strip of Elastoplast. Elsewhere I heard Mum shouting at Brother Nothing and James to go downstairs. Dad wrapped me up in my dressing gown and for a moment he hugged me, it seemed with all his might. Then we joined the others in the lounge, the floor of which was covered in yet more splintered glass. That didn't matter. We were all there, safe.

Mum was on the far side of the room. I ran over to her. "Look Mum," I shouted excitedly. "I'm wounded."

She glanced at me, half smiled, and then resumed straightening the pictures. I showed my wound to Gran instead. She was calm and very sympathetic, but she too had a clear order of priorities. She was clutching her bottle of Ganges holy water.

I looked around at the others. James was fully dressed, complete with his school cap, as though ready to walk off down the avenue. Brother Nothing was still in his pyjamas with his gas mask on. Suddenly I began to laugh. I knew I shouldn't, but I couldn't help it. He looked such an idiot. Why he thought that he alone should wear a gas mask, I'd no idea. Already the cellophane eyepiece was clouded over so that he couldn't see anything and every time he breathed out he blew loud raspberries out the side of the mask. Funniest of all, he was groping around the place as though playing Blind Man's Bluff, calling out in muffled tones through his snout: "What's happening, Dad?"

My God, how I giggled. It was relief and shock, I suppose. Mum shouted at me to stop being so silly, but every time Brother Nothing bumped into someone else and asked: "What's happening, Dad?" I giggled until tears ran down my cheeks.

For quite a time we just stood around, not knowing what to do. Then Dad went around the house a couple of times to inspect the damage. His verdict was that it was superficial, mainly broken windows. The worst damage had been in my room where a piece of shrapnel as big as a fist had torn a hole in the wall about two feet above where my head had lain.

Next, Dad went out to see what was happening in the avenue. We heard him speaking with several neighbours so we ventured out. The avenue was full of people, everyone in disarray: hand torches were being flashed about despite the regulations, and people were in various stages of dress and undress, some still in night clothes, men in trousers and vests with highly coloured braces showing. Others were arriving by the second, most of them fully dressed with tin hats on, a few even running down the road with stirrup pumps. As for actually doing anything... Well, mainly people were just looking in horror at what had happened, at what had once been their neighbour's house, searching for somewhere to start digging.

Before long two ambulances came dashing down the avenue in opposite directions. They were going so fast, and could see so little because of their blinkered headlights, that they passed each other and overshot the bombed house. Some people, expecting them to stop, nearly got run over. Everyone shouted and waved at them and the ambulances screeched to a halt and reversed back to where they were needed. Simultaneously, Dad's ARP colleagues put in an appearance. They were on their bicycles, newly painted with white mudguards. They too were travelling at speed. They didn't look at all steady due to the football rattles they were rotating above their heads. As they wobbled along they were shouting: "Air raid! Air raid! Take cover!"

Dad regarded them with utter contempt and muttered: "What a bunch of wallies," and I burst into fresh giggles.

Eventually, whilst Mrs Cohen took Lucky into her home to dress his wound, I was bundled into one of the ambulances with Mum and taken to hospital for a check-over. There, they shaved off a semi-circle of my hair, poured more iodine on my wound, bandaged it, and put me to bed in the children's ward. I'd hardly had time to go to sleep before Mum was back again, telling me to get dressed. We were going back home to collect essential belongings and would then be given temporary accommodation. She also told me that Dad had insisted on reporting for duty with the ARP. They were digging as hard as they could in the house opposite, hoping to find survivors.

We duly collected various things from Number 49 and then stood in the driveway, waiting for a taxi to take us to our new accommodation. Lots of people were helping the police and ARP with rescue operations. Prominent among them were our Jewish neighbours. Mr Greenbaum was clawing at the rubble with his bare hands, perspiration cascading down his face, and Mr Cohen and Mr Goldsmith were with Dad, part of a human chain clearing the rubble out of the way. In the background, in a wide half-circle, stood the Jewish women, many of them leaning on each other for support, most of them weeping. Then came excited shouts. The family had been located, all of them still in their beds. Men surged forward. Heads went down, backs bent double, and debris was soon shooting backwards in the same way as soil flies when rabbits burrow.

Before long the family was dragged out, one by one. They were complete and bloodless, but ominously still. They were laid out on stretchers in their driveway and a doctor went from one to another, examining them, each time concluding matters by pulling blankets over their faces. With each tragic declaration the Jewish women howled rather than wept and several of them tried to dash forward, only to be restrained by the police. Others simply stared, struck dumb. To this day, I know of few things more shattering than blankets being drawn over bodies, declaring no hope.

As the corpses were loaded into an ambulance, the rescuers withdrew, knowing that all the utilities had been turned off and that until daylight nothing more could be done. They were given cups of tea by Mrs Cohen. I joined Dad among the main group of rescuers. For a time no one said anything. Then there were generalisations, everyone searching for words of consolation. When they'd run dry of the usual cliches, Dad gave a loud sigh, as though he at least would be able to contribute something original and meaningful.

"Well," he said, "you've certainly got to hand it to old Adolf. He's a bloody good shot. First bomb on London and he's already got four Jews."

There was a stunned silence.

Everyone stared at Dad in disbelief.

Dad laughed selfconsciously, as though to make light of it, but that only made matters worse.

Of course, there was no excuse for what he'd said. He knew it as soon as the words left his mouth. He would have done anything to withdraw the remark, but that was impossible. Retractions and apologies, and assurances that it was only said in jest, were futile. Such a cruel, racist quip meant the words would never be forgotten, or forgiven.

Yet I will defend Dad until the death. He wasn't a racist nor a callous man. As an Untouchable in India he'd had no alternative but to be blase towards death; and as a veteran of Flanders, who'd seen men slaughtered in their thousands, he had acquired the false bravado of cannon fodder – the pathetic jokes which sought to minimise disasters. In the trenches it was commonplace. Among those who faced death all day and every day, it worked. It was routine, something they did before claiming the dead man's boots and sharing out his Woodbines and his Wills Whiffs.

However, the rights and wrongs of the situation were immaterial. Dad had sufficient sense to realise that we had no alternative but to move out of the area.

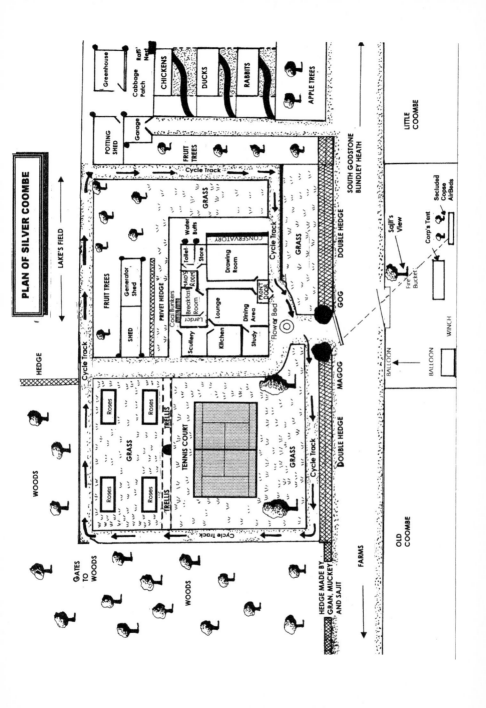

PLAN OF SILVER COOMBE

12

Silver Coombe, our new home – An ideal location for resisting invasion – Enter Mr Muckey – Sparks fly between Mum and Muckey – Muckey's prize marrow – Gran intercedes and love is born.

We moved to Silver Coombe, a magnificent eight bedroom house with two acres of garden and extensive woodlands between the Surrey villages of South Godstone and Blindley Heath. It was an idyllic location, situated midway up a country lane liberally scattered with what estate agents used to call 'Substantial Gentlemen's Residences', but which they now strip of gender and refer to as, 'Ideal Executive Homes'. It was secluded but not isolated. Dad bought it for £999.19s. 11d. It was going cheap because of the invasion scare. Some faint-hearted people were so convinced that the Germans would wipe out the RAF and then invade us that they were selling up and clearing off as quickly as possible, and the nearer they were to the south coast the quicker they were going and the cheaper they were selling.

The threat of invasion was real enough, of course. Dad's theory was that if we were invaded we'd all had it anyhow, that at the best we would spend the rest of our lives in slave-labour camps. He intended to go down fighting and had already declared his intention to change allegiance from the

Gran and Mr Muckey

ARP to the Home Guard so that his last act on this planet would be firing a rifle, not squirting a stirrup pump.

In truth, Dad was confident that when the inevitable showdown came for the command of the air, the RAF would do their stuff and see off the Luftwaffe. Then, an invasion would be impossible and an eight bedroom house with lots of ground in the heart of Surrey, on a direct Green Line route to London, would become a pot of gold. (He was right.)

Dad's reasoning was far too long term for me. I could think no further forward than the invasion; and even now I recall with complete clarity my single-minded determination to be among those who repelled the Krauts. That's why I was so keen to live at Silver Coombe. It had tremendous potential as a defensive position. I had gained a limited knowledge of good defensive positions from Champion, a comic that had regular articles about the Commandos, and I at once realised that Silver Coombe's elevated position gave it brilliant fields of fire covering the route the Krauts were bound to take, coming up from East Grinstead, Lingfield, and Blindley Heath.

On either side of the large, wrought iron gate of Silver Coombe were two odd-looking deciduous trees. Their bare trunks rose arrow straight for about thirty feet and then sprouted thin branches in a circular manner, leaving a bowl at the top. Dad called these trees Gog and Magog. I decided straight away that they would be perfect observation posts, and even before contracts for the house had been exchanged with Mr Pertwee, I had everything worked out. I would fix rope ladders to the trees for easy access. Then, using Dad's old army binoculars, I would relay the disposition of the advancing Krauts to James who I was relying on to man the Silver Coombe headquarters, which was to be a small tree house in a copse beside the tennis court. Communications would be via a walkie-talkie – two empty Baked Beans tins connected by string. Another great attraction about Silver Coombe was that along the front boundary were thick, double hedges, and although I conceded that these didn't provide protection from blast and flying metal, they did give cover from view and, in my imagination, they were so like proper trenches that I fancied our chances of holding the Krauts at bay until the army could mount a counter attack and push them back into the sea.

When we moved into Silver Coombe James, who had been my chief accomplice, suddenly withdrew all offers of help. He became terribly practical. He kept saying, "But what happens if you're outflanked?" and "How are you going to stop tanks?" and "You haven't even got any weapons...The Germans won't be using pea shooters, you know..." I had no answers, of course, but I still wasn't prepared for his final comment. "Sajit, being a fanatic is one thing. But you're just plain stupid."

All my plans and aspirations disintegrated.

Then I met Muckey.

He was our inherited gardener. Muckey brought hope. Through him were born fresh plans.

When we acquired Silver Coombe, Mr Pertwee warned us that Muckey was a difficult man to handle and that it might be a nice gesture if we all called him 'McKay', rather than Muckey. He added, however, that whatever we called him he had his own way of doing things and refused to take orders from anyone, particular women. Men giving him orders were ignored, women trying the same thing got a mouthful of foul abuse. In fact, Mr Pertwee advised that all women in the household should avoid Muckey like the plague.

Despite these warnings, Dad went round to the potting shed to check the garden inventory and I accompanied him. Muckey wasn't pleased to see us. As Mr Pertwee had intimated, Muckey considered everything about Silver Coombe (apart from the house and contents) to be his sole concern and responsibility. In particular, the potting shed was sacred ground. I doubt if anyone else had set foot in it for years. Muckey confronted us in the doorway and Dad literally had to barge his way in. He then discovered that numerous tools were missing. All those which could be considered dangerous in the wrong hands (such as pitch forks, scythes, sickles) had vanished. Muckey's explanation was always the same. "Bloody Home Guard's got the bugger."

Dad accepted this. Everyone knew that the Home Guard had no proper weapons and were improvising in whatever way they could, but when Dad asked Muckey why he'd taken it upon himself to arm the Home Guard, Muckey replied: "Because I'm the bloody platoon sergeant."

That was why Muckey became my great hope. It was the foundation stone of a marvellous friendship, one I will treasure all my life. I reasoned that if a decrepit old man like Muckey could be platoon sergeant, then surely there was room somewhere, in one capacity or another, for a fit young bloke like me. After all, I was now knocking on seven years old. So I decided that Muckey was a man whose favour I would have to curry, and before I go any further I'll tell you what a wonderful old chap he was.

Muckey had the bends. Not the decompression sickness divers get, but the bends old men get due to arthritis. He walked with his legs bent in two directions, forward as though in preparation for the high jump, and outwards as though he'd forgotten to mount his horse; and as he went about his business in the garden, his entire body was bent forward at the waist as though searching for a six penny piece he'd dropped the previous day. His arms were usually loose at his side, bent in the manner of Tommy Farr when about to deliver left and right hooks, the dreaded 'one-two'.

At one stage Muckey had served in the army (he had a DCM but I was the only person he ever told, and I was sworn to secrecy) and he had a large chunk out of the tip of his boxer's nose where shrapnel had caught him. Below his nose, as though to take attention away from it, was a bandito moustache, an unkempt nicotine-stained growth which had the texture and colour of last year's hay and which was so rarely trimmed or attended that it hung over his lower lip

John Hollands

and acted as a strainer, leaving considerable evidence of what he had last eaten. It rendered his speech – which was already hard to follow because of his Surrey country dialect – incomprehensible to all but his intimates.

His vocabulary revolved around three swear words, 'bloody', 'bugger(ing)', and 'bleeding", and the key to understanding him was to ignore the swear words and concentrate on what little remained. He wore what was essentially a uniform since it never varied: Wellington boots (boasting numerous 'Dunlop' repairs), faded blue dungarees, a loud, Canadian-style lumberjack's shirt, and a dirty old dun-coloured flat cap which lay on his head like a crusty cowpat. When it rained, the cap changed colour, drooped, and looked like a fresh cowpat. On the frequent occasions when he removed his cap to scratch his scalp, he had a full head of fine, silver hair.

His trade mark was a briar pipe. It had a huge bowl and a broken stem bound ineffectually with insulating tape. Both the stem and bowl billowed smoke like a power station, smelt like God knows what, and gurgled and rumbled like an empty stomach. It was seldom out of his mouth and when he spoke it jumped about. His false teeth jumped in tandem, but were never seen, of course, only heard, a soft thud each time the pipe went up and down. It was just one more distraction to be ignored if he was to be understood.

Muckey was well into his seventies and had been a gardener at Silver Coombe for so long that he was a fixture. One of the covenants covering the sale of the house was that he should be employed until he chose to retire or until death.*

In our lane there were four 'Coombe' houses: Silver Coombe, Carlton Coombe, Little Coombe, and Old Coombe, and by a curious coincidence the names of their gardeners had an odd similarity or connection, being (respectively) Muckey, Muddle, Smart and Tidy. All shared one great obsession in life, growing giant marrows. There was vicious

---

* Mum said it was a great comfort to know that we had no obligation to employ a dead gardener.

rivalry between them, going back over twenty years, and every year it surfaced at the Blindley Heath Flower and Produce Show. Feelings became so intense, and the locals so involved, that the winner became the gardening champion of the village. Whilst Muddle boasted the most wins (10), Muckey had dominated the last eight years, even though Tidy, a man with horticultural qualifications, was never more than a fraction behind. Indeed, so narrow were Muckey's victories that his relationship with Tidy had deteriorated to a state of pure, unadulterated hatred. They even accused each other of cheating. Muckey said Tidy grew his marrows in a vacuum and Tidy accused Muckey of injecting his with steroids.

In reality, neither cheated but each had a secret formula for forcing the growth of their marrows, secrets which they guarded jealously. First thing every morning, Muckey went to his vegetable garden with a piece of sacking over his arm, hiding his secret ingredient. He would then pour his magic potion out from beneath the sacking, revealing nothing. Yet it could be that he had an additional secret. Like many gardeners, he spoke to his plants, but instead of coaxing his marrows along with pleasantries and flattery, he unleashed on them a torrent of foul, lower-rank military abuse.

When we discovered all this about Muckey it was predictable that some in the family assumed him to be a bumbling old idiot. In typical Contractor style (I'm ashamed to say), they found him so amusing, and such an inviting target, that they made plans to have fun at his expense. The truth was, however, that although Muckey looked the very epitome of a senile country bumpkin, he had more peas in his pod than people ever suspected.

Muckey and Mum fell out as soon as they met. They were such complete opposites that it was entirely predictable. Since moving to Silver Coombe Mum had not been in the best of tempers. Life in the country was not to her liking. It was far too disorganised and messy. Leaves and seeds and things were forever blowing about the place, out of control, multiplying and decomposing. She liked things to be stationary and cleanable, preferably polishable. The house was far too big and rambling and the only time she tried to spruce up the outside by playing her hose over it, paint on the woodwork peeled off. The garden was in a terrible state with literally hundred of trees which would have to be chopped down and disposed of by autumn if we were to be saved from a deluge of dead leaves and windfalls.

She won a partial victory when Dad agreed to employ a maid and although there were dozens of applicants, Mum declared them all to be 'gormless'. However, she did appoint one, Mary. She was the least gormless of them but – as we shall soon see – she was gormless nonetheless.

What really infuriated Mum was the nerve of the previous owner, Mr Pertwee. The way he assumed to have some lingering interest in Silver Coombe made her tremble with anger; and his advice that she – as a mere woman – should keep clear of the gardener filled her with such fury that it made her doubly-determined to get involved right up to her neck. The very idea of someone in her household not obeying her orders and not abiding by her set rules was nothing short of heresy. If she was capable of making Dad toe the line she certainly wasn't going to let our gardener (who she'd been forced to employ, and over whom she lacked the power of dismissal) get the better of her. She was going to make sure she got her money's worth out of the Old Fart if it was the last thing she did; and as for the nonsense about pronouncing his name 'McKay', she was highly contemptuous of the very idea and forbade any of us even to think about it.

"He's bloody mucky by nature so he stays bloody Muckey by name. Got it?"

Like my brothers, I chorused: "Yes, Mum," but I already knew that Muckey didn't give a damn what he was called.

Mum made no secret of the fact that she considered the garden to be a shambles and if it hadn't been for the covenant she would have gone straight across the road to Old Coombe to head-hunt Mr Tidy, who organised General Westlake's garden so beautifully. In particular she couldn't get over the state of our lawn edges, the weed-ridden flower beds, and the uncut hedges; and the thing she intended to sort out above all else was the potting shed. It stank to high heaven.

"You can smell it a mile off," declared Mum.

"I think you'll find that it's fertiliser, Mum," I said, determined to defend Muckey.

"Bull shit!"

"No, Mum. Horse shit, actually..."

That earned me a whack around the ear, so from thereon I just listened to Mum's ravings and kept quiet.

The thing none of us will ever forget was their initial confrontation. We'd all been awaiting it with keen anticipation. At that stage I was the only one (apart from Dad) to have encountered Muckey, so I alone gave the old man any chance of surviving the encounter. We had to wait nearly a week. On a matter of principle, Mum and Muckey avoided each other, refusing to make the first move, like two boxers circling the ring. Eventually, Muckey had to give way in order to collect his wages.* When he entered the scullery he had thick mud on his boots and chunks of manure flaking off the spade tucked under his arm. Deliberately, Mum kept him waiting. He didn't seem to mind and occupied himself by filling his pipe with unrubbed Egyptian tobacco. As a preliminary he knocked out his pipe in the scullery sink, despite it being half full of unwashed crockery. When Mum heard the noise she hurried in with his wages. When she saw all his old pipe muck floating about in her washing up water, she couldn't credit such disgusting behaviour. She flew at him like an enraged cockerel, but instead of getting the cowering reaction she was accustomed to from the rest of us, Muckey stood his ground, went on knocking out his pipe, and made a very good pretence at not having heard a word she yelled.

* Two pounds a week would you believe!

When she eventually offered him his wage packet he ignored it, making her wait. Instead, he took out his pen knife to decoke his pipe. This was an ear-shattering operation that sent chips of charcoal flying in all directions: on to the floor, into the crockery, and even reaching the kitchen. He scraped the bowl in a circular motion and knocked it out each time he'd completed a rotation. Eventually, having decided there was now room for a decent refill, and he made a big palaver of lighting up. He used three matches (the remains of which he dropped on the floor), and he didn't stop sucking loudly until a vast cloud of toxic fumes filled the scullery. With Mum coughing and spluttering and backing away, Muckey grabbed his wage packet off her and said: "What in the name of buggery has bitten you, woman? This is all I need, a bloody woman spearing around the bleeding place..."

Fortunately, Mum didn't understand a word he said. She turned to me for a translation but I wasn't going to get involved. "No idea, Mum... Thanks very much, I think."

Muckey took advantage of the pause and shuffled off, happy at having had the last word; but a few minutes later he was forced to return.

"Seen my bleeding spud, woman?" he called out.

"Spud?" repeated Mum, who was up to her elbows in Domestos and Vim suds, scrubbing and disinfecting the scullery sink. "Your spud?"

"Yes, my bleeding spud, woman."

"Your potato?"

"Not taters, woman. My bleeding spud."

Mum was still trying to work out what he was talking about when Muckey saw that she had removed his spade from the scullery, cleaned it and polished it, and it was now leaning against the Easiwork just inside the kitchen, ready for a display cabinet. Muckey pushed his way past her to retrieve it. "Just leave my bleeding spud alone," he cussed. "Spuds are like frying pans, woman... You never clean the buggers."

Gran and Mr Muckey

"If you're suggesting I don't clean my frying pans you're very much mistaken. Now push off, you dirty old grampus. And never light up that filthy camel dung in here again... Go back where you belong, to your stinking shotting ped..."

Muckey turned to me. "What's the woman bloody spearing on about?"

From thereon similar rows occurred almost daily. If anything, they got worse. Mum soon understood every word Muckey uttered and his profane and disparaging remarks only served to provoke her into demonstrating that when it came to a good, old-fashioned slanging match her background among the rough-and-tumble of the Rhondda mining community made her a match for anyone.

The rest of us never actually watched these rows. We took the cowardly way out and sat in silence around the kitchen table and eavesdropped. When my brothers or I started to laugh, Gran silenced us with a finger to her lips, fearing that any off-stage noises might put an end to things. When the rows finished we dispersed quickly and silently, without comment, as though not interested; but events that followed soon made our attitudes and loyalties abundantly clear.

Brother Nothing and James regarded the rows as open licence to embark on baiting and tormenting Muckey. I suppose some would excuse them with the old cliche, 'boys will be boys' and argue that they were at a mischievous age and were only standing up for their mother. Whether justified or not, they spent most of their days stalking Muckey as he went about his duties, dreaming up ways of sabotaging his efforts. Their favourite trick was to sneak up behind him whilst he was bending down with his spade or some other tool laid aside, and then nip forward silently and pinch it. Once safely back in their hiding place, they watched with great amusement as Muckey struggled against his arthritis to straighten himself up, turned around with equal deliberation, and then searched in bewilderment for his missing tool. Similarly, they would watch him go about some task or other and then, when he'd gone off to do something else, reverse what he'd just done. Another trick, usually after a day of heavy rain, was to pull the plugs out of his numerous water butts so that when he went to fill his watering can he found them bone dry. On another occasion they drilled small holes in the bottom of his watering can so that once he'd filled it he'd trudge off with it leaking like a sieve.

Naturally, he soon got to know what they were up to and kept a beady eye out for their pranks. However, they invariably got the better of him. Once, while Muckey and I were busy on the compost heap, they sneaked around behind the garages where he kept his two wheel barrows (burrows, to Muckey) and painted slogans on their sides. One had, 'Go To it!' on one side and, 'Give Us The Tools And We'll Do The Job' on the other. On the second barrow it was, 'Dig For Victory' and 'We Can Take It'. On another occasion James wrote out posters in huge capitals and pinned them on the potting shed door. The first read, "Abandon Hope All Ye Who Enter Here' and this was followed by 'Illigitimus Nil Carborundum', which Muckey had no way of knowing was supposed to mean, 'Don't let the bastards get you down'.

Their campaign reached a peak when Dad took it into his head to buy them Daisy Air Rifles. (At first, I was considered too young to handle such feeble weapons.) A proper target went with these rifles but my brothers soon found shooting at a stationary target far too boring. They decided it would be more fun to shoot at Muckey. They would hide behind the privet hedge in front of the generating shed and wait for him to come along the path at the rear of the house, heading for the scullery. Just before the scullery door were two large, galvanised coal bunkers. When Muckey was within a few feet of these they blasted off pellets with rapid fire. They made loud 'pinging' noises as they hit the bunkers no more than an inch or two in front of Muckey. He never flinched, merely shouted: "You young buggers. I'll skin you alive if I bloody catch you."

Gran and Mr Muckey

He had no chance of catching them, however. They were up and away in a flash, splitting their side with laughter. When he re-emerged from the scullery, they'd be back in position, ready for another go at him.

Another trick was to lay trip wires across the narrow path leading to the potting shed, but since Muckey was always looking at the ground, searching for that elusive six penny piece, he spotted them and kicked them away contemptuously.

Whilst all this was going on I was creeping up to old Muckey as hard as I could, still hoping that he would involve me with the Home Guard. Lucky and I spent a lot of time with him, not only doing small chores for him, but sitting with him in the potting shed. Muckey and I yarned about all sorts of things and consequently we were soon great pals. Although he wasn't going to admit it to anyone but me, Muckey was amused by my brothers' antics. They were, after all, pretty harmless and from what he told me, he'd obviously been a bit of a lad himself in his day. Anyhow, I became his spy and told him what to expect next, which meant that most of their pranks began to misfire.

Once, Muckey got his own back with a vengeance. I tipped him off that they'd loosened the nuts on the wheel of his wheelbarrow, so when they sneaked around after him, waiting for the moment when the wheel fell off, he steered his barrow around the corner by the conservatory. What they didn't realise was that Muckey had his hose connected and running full blast. Once around the corner, he dumped his wheelbarrow over and cursed out loud. Then, when they came dashing around the corner to see the fun, he caught them with his jet fair and square, smack in their faces.

Then two things happened which soured Muckey's attitude, particularly towards Brother Nothing. The first became known in the family as 'The Rats Incident'.

In a sense, Lucky was responsible for this. Taking his cue from me, Lucky had taken to Muckey in a big way and on a couple of occasions he'd gone back to the potting shed with dead rats and laid them before Muckey as presents. The truth was that around the chicken and duck houses (we kept 36 chickens and 20 ducks) there were lots of rats and keeping their numbers down was one of Muckey's constant battles. When he realised what a fine ratter Lucky was, the three of us combined to seek out the rats' nest and exterminate them.

It was in the middle of a very wet spell and Brother Nothing and Mum had occasion to go looking for Muckey. They couldn't find him anywhere and eventually they ended up walking along the duck board in the chicken run, on either side of which was a sea of mud. What they didn't realise was that some fifteen yards further on, around the other side of the chicken house, Muckey, Lucky, and I were at the crucial stage of a delicate operation. We were sneaking up on the rats' nest, about to launch our attack, an all-or-nothing assault.

When we struck, Brother Nothing was still leading the way along the duck board. Suddenly, without warning, he was confronted by a pack of frenzied rats haring around the end of the chicken house like greyhounds unleashed from their traps at the White City. Lucky was in hot pursuit, with Muckey and I bringing up the rear, lagging well behind, still on the far side of the chicken house.

"Rats! Rats!" screamed Brother Nothing.

He turned and sprinted away for all he was worth. He was so crazed with fear that when he found Mum barring his way on the duck board he stuck out an arm and swept her to one side. She went flying and landed on her back in the mud, directly in the path of the fleeing rats. She claimed that four of them ran straight over her. Whether or not this was correct I don't know. The only sure thing was that Brother Nothing kept running until he was safely back in the house.

Gran and Mr Muckey

For some reason Mum put the entire blame for this incident on Muckey and every time he went into the scullery she would jeer: "Are you alone, Muckey? Or have you got some of your rats with you?"

Brother Nothing and James found this hilarious and jokes about Muckey and his rats became an integral part of the anti-Muckey campaign. Gran and I never joined in. Even if Mum said something genuinely funny (as she sometimes did) Gran wouldn't laugh on principle, and the more rows she witnessed between Mum and Muckey so her admiration for the old man increased. She loved the way he stood up for himself and traded insults with his bullying employer. She told Mum straight that Muckey was the type of man who would be venerated in India, to which Mum replied: "I dare say. With all the rats you've got out there, he'd be in his element."

The other thing to sour Muckey's attitude came about because of Gran's eagle-eye. Since we'd moved to Silver Coombe, she hadn't stirred outside the house but she had (as you'll have gathered) taken a keen interest in the rumpus with Muckey. Although she'd never spoken to him, and had even kept out his sight, she regarded him as an ally, someone to be defended at all costs, right or wrong.

She was particularly disgusted by the behaviour of Brother Nothing and James. When she reprimanded them they took no notice. After all, they had Mum's blessing. This so incensed Gran that she embarked on a systematic scheme of spying on them, logging every one of the nasty tricks. She was able to do this by roaming from bedroom to bedroom since all parts of the garden were visible from one bedroom or another, the attic bedroom being a particularly good observation post. She soon had a damning indictment of their behaviour and when Dad came home in the evenings she would pass on everything to him, even though he was too tired after his exertions in Camberwell to be bothered about minor frictions at home.

John Hollands

When I was in the garden, either playing on my own, or helping Muckey, I often looked back at the house and there Gran would be, standing a little back from one of the windows, half-hidden in the shadows, a secret, prying figure, a Mrs Danvers of the Orient. Like Dad, I got a full run down on her findings, but with me she went one step further and made no secret of her interest in Muckey and her deep sympathy for him; how impressive she found him, what a conscientious worker he was, and how, in India, he would be regarded as the salt of the earth.

What infuriated Gran most about my brothers' tricks was that they often carried them out behind Muckey's back, once he'd returned to his thatched cottage in South Godstone.

She considered that cowardly, so typical of Brother Nothing.

In fact it was on a fine Sunday afternoon that Gran noticed Brother Nothing acting in a suspicious manner, putting on a pair of gum boots. She went up to the attic bedroom and very soon saw her grandson making his way to the vegetable garden. Even though he had no idea he was under observation, the evil way he slunk along told Gran that he was up to something especially nasty. She had no idea, of course, just how treacherous he was being: that his mission was nothing less than scuppering Muckey's chances of winning 1st prize in the marrow section at the Blindley Heath Show. All she saw was him rummaging around amid the vegetables, pulling back leaves in search of something. She soon realised that he'd found whatever he was looking for. He spent several minutes in a crouching position, busying himself very intently, and then he jumped up and ran back to the house.

Gran waited for an hour or so and then, when there were no further developments, she got me to go to the vegetable garden to investigate. I soon found Muckey's potential champion. It was lying beneath the shade of giant leaves, probably the finest marrow Muckey had ever propagated and nurtured. On the side of the marrow, in bright red letters, Brother Nothing had written in great capitals:

"UNEXPLODED BOMB!
CALL THE UXB
TELEPHONE WHITEHALL 1212."*

When I told Gran she was so furious that as soon as Dad returned from Camberwell she told him what had happened. She was so upset that this time Dad took some notice of her. He went out to see for himself. He came back even more angry than she was. We were all assembled in the lounge. Dad was a frightening sight. He already had his leather belt out of his trousers. He pointed at Brother Nothing and demanded: "Did you do that to Muckey's marrow?"

Brother Nothing remained silent.

"Did you?"

He still said nothing.

"It's only a marrow," said Mum.

"Only a marrow? What are you talking about? That's old Muckey's greatest pride. It's his life's work."

"Life's work," scoffed Mum. "It's nothing but a bloody marrow. What difference does it make?"

"It makes all the difference in the world to Muckey."

"Anyhow," ventured Nothing. "It's time Mr Tidy had a chance to win."

"It's a joke, for God's sake," said Mum.

Dad's temper snapped. It had never happened before and I never knew it to happen again. It was awesome. In one motion he grabbed Brother Nothing, put him across his knee, and gave him a vicious thrashing. Mum yelled at him to stop, but he carried on until Brother Nothing was screaming out in pain. Eventually he cast him aside with contempt.

*UXB was the Unexploded Bomb Division of the army. Whitehall 1212 was the telephone number one rang whenever confronted by a national emergency.

As Nothing scrambled back to his feet, Dad added: "Don't you ever, ever try to destroy a man's pride." Then he turned on James and me. "And that goes for you two as well. A man needs to excel at something, whether it's a bloody marrow or re-treading a giant tyre."

"Say you're sorry," advised Mum, comforting Brother Nothing.

"Him say sorry!" bellowed Dad. "It's no good him saying he's sorry. That'll be a bloody insult. I'm the one who's got to say sorry – sorry to Muckey for the despicable behaviour of my own son." Mum went to speak again but Dad shouted her down. "I don't want to hear any more about it. Just hold your tongue! When I see Muckey at the Home Guard parade, I'll apologise. Knowing him, he'll take it in his stride. And his loss will be nothing to our shame. In future, just leave the old man alone."

Brother Nothing was sent to bed in disgrace and for the rest of the evening hardly a word was spoken. First thing in the morning, as soon as Dad had left for work, Gran ventured outside the house for the first time. She went across to the vegetable garden and examined the marrow. She came back highly excited. She sought me out and said she thought she could remove the graffiti without damaging either the texture or the colour of the marrow. Her optimism was based on the fact that the skin of the marrow hadn't been pierced.

"But Muckey will already have seen it," I pointed out. "He feeds it first thing in the morning. He'll have seen it even before we were up..."

"Never mind. We're going to see what we can do."

So together we gathered up a bucket of warm soda water, a bottle of Sarson's Apple Vinegar, and a wad of wire wool, and set off for the vegetable garden. As we passed Mum on the way out she taunted us: "Well, well, well... The healers go forth. The Virgin Mary, off to cure the pilgrims at Lourdes."

Gran and Mr Muckey

Once we'd located the marrow, Gran bathed it in the soda water, applied the vinegar generously around the writing, and then rubbed it gently with the wire wool. By the time she finished, the marrow was restored to its former condition, except for faint indentation marks. When I pointed these out, Gran said they'd disappear in time if the marrow was massaged regularly. Then we stood back, satisfied that at least all was not totally lost. It was then that we saw Muckey watching us. He was some twenty yards away, half-hidden behind a large gooseberry bush, looking like a Corsican bandit. Gran beckoned him over. He came slowly, suspiciously, but when he examined the marrow he too was well pleased. Beneath his moustache lurked a smile of gratitude. I could tell by the way his ears waggled backwards.

"Sajit, aren't you going to introduce us?" said Gran.

"Oh, yes. Sorry. Gran, this is Muckey. Muckey, this is my Gran, from India."

"Mister Muckey, Sajit. Mind your manners, please."

"Well, yes. Mr Muckey."

I looked at Muckey and muttered apologetically but he didn't hear a word. Metaphorically, he was miles away. Then a most extraordinary thing happened. At least, I think it happened. Muckey's face was suddenly rejuvenated. Even the empty folds of skin hanging around his neck disappeared. I looked back at Gran and she too was different. It was as though a magic pall had swept over them and banished the defects of time. My eyes flicked from one to the other. Muckey's cap was now off, revealing auburn hair, and he was upright and muscular. Gran was slim and elegant, her bare midriff as level and soft as the back of a bar of warm milk chocolate.

Then Gran spoke and the spell was broken. Yet in a way I knew it wasn't a spell. What I had imagined was what they had seen: each other in their prime.

"Mr Muckey, you have the most lovely marrow," said Gran.

"So I like to think, Lady."

"Quite the most magnificent specimen I've ever see, Mr Muckey."

"Thank you, Lady... And thank you for fixing it."

"Not entirely fixed, Mr Muckey. But if we nurse it along, I think it will recover... Perhaps if we could feed it a little liquid dye it might make it darker so that the marks become less noticeable."

"Gran grows the most marvellous Sweet Williams, Muckey," I said proudly.

"Then you're a keen gardener, Lady?"

"Oh, yes. Especially when I was in India. May I pass on a tip from India, Mr Muckey?"

"Of course, Lady."

"In India, if gardeners are anxious for special results they usually urinate on things..."

That struck me as very rude. In fact, rather disgusting, but Muckey was unmoved, no doubt accustomed to the ways of India. Then he amazed me by letting out his great secret, which only goes to show what putty men are in the hands of women they fancy. "I've often heard talk of things like that, Lady. But between you and me, I always use Friary's brown ale. A bottle of Friary's Best Brown first thing every morning, before sun-up."

"Well bear my suggestion in mind, Mr Muckey," urged Gran.

"Maybe I will... But to tell you truth, Lady, there 'baint be much difference between Friary's Best Brown and my urine. Maybe Friary's is a tad more concentrated than Muckey's."

With that they laughed and wandered off towards Muckey's potting shed. Instinctively, I left them to it.

Whether or not Muckey took Gran's advice I never discovered, but some weeks later he certainly triumphed over Mr Tidy at the Blindley Heath Show. We cheated a little. Despite Gran's and Muckey's efforts, a few indentations still remained on the marrow, so when we put it on the display table for the judges' attention, we placed it with the indentations to the rear, against the wall. When Muckey shuffled forward to receive his award from Admiral Sir Archibald Cook, cap off, hair combed, moustache trimmed, I was sitting between Dad and Gran in the front row of the audience. Admiral Cook made a little speech in which he referred to Muckey as "my brother-in-arms, Sergeant Muckey," and Dad called out, "Bravo!".

As the winner's rosette was pinned to Muckey's shirt, I glanced at Gran. She was clapping harder than anyone: happier than anyone. Even an ignorant young kid like myself could see that the sparkle in her eyes burst the boundaries of pride and affection. It was love, and strangely enough it didn't strike me as in the least soppy.

13

Despatch Rider for the Home Guard –An elite platoon –
LET and MOANS – Admiral Cook causes chaos –
Sergeant Muckey leads the charge – Dad does his bit
and we get a laugh.

A s the weeks passed I was still stuck with the problem of how to become actively involved in repelling the coming Kraut invasion. James, my old ally, was now so closely in cohorts with Brother Nothing that he'd lost all interest in the war effort. Anyhow, I still hadn't forgiven him for calling me stupid.

All this left me at a dead end until I had a stroke of luck. I was helping Muckey and Gran sort out some lawn seed in the potting shed when there was a knock on the door. We looked up to see a very distinguished gentleman with a black Labrador at his side. It was Major General Westlake, who commanded the South Godstone platoon.

Muckey touched his cap. "Morning, General..."

"Morning, Muckey, Madam, young man. Sorry to disturb you all... Bit of a problem with tonight's parade I'm afraid, Muckey. Been cancelled. No doubt you can get a message to Mr Contractor, but I've having trouble with some of the others. I've rung round most. But two are out and the Admiral can't hear his bell, of course. Any suggestions?"

Gran and Mr Muckey

Muckey didn't look very helpful. I could see that he had no intentions of volunteering to be a messenger, so I grabbed the chance of ingratiating myself. "I could take messages around on my new bike, sir. It's got 24 inch wheels..."

"Oh, splendid. Good show. Can you spare the young fellow, Muckey? Good show. Come round to my house in about half an hour, young fellow, and I'll give you all the gen."

So it was that I became the unofficial messenger of the South Godstone platoon, what Dad called their 'Don R' – despatch rider. At first, all I did was take messages to private houses but then, as I rode past the General's house and saw him in the garden, I'd pop up his immaculate drive and ask politely: "Any more messages for the Home Guard, General?", and sometimes there were. Twice I had to cycle all the way into Godstone to leave messages for the company commander who never answered his telephone because he was up in London on business.

These tasks gave me General Westlake's seal of approval, which meant that Muckey would often put work my way as well, and before long I began to feel part of the organisation. If I turned up at one of their parades, or when they were on one of their local exercises, no one questioned what I was up to or told me to clear off. Dad also entered into the spirit of things and although, as a private soldier, he had no authority to send me on errands or messages, he fed me details of what the platoon was up to, what the other members were like, and how to make myself useful.

The Home Guard started the war as the LDV (Local Defence Volunteers) but it was later changed to Home Guard to give it greater credibility as a national organisation. Of course, after the war it changed its name again and in most people's minds became *Dad's Army* after the highly successful and oft-repeated television series. As in all good humour, *Dad's Army* was outrageously bizarre but managed to retain a modicum of truth. Out of necessity it was made up of stock comic characters designed to give all sections of the community a fair go: a bank manager, a clerk, a butcher, a Scotsman, the inevitable spiv, an old man with water works trouble, and a young man without a clue.

With the South Godstone platoon this was far from the case. Because of the wealthy nature of the area, and a clash of personalities among the local residents, the platoon consisted (apart from Muckey and Dad) of retired service officers. The lack of working class volunteers was due to Muckey. The shopkeepers, farm workers, jobbing builders, and gardeners, who would normally have made up the rank and file, refused to join because Muckey got in first and was appointed platoon sergeant. Headed by his arch rival, Mr Tidy, the others stormed off in high dudgeon and joined vastly inferior outfits under the general classification of Civil Defence. This left only retired officers. They were all grossly overqualified for an infantry platoon, but that didn't worry them in the least. They were delighted to be serving at the grass roots. Like Dad, they were determined to be involved in real fighting, to actually have the satisfaction of lining up Krauts in their sights and shooting them dead. Major General Westlake was typical. He was happy to come down from a divisional commander to a platoon commander, a position usually held by a 2nd Lieutenant – the LFL in the PBI.*

Actually, even General Westlake shouldn't have been in command. On seniority alone, the commander should have been Admiral Sir Archibald Cook. He was the senior man and in the senior service, but he deferred to the General on the grounds of age (72 to 68) and the fact that the duties required were land-based, and whilst General Westlake was an expert at crawling around in the mud and issuing order from a recumbent position, Admiral Cook felt lost unless standing on a ship's bridge with the tang of salt up his nostrils.

*The Lowest Form of Life in the Poor Bloody Infantry.

Gran and Mr Muckey

The three section commanders in the platoon (usually corporals) were retired brigadiers. One was a former Bengal Lancer and India's champion pig-sticker 1932-34; another had been in the Royal Horse Guards and was renowned for having sat on a horse outside Buckingham Palace for a total of seventeen years; and the third was from the 14th/20th King's Hussars, an oddball who only ever drank alcohol out a replica of the Emperor Napoleon's chamber pot, the real thing having been captured off the Emperor by the 14th/20th.

The platoon boasted the biggest collection of military decorations ever known in a single platoon. There were twelve DSOs, one DCM (Muckey), sixteen Military Crosses, four Croix de Guerre, an American Medal of Honour, a Purple Heart, and one MiD (Oak Leaf, Dad). In fact, just about every gong going bar the Victoria Cross.

When Dad enrolled with the platoon he soon got used to having Muckey as his platoon sergeant. He was the only ex-sergeant among them and he alone understood the duties of that exacting position. All the others (except Dad) had spent most of their adult lives saying, "Carry on, Sergeant." Yet what the sergeants then actually did was a complete mystery to them. Whilst the sergeants were 'carrying on' they were already back in the officers' mess having a drink.

Other factors in favour of Muckey being platoon sergeant were his unequalled knowledge of local terrain and the fact that most of the platoon were armed with tools out of his potting shed. If Muckey took umbrage and buggered off like Mr Tidy and the others, the platoon would have been left without a decent pitch fork between them and, as they all agreed, there was nothing the Krauts feared more than cold steel, especially the duel thrust of a long-handled Spear and Jackson pitch fork. In those days, when there were no firearms available to the Home Guard, it would have appeared to an impartial observer that the strategy of the South Godstone platoon was based on pitch forks being to the invasion of Britain what the long bow had been to the Battle of Agincourt.

Because the village of South Godstone was little more than a single track railway station, it was considered unsuitable for the headquarters of the platoon, so they paraded three times a week at the Blindley Heath Cricket Club, known locally as The Oval.* Here, the cricket ground afforded plenty of level ground for drilling on. It also had a pavilion in which to shelter in the event of rain, or in which to sit in comfort for tactical discussions and lectures. The Anchor, just down the road, was also an excellent pub.

On the day Dad enrolled in the platoon it was raining so heavily that they had a tactical discussion. A beautifully made sandpit model of the area was brought out by General Westlake and he gave a detailed explanation of their role in the event of invasion, including precise dispositions of regular units, based on the 6th Canadian Division which would shortly be arriving from across the Atlantic. Dad said he was left wondering what had ever happened to the 'Careless Talk Cost Lives' campaign.

"But no one is going to say anything, Dad," I protested.

"Your father just has," observed Mum. "Now you know and you can never keep your mouth shut."

Dad became one of the keenest members of the Home Guard. He thought the other members of the platoon were marvellous, just the type of English gentlemen he would be happy to fight and die alongside. He made tremendous efforts to get back from Camberwell in time for the parades but if ever he was liable to be late he would telephone through and I would dash up to the Oval on my bike to let

*The South Godstone platoon was responsible for one of cricket's favourite jokes. They were playing at the Oval (Blindley Heath) and were in the field against the East Surrey Regiment. Suddenly, a top edge sent the ball high into the covers, an easy catch. General Westlake, the captain, shouted: "Yours, Colonel!" and all six fielders on the off-side went for it, collided, and missed it. Since then, the incident has often been attributed, quite erroneously, to an MCC match against unspecified opponents.

Gran and Mr Muckey

General Westlake know. Then I'd hang around, hoping there would be something else for me to do.

The platoon still hadn't been issued uniforms but most of them overcame that by using their regular army ones with ranks and insignia stripped off, and these, together with their Home Guard armbands, gave them status in the community. So too did their 'exercises'. Whilst the regular army stuck to 'TEWTS' (tactical exercises with(out) troops), the Home Guard exercises were split into two categories, known in the South Godstone platoon as LETs (local exercises, tactical) and MOANS (manoeuvres on a national scale). LETs were popular but MOANS were dreaded, although none of them admitted it. Dad told me these exercises were a waste of time since war never followed a pattern, but he added that they did them because that's what the military mind demanded and it was a good way to weld them into a team.

In LETs, the South Godstone platoon was pitted against the regular army and, by arrangement, they never failed to come off best. As I hung around in the background on my bike, ready to dash off on messages between the sections, I saw things at close quarters. General Westlake was a great organiser, but when it came to instant orders in the field, Sergeant Muckey took control. He told them what to do without any compunction and hearing these senior officers responding: "Yes, Sergeant!" was an absolute scream.

LETs revolved around setting up a road block at Anglefield Corner, the junction where our lane joined the A22 road to Eastbourne. The theoretical objective was to bring the enemy Bren Gun Carriers advancing along the A22 to an abrupt halt at the road block and then annihilate them with a flanking platoon attack. General Westlake and Muckey took command of the assault sections. They concealed themselves in Byers Lane, just to the south of Anglefield Corner, and once the Bren Gun Carriers had been halted at the road block, and were trailing back along the road, a whistle was blown (my job since I had more breath than the rest of them put together) and the assault sections charged forth, brandishing their pitch forks. Muckey was always in the forefront of the charges but by the time they reached the far side of the A22 he was well to the rear, yelling: "Keep going, you buggers!" Having run through the enemy (well, run past them) they consolidated in a defensive position in Walker's Landscape Nursery. A neutral umpire from a neighbouring Home Guard unit then declare all the regulars dead and that would conclude another LET.

Undoubtedly the best part of LETs was watching the detachment under Admiral Sir Archibald Cook. Their task was to create the road block at Anglefield Corner. In the event of a real invasion they would no doubt have used farm carts and tractors, but during LETs they relied upon passing traffic. They stopped cars, lorries and other forms of transport coming down the road from Godstone (the ones from Blindley Heath were let through a small gap so that the Bren Gun Carriers didn't get held up). Only buses and Green Line coaches were exempt. The rest were commandeered and lined up across the road.

These days, people question if anyone would have stood for such treatment, but the truth was that the local inhabitants were aware of what was going on and kept well clear. Thus it was only the odd strangers who became involved. Some of them shouldn't have been running vehicles anyhow, so when they came round the bend from South Godstone and were confronted by a distinguished-looking figure, in what had obviously once been the uniform of Admiral of the Fleet, waving a red flag at them, they drew up. Admiral Cook then told them that an enemy armoured division was advancing from East Grinstead. Predictably, this brought instant obedience and it wasn't until they were out of their vehicles and being bustled towards the bus shelter that any of them wondered why the church bells hadn't been rung or – alternatively – why they couldn't get back in their vehicles and make a run for it. By then their protests were too late. Their vehicles were already an integral part of the road block and the lance corporal who was second-in-command of the section (Colonel Matthews-Spencer, DSO and Bar) would allow no exceptions. In his booming, authoritative voice he made it plain that they were to remain in the bus shelter until further orders. If anyone argued, he rotated his football rattle once and barked: "You're dead. Be quiet."

MOANS were a very different story. I was never allowed to help in these and the South Godstone platoon would be but one small, insignificant unit in a divisional or even corps exercise run by the regular army, covering most of southern England. It meant that they seldom had any idea of what was happening and they never did anything of any note. Time and again their role was to lie in a water-logged ditch halfway up Godstone Hill. For 24 hours the only food they received was hard rations (dried biscuits), with drinks confined to what they carried in their water bottles.

Whenever MOANS were in operation, Brother Nothing, James, and I took a trip into Caterham on one of the double-decker buses. As the bus laboured up Godstone Hill, we never failed to see Dad and the rest of the platoon lying in the roadside ditch. Rain would be tamping down on them and they would be soaked to the skin and knee-deep in water. As young sons we found this hilarious. We waved like mad and Dad always waved back. He made no complaints. He was doing his bit.

14

*Gran and Muckey – Close-up on the Battle of Britain –
My new school at Caterham – Miss Openside – Wreckage
found in the woods – An unpleasant surprise on a nature
walk – Sex education of sorts – The war strikes with tragic
consequences.*

The Home Guard was only a spare-time occupation, of
course, and throughout the country members carried
on with their normal work. Dad was busier than ever
at the Works. He slaved away all hours and the strain of it
soon showed. Flecks of grey hair appeared around his temples and I often noticed dark bags under his eyes. He set off
for London on the first Green Line and came back on the
last (except on parade days) and no sooner had he had
something to eat than he went to bed and crashed out.
Theoretically, he had the weekends off but hardly a
Saturday or a Sunday passed without an emergency call
from his foreman, Old Percy. Mum pleaded with him to get
someone else to sort things out, but he wouldn't hear of it
and off he'd go again.

For Muckey things were far more orderly and sedate. His
Home Guard duties were more than compensated for by the
help he received in the garden from Gran. Every morning
she was up with the lark and straight out into the garden,
and as evidence of her interest in Muckey she went into

Caterham and bought several gardening outfits, all of them based on Wellington boots, dungarees, and coloured shirts similar to Muckey's, the first time we'd ever seen her in anything but a sari. Another sign of her devotion was the way she followed him around the garden. It was very similar to the way Lucky followed around after me; and just as I loved this devotion from Lucky, so Muckey loved it from Gran. Whether work was needed in the vegetable garden, among the fruit cages, in the orchard, or feeding the livestock, they did it together. They rarely spoke, just worked side by side as though in harness.

At lunch time Gran helped herself to two platefuls of curry, with generous dollops of chutney, and then ate with Muckey in the potting shed. I often wanted to join them, but Mum wouldn't let me. "Just stay exactly where you are. I don't want you poking your nose in and spoiling things. Can't you see that they deserve each other?"

I knew what Mum had in mind. Muckey was a bachelor and she wanted to be rid of Gran for ever. If Mum's wishes came about and they got married, I wouldn't have minded a bit. It would have made Muckey some kind of honorary grandfather. I could think of nothing better.

Midway through the summer came the Battle of Britain, what was obviously going to be the most decisive battle of the war. Everything was on a knife edge: if we lost, Germany would be all-powerful, the ruler of Europe, the greatest power in the world. I knew this because Dad encouraged me to listen to every word broadcast by the prime minister, Winston Churchill. When the battle started the prime aim of the Luftwaffe soon became clear. They were out to destroy our aircraft on the ground by bombing airfields such as Tangmere, Biggin Hill, Kenley, West Malling, Manston, and Hornchurch. The RAF, with the help of radar, soon got the hang of intercepting them, either over the channel or the home counties. As always, the BBC Nine O'clock News was our main source of information and now, instead of keeping war maps, I kept charts recording losses on both sides. Although we didn't start too well, we soon improved. Before long we were flinging every available plane into the struggle and the Krauts were doing the same. We grew accustomed to formation after formation of Heinkel and Dornier bombers roaring overhead. They were wing-tip to wing-tip, tail to nose, a swarm of metallic locusts after easy pickings, sometimes so low that we could see the pilots in the cockpits.

As they droned overhead they appeared indomitable, but then a squadron of Spitfires would suddenly appear out of the heat-haze surrounding the sun. They would wheel towards the Hun with majestic precision, peeling off and opening up like a giant fan, swooping straight into them, the purr of their Merlin engines sweet music to my ears. The German formations would stutter, buckle, and then disperse, every man for himself. Standing below, ignoring Mum's yells to get back inside before I was killed, everything was so vivid that I could imagined the Germans screaming: "Achtung Spitfire! Achtung Spitfire!" over their intercoms. I tried to keep a tally of those I saw shot down or crippled, until eventually the whole mass of them would go on to a final showdown over Kenley, Hendon and Biggin Hill.

At other times I saw individual dog-fights. Some spilled over from the Sussex and Kent airfields but more often than not Spitfires ripped into German bombers which had dropped their loads further north and were speeding back to base. The most exciting dog-fight I ever saw was between a Spitfire and a Messerschmitt 109, one fighter against another. It was a personal duel, both of them having become detached from their comrades, both clearly determined not to give way: a fight to the death. Vapour trails were left in the sky, creating a dizzy pattern of circles and loops like tangled string. Our hopes were high. We could see that the Spitfire had greater speed and manoeuvrability. It kept zipping up beneath the Messerschmitt, tearing into its soft, unprotected underbelly. At other times it would slip in behind the German plane and fire short, sharp bursts, but with no apparent results. Surely our man couldn't be missing the whole time? Why didn't he blast the Kraut out of the sky? Then the German plane got the advantage but he also appeared to be shooting wide. Finally, the Spitfire went into the attack but nothing happened: he was out of ammunition. He pulled away, made off while the going was good. Then, as my heart sank and I thought our man had failed, and would be pursued and torn from the sky, the Messerschmitt blew up. It became a great ball of orange fire, tinged and circled by inky black smoke. No parachute blossomed and what was left of the plane disintegrated into fragments and plunged to the earth like bits of a toy, a wing here, a piece of wooden tail there, sometimes just solid balls of smoke-trailing metal. The Spitfire wheeled round and returned, swooping low over the ground before doing a victory roll. It wasn't appropriate. I remember wishing he hadn't done that. There was no need. Total destruction was comment enough.

You may wonder what had become of the Contractor boys' schooling during this period. Well, here's the situation. Having moved from Edgware, we obviously had to start at new schools. Realising that his University of Life education was on hold because of the war, Dad tried to get us the best education that money could buy. For my brothers he turned to Harrow and Eton but both said they were oversubscribed and mentioned that they had no record of their names having been entered at birth; and other great public schools likewise found excellent reasons for turning them down. I suffered a similar fate at several leading prep schools. One offered me an interview but when I went with Mum the meeting turned out to be very short, presumably because the headmaster had no wish to become involved in the complications caused by a coloured pupil. However, Caterham School had no such reservations. At very short notice they welcomed us with open arms on the payments of a year's fees in advance. Brother Nothing and James went to the public school and I attended the prep school, situated beyond the former at the very end of Harestone Valley Road and bordering on to what was then a wild part of the North Downs.

I have very fond memories of Caterham Prep School even though I was only there for two terms before being removed. The headmaster was Mr Denham and because his initials were S.O. (Stanley Oliver) he was known through the school as SOD, and a sod he most certainly was. Like many school masters of his generation he knew that there was nothing better for keeping small boys in order and working hard than a good caning, and as though to remind us of this SOD was never seen around the school without his silver birch. He would hold it out in front of him, as though divining water, and then waggle it from side to side with a whippy wrist action, making it quiver and hiss like an angry snake.

The remarkable thing about SOD, and the reason why we forgave him everything, was that the staff he employed (because of the war) consisted of the most delectable young ladies. Our form mistress had the unusual name of Miss Openside and she was absolutely gorgeous. To paint an adequate portrait of her in words is impossible. I would only be accused of exaggerating. Nor, in truth, do I want you to know how lovely she was. I prefer to keep the memory of her perfection to myself. Suffice to say that it was rather like being taught by Marilyn Monroe, although Miss Openside was a natural blonde with nothing synthetic about her, and her legs were longer and more shapely, and... Enough said.

Due to Miss Openside's influence, I've never known small boys develop and mature so quickly as we did. Nor a class of boys who looked forward to their lessons so eagerly. Our class consisted mainly of local boys, but there was also a small clique of refugees from various European countries, which was normal during that time. Some spoke good English, others struggled to start with. With one exception they were nice lads who fitted in well. The exception was a most suspicious character named Hermann von Pletenburg. It was the sinister 'von' that earmarked him as highly questionable. Also, the fact that he wasn't a Jew. Our theory was that his father was a crook who had fled Vienna because of fraudulent financial dealings and that his asylum was accomplished by bribery. In our eyes his son showed distinct Germanic, if not Nazi, sympathies. He was a year or so older than the rest of us and easily the most intelligent, coming first in every subject in every exam or test, a success he shrugged off with infuriating arrogance. "Of course I vin," he crowed. "It's so easy." He might just as well have added: 'Vot else do you expect from zer master race?'

However, it wasn't his intellectual superiority we found so intolerable, more his cynicism and lack of respect towards Miss Openside. This he disguised beneath a veneer of German manners. Whenever he spoke in class he jumped up from his desk, stood to attention, and clicked his heels together, just as the German aristocrats had done in Switzerland. Another odd thing about von Pletenburg was that although he was capable of good English he insisted on retaining a few key German words, such as 'Actung!', 'Guten tag', 'Jawohl!' 'Gut', and – when referring to the headmaster, SOD, 'Der Fuehrer'.

Admittedly, this did once give us a good laugh. He came into class very late and when Miss Openside asked where he had been he gave her a cock-and-bull story about being told to report to the school porter. When Miss Openside questioned this, von Pletenburg retorted indignantly: "But Miss Openside, mine orders came direct from der Fuehrer..."

More typical of von Pletenburg was the time he jumped to his feet, clicked his heels, and then, when asked what he wanted, said: "Miss Openside, last night I dreamt about you."

"How nice, Hermann," replied Miss Openside, feeling flattered. "I hope it was a pleasant dream?"

"Jawohl! All the time you had no clothes on..."

Naturally, some of the class laughed. Miss Openside struggled to conceal her distaste and embarrassment. I thought it was more than a bit off and after class I made my feelings very clear to von Pletenburg. Even though he towered above me, I said: "Any more of that, Pletenburg, and I'll give you a darned good bashing up."

Because of staff shortages, Miss Openside took us for every single lesson, covering the full gamut of subjects. She even took us for basket ball in the gym. She always dressed the part in a natty little tennis skirt she'd outgrown by some years, satin knickers, a tight, pale blue polo-neck jumper, and white ankle socks. I used to run around after her far more than I ever did after the ball, and I wasn't alone in this.

Miss Openside was aged eighteen and she was terribly naive. At first she would never come into the changing room or the showers to make sure we got on with things and didn't muck about. She'd stand at a chink in the doorway, her eyes averted, trying to control things from there. Eventually, when we became involved in a fierce towel-flicking fight, there was so much noise going on that SOD came thundering along the corridor, his cane swishing, to sort things out. Unceremoniously he pushed Miss Openside in among us. The fight stopped instantly and although others didn't mind her presence I immediately wrapped my towel around my waist. For her part, Miss Openside blushed deeply and never let her eyes drop below shoulder level.

By attending Caterham School I by no means missed out on the Battle of Britain. At South Godstone I saw dozens of dog-fights but it was at Caterham (the start of Greater London) that bombs began to fall in earnest. There were lots of casualties in the town and a boy at the prep school was killed by shrapnel when running towards the shelters, which were some distance from the classrooms. Lessons were often interrupted by raids and it was not at all uncommon for Germans bombers to swoop over the school before we had time to get down to the shelters. Then, Miss Openside made us get beneath our desk and she kept up a stream of reassuring remarks, even though she was just as scared as we were. She could easily have sheltered under her stout oak table but she deliberately chose not to. She would be down on her hands and knees, moving from one desk to another to comfort us. When the raids were over she went round the entire class giving every boy a reassuring hug.

During one of the worst raids several bombs exploded in the school grounds. Windows were broken and several of our class were reduced to tears. Some even wanted to make a run for it and go home to their mums. I wasn't among them. In fact, I did more than most to restrain and comfort those who were on the verge of panic. Afterwards, Miss Openside complimented me on my composure and by way of explanation I told her how I'd already been bombed out at Edgware. I even showed her my scar, which was still quite pronounced. To my surprise she made me stand before the class and relate the experience. This I did willingly enough, although I played down the dangers involved. I explained Dad's theory that a bullet and/or a bomb either had your name on it or it didn't; and that's all there was to it. "And that means I'm okay," I concluded. "The one with my name on it only nicked me..."

"And I'll be all right as well," declared my friend Harry Kicks. "The Krauts will never have heard of a stupid name like Kicks."

"Same with me," said a kid called Michaelthwaite.

"Well what about Openside?" quipped Miss Openside, and we all laughed with her.

"And they'll never be able to spell my name, even if they have heard of it," chipped in a Dutch refugee named Claus Schillebeechx.

"Thank goodness no one in the school is called Charlie Smith," joked Miss Openside and again, we all laughed.

*****

On the occasions when the sirens gave us a chance to get down to the shelters before the German bombers roared overhead, the atmosphere created by Miss Openside was very intimate. Each class had its own shelter and, without exception, they were damp, chilly, full of creepy-crawlies, and without any lighting. However, there were plenty of candles and Miss Openside always took along her powerful torch which meant that we had sufficient light to track down the creepy-crawlies and kick hell out of them, much to the relief of Miss Openside. We each had a small wooden stool to sit on and Miss Openside would get us to draw them up in a tight circle around her, and as we sat there, knees-to-knees, she would read us stories. The ack-ack guns stationed in the school grounds loved to blast off as hard as they could and their efforts always attracted additional bombs. Usually, Miss Openside read on, as though oblivious to them, and we soon became equally as blasé about the dangers. The first book she read was Robinson Crusoe, then Treasure Island, followed by extracts from Alice in Wonderland. Very occasionally, if the guns and bombs

became so ferocious that Miss Openside faltered in her reading, we had sing-songs, including topical ones like '*Run Rabbit*' and '*Roll Out the Barrel*'. At other times we fell back on the old classics like '*Michael Finnegan*' which was our favourite.

"There was an old man called Michael Finnegan
He grew whiskers on his chinigan
The wind came along and blew them in again,
Poor old Michael Finnegan
Begin again.
There was an old man called Michael Finnegan..."

If Michael Finnegan failed to lift our spirits, Miss Openside turned to me. I'd gained a reputation in the class as a storyteller. It was because of my cavalier approach to having been bombed out, and also, as a skinny little fellow who was clearly Indian, but claimed to be English, despite traces of a Welsh accent, I cut a comic figure among my peers. Anyhow, when the bombing became really intense, with the Germans going for the Brigade of Guards Barracks on Caterham Hill, Miss Openside would stand me on a stool, pin-point me in the beam of her torch, and encourage me to get everyone laughing at my stories. I told them about my experiences as an evacuee: the group photograph at Paddington, the disappearing Bloggs twins, the boy who became Lost Property, and how Lucky blew up the police station. I told them Dad's story of Flippy-Floppy and invented yarns in a similar vein, all centred on small animals that overcame various handicaps. I even gave them a highly exaggerated version of the love affair between Gran and Muckey, and the saga of Muckey, Mr Tidy, and the prize marrow that was fed on nothing but Friary's Best Brown and which had, at one stage, been classified by Brother Nothing as an UXB. Even though I say it myself, the stories went down very well. I found storytelling easy. They flowed, one exaggeration leading on to even bigger ones, until eventually I'd go way over the top and the other kids would laugh and shout with glee, singing out: "Tell us another one, Saj! Tell us another one do!"

During these stories there would be so much noise going on outside that it was impossible to tell the bombs from the ack-ack guns and shrapnel often clattered down on the reinforced roof. Once, a raid was so vicious that I had to pull out all my best stops to keep the class's mind off the bombs, so I told them of our mountaineering exploits in Switzerland, and how we'd been trapped on the Devil's Ledge with ibex in front of us, a grizzly bear behind us, a sheer rise on one side, and a sheer drop of 5,000 feet on the other. Thankfully, the raid ended before I had to find a way out of our predicament.

Miss Openside waited until everyone was running back to the classroom and then called me over. She squatted down in front of me and took me in her arms, burying my face in her bosom. She squeezed me hard and rocked me from side to side. "Oh, Sajit! I'm so grateful to you. That was wonderful... Wonderful... And I want you to promise me one thing. Always keep telling your stories. They're marvellous..."

"They're only things I make up, Miss," I muttered into her soft jumper.

"Don't be so modest, Sajit. You have a gift, a great imagination."

"Not much is real, Miss. Like you said, just imagination."

"But imagination is real. It's as real as anything else, Sajit. Everything that goes on in your mind is real. Where would Newton have been without his imagination? And aren't all great symphonies real? Isn't the Mona Lisa real? They all come from the imagination. One day, Sajit, you could write novels..."

She gave me an extra squeeze and as my nose sank into what was clearly her nipple I thought: 'And they'll be rip-roaring best-sellers at this rate'.

"Promise me you'll never stop imagining things, Sajit," she continued. "Imagination makes the human race unique.

Only human beings have such power... One day you could become a great novelist and novels are the highest form of art."

She released her embrace, even though I did my best to cling on for a few more precious moments. When I re-emerged her eyes were misty with tears: the joy of antic-ipating a famous pupil, I surmised. That was the birth of my ambition to become a celebrated novelist. My deepest regret is that – despite the odd success – I've failed Miss Openside so miserably, but I'll never lose faith with her and stop trying.

Teaching was a vocation to Miss Openside and she went to enormous pains to make everything interesting. We were with her all day, every day, lesson after lesson, yet we were never bored and her pride in our progress was obvious. Being so young, we were highly impressionable and we soon came to love her, the type of love properly called Agape. Maybe some of us regarded her as a perfect elder sister, but I prayed that I would be endowed with a magic spell with which to make her ageless until I caught up with her and could claim her as my girlfriend.

As it happened, she already had a boyfriend. He was an Australian named Eddie and it was no accident that the most prominent wall display in our classroom was an enormous pink map of Australia. It had a giant-headed coloured pin stuck in the back-of-beyond, somewhere between Bathurst and Broken Hill, representing the sheep station Eddie lived on. Before we even met him we knew that she was desperately in love with him and when we came to know him we understood why. He was a smashing bloke. He was well over six foot tall, as tough-looking and bronzed as a roasted conker, and very nearly as handsome as Miss Openside was beautiful. He was a Spitfire pilot stationed at Kenley and, whenever his duties allowed, he picked up Miss Openside from school. Twice, he came to the school with another Australian pilot and gave us a talk on their training

and exploits against the Germans. On another occasion
Eddie told us about sheep-farming in Australia and how
both he and his friend had covered thousands of miles on
horseback as jackeroos. On each visit they concluded
matters by taking us down to the gym to teach us how to
play basket ball properly, not the namby-pamby way Miss
Openside insisted on. They even made her play with us, and
that really made our day.

Every afternoon when lessons were over, our class
walked down to Caterham to catch our various buses home.
Miss Openside always walked in our midst. As we drew near
the large, wrought iron gates of the senior school at the start
of Harestone Valley Road, everyone strained to see if Eddie
had come to collect her. If he had, he'd be in his superb
little sports car – a six cylinder Wolseley Hornet – and we'd
rush towards him. He may have been Miss Openside's
boyfriend, but he was also our hero. He was more interested in kissing her than larking about with us, of course, but
whilst he was enjoying a couple of lingering kisses he'd let
us scramble over his car. Then he'd take take two or three
of us down the road to show off the Wolseley's paces. It went
like a rocket, so fast (around 70 mph) that Harry Kicks reckoned he'd syphoned special air fuel out of his Spitfire.
Eventually, Eddie would help Miss Openside into the car
and drive off for the next round of their platonic courtship.

One of Miss Openside's great virtues, and one which singled
her out as an exceptional teacher, was patience. We may
have been attentive in her classes but some of us were right
little devils and obsessed by the war, something she tried to
curb. I was one of the worst, and so was Harry Kicks; but in
fairness to us it was a unique period in our national history when the most extraordinary things were happening all
around us, all the time.

The raids over the area were only a start. Every day
between fifty to a hundred planes were shot down over
southern England and each one created a drama all of its

own. Many planes crashed in remote spots where they weren't located for maybe months and this was the reason why RAF pilots were often accused of overstating their kills, simply because no one could pin-point the wreckage. Harry Kicks and I got involved in just such a case. The whole thing was purely accidental, due to our love of exploring the surrounding woodlands. One free Wednesday afternoon we went to a remote area of the North Downs. The first indication of anything unusual was a repugnant smell, something we'd never encountered before. Then we noticed that a broad swath had been ripped through the woods. Sunlight was streaming through and when we followed the line of the dust-bespangled rays we saw that a Dornier had ploughed through the woods and undergrowth and was now lying there, wingless, like a great grey turd. On closer inspection we saw German crosses on it and how the fuselage was riddle with bullet and shrapnel holes.

We stopped, hid behind trees, and listened for signs of life. Apart from bird song there wasn't a murmur. I wanted to turn and run but Harry was made of sterner stuff. He stood fast, so I stuck with him. Then, advancing a foot or so at a time, we got right up to the plane and ducked down and entered through a gaping hole in the fuselage. God, it was spooky! It was as though we'd entered the very heart of the German war machine. The relative darkness inside made it even more terrifying, but gradually, as our eyes became accustomed to the light, our fear subsided.

We soon realised that the awful stench came from dead bodies. As we spotted the first one we recoiled and clutched each other. Then morbid curiosity got the better of us and we took a closer look. He was obviously the navigator, still sitting at a tiny table with maps and charts trapped below his sprawled body. Then we saw the pilot, still at the controls. He was leaning backwards, his eyes wide open, blood stains coming from his mouth. A third man was lying on the floor, his arms outstretched as though trying to make his escape. All three were caked in dried, brown blood and they had a strange, waxy look about them. We kept as good a distance from them as we could and went right forward into the cockpit. Suddenly the fuselage gave a lurch on account of our weight. We panicked and got out quickly. Once at a safe distance, I said: "Poor devils."

"Yes," agreed Harry. "They're all good Germans."

"How do you know that?"

"Because they're dead. All dead Germans are good Germans."

After a pause to collect our wits, we circled the plane once or twice and came across another body, accounting for the crew of four. He'd been thrown clear and had gone face first into an elm tree. He looked as though he was trying to hug it. Eventually we convinced each other that there was nothing to be frightened of. Apart from their smell, the Krauts couldn't hurt us and the plane itself, after at least a couple of days of lying there, was now nothing but an inert lump of scrap metal and certainly not liable to blow up.

Harry was the mechanical type of kid and he was determined to dismantle some part of the plane and take it back to school as evidence of what we'd found. Much to our surprise the easiest part to take was the machine gun in the forward turret which the impact of the crash had wrenched free of its mountings. The fact that it was near one of the dead Germans didn't deter us. We dragged it out of the plane, gathered up some ammunition belts that were attached to it, and set off back to school, shouldering the machine gun between us with the belts of ammunition draped over the barrel.

At school, everyone had gone home, but the classrooms hadn't been locked by the porter. So we put our trophy on Miss Openside's table and went off down Harstone Valley Road to catch our buses home.

To us, that seemed a perfectly natural thing to do, but the reaction of others the following morning was very different. Miss Openside was the first to entered the classroom and when she was confronted by a German machine gun with live ammunition in it, pointing straight at her, she fled to SOD in terror. SOD telephoned the police and the RAF, demanding that they should sort things out. As each pupil entered the school hall he was confronted by a policeman and asked if he knew anything about it. None of them did, of course, until Harry and I claimed the credit. We were then rushed to SOD's office and questioned by RAF officers. Naturally, we told them all we knew and then listened to a long lecture on, 'Didn't you realise it could have blown up at any moment?' and 'Didn't you know that the machine gun was cocked and ready to fire?' and 'Why didn't you report it to the police straight away?' Despite this, the senior RAF officer had a sneaking regard for what we'd done and arranged for the machine gun and ammunition to be laid out in the assembly hall so that the entire school could file past and inspect the trophies. Harry and I were allowed to keep a souvenir. I chose a chunk of fuselage with a German cross on it. I've still got it.

That wasn't our only brush with the Luftwaffe.

Miss Openside's favourite subject was nature study and there was nothing she enjoyed more than taking us on nature walks, each one having a specific objective. We had to look for the 'plant of the week'. On this particular walk the plant was Shepherd's Purse. To make things more exciting we were given points for general naturalist observations (such as 'Look, Miss, there's a Nuthatch'), and a ten point bonus for the boy who found the most 'plant of the week'.

As it happened, I spotted a Shepherd's Purse almost as soon as we left the school grounds, but otherwise there was a complete dearth of them. As we went deeper and deeper into the woods and still found nothing, so the tight formation Miss Openside usually insisted upon broke up and we wandered all over the place. Inevitably, Harry Kicks and I foraged well ahead of everyone else. As we ran round a bend in a narrow, wooded path we bumped straight into a German pilot who'd been shot down. He was in a terrible state, his head cut, his blond hair matted by dried blood, his right arm hanging limply at his side. We halted abruptly and stared at him in horror. I was behind Harry and I saw the hairs on the back of his neck stand up on end. Then we saw that the Kraut had a pistol in his left hand. Harry (who knew about these things) identified it as a Luger. This was very different from the crashed Dornier. This wasn't a good German. This one was alive and kicking and trying to raise his left arm in order to point his Luger at us. We were off like startled rabbits, desperate to get back to Miss Openside and the others to raise the alarm. As soon as we saw them tripping about amid a bank of wild nasturtiums, we bellowed: "A Kraut! A Kraut! Run for it... He's got a gun!"

When the others saw two ruffians like Harry and me scared witless and sprinting for our lives, instinct made them follow without further prompting – and how! Blind terror gripped their minds. Miss Openside brought up the rear, protecting her brood. God how we ran. How Miss Openside ran, scratching her lovely legs on brambles and twice falling over as she urged us on. When we got back to school she grabbed the bell in the assembly hall and rang it and rang it. She swung it from over her head to between her legs until the entire school came dashing out to see what had happened.

Poor Miss Openside: having got everyone assembled, all goggling with excitement and curiosity, she hadn't got enough breath left to tell them anything. Even when she'd recovered her breath she was so upset that she couldn't talk coherently. It was left to Harry Kicks, who was never short of breath, nor lost for words, to explain that there was a wounded, but armed, Kraut on the loose.

That was when SOD took control. Whilst his secretary telephoned the police, SOD grabbed a shot gun from his stationary cupboard and went in search of the German airman. He realised that if was only half as badly wounded as Harry Kick said, he'd never offer any resistance: no mug, old SOD.

Gran and Mr Muckey

By the time a policeman and a sergeant from the Home Guard arrived at the school, SOD had captured the German and was prodding him down Harestone Valley Road. He brushed aside all attempts to be relieved of his prisoner and marched him down the valley and into Caterham so that everyone in the school and the town became aware of his heroism. He even posed for a photograph outside the police station, handing his prisoner over to the duty sergeant. He sent the film to the Surrey Mirror for developing and when it appeared in the next issue with a long story, SOD cut it out and stuck it on the school notice board. There wasn't a word about Miss Openside and her class.

Directly after this incident, when we were back in our classroom, and everyone had calmed down, we had a good laugh about it and got Miss Openside to show us the scratches on her legs. Then she said how proud she was of us and she came round giving us hugs like she did after the air raids. When she returned to her table Harry Kicks stood up and said: "Miss. I think Sajit and I should get extra bonus marks for spotting the Kraut."

"I'm afraid not, Harry. We were on a nature walk, looking for Shepherd's Purse. Not Germans."

"But Miss! That's not fair. A Kraut airman is far rarer than some mangy old Shepherd's Purse."

"I'm afraid not, Harry..."

"But miss..."

"Harry Kicks," she shouted. "Can't you understand? This isn't a game. That man could have shot us. He could have killed us. Don't you understand, Harry? It's not a game!"

Then, to our amazement, she burst into tears and ran from the room.

I'm ashamed to say that that wasn't the only time we reduced Miss Openside to tears.

The second time was due to Hermann von Pletenburg. A boy called Jensen started it all by saying that his Mum said sex education should be compulsory in all schools. We giggled like mad and urged Miss Openside to start right away. As was her nature, she went along with our skittish mood and agreed to discuss the subject during our next General Affairs lesson. Needless to say, this was eagerly awaited and she started off by stressing that there was nothing secretive about sex and it certainly wasn't anything to get silly about. Nor was it something of immediate importance to us since sex was something strictly reserved for married people. It was a bond between husbands and wives and an expression of the deepest spiritual significance. She then explained that men and women were different because God wished us to perform separate functions.

Eventually, someone asked the inevitable question. "But, Miss... How exactly do babies come into the world? I mean, where from, exactly?"

Miss Openside's cheeks went crimson. Then she touched her rump and said: "From here... Out of the lady's bottom."

At this, the know-all Kraut, Hermann von Pletenburg, jumped up and clicked his heels. He had already been through early sex lessons in Vienna, no doubt receiving instructions by numbers on how to produce the next generation of the master-race. Also, his mother had recently acted as midwife for their neighbour who had needed an emergency delivery. Von Pletenburg, who had been required to rush up and down stairs with fresh supplies of hot water, had seen more than he should have.

"Miss Openside," started von Pletenburg. "I beg to differ. Mrs Burntside, who lives at Westside, the house on our right side, had her baby through the front side of her backside, whilst sitting on the far side of her bedside...."

"I'm sorry Hermann, but that's quite impossible..."

Von Pletenburg clicked his heels again, refusing to give way. "Miss Openside, whilst the front side of a lady's backside might seem a little on the small side, the anatomy of the inside of a lady's backside..."

Gran and Mr Muckey

At that point Miss Openside's modesty overwhelmed her. She let out a cry of distress and once again ran from the room in tears.

We all turned on von Pletenburg. Teasing Miss Openside was one thing, but crudity that drove her to tears was quite another. So we did what we'd been longing to do for weeks. We beat him up. I gave him a bunch of five straight down his big Kraut kuchen hole.

The following morning it was clear that Miss Openside had checked matters in a medical encyclopaedia. She apologised to von Pletenburg and admitted that he was perfectly correct. Babies were, indeed, delivered via the lady's vagina, not her rectum.

However, none of us said sorry to von Pletenburg for having beaten him up. We may have been bullies, but we weren't hypocrites.

Two days later a vicious air raid lasted all morning. German planes, chased by Spitfires, swooped all over the sky, in and out of cloud formations, engaged in a deadly game of hide-and-seek. We spent nearly three hours under our desks. At one stage nearby windows were shattered. As always Miss Openside was fantastic. Most of the time she had us playing 'I spy'. I won because no one could guess 'FB': floor boards. It was easy but no one could concentrate.

During the afternoon, when things were back to normal, Miss Openside was called into SOD's study. Some time later SOD came into our classroom. Straight away we could see that something was wrong. He didn't have his silver birch cane with him. He told us that Miss Openside's young man, Eddie, had been killed. He had advised her to go home and stay away for as long as was necessary. He then explained that during the morning's air battle, Eddie had run out of ammunition in the middle of a dog-fight, but rather than let the enemy escape he had rammed a Dornier and sent it spinning down in flames. His Spitfire was already badly damaged, trailing smoke, and would have gone down anyhow, but it was possible that he could have saved himself if he'd tried to bail out.

Instinctively, Harry Kicks said: "Why did he do it, then?"

"He did it, Harry," said SOD, using a Christian name for the first and only time, "for the sake of you. And me. And everyone else who values freedom."

The following morning Miss Openside came back to see us. Her eyes were like tomatoes. One by one, in a completely spontaneous gesture, we went up to her table and hugged her. At the end of it all she was crying so much that SOD came in again and escorted her out and arranged for someone to take her home. That was the last I ever saw of her.

I often think about her. She was the most beautiful English girl I have ever seen and certainly the bravest, most dedicated, and talented; and these days, when I hear incessant, aimless, chatter about female equality, I smile ruefully. Who, male or female, young or old, could ever have been the equal of Miss Openside?

HATS OFF!

15

The end of summer term – Corporal Fletcher moves in –
Brother Nothing's new theory – Mary takes trips across the
road – On the look-out for Corp – An unfortunate event and
speculation is rife – A token of appreciation.

The summer term at Caterham ended a couple of days later. We all went home with heavy hearts, even though SOD assured us that Miss Openside was taking Eddie's death as well as could be expected and would certainly be coming back at the beginning of the autumn term to continue as our form mistress.

What I had no way of knowing was that I wouldn't be there. I was destined for the wilds of Exmoor.

The first surprise of the summer holidays – and there were several during that long stretch of perfect weather – was that a huge RAF lorry drew up outside Silver Coombe and an officer and a corporal by the name of Fletcher came in to see Mum. They had with them a great screed of papers from the War Office which authorised them to put a barrage balloon in the small field directly opposite Silver Coombe. The fact that Dad had bought the field to stop anyone building there was beside the point. As usual, we were in the hands of the bureaucrats.

The first thing that struck me was that this would interfere with the Home Guard's field of fire. If the Germans were able to dodge about behind a barrage balloon lying on the ground like a great fat elephant, it would make things horrendously difficult. I dashed round to see Muckey. I found him in his potting shed enjoying his morning break with Gran. He was pretty concerned but – like Drake with his bowls – he wasn't going to let his Friary's Best Brown be hurried by a national emergency. However, once he'd drained his bottle he shuffled round to the scullery to sort out the Brylcreem Boys. When I introduced him as the platoon sergeant of the South Godstone contingent of the Home Guard, Mum snorted contemptuously and the Brylcreem Boys smiled indulgently. When Muckey had said his piece about not having been bloody well told by any bug-gers about any bleeding balloons, the officer replied: "Don't worry, Grandad. The war is going to be won in the air, not the ground. Corporal Fletcher here will be in command and his contribution will be inestimable."

So it was, but it had damn all to do with the balloon.

Corporal Fletcher was a sex maniac.

I'd never met a sex maniac before, so I had no way of knowing one when I saw one. Nor, apparently, had anyone else. Corporal Fletcher was so mannerly that he fooled us all. Mum was completely taken in by him. When Corporal Fletcher complimented her on the state of the house she preened about like a purring cat, and when he became more specific and said: "Such beautiful polished surfaces, Madam," she might just as well have rolled over on her back to have her tummy tickled. He won over Mary, our maid, even more easily. For a moment or two he studied her as though he was a qualified beautician, then he went up to her, drew her long hair back, and exclaimed: "Mrs Contractor, have you ever seen such exquisite ears?"

Having been told she had beautiful polished surfaces, Mum would have agreed to anything, so she ignored the fact that Mary's ears were like stunted pink banana leaves gone curly at the edges, and replied: "No, now you mention it, I don't think I have."

Apart from his way with women, there was nothing impressive about Corporal Fletcher. He wasn't big, not even muscular. He wasn't rich and he certainly wasn't powerful, unless one had the misfortune to be an aircraftsman under his command. He might even have been a case of schizophrenia, with a split personality. When in the presence of Mum or Dad, or one of his officers, he was shy, retiring, formal, well-spoken and terribly polite; whereas when alone with women of a shaggable age he was bright and breezy, a regular 'cheeky-chappie' of the Max Miller mould, with flashing green eyes and the ability to adapt his accent and language according to the girl. He'd suddenly blossom into phrases such as, "'Ello, darling! Wot yer doing tonight, then?", or, "Fancy coming round to my place, gorgeous?" I also had it on good authority that when walking down the main street of any town he could stir up youthful female hormones merely by raising an eyebrow, flashing a cheeky smile, or letting out a soft wolf-whistle.

(A word of explanation. Corporal Fletcher was indicative of the times. British sexual mores were in a state of flux. This was the people's war and the people – male and female –wanted the pleasures as well as the dangers, and whilst the brave wanted to get to grips with the Krauts, the amorous wanted to get to grips with each other. Nor must the Kraut influence be underestimated. In his regular broadcasts from Germany, the traitor Lord Haw Haw (William Joyce), who usually lied through his teeth about the sinking of the Ark Royal, told perfectly true stories of toffs and top brass enjoying the most blatant debauchery at such places as the Savoy, the Ritz, and the Trocadero. He wasn't even exaggerating. He pointed out that whilst the rank and file suffered, and Tommies in the Western Desert got sand up the most indelicate places, foreign officers in bizarre uniforms ruled the roost in London's West End.

Indeed, the more bizarre their uniforms, the more mind-blistering their sexual exploits. Polish cavalry officers in pointed hats, tight riding britches, leather boots, silver spurs, and carrying whips, were taking their pick of prime British female stock.

Of course, there's never been a more potent aphrodisiac than the knowledge that others are getting far more than their fair share when you're not getting a share at all; thus what happened at the Silver Coombe balloon site was not untypical. It was by no means the end of Victorian Puritanism, but – to misquote Winston Churchill – 'it was certainly the beginning of the end. Here endeth the explanation.)

Once Corporal Fletcher's balloon had been hoisted with the aid of a squad of airmen, and the monster was high in the sky, tethered to some kind of winching machine, he got himself properly organised. First, he surveyed the field – the female field, that is. Inevitably, his evil designs settled on Mary. She was the most readily available female and he was in a hurry. His overtures were greatly assisted when Mum granted him use of our downstairs toilet and wash basin. This meant that he was in and out the whole time and he made sure his visits (stripped to the waist with a towel tossed over his shoulder) coincided with Mary's presence in the area. That wasn't difficult because she was always on the look out for him in exactly the same way, sporting a new hair style, with every strand swept back, revealing her sexy ears.

Mary was seventeen and had never had a boyfriend. Her social life was confined to the monthly Blindley Heath 'hop'. These functions were notoriously tame and instead of providing an outlet for her ever-increasing sexual appetite they only served to aggravate her physical frustration, especially since the local manhood (exclusively pimply youths) considered her to be so plain that she was a perpetual wallflower. However, Corporal Fletcher, with his uncanny talent for mentally undressing women, soon spotted what others missed, namely a good body, long legs, and an abundance of twitching erogenous zones. He wasn't worried about the poor girl's phizog. He adhered to the old adage: 'You don't look at the mantelpiece when you poke the fire'.

He knew that the way to Mary's heart was to ask favours of her, to make her feel important, as though, by helping him, she was furthering the war effort and hastening the downfall of Adolf Hitler.

"Now look, darling," he explained earnestly. "When the time comes for a tea break, instead of me wasting precious RAF time and coming over here, or trying to brew up on my own in the field, and maybe blowing everything sky high, what about you nipping across the road and slipping me ... (wink, wink)... a cup of tea?"

Hence Mary was soon tripping across the road with cups of tea. I often saw her going backwards and forwards but in my innocence thought nothing of it.

Perhaps the reason why I was so slow in the uptake was because at the time I was very worried: the whole family seemed to have abandoned me. Brother Nothing and James would never play with me on the grounds that I was too young and getting more childish by the day; Mum and I never got on, anyhow; Dad was so busy in Camberwell that I saw hardly anything of him; and whilst Gran and Muckey were as friendly as ever, they were totally wrapped up in each other and I didn't like to intrude.

In desperation I reverted to practicing my leg breaks and googlies on the tennis court. Due to Gran's influence, Muckey lowered the blades on the Atco and created three pitches for me, each separated by three yards. Once they'd been cut, Gran and I got an old roller out of the potting shed and rolled the pitches maybe a hundred times to get rid of the bumps. Then I got on with my bowling, with Lucky retrieving the ball for me, and for a week or more I was eminently happy.

John Hollands

Then Brother Nothing and James got a new craze. Dad gave them each a set of bows and arrows. He'd come to the conclusion that the Daisy Air Rifles were feeble, so feeble that I was allowed to have one at long last. Now, it was bows and arrows I was judged too young to handle. Not that I was greatly surprised. These weren't toys. They were the genuine article, so much so that neither Brother Nothing nor James could 'draw' them to their full potential, which was just as well. Dad had intended them to confine their archery to a highly coloured, ringed target, but having failed to hit it with a single arrow after a whole day of trying, they decided on something more exciting. They set off like a couple of Red Indians and arrows were soon flying around like loose porcupine quills.

They shot at practically everything, including low-flying Hurricanes. As always, it was Muckey who took the brunt of it. Anything wooden was considered fair game and by the end of the second day all his beautiful water butts were leaking like sieves. Gran kept chasing after them with a rake, and Muckey swore at them more ferociously than ever, seeing these steel-tipped arrows as a far greater threat to his safety than the Daisy Air Gun pellets ever were. Mum was so fearful of the consequences that she stomped around the house cursing out loud: "Their father is mad. Bloody mad! Does he want them to kill themselves? First air rifles. Now bows and arrows. Next it'll be a battery of bloody Gofar Buns."

Before long, Brother Nothing came up with another of his famous theories. This time he reckoned that if he stood in the middle of the tennis court, pointed an arrow straight up in the air, twanged it off, and then remained stock still, the arrow, on its return to earth, would always miss him on account of having to 'flip-over' between going up and coming down. James committed the problem to paper and the equation he used indicated that this was indeed the case, every arrow would miss by precisely eighteen inches.

Gran and Mr Muckey

One might be excused for thinking that this was the end of the matter, but not with Brother Nothing. He had to prove his theory. I pleaded with him not to. So did James, who was sensible enough to concede that his calculations might be wrong; but Nothing spent at least half an hour each day on the lawn, standing stock still, twanging arrows into the sky and watching them as they reached their zenith of about 100 feet and then streaked down towards him before burying themselves deep in the ground, sometimes in front of him, sometimes behind, occasionally to one side, but always precisely eighteen inches away.

Whenever he saw me after these sessions he shouted: "There you are, squirt. KCYS!"

However, his success didn't impress me and I never dared to watch him. Whenever he had another go I wandered around the garden in agitation, expecting at any moment to hear a piercing scream and then see Brother Nothing rushing for Mum with an arrow sticking out the top of his head. I even visualised it going right through his head. Even disappearing into his body and then reappearing out of his arsehole.

God, how awful! What a mess that would make. There would be blood and shit all over my newly mown pitches.

My attention was eventually diverted from this frightening scenario, and banished from my mind, when I saw Mary returning through the front gate after a visit to Corporal Fletcher. She had empty cups and saucers in her hands and a smile on her face which was, to physical delight, what the Bisto Kids' smile was to Irish Stew. As she passed me I saw that her pleated skirt had got caught up in its waist band and was hitched up. It revealed that he wasn't wearing any knickers and that she had a very handsome, well-rounded bottom.

Although a sight to behold, I was embarrassed. Even in my innocence, a lack of knickers indicated something pretty naughty going on. I saw it as a challenge. If I was crafty, maybe I could find out what she was up to; and that meant my first task was to save Mary from Mum. If Mum saw her walking about the house without any knickers, showing off her backside, she'd very likely sack her on the spot, no matter how handsome and well-rounded it was. So I ran up behind Mary and pretended I was starting a game of 'tag', which we sometimes played. This time, instead of tapping her on the shoulder, I slapped her in the small of the back and managed to jerk her skirt free without her suspecting a thing.

Next I formed a plan of action. My excitement was hardly containable. I knew I was about to witness something depraved and that made it all the more irresistible. I felt sure it would be a turning point in my life, an illuminating glimpse into adulthood. Everything would be down to observation. I decided that as soon as I saw Mary making tea I would shin up the rope ladder attached to Magog and then, using Dad's old army binoculars, watch every move.

Corporal Fletcher had an ideal lair. He'd pitched his camouflage tent at the far side of the field, well away from the winch and other equipment used for raising and lowering the balloon. It was just in front of a lovely little copse of fir trees with a convenient bank of brambles and blackberry bushes at the rear of it, hiding it from the lane on the far side of the field. He had improvised with ingenuity. He had three air beds strung together to form a king-size bed, a portable gramophone with a large collection of Ambrose and Geraldo records in order to create suitable atmosphere, and camp chairs and a table for elementary wining and dining.

Mary went across twice a day and thanks to Dad's binoculars I saw everything that came off and went on, usually to the strains of 'Love is the Sweetest Thing' and 'Don't Say Goodbye'. My expectations were entirely fulfilled. I knew I was being a right little nark, but that didn't stop me. I doubt if it would have stopped anyone. On my second morning of observation, Mary had only just returned to the house when I heard a tractor coming down the lane. It was pulling a hay

Gran and Mr Muckey

cart and sitting on top of the hay were five Land Girls dressed in cord riding britches, tight green sweaters, and wide-brimmed felt hats, real daughters of the earth with rosy cheeks, callused hands, and the healthy odour of the farmyard. By the time the tractor had drawn level with Corporal Fletcher's gate, he'd pulled up his trousers, buttoned his flies, and struck what he obviously considered to be a manly pose.

"'Ello, darlings. Making hay while the sun shines?"

There were shrieks of laughter and then one of them shouted back. "That's right, handsome. And what about you?"

"Don't worry about me, gorgeous. I'm working the land the same as you are. Sowing a few wild oats... Like to help me?"

There was another outburst of giggles and saucy banter, their natural reticence dissolved by strength in numbers; and although by this time the tractor was well past the gate I was pretty sure it wasn't going to be the end of matters. Nor was it. The Land Girls must have drawn straws and a minute or two later one of them came running back up the lane, giggling away to herself and all parts of her generous body wobbling and shaking in anticipation. Within five minutes Corporal Fletcher had her blowing more air into the beds so that they didn't 'bottom out' and then, before she could get her breath back, she was lying on a bed of her own making.

Near lunch time, when I climbed down my rope ladder, I found Corporal Fletcher waiting for me. "I thought so, you little devil," he said. "You've been spying on me. I saw the glint of your binoculars."

I was too scared to reply. I didn't know what to expect. Would he beat me up?

"Don't look so frightened, youngster. Come over to the field. You and me had better come to an arrangement."

The arrangement we came to was that whilst perched up Magog I would be his lookout man. He put it very convincingly. We were to be partners, a couple of men sticking together, comrades-in-arms in our ordained role as the sowers of seed and the alleviators of female frustrations by utilising the panacean gift granted to men by God. I didn't understand a word of that, of course, but I was more au fait with things when he warned me that women were curious creatures who invariably had dozens of boyfriends but expected all of them to be faithful to them, and them alone.

"So what I suggest you do," explained Corporal Fletcher, "is this. You take your air rifle up the tree. And every time you see a girl coming who shouldn't be coming, on account of me being with another one, you fire at an empty bucket I'll hang near the gate. Then, whenever I hear a 'ping', I'll have time to take the necessary action. Can you hit a bucket from here?"

"You bet I can."

Corp – as he insisted I called him – hung an empty bucket from the branch of a handy tree and when we tried things out I hit it every time. The only thing I had to be careful of was that I got my shot in as soon as possible so that the sound of the air rifle and the 'ping' didn't give the game away to the approaching girl.

Within a few days, Corp's visitors became a regular procession. If it wasn't Mary or one of the Land Girls, then others girls, who'd heard the whisper go around, turned up for a piece of the action. As it happened, I rarely had to use my air rifle, but I logged each girl in and logged each girl out. Soon, I felt I was getting to know them. I invented special names for them, some affectionate and flattering but others – I'm ashamed to say – betraying a young boy's artless crudity, such as 'Fat Arse', 'Chicken Legs', 'Baggy Drawers', 'Fried Eggs', and 'Big Blobbs'. Whatever I christened them they went away happy and always returned for more: an early lesson for me that a healthy sexual appetite is by no means a male prerogative.

*****

Gran and Mr Muckey

What amazed me (and probably does you as well) was Corp's stamina. It just didn't seem natural. It puzzled me so much that I consulted James. "How often can human beings do *it?*" I asked as casually as possible. "I mean in quick succession?"

"Females can do it often," replied James, preparing to fire an arrow into the door of the generating shed, in which Muckey was topping up the petrol tank. "Almost as often as they like. But the performance of males is strictly limited. Apart from odd insects, the only male species well-known for their ability to copulate in such quick succession that they can satisfy a whole gang of females in one sitting, is lions. Lions just go on and on... No end to it."

This answer (although spot-on biologically) solved nothing. Corp was no lion. Was he a freak? A modern-day Rasputin?

All this had been going on for some time when Mary didn't turn up for work. I asked Mum what had happened to her but she didn't know. I was scared out of my wits. For two days I conjured up all kinds of unlikely possibilities. Then Mum told me that Mary was going to have a baby.

"Is that all?" I said.

"Is that all?" yelled Mum. "What are you talking about?"

"Well, she could have been murdered..."

"Murdered. Don't be so ridiculous."

"What will happen now, Mum? Will she get married?"

"Normally. But it seems she won't say who the father is."

I changed tact. "Well now she's going to have a baby, they'll give her somewhere to live, won't they?"

"Sajit..."

"And enough money to look after it..."

"Sajit, you really are an incredibly stupid little boy. Who are 'they'? And why should anyone give her anything? She's sinned. Brought shame on her family. On everyone. You just have no idea."

Mum was right. I had no idea of the implications of pregnancy in those days. The first thing that happened

223

was that Mum sacked her: no written month's notice, no references, no redundancy package, no compensation, just 'bugger off'.

Locally, Mary's downfall caused a great scandal, but her refusal to name the father came as no surprise. Everyone assumed she didn't know who he was, and after the way she and other local girls had been behaving lately, no wonder. Ever since the 6th Canadian Division had arrived in the area the Blindley Heath 'hops' had degenerated from gentle gyrations to the records of Henry Hall into bebopping orgies to the discordant, animal-like vibrations of a transatlantic jazz band. When two other girls fell pregnant, blank walls in Blindley Heath and South Godstone were daubed with graffiti saying: 'Lock up your wives and daughters', and the Canadians, who fathered numerous infants in the area during their stay, took great delighting in adding, 'And your sisters, and your aunts, and your mothers'.

The worst thing for Mary was that her parents disowned her. They sent her to a home for 'fallen girls' in Hertfordshire. She had to stay there until the baby was born and had been adopted. It was all so blatantly unfair that I could hardly believe it, and I was terrified that at any moment someone – probably Mum – would question me about Corp. If that happened, should I betray him? I worried about it so much that I went round to the potting shed to talk it over with Gran and Muckey. I never actually told them what I'd seen, but I hinted pretty broadly at who the father was. Muckey kept quiet, knowing that Gran would have far more finesse on such a subject. She told me not to worry about Mary; that such things had been happening since the beginning of time. It was her body and hers alone and she had to take full responsibility for it. Females had the gift of intuition and this spelt out the dangers of illicit love clearly enough right from a very early age. It was only those who chose to ignore and defy this inborn wisdom, and who opted for the desires of the flesh, that ended up with self-inflicted misery.

*****

So only one mystery remained: how did Corp manage to satisfy all those girls so regularly and over such a long time? I'll give the answer now, even though I was left wondering for many years. I was approaching my twenty-fourth birthday when I had a parcel and a letter from a solicitor in Birmingham. The letter explained that he was executor to the last will and testament of Harold Sylvester Fletcher who had passed away after a long struggle against cancer. In the package was a note from Corp thanking me for my help and loyalty whilst he was stationed at South Godstone, and stating how proud he was to have been an important part of my sex education. He said he'd read and thoroughly enjoyed *The Dead, The Dying and the Damned* – my best-selling novel of the Korean war – and he felt sure the degrading sex scenes I'd described in such brilliant and lurid detail among the whores of Tokyo were indebted in no small measure to what I'd learnt from him. Finally, he added that he was enclosing a small token of his appreciation. When I unpacked this token there were two hard, brownish-grey lumps that looked and smelt like dehydrated donkey droppings.

Thankfully, they weren't. They were rhino horn. During his pre-war RAF service he had been station in Nairobi and it was there that he'd purchased two horns. All he had to do (and I often watched him do it without realising what he was up to) was file off a small quantity and mix it with his stew or Gran's curry, which he often dipped into. Within ten minutes he was raring to go, the answer to a nymphomaniac's dream.

Viagra and Ginseng have nothing on rhino's horn and if this book does nothing else, I hope it will convince you – my readers – of the vital importance of preserving the rhinoceros as a species. As things stand today, with modern women having cast aside the hypocritical anachronism of virgo intacto, men will need all the horns they can get.

16

Worries about sex – Back to cricket – My imagination comes in for criticism – A conspiracy is confirmed – Dad offers a helping hand.

Whencc I considered the dire consequences of sex outside of marriage, I became very confused. I recalled what Miss Openside had taught us: that sex was for married people only. We all took that with a pinch of salt of course, but when I visualised Miss Openside carrying on like Mary I was so shocked that I felt positively sick. Yet I couldn't deny that I'd enjoyed being a cheap voyeur, and neither could I bring myself to condemn Corp for taking advantage of what was so freely offered. Yet it surely couldn't be right? Weren't there any sensible and enforceable rules for these matters? I went across to Corp and asked him a few questions. I wanted to know if sex was really so sensational that it was worth all the risks.

"Saj, I don't know how to answer you," he replied, smiling softly. "There are those who can control it and those who can't. Depends on how God made you."

I tried desperately to recall the exact words of Miss Openside had used to us. "But doesn't sex have any meaning, Corp?"

"Meaning? No, it's just an urge... Something we all have. It guarantees that the world keeps going."

"But isn't it spiritual?"

"Spiritual? Oh, yeah. Definitely. Keeps your spirits up something smashing. When you're down in the dumps, nothing better than a bit of the other."

I gave up. That wasn't what Miss Openside meant at all. I told Corp I didn't think I should be involved any more. He understood. He shrugged his shoulders and said that he'd miss my help, but he'd just have to take a chance on things. I think that by that time there were so many girls trooping around to see him that he couldn't have cared less even if one did catch him at it with another and desert him. What haunted me was how I would turn out. Would I be able to control it?

I took refuge in cricket, something I've often done in life when perplexed and out of my depth. Muckey and Gran continued to help with the maintenance of my pitches and this was important. I knew Mum was on the look out for trouble, itching to tell Dad I was ruining the lawn. She had a point. The area around where I delivered the ball did become very worn. In fact, large holes kept appearing. When they got ankle deep I transferred to a neighbouring pitch whilst Muckey returfed the damaged zone and sprinkled it with grass cuttings, thus making it look as good as new from the house.

I started my bowling run-up from the far end of the court and, when nearly halfway, I had a stump stuck in the ground to mark the beginning of the pitch. From that point, I bowled towards the house and the ball would go into the stout wire netting that separated the court first of all from a broad flower bed and then the driveway, outside the kitchen window. After every delivery, Lucky would dash down the pitch to retrieve the ball and I would start again.

Whilst I practised, Mum would be indoors with her new maid, Rose, yelling at the poor girl to use more elbow grease. James was in one of his more studious spells, usually sitting in the window of the small bedroom directly above the kitchen; and Brother Nothing would be roaming the woods with his Daisy Air Rifle slung across his shoulders and his bow at the ready, half drawn back for an instant shot at any blackbird or other unsuspecting small creature he was bent on exterminating.

Poor old Nothing! He liked to think he was Robin Hood in Sherwood Forest with his merry men. One day, when Muckey and Gran were in the woods, they heard him rummaging around and then calling out in a piece of make-believe: "Is that you, Little John? —— Over here, Robin..."

Normally I kept quiet about this inside knowledge, but when Nothing came over to the tennis court to torment me with fresh threats to throw my cricket ball away, or by shouting out silly remarks like, "How's that?" and, "No ball!" every time I bowled, I retaliated by singing:

"Robin Hood, Robin Hood,
Crawling through the grass,
Up came Little John
And shot him up the arse."

That soon shut him up.

On the whole, however, we left each other alone, except when gathered around the lunch table. There was some-thing about our lunch-time gatherings that sparked off animosity. I was always the butt of everyone's ribbing, probably because I made the mistake of volunteering what I'd been up to during the morning. To sit around the table in stolid silence when I'd just experienced one of the most thrilling sessions ever played at Lord's was quite impossible. Maybe Brother Nothing could resist telling us about his triumphs over the Sheriff of Nottingham, and James could conceal that he'd just cracked Einstein's Theory of Relativity, but damned if I could hide the fact that I'd clean bowled Wally Hammond for nought.

They were so ignorant about cricket that they didn't know who Wally Hammond was and the only message that got across to them was that I had a very high opinion of myself.

"Don't be such a dirty little swank," Brother Nothing would start off.

"I'm not."

"Oh yes you are. I've heard all about you at school. Miss Openside's little pet..."

"I'm not."

"Oh yes you are. Always kissing and hugging her. And what about when you and Harry Kicks tried to claim the credit when SOD captured the German pilot?"

I had to gloss over that before Mum heard too much about it. Likewise, the story of the Dornier machine gun. Not that my silence did any god. Instead, Brother Nothing came out with his versions of them. These either exaggerated or played down my role according to whichever he thought would annoy Mum most.

"And Harry Kicks has told me all about your lies in the air raid shelters. Mum, Miss Openside gets him to stand up on a stool and then he tells a whole lot of lies about us."

"No I don't."

"Yes you do. Harry Kicks has told me. Like when you told them that shrapnel demolished the wall behind your bed?"

"I didn't."

"Of course you did. And those lies about when we were on the Devil's Ledge... Surrounded by grizzly bears."

"They weren't lies. It was imagination. Miss Openside says I've got a marvellous imagination."

"You mean you're a dirty little liar."

"I'm not. Imagination is like an extra dimension. Something no one yet understands properly..."

That made them roar with laughter, Mum leading them with a shriek of scorn. I refused to let Miss Openside's views be belittled so I stammered out her points about human culture being founded on imagination. Frankly, James soon demolished that theory. According to him such things were achieved by hard work, discipline, and training from those who knew better, and that a young, untrained, wartime stop-gap kindergarten teacher like Miss Openside didn't know the first thing about it.

"And I know all about her," crowed Brother Nothing. "Harry Kicks told me. She doesn't even know which side is which."

I blushed crimson and kept quiet.

"What do you mean by that?" demanded Mum.

"Oh, nothing," smirked Nothing.

"What?" yelled Mum.

"Nothing, Mum..."

"Tell me, look you!"

"She doesn't know which side her bread is buttered," said James, saving the situation.

Such a narrow escape didn't stop Nothing from goading me further. He told Mum every one of my stories during the air raids and by the time he'd finished all I could mutter was: "Well Miss Openside says I'm good at stories. That one day I'm going to be an author and write novels."

That caused great mockery and to this day I can remember sitting there, crying into my semolina pudding.

Before long I sensed that even Dad was viewing me with concern. Normally, he came back from work totally exhausted. Sometimes he didn't come back at all through having to fire-watch at the Works. It meant that he hardly had time to speak to any of us, yet all of a sudden he went out of his way to bombard me with a whole lot of probing questions. He interrogated me about the remarks Brother Nothing had gleaned from Harry Kicks, and it soon became obvious that Mum had nagged him into conducting this cross-examination. At one stage he said: "Your mother tells me that your teacher says you could become a writer."

"Yes, Dad. Is that a good idea?"

"Yes. Very good. It means you can get up any time you like. And you can do it wherever you are. All you need is plenty of paper and a pencil. As a matter of fact, I'm going to write a book when I retire."

Gran and Mr Muckey

"Then I can follow in your footsteps, Dad."
"You could. But you've got to know something about life."
"Like the University of Life, you mean?"
He smiled, proud of me for remembering it. He was looking at me in a new light, as though he'd discovered hidden talent. "You're only a little fellow, aren't you, Sajit."
"Yes, but I'm tough. I was conker champion last year."
"Were you? Good...But do your brothers ever hit you? I know they're always teasing you, but do they hit you?"
I hesitated. As it happened, Brother Nothing did quite often, but I always gave back as good as I got – well, nearly. Not that I was going to mention it. I was already brainwashed by the schoolboy ethic that you didn't squeal. You fought your own battles.
Dad respected my silence. "You know, Sajit, I think it would be a good idea if you came up to the Works with me."
"To Camberwell Green?"
"Of course. Would you like that?"
"You bet I would."

17

Back at the Works – A look around the East End –
The Krauts move west – The skinniest man in south
London goes ferreting – Mugs of tea and a touch of the
Gunga Dins.

The date on which the Battle of Britain became the London Blitz is a matter of historical record: the night of September 7th.

It was the following morning that Dad took me up to Camberwell Green. During the night we'd heard the rumble of distant bombing, but we had no idea that it was the start of the Blitz. Had we gone into the garden and looked north, across Lake's field and over Tilburstow Hill, we would have seen a bright glow, a vast semi-circle of raw, pulsing redness, which was much of London's East End burning to the ground.

We snatched an early breakfast and then caught the first Green Line of the day. It was standing-room only until a few locals got off at the Godstone bus station and it was then that some copies of the *Daily Express* were tossed aboard for delivery further up the line. Giant headlines told us what had happened but naturally no one commented on it. Even those who got on board further on, who must have had a very disturbed night, merely read the details in the various morning papers they'd brought with them and kept their own counsel. It wasn't until the drivers 'swapped' at East Croydon that anything was said. The departing driver then said to his successor: "Our turn soon, mate."

"Bollocks to 'em. They can bomb us all they like. Won't do them any good."

"Bugger the bombing. I'm talking about the night shift. We're on it next week."

When we eventually arrived at the Works everything was perfectly normal. The men were retreading tyres, hauling them from one place to another, and loading lorries. In the battery shop, a new bank of formation had just been turned on and this, as always, brought on bouts of coughing. As Dad did a tour of the Works with Old Percy, he got the usual cheery greetings and I also came in for quite a few, mainly "'Ello, Nipper. Good to see yer again, me old mate."

Dad took me over to a corner of the stables which had previously been unused. Now, it was occupied by two enormous vats of molten lead with gas-fired burners roaring beneath them. They had hoods over them, with noisy extractor fans drawing off the fumes and pumping them through chimneys. An incredibly thin young man was in charge of things. Even though he was dressed from head to toe in rubber overalls with tight-fitting goggles to protect his eyes from splashing sulphuric acid, I could see that he was all skin and bone. Yet he seemed tough enough. To one side of the stable was a large pile of old car batteries and he was breaking their black boxes with a sledge hammer and then extracting the lead plates and lowering them gently into the vats.

"This is something new," explained Dad. "We're reclaiming our own lead. It's the first part of the process. We have to use every trick in the book these days. And there's more money in scrap lead than making new batteries."

Dad's mercenary attitude didn't greatly interest me. I was fascinated by the man breaking up the batteries. After Dad had passed on to his office, I continued to watch him. When he stopped for a breather he peeled off his goggles. "So you're the Guvner's nipper," he said. "Glad to meet you, youngster. I'm Charlie Smith."

I was stunned, unable to answer. I felt faint. Charlie Smith! It was as though I'd had a presentiment. Indeed, there was no 'as though' about it. I had had a presentiment. Charlie Smith would be written on thousands of Kraut bombs. "Nice to meet you, Charlie," I managed to say eventually. "My name is Sajit."

"See you around then, Saj."

With that he replaced his goggles and resumed smashing up the batteries. Then he carried the plates over to the vats and lowered them into the molten lead very gently, showing it great respect.

The lead refining wasn't the only change Dad had made since my last visit. He had a new office which was very smart, and a new secretary who was even smarter and far more friendly than the previous one. She knew all about me being the 'Don R' for the Home Guard and also about my interest in cricket. "And what are you going to do whilst you're up here with your Dad?" she asked.

"I don't know."

"You're going to be the char wallah," said Dad. "At tea breaks, Margaret makes it and you're going to take it round."

I didn't think much of that but I didn't argue because I thought Dad was joking, but he wasn't. At eleven o'clock Margaret made an enormous pot of tea and I was sent round with a tray of mugs which was so heavy I could hardly manage it. The same thing happened at four o'clock. It could have been really demeaning but thankfully the men had a laugh and joke with me and promised that when things were less hectic they'd let me have a go at their jobs.

"Will I get paid?" I asked.

Gran and Mr Muckey

"Blimey, Nipper. Yer just like yer old man...Nothing but money...Tell yer what. When yer 'alf as good as wot 'e is at retreading tyres, we'll pass the 'at round for yer."

I didn't know whether to take the remark seriously but since everyone laughed, and so obviously welcomed my presence, I didn't worry about it.

For two nights we went home as usual and whilst we slept peacefully the East End continued to be systematically flattened, and all against very little resistance from night fighters or ack-ack guns. The East Enders just had to sit there and take it.

On my third morning at the works there was considerable excitement. A lorry load of retreads had to be taken to the Rotherhithe wharfs for shipping to the middle east. There was a query about the paperwork, not for the export, but merely to get into the dockland area. "I'll take them myself," declared Dad.

I knew why Dad decided to go. He wanted to see the state of the East End. So did I, so when a van had been loaded I jumped up into the cab next to him as though it was the most natural thing in the world.

I rate that journey as one of the most extraordinary I've ever undertaken. Until we got to the junction which linked Bermondsey Street, Tower Bridge Road, and Grange Road, not a single bomb had fallen. Only on the other side of the junction was there any damage, and then what damage! It was a very calm morning and the smoke was rising straight into the sky, showing no signs of dispersing. As we waited at the junction for police permission to proceed, Dad kept getting out of the cab to stretch his legs. Each time he got into conversation with people and he kept telling them: "It's precision bombing. They come straight up the line of the river and drop bombs on either side of it... Easy navigation, and you know what that means..."

Eventually, after we'd had our papers examined, we got police permission to try to get to our destination. We were warned that we might not make it and advised as a first step to proceed along Grange Road. From there on we came across road blocks and diversions every hundred yards or so until Dad soon had no idea of where he was. Progress got slower and slower: stop, start, turn around, try some other route. At one point we followed a local van, thinking it would know how to get through, but it turned out the driver had no more idea than we did. When we drew up alongside him at one stop, he called through his window: "Any idea how to get to Brixton, mate?"

Wherever we went great rows of buildings had been demolished – now huge piles of rubble in the middle of the roads – and fire engines were straddled across our path with a mass of bulging hose pipes trailing in all directions like spilt spaghetti. Water was gushing about everywhere with firemen still up their extended ladders, spraying down buildings from which smoke belched as though they were erupting volcanoes.

One halt was very different to others. ARP wardens came rushing down the road towards us, blowing their whistles and shouting, telling drivers to reverse and get back as far as they could. They cursed and swore at anyone who was slow to obey or who held up things by demanding an explanation. Dad crashed into reverse and weaved his way backwards, dodging about and never hesitating to mount the pavement if it was necessary. Once we'd halted, we got out and walked back up the road to see what was happening. We soon came to a police barrier. Everyone was straining against the rope, anxious to find out what the panic was all about. In front of us was a shopping parade with eight-storey buildings on either side of the road. They were expected to collapse at any moment; and even as a policeman was explaining this, the buildings let out a series of sharp reports, like the cracking of whips. Then both sides, for as far down as we could see, suddenly sagged, suspended in limbo, and then sank down with a gentle 'swoosh' before hitting the ground with the boom of thunder, sending dust and flying debris billowing into the air. Within seconds everything had disappeared beneath the dust, and since a great cloud of it was heading in our direction, we ran back to our vehicle.

That caused another major delay and diversion. This time we went through a maze of side streets and here we saw a more personal side to the tragic events. Long residential roads were studded with gaps where bombs had fallen. Each gap was quite distinct, like a tooth extraction, and they were dotted down the road at regular intervals, sticks of bombs having scarred them with the precision and neatness of buttons on a waistcoat. The houses in between, although still standing, were mere shells: no doors, no windows, and roof slates missing.

Invariably, the residents were moving out. Heaps of furniture and personal belongings were dumped outside their front doors, each pile jealously separated from the others. Some families were just standing there, as though on guard, waiting for God knows what, others were attempting to get the debris into piles, and some were in the process of moving off, loading their chattels into prams, barrows and home-made carts which had served as toys for generations of kids.

In another street, where a land-mine had drifted down on them by parachute, an entire terrace of houses had been blown away. It must have happened on the first night for here, no one stood around, no rescuers shifted through the half-cleared rubble. All hope had been abandoned.

Once, a policeman waved us to a halt because rescue operations were in progress. Dad was told to turn his engine off and make no noise and we sat there in silence and watched ARP men and police standing atop bricks and chunks of broken walls, knocking on exposed pipes, then waiting tensely to hear if there was any response. We saw the rescue brought to a successful conclusion. As near as damn it, it was a repeat of Edgware, except that this time a

John Hollands

whole family, numbering seven, with a babe in arms amongst them, was dragged out alive.

Halfway along Jamaica Road, right smack in the centre of everything, there was an enormous crater, with a double-decker bus protruding from it, standing on its back end, exposing its underbelly. The driver's cab and the front wheels were resting in the bay window of someone's front bedroom with a picture of a mountain (probably Ben Nevis guessed Dad) on the far wall. The adverts on the bus told us: 'Good Taste Demands Hovis, Not Just Brown'. Dad said the tyres needed retreading.

Eventually, when we got to Rotherhithe and made our delivery. One of the men who helped us off-load offered me a large piece of shrapnel as a souvenir.

"This bit is special, Nipper, isn't it?"

"Why is that, sir?"

"Because it killed the bloody foreman, didn't it?"

"Did it?"

My eyes must have bulged. He laughed, threw the shrapnel away, and gave me a tanner instead. As we drove off I asked Dad if it was all right for me to accept tips. He replied in broad cockney. "Tea boys take wots going, mate. Don't they?"

"Do they?"

"Sajit, Londoners always end everything with a question, don't they? They don't expect you to answer though, do they?"

When I didn't reply he slapped my knee playfully. "Good boy. Yer learning, mate. Aren't yer?"

On the way back things were a little easier. It was incredible how quickly the fires and wreckage were brought under control and cleared. Mainly, we saw knots of gossiping women standing around forlornly, while their urchin kids rushed around them, already on to some fresh game. Their men folk were laying siege to pubs, waiting impatiently for them to open, banging on the doors and yelling out: "Come on, you old bugger! Open up. We know you're in there."

Many older boys were clamouring over the wreckage, scavenging, looking for belongings of any value, yelling at each other excitedly as they found something of worth or which caused amusement. One group pulled out a long line of washing, a family's clothes torn to shreds.

Several times we passed schools or church halls where people were being given emergency accommodation. They were easy to spot, their prams and carts parked outside. All the bigger items, such as pianos and sofas had been left behind, but I was amazed to see how many clocks were being carted around. "Family heirlooms," said Dad. "Given to their fathers and grandfathers for fifty years of devoted service to the local coal, gas and coke company."

Near the end of our journey, when we were diverted to London Bridge, we saw people clustered around the Underground Station. The story had gone around that the Underground offered the best shelter and, although no official permission had yet been granted, people weren't going to be denied such safety and as things turned out, nor were they.

Only once did we come near to being embroiled in a nasty incident. We were stuck in a queue of traffic opposite a typical group of bombed out residents. A rough-looking fellow in a flat cap with no shirt and a dirty vest, saw us looking at them. He pushed members of his family aside and came striding over to us. He was all hair and gut. "Wot's yer game then, mate?"

"Nothing," said Dad. "Just stuck in the traffic."

"Then stop your gawking and bugger off. All right for you lot, but we've lost bloody everyfink."

"We've been bombed out too," said Dad calmly.

"Oh yeah? Where was that, then? Katman-bloody-du?"

"Edgware."

"Norf London? Among all them Yids?"

"Yes. Four of our Yiddish neighbours were killed."

The man touched his cap in respect. "Oh, sorry, mate..."

"That's all right," said Dad. "We're all in this together, you know. If you've lost everything, can I give you a few bob... Just for a drink... No hard feelings..."

"Oh, no, no. Don't worry about that, mate. Matter of fact, the Nags Head caught it last night and there's that much looted booze doing in the bloody rounds that we'll all be pissed tonight, won't we?"

"Sounds like it," laughed Dad.

In fact, the East Enders resented nosy-parkers. They didn't mind visits from the King and Queen, or Winston Churchill, but all others were given very short shrift. During another hold up, Dad and I came across a well-known politician trying to spread comfort. Taken aback by his frosty reception, he went over to a small boy who was sitting alone, leaning against a lamp post, crying quietly. The politician knelt beside him and asked what the problem was.

"My Mum, Guvner! She got burnt yesterday, didn't she?"

"Oh dear," sympathised the politician. "Was she burnt badly?"

"Bloody 'ell yes, Guvner! They don't bugger about at them crematoriums, do they?"

Everyone laughed and the boy's face spread into a cheeky grin. No one knew whether he was kidding or not. The politician certainly didn't. He strode back to his limousine, flushed and embarrassed. "Back to the House!" he instructed his chauffeur haughtily, but they were stuck in the traffic the same as everyone else, so he just had to sit in isolated splendour on his back seat. Within seconds his limousine was surrounded by local urchins, all laughing and jeering at him.

I continued to go up to Camberwell Green with Dad every day and the pattern remained the same: enormous raids overnight with the East End catching everything, and still no real defence mounted against it. A few bombs strayed into south London, but that was all. One morning, as I took the men's tea around they were discussing how long the

Gran and Mr Muckey

East End could take it, and how accurate the bombing was, so I explained to them: "It's precision bombing. They just come up the line of the river and drop bombs on either side of it... Easy navigation... And we all know what that means..."

This was well received until I repeated it to Charlie Smith and some of his mates. Having listened attentively, Charlie said: "No Saj... I don't know. What does it mean?"

"Well... Er... You'd better ask my Dad..."

They laughed so loudly that from then on I kept my mouth shut.

When Dad's turn came for fire-watching we stayed at the Works overnight. Mum didn't mind. She knew the bombing was confined to the East End and she had no idea that Camberwell Green was within spitting distance. To her, the East End was to Camberwell what Barry Island was to Cardiff. If she'd known the truth she would have had kittens, just as she would have if she'd known what the Works were like. She'd never been there and thought it was like a mini ICI factory, full of changing rooms and showers and spotless canteens, not a collection of tumble-down converted stables, quite liable to collapse under the force of a strong wind, let alone Kraut bombing.

On my first night at the Works everything changed. The Krauts gave their bombers a free hand and they bombed all over the eastern half of London. At the same time ack-ack guns and searchlights had at last been brought into London from all over the country, thus ensuring that the Krauts got what the Londoners loved to call: "A bit of the old whatfor!"

The sirens sounded early, long before I'd even thought of settling down on the camp bed Dad's secretary had prepared for me in the office. When we went up on the roof to see what was happening dozens of pencil-beamed search-lights were thrusting into the sky. Even so, none of them had yet picked out any Dorniers or Heinkels even though we knew, from the distinctive drone of their engines, that they were up there somewhere. The ack-ack guns weren't deterred by the failure of the searchlights and they opened up, determined to have a go, even if they were blasting away at nothing in particular. They came from all quarters of London and made an enormous racket. In *Their Finest Hour*, Churchill summed it up: 'The roaring cannonade did not do much harm to the enemy, but gave enormous satisfaction to the population. Everyone was cheered by the feeling that we were hitting back.'

Dad and I were among those cheering with enormous satisfaction, but what Churchill didn't mention was the shrapnel from the ack-ack shells came down like confetti, often with dire consequences. It took Dad, with his war experience, to point out that these were self-inflicted wounds and he quoted the old army maxim: 'There's no such thing as friendly fire.'

Then, gradually, the searchlights began to pick out the elusive bombers and it was obvious by the way they took immediate evasive action, swinging first one way and then the other, that they didn't like it one bit; and furthermore the ack-ack guns quickly got in on the act and peppered the area. This was more like it! The most dramatic moment I witnessed throughout the night was when a Heinkel was caught fair and square in three searchlight beams.

"The poor bugger must think he's the star turn at the Palladium," said Dad.

Actually, the way it was lumbering across the skyline, it reminded me more of an old ham actor being booed and pelted off stage. It was gross and cumbersome, an engine trailing smoke, listing to one side with what seemed like every gun in town trying to finish it off. Then the dirty swine relieved itself right across the Elephant and Castle. With stark clarity, I saw the bombs falling, and when their explosions illuminated the Camberwell skyline they left imprinted on my mind a vivid negative picture of chimney pots and church spires.

Gran and Mr Muckey

Things were getting too dangerous to watch any longer so we returned to Dad's office. His secretary had plenty of water on the boil, all set for brewing up in a vast tea pot. "You two char wallahs will be essential," said Dad. "When things go wrong and people get hurt, the whole neighbourhood suddenly needs cups of char."

For a time we just listened as the bombing increased and the ack-ack thundered on. This was very different from the raids I'd experienced at school. Then, we'd been on the periphery, an accident waiting to happen, whereas here we were the epicentre, the target, the very people the Germans were out to kill, whose morale they were determined to break. Dad said it reminded him of Flanders before a Kraut attack, and he assured us that the only sensible thing was to remain still and calm, knowing that those who rushed out to try to do something positive only further endangered themselves and did no good whatsoever. So, with high explosive bombs and land mines falling all around the Camberwell, Lambeth, Brixton, Battersea, and Herne Hill area, the three of us sat tight, praying silently, but not letting on.

Bombs began to fall so near that we ducked under the office table. Our closeness was comforting. Dad had one arm around me and the other around his secretary. He seemed to enjoy cuddling her and I don't think she minded either. Then there was a deafening explosion and the whole building shuddered, its very foundations quaking. Dust and debris fell away from the ceiling: great chunks of plaster and narrow strips of timber crashed on to the table top. Windows were shattered, the sound of splintering glass as loud as a pile of crockery going over. There were screams and then shouts of warning, all far too late. We wondered just how much would be left of Lomond Grove by the time it was all over.

When things seemed about as bad as they could get, bar a direct hit, we heard someone approaching, footsteps scurrying down the pavement outside. Doors were flung open and then slammed and eventually, from beneath the table, we saw a pair of legs in the doorway. It was Charlie Smith from battery reclamation. "Get under the table, Charlie," yelled Dad.

When Charlie joined us it was such a tight fit that all our backsides were left sticking out, prime targets. "What the hell are you doing rushing around the place?" demanded Dad.

"I was going around to see if my old lady's okay."

"Oh, come on Charlie. For God's sake. She's in the cellar of the Beggar's Roost with the rest of the regulars. She'll be as pissed as a bloody newt by now."

Charlie laughed. "Yeah, I know that, Guvner. Truth is, I got the wind up. It's bloody murder being on your own."

Charlie was pressing hard against me. He was as skinny as a whippet and was shivering, as so many of them do.

We didn't wait for the all-clear. As soon as the sound of the bombers died away and the ack-ack guns tailed off, we went outside to see what had happened. At the end of Lomond Grove, near the Green, most of the houses were ablaze. The residents were out in the road, women and children clinging together, their men making futile attempts to retrieve belongings or to fight the flames with stirrups pumps and buckets of water, the latter being passed along in a human chain, hand to hand.

The worst hit areas were Church Street, leading into Peckham Road, and Camberwell Road, heading for the Elephant and Castle. In both areas the tall buildings flanking the road were now empty shells with infernos raging inside, all of them about to collapse, just as we'd seen in the East End. Then came the sound of approaching fire engines, the drivers' mates seizing their chance to clang their bells like the very devil, no doubt fufilling boyhood dreams. Soon there were fire engines everywhere. Men were jumping down into the road, rehearsed and efficient, know-ing exactly what to do. Hose ends were clicked into water

mains and powerful jets of water were soon streaking sky-
wards, directed at the top of buildings. The higher the jets
went, the more the wind caught them and spread a fine
spray over the entire area, soaking everyone: but no one
noticed, let alone cared.

Dad ordered me back to the Works to get cracking with
the tea. Margaret was already pouring it and I was soon
staggering out on to Lomond Grove with a huge tray of
mugs. I wasn't at all sure who I was supposed to offer them
to, but I needn't have worried. I'd hardly gone any distance
before they'd all been seized upon, people helping themselves as though it was a cocktail party and I was one of the
flunkies; and for the rest of the night that's all I did. I kept
going in and out, in and out, with Margaret replenishing the
mugs. Miraculously, we accumulated more mugs, not lost
our original ones as I'd feared. How that happened I'll never
know, nor how far afield I went. Well down the Peckham
Road and halfway to the Elephant, I should think – such a
distance that by the time I'd been relieved of my last mugs,
the tea must have been stone cold. Not that anyone minded. Some firemen drank so many cups that I got to know
them quite well. All of them had a cheery word for me and
as soon as they'd scoffed their tea, straight back in they
went, heedless of the dangers.

My main area was around the Green. That made me
smile. The last time I'd been there, the old pros had been
dotted about the place, praying for a bit of action. Now, the
only one to be seen was the best known of them all, a classy,
well-bred ex-actress who'd fallen on hard times, known to
everyone as Ten Bob Tina. She spent the whole night
wandering the streets in her dressing gown, looking for
Romeo, her randy old ginger tom who everyone else said
should have been called Casanova. As she roamed, she
clashed together Romeo's feeding bowl and a saucepan lid,
hoping he'd think it was feeding time.

I kept bumping into her, even though she never had any
tea off me. At about three o'clock in the morning, I was at

the Elephant end of the Grove. Things were pretty tense. A couple of houses had just collapsed in Bowyer Place and it was still unknown if anyone was trapped. Several firemen, who'd been driven back by the smoke and flames, were recovering from their efforts. Between their coughing and spluttering, they were helping themselves off my tray. Then we all looked around as we heard Ten Bob Tina approaching. At the far end of the Grove, she was tip-toeing daintily through the debris and hoses, trying to keep her feet dry, and she now had an umbrella up, seeking protection from the spray. To cap it all, every ten yards or so she clashed the feeding bowl and saucepan lid together and called out for Romeo. When she got right up to us, she surveyed us pleadingly and asked: "Have any of you gentlemen seen my pussy?"

The firemen regarded her sympathetically and murmured in the negative. Then, from directly above us, through a broken window, a mature female voice, reminiscent of aggregate sliding from a tip-up truck, yelled down: "Christ all bloody mighty, Ten Bob. Every young Prick in Camberwell has seen your pussy, but yer don't expect them to admit it, do yer?"

One fireman was so amused that his tea went down the wrong way and came spurting back out in an unsightly mess. Ten Bob straightened herself, raised her chin in contempt, and strode off with all the dignity she could muster. She clashed her cymbals together harder than ever and, with the clarity of Edith Evans, she called out: "Romeo! Romeo!"

However, the old biddy above us had the last word. She let out a bellow that soared above all the noises of war: "For Christ's sake, Romeo! Wherefore fucking art thou?"

At an early stage, the Green was established as the field headquarters of the fire brigades, with everyone rushing around, giving and receiving orders. Buildings were collapsing all the time and the firemen were uncanny in the way they knew exactly when it was going to happen. People invariably got clear in time, but the great heaps of rubble that cascaded down into the road ripped many of the hoses to pieces and put rescue work back hours.

Twice, I came across Dad. The first time he was a few rungs up a fire ladder wearing a fireman's brass helmet which was about three sized too big for him. It was just as well he had a good pair of ears or he wouldn't have seen a thing. He was soaking wet, as though he'd been on the receiving end of one of the jets, and through his shirt his muscles bulged like knotted ropes. He took a mug of tea off me and winked broadly. "Keep going. You're doing a great job, Gunga Din!"

Others in the area heard and the name stuck. Soon, wherever I appeared I was greeted with, "Here comes Gunga

Din!" Once, on the Green, a bloke dressed up like a general, with a silver helmet instead of a brass one, shouted at me: "Hi, you! Gunga Din! More tea for that old lady over there. The one on the curb...Wearing a straw boater..."

On the second occasion I bumped into Dad he was back in the office. Charlie Smith was with him, looking very pale. He had an absurdly small tin hat on and the skin around his temples was so wet and translucent that I half expected to see his brain ticking over inside. Dad was pleading with him. "Come on, Charlie...Someone's got to do it. There's a whole family down there, somewhere. We can hear them. And you're the skinniest bloke south of the Thames, you know that..."

"But what about the building, Guvner? Could it collapse?"

"It could... Of course it bloody could..."

"Then what would happen to me?"

"Same as'll happen to the others if you don't go down. Charlie, you're our only hope, but you don't have to..."

"I'll have a go, Guvner... You know that. But I'm allowed to be frightened, aren't I?"

"Good lad, Charlie. Let's get down there quick."

By the end of the night, Charlie Smith, the skinniest man south of the Thames, had established himself as the local ferret, expert at squeezing through tiny gaps and into buildings or basements where people were thought to be trapped. He went in on the end of a rope, with a Woolworth's Everready torch clutched in one hand, and on his say-so the strategy of rescue was based.

Dawn came very quickly. Suddenly, there was an uncanny, spooky stillness. As light spread, a mantle of muck and slime was seen to be covering everything. People were walking about like chalky ghosts, their hair in rat's tails, rivulets streaking their faces. There was a cocktail of smells, high explosives mingling with mortar dust and charred timber. Somehow, daylight made the damage seem less, the fires smaller, the leaking water on an ebb tide. The only trouble was that a chorus of sirens sounded again: the Krauts were back. This time, instead of the ack-ack blazing away, a squadron of Spits screamed out of a Japanese-style morn and saw the bastards off with no trouble: cut them to pieces. We cheered and shouted as four of the Krauts plunged earthward. Then we heard and felt the explosions as they impacted on some poor devils and our shouting died away.

By this time Margaret was nearly out of tea and although she had been at it all night she looked highly elated. Dad brought several of his workers into the office to shelter from the bombing. Their clothing was torn and many were bleeding or bandaged. Charlie Smith had a long, shallow gash across his forehead. His lifeline rope was coiled over his shoulder and his torch was tucked into his belt. I'd never seen such a filthy, wet and weary lot: exhausted, contented, and proud: 'And peace of mind, all passion spent.'

As I took my final tray of teas into the office, they cheered me and Old Percy led them in a poorly rehearsed chorus Dad had put them up to:

"Din, Din Din!
Where the bloody hell yer bin?
They've bombed yer and sprayed yer,
But by our old Guv who made yer,
Yer a better man than them Krauts are,
Gunga Din!"

I sat down. It was a great moment.

For a time there was silence. Then Dad went round splashing great slurps of brandy into their mugs of tea and gradually they reverted to type and began to laugh and joke about the night, relating the funnier incidents, invariably starting: "'Ere, I'll tell yer wot..."

Dad came up with the best story.

"I was halfway up this ladder, holding the hose, when all of a sudden another ladder goes up right beside me. And when a bloke gets level with me I can see he's come up from Bournemouth with the South Hants Brigade. He looked at me quizzically and then asked: 'Where you from, mate?' So I waggled my head and rolled my eyes and replied: 'From India.' 'Bloody hell,' he said. 'Your lot got here quick.'"

Later in the morning things got back to what passed for normal, with men retreading tyres and making batteries. On and off, Dad kept trying the telephone. When the lines were eventually restored, I heard him say: "Yes, dear... Yes, dear.... Nothing much, dear... Just a few stray bombs... No, honestly, he's fine... Slept like a log..."

When Dad put the receiver down I knew I was about to be sent home. "It's no good arguing," he said. "You should never have been here in the first place. And when you get home, play it down. Keep your imagination in check."

It seemed to escape Dad's notice that I was soaked to the skin and as filthy as the rest of them. My trousers were torn, my socks around my ankles like soggy dishcloths, and whenever I walked anywhere my shoes squelched, left wet footprints, and I must have looked as though I'd wet myself. About the only good thing was that my pockets were stuffed with really wicked pieces of shrapnel which would make me a fortune when I got back to my pals at Caterham.

Mum wasn't fooled, of course. She met me off the Green Line, marched me back home, yanked the clothes off my back, and dumped me in a hot bath. Her diatribe about Dad as she threw away my shrapnel was quite unprintable. As Dad had suggested, I denied everything but she didn't believe a word.

For the rest of the morning I felt very strange. Indoors, Mum was in one of her impossible moods, dashing from one piece of furniture to another and yelling at the unfortunate Rose. Outside, it was a gloriously hot day. Everything was peaceful. The only sounds were chirping birds and droning tractors. I felt completely disorientated. The events of the night were in constant replay in my mind, which made the tranquillity of the countryside false and hollow, as though I had been dumped in a vacuous dream.

I mooched about with Lucky at my heels, wondering what to do, trying to visualise how Charlie Smith was and how the men were getting on with their normal jobs. I looked around for James and Brother Nothing, but they were somewhere in the woods, pinging away with their bows and arrows. I wandered across the road, hoping for a chat with Corp, but he was dallying with some girl I'd never seen before and so intent on work in progress that I realised it would be best to call back later.

I went over to the vegetable garden and found Gran and Muckey hard at work, digging up potatoes. They were pleased to see me but they were so busy that they just waved and carried on with their labours, Muckey forking the spuds from the ground and Gran carrying them to the potting shed, using a large wicker basket on the top of her head, Indian style. I hung around watching them until lunch time and then joined them for curry in the potting shed. I told them everything, of course, especially Dad's joke and how Charlie kept going down into the rubble through little openings, contacting people who were trapped. I also told them how I'd been nicknamed Gunga Din and all the hundreds of mugs of tea I'd taken round. They listened to every word, but eventually Muckey delved into his haver-sack and produced a *Daily Express*. The headline was 'Now South London Gets it!', and a picture showed smoke billowing around the Elephant and Castle.

No wonder Mum hadn't believed a word I'd said. When I went back in the house I tried to justify my lies by telling her that all I'd done was take mugs of tea around. "And who did the washing up?" she asked calmly.

"Washing up? No one did any washing up. We just refilled the mugs with tea and took them out again."

"Well I really don't know," sighed Mum. "Anyone would think that you were dragged up in the gutter."

I was beginning to wish I had been.

That afternoon, whilst having our usual formal tea, I really put my foot in it. Apart from James telling us how many pieces of bread and butter there were each, how many scones each, and how many fairy cakes each, no one said a word. No doubt their minds were total blanks. In contrast mine was working overtime, re-enacting events of the night. Suddenly, as I recalled that moment when I went back into the office with the final tray of teas, I blurted out:

"Din, Din, Din,
Where the bloody hell yer bin..."

I could have kicked myself, really bitten my tongue off.

The way Mum reacted you'd have thought that I'd gobbed into the tea pot. I was sent to bed in disgrace and after I'd been left to stew for an hour or so Mum – who was familiar with Kipling – came up and lectured me on what an insult it was to let anyone (particularly ignorant working people from London) call me Gunga Din. I didn't dare tell her it was Dad who'd started it. Nor, at the time, did I have the knowledge to realise that whilst Mum might know the words of Kipling's famous poem, Dad understood them. Now, looking back over the years, of all the names I've been called (and there have been plenty!) none gives me greater pride than Gunga Din.

Whenever Dad came home I'd ride down to meet him off the Green Line. He'd tell me of everything that had been happening: how the raids were continuing and how most people were now heading for shelter in the tube stations. I always asked him one particular question: "How's Charlie?"

Dad said he was doing wonders. He stood by for rescue work all night and every night. They'd already lost count of the number he'd saved. "Why are you so concerned about Charlie?"

"Just wondered, Dad..."

"Come on, Sajit. Tell me why?"

"Because of his name... The Krauts are bound to write Charlie Smith on a bomb."

Dad sighed with disappointment. "I thought you'd grown up a bit. They don't really do that... It's just a saying..."

I knew that. Of course I knew that, but how could I tell Dad that I'd had a premonition about Charlie?

The moment I'd been dreading came soon enough. I met Dad at Anglefield Corner and as we walked back up the lane, he was full of the latest German losses. Going through the gate, between Gog and Magog, he said: "Better come into the study... I've something to tell you."

I listened attentively but I already knew that Charlie was dead. The most ghastly thing was how he died, something Dad wouldn't tell me, but which I found out later. A daylight raid was on and he'd gone back to the lead reclamation shop to turn off the gas beneath the two vats of molten lead. A bomb then went through the roof of the building next door to the Works. The blast threw Charlie to the ground, unconscious. It also overturned the two vats of molten lead. The lead flowed all over Charlie.

After the raid, when they were clearing up the mess, no one could account for Charlie. The last place they thought of looking was in the middle of a huge slab of lead which had solidified on the floor. That's where he was, though.

I went to Charlie's funeral, together with Dad, all Charlie's work-mates, and his mother. She was drunk again but only her friends realised. The others thought she was being supported because of her grief. Dad had a beautiful headstone erected over Charlie's grave. It read:

RIP

CHARLIE SMITH
(1920—1940)

Charlie was a Londoner,
Loyal through and through.
But to him came no honours
As were lavished on The Few.
Into fickle bomb wreckage
On his own volition he crawled,
Pulling out survivors, his
Back bleeding as if keelhauled.
He betrayed his fear to no one,
Nor protested as he strove:

<u>Charlie Smith</u>
<u>'Spirit of London'</u>
<u>Né The Works at Lomond Grove.</u>

The headstone stood there at the Old Camberwell Municipal Cemetery until September 7th 1990, on which auspicious date vandals took a sledge hammer to it. On the 60th anniversary of the Blitz, I tried to reinstate it, but the local authority refused permission. I was informed that, in view of the current European political climate of peace and reconciliation, it was inappropriate.

18

The trauma of Charlie's death – Test Matches against
Australia – Alf Gover causes chaos – Mum draws the line –
I see a 'special' doctor – Caterham is ruled out –
A long winter – Farewell to Corp.

Few things have affected me more in life than Charlie
Smith's death. It was the waiting, knowing that he
was about to die, that was so appalling. How did I
know? Was it just a guess? Had my subconscious merely
linked two names and a feeble joke? Or was I cursed by
some mystical power? Had my overdeveloped imagination
elevated me to the ranks of the clairvoyants?

More than anything, I felt humility. I knew how
frightened Charlie had been. As Dad had told him, he was
under no obligation to risk his life, not even once, let along
countless times. Yet he sought no credit or acclaim: there
were no newspaper articles about him, or local dignitaries
putting his name forward for decorations. He just did what
needed to be done. He didn't asked for time off work in
which to recover, nor was there any talk of traumatic experiences. It was at his funeral that I discovered the details of
his death and it haunted me. How did they get him out: chip
him out, or melt the lead?

*****

It was with these thoughts pulsing through my mind that I wandered Silver Coombe. Mostly, I tagged along with Gran and Muckey. They were highly sympathetic and insisted that the best thing was for me to help them, to do something useful, but before long I realised I was getting in the way, a nuisance. I went in search of James and Brother Nothing and when they showed no sympathy and told me to shove off, I went to Corp instead. He helped a lot. He was a good friend. He made me laugh, but as often as not, just as I was about to get back to something approaching normal, one of his girlfriends would come round. He never pushed me off like my brothers did, but eventually I became so aware of the girl's impatience that I made an excuse and wandered off.

Mum showed the least understanding. She got really ratty. "You're like a bloody lost soul," she shouted. "You've got to pull yourself together, Boyo." Then one day she exploded: "I've had enough of this. Get out from under my feet. For God's sake get that cricket ball of yours and go and throw it up and down the lawn."

So that's what I did. I practised my bowling and it helped a lot. Once I'd got into the swing of things, with the ball turning this way and that, I soon felt the need to test my skills against the great players I'd read about. In the end I took things to the ultimate and transposed myself to Australia for a five Test Match series.

After listening to Eddie's tales of Australia at Caterham School, I was fascinated by his homeland, especially the vastness of it and the paucity of the population. He had made Australians seem like a breed apart, as though we, the British, had spawned a race we would have loved to have been. I visualised their cricket grounds as entirely different to ours: far, far away from dreary, rain-stopped-play suburbs; completely divorced from honking buses, clanking trams, and smelly gas works. To me, Aussie cricket grounds were vast arenas, stuck in the back-of-the-beyond, packed to suffocation with leather-faced bastards in cork-bespan-

Gran and Mr Muckey

gled bush hats and worn-out shorts; men in boots without socks, with oak-tree legs scarred by snake bites; men who appeared from God-knows where, having set off on walkabout weeks before, leaving notes for their Sheilas pinned to the fly-screen doors of their corrugated iron shacks: 'Gone to watch The Don!'

As I prepared to open the bowling for England on the first day of the second Test at Sydney, I looked around me, up the long slope of the Hill. I saw nearly 50,000 bastards shoulder to shoulder, all of them yelling and cursing, swaying forward towards the playing area, threatening to overpower the wooden pickets as they bayed for English blood; and all the time the naked sun beat down on them, not an inch of shade in the whole ground.

Most days I stayed on the tennis court from after breakfast until Dad came home, by which time it was usually getting dark. I only broke off when Mum called me in for meals. I gave the others full reports on what had happened and how many wickets I'd taken. When I'd done this before I'd been treated with contempt, but now there was a subtle difference in their attitude. My brothers egged me on and they were full of sniggers, sidelong glances, and snide remarks, such as: "And what did Jack Hobbs have to say about that?" Mum was just as bad. She rarely said anything but the fact that she never stopped them was tantamount to blatant encouragement.

It was one of the best-known English players, Alf Gover, who brought it all to an abrupt and unhappy end.

*(A word of explanation. For those sketchy on cricket history, Alf Gover played for Surrey and England and then ran a world-famous indoor cricket school above a garage in Wandsworth. Alf was a fast bowler and during his career he had more '**ever-known**' accolades tagged to his name than any other player. His run-up was the longest **ever-known**. His bowling action was the wildest **ever-known**. He was the*

*most natural number eleven batsman **ever-known**. He was the most non-bending Test Match fielder **ever-known**. Also, he was the only player **ever-known** to bring a first-class match to a halt and cause a riot single-handed.* I only mention the uniqueness of Alf to illustrate that it was predictable that he should prove instrumental in my downfall. Here endeth the explanation.)*

As captain of England I only ever used Alf in short bursts, usually one over at a time. In the Test Match in question, I gave Alf the ball for the first time when Australia were 595 for 9 in their second innings with two runs needed for victory. Tiger O'Reilly, their number 11 batsman, was 3 not out and facing. At the other end, Don Bradman was 295 not out and looking pretty settled. As Alf started off towards the distant sight screen to start his run-up, I said to him: "Gover (he was a professional, of course), what England expects is the fastest ball **ever-known**. And you're just the man for that."

Thus inspired by his skipper's confidence, and with a glint of desperation in his eyes after four days of pounding the fine-leg and third-man boundaries, Alf stomped back for his run-up, going further back than **ever-known**. When he reappeared from behind the sight screen he was galloping like a stag, and when he reached his delivery stride he let out a cry of excruciating effort which would have done justice to the Dervish whose spear pinned General Gordon to the door of the High Commissioners Residence in Khartoum.

The result was the fastest and highest overhead wide **ever known**. Alf had done it again. Even at Melbourne and Kennington Oval it would have soared over the fine-leg boundary for six wides. At Silver Coombe it streaked over the tennis court wire netting, did a meteoric flash across the drive, and went straight through the kitchen window.

---

*The full story is told in 'The Long Run', Alf's autobiography.

Gran and Mr Muckey

The initial CRASH!, the noise of splintering glass, and the human cries of terror, were horrendous. It was as though a German bomb had just scored a direct hit. I was back from Australia in a trice. Before you could say Mahatma Gandhi I was standing in the drive, staring through the broken window. The sight I beheld made me marvel at the destructive capabilities of a high-velocity 4¾ ounce cricket ball.

It was sheer bad luck that Mum, Rose and James were in the kitchen at the time. Rose was preparing a beef casserole. Mum was adding the final touches to a work of art, squirting little cream blobs on to a sherry trifle. James was sitting around, licking discarded mixing bowls. On the central table was nearly a week's food rations. The whole lot was speared by glass. Rose, Mum, and James were cut. All of them were bleeding profusely. All were hysterical, rushing around in circles, aimlessly. Rose was the first to become *compos mentis* again. She resigned on the spot. Still bleeding and crying in pretty equal volumes, she ran from the house, jumped on her bike, and raced home, never to be seen again.

Mum, with her wounds untended, blood still flowing freely, frog-marched me to my bedroom. More than that, she locked the door on me, as though I was some kind of maniac. I didn't even know she had a key, but she did, obviously kept for just such an eventuality. I quite expected her to telephone the police or call Whitehall 1212. Instead, she turned to Brother Nothing, who by this time was loitering with delight. "Stay outside his door and make sure he doesn't escape."

Half an hour later I squinted through the key hole. There was old Nothing parading up and down the landing like a Nazi stormtrooper at Stalag Luft III, his Daisy air rifle at the high port, cocked and ready for action. What a prat!

Four days before the Autumn term at Caterham, Dad told me I wouldn't be returning there. I was devastated. What about Charlie Kicks and my other friends? Worse still, what

259

about Miss Openside? When I asked Dad why, he said it was because I needed to see a doctor in London, a special doctor, the type who would chat to me and discuss things, not pull and prod me about.

I may have only have been a youngster, but I realised that taking me to see a 'special' doctor was tantamount to declaring me soft in the head. I knew it wasn't Dad. It was Mum. After the Alf Gover full toss she thought I was one wicket short of a hat-trick. Yet there was a lot more to her vindictiveness than that one incident. Whatever I did she despised. There was my relationship with Gran and Muckey, the way I called myself a 'Don R' with the Home Guard, glorying in being Gunga Din at Camberwell, the stories I told the other kids at Caterham, my obsession that one day I'd be a novelist, and – always lurking in the back-ground – her resentment that I was a boy and not a girl.

Dad told me it was no use arguing. Mum had already written to SOD telling him that I wouldn't be returning to Caterham Prep School. During the next day or so Mum came over all smarmy and tried to minimise her treachery by telling me that the doctor had his clinic in Harley Street. This piece of geographic information was supposed to send me into ecstasies of delight.

"Sajit is going to see a doctor in Harley Street," she told my brothers. "And not many young boys can claim that."

"And not many young boys can claim to have gone round the twist," observed Brother Nothing.

The day after James and Brother Nothing went back to Caterham, I was dressed up in my best suit – a prickly utility monstrosity that was like wearing cardboard – and Mum took me by Green Line to Victoria and then by taxi to Harley Street. The psychoanalyst turned out to be a very friendly gentleman. He insisted on calling me, "Sajit, old chap," and the first thing he did was to interrupt Mum and tell her to go back into the waiting room and wait. "Probably for rather a long time, Madam," he added with heavy emphasis. She didn't like that a bit and resumed volunteering what she considered to be vital information about my failings, but the psychoanalyst reversed her out until she disappeared behind the door, her voice finally trailing away.

"Now then, Sajit, old chap. Peace and quiet at last. I understand you enjoy cricket?"

That was a promising start. At a stroke it demolished all the defensive positions I'd dreamed up in my mind over the past few days. In fact, Doc and I were soon enjoying a lovely conversation. It turned out that he was a member of the MCC and knew far more about cricket than I ever did, or was ever likely to. His information came from playing for Oxford University for three season. Since my knowledge came from cigarette cards I felt pretty humble.

We soon got to the crux of the matter: my imagination. We went through some of the points Mum had already mentioned. I also told him several other things no one else knew anything about. How, when I'd introduced Gran to Muckey, I'd suddenly seen them in their prime. I also made no secret of of my premonition about Charlie Smith being killed in the blitz.

Of course, I was putty in his hands. He soon knew everything there was to know about me. Not that it mattered. Indeed, it was the best thing that could have happened. Many years later, when I was going through Dad's effects, I came across his report. It said, in essence, that I was lonely. That although it was unusual for a boy of my age, with two brothers, to have imaginary friends, my cricketers were different in that they were an integral part of imagined events. Other incidents of odd behaviour he put down to my worries about the lack of harmony in the family, especially the clash between Dad's thirst for adventure and Mum's fanatical desire for domestic perfection. This ever-present chasm left me in a void which – due to a lack of sympathy and understanding from my brothers – I sought to escape by inventing a world of my own.

What caught my eye in particular was the paragraph: 'Sajit's ambition to become a writer might seem outrageous at the moment, but it should neither be encouraged nor discouraged. Let him float to the surface on his own.'

His conclusion was that I needed to escape the conflicts at home and enjoy an environment which embraced my personal interests, a school where my capabilities could be expanded in a competitive atmosphere among boys of my own age. 'I can think of no place more suited to Sajit's requirements,' his report ended, 'than Hillhead Prep School run by Geoffrey Steele with the aid of George Warbutt, an old friend of mine. Sajit needs to be a full-time boarder and, since the school is situated on the very edge of Exmoor, this would be essential anyhow'.

I had to wait until the start of the summer term before Hillhead could take me. During the interval three tutors came and went in quick succession. None of them contributed anything to my education. However, they kept me quiet and out of Mum's way, which was all she required of them. Dad was far too busy working by day, and fighting the Blitz by night, to become involved.

Yet that six month period was far from wasted. At every available opportunity I fled my tutors and sought out Gran and Muckey, and thanks to them I learnt basic country skills which have stayed with me ever since. They taught me to embrace nature and flow with it, never resist it. They told me when to plant things and how to promulgate seedlings, when to transplant and which plants need to go in the greenhouse. Muckey taught me how to outfox foxes when it came to breaking into chicken runs. He took me out ferreting and showed me how to kill rabbits humanly by whacking them on the back of their necks, directly behind the ears; how to skin them and gut them and then preserve their pelts. He also passed on the skill of tracking down pheasants by observing their droppings and then setting traps which killed them instantly.

John Hollands

Gran was an expert at pruning and grafting. When it came to thatching, Gran and Muckey had different methods, just as they did with wattling and hedge-making. Using Muckey's traditional English method of splitting young branches and then bending them and interlacing them as though plaiting hair, the three of us made a beautiful hedge where the woods bordered the lane. It's still there today.

We worked on that hedge through one of the coldest January spells on record, wearing mittens, never gloves, and it was then, more than at any other time, that I was able to observe the curious relationship between Gran and Muckey. They were slow, plodding workers and all the time they watched each other surreptitiously, eager to go over to help the other one with tricky bits, and then they loved to stand back and admire their joint efforts. After a pause Gran would take his hands in hers and blow on his fingers to warm them and old Muckey's ears would betray the broadest of smiles.

When we broke off for lunch and returned to the potting shed, Muckey lit his paraffin heater and while he and I huddled over it, trying to thaw out, Gran – who must have felt the cold far more than either of us – hurried off to fetch huge helpings of curry. They warmed us up far more than any paraffin heater.

I continued to make trips across the road to Corp. Despite the weather, his girls turned up as regularly as ever and I got to know most of them well. I couldn't understand why they demeaned themselves by being shared around, especially since Corp's tent offered no comforts and he certainly held out no prospects for the future. What I was too young to grasp was that his activities merely affirmed the two prime stimulants of human nature: the in-built, God-inspired yearning to copulate and the insatiable desire for more of the same when that lust is more than adequately satisfied by a master-craftsman – a combination which

Gran and Mr Muckey

(God knows!) has brought down saints, governments, kings, queens, emperors, generals and admirals, to say nothing of Corp.

I include Corp in such an illustrious line-up because one day, without warning, the same huge RAF lorry that delivered the balloon reappeared to remove it. Corp went with it. When he said good-bye to Mum he said it was all a matter of re-deployment, but when I took him around to see Muckey he told a different story, the truth. A couple of days before an officer and a squad of WAAFs had arrived to lower the balloon and overhaul the winching machine, and instead of finding Corp waiting to assist, as per written orders, they caught him red-handed bouncing up and down on his air beds with one of the land girls.

Muckey listened with scant sympathy. "The buggers never caught me. In the Sudan we pulled the bints up the walls of the fort in wicker baskets. We had a pulley system. As one used bint went down, a fresh bint came up. The bloody officers thought it was our laundry... So the buggers never caught us..."

"I'll bet they didn't, my old mate," rejoined Corp. "But don't get too cocky about it. From what I hear, you're not out of the wood yet... So keep your wits about you..."

"Cheeky young bugger," said Muckey as Corp swaggered off.

Despite Corp's unquenchable good spirits, I felt guilty. If I'd stuck to my duties as KV man he would never have been caught. Corp would have none of it. As I saw him off, shaking hands with him warmly through the passenger's window, he merely asked me to explain to his girls that he'd gone to get his knees brown. He then thanked me for my help and assured me that one day he would show his gratitude in a fitting manner.

As you already know, he did.

265

19

The Hillhead clothing list – My Montague Odd cricket bat –
A new method of oiling – Racism in Knightsbridge –
Humiliation at Harrods – My bat causes concern.

Our first indication that Hillhead was going to be
something special came when the school clothing
list arrived. As Mum read it, her expression changed
as though she was a new type of chameleon. First there was
great pride, with a beaming smile. Then there was concern,
with a tight frown. Next there was anxiety and she chewed
her lip. Finally there was outright desperation and she
savaged her scalp as a hot flush took control.

I was delighted. Leaving Caterham and never seeing my
friends and Miss Openside again was all her doing, so I
considered it only right that she should have her share of
troubles. The list stipulated that everything had to be
purchased from the Harrods School Clothing Department
where a Hillhead 'bay' was maintained. This was what
infuriated Mum. She hated Harrods. More accurately she
was in fear of the place and had refused to go near it for
years. What made matters worse was that the clothing list
threatened to use up the whole family's clothing coupons for
the rest of the year. Also, the list went far beyond mere
clothes. She had to produce a fully stocked tuck box, a
saddle, a riding crop, Cotton Oxford rugby boots, black

266

rugby socks (only to be worn when awarded colours), and cricket clothing and equipment. This included a Montague Odd cricket bat, the only item not available at Harrods.

The extent of the cricket equipment struck me as very promising. Even Dad's concern over the Montague Odd bat was solved when he discovered that Mr Odd had a retail shop at London Bridge Station. Mr Odd lived up to his name. When Dad walked into his shop and asked for a cricket bat for his son, Mr Odd didn't even ask how old I was. There was no mention of size, weight, long-handle, or short-handle. He just went over to his enormous rack of new bats and picked out the most expensive. It was a full-size, long-handled monster, one of his *Frank Woolley Anti-Yorker Specials*.

It was no doubt an excellent bat, but only in the right hands, and I later discovered that the only other bats he'd ever sold in the edition were to Big Jim Smith of Middlesex and Arthur Wellard of Somerset, both renowned sloggers of huge sixes and men of immense size and strength.

Mr Odd obviously saw Dad coming. Why else had he sold him such a bat and then have the gall to add a gallon of linseed oil to go with it?

Mum insisted that the bat should be my Christmas present. I thought that was a rotten trick, about as mean as any mother could get. After all, it was part of my official school equipment. It also meant that the first I saw of it was when it was unwrapped. I pointed out to Dad as politely as I could that it was far too big, but by that time he'd lost the receipt, so there was no question of taking it back for a refund or exchange. Dad said I'd just have to grow into it, the same as I did with Brother Nothing's and James's cast-off clothing. I suppose to him an oversized cricket bat was no more ridiculous than shirt-tails which reached down to below my knees.

When I asked him if Mr Odd had given him any instructions about oiling the bat, he laughed. "Oiling instructions,

Sajit? What do you think I am? Why do you think I bought a gallon of linseed oil?"

That was precisely what I'd been wondering. A gallon of linseed oil was enough to keep the entire County Cricket Championship going for a couple of years.

The oiling took place in the generating shed. Dad had every-thing lined up as though for a surgical operation. There was a vice, a claw hammer, a six inch nail, and an umbrella stand. He told me to stand well back. He then secured the bat in the vice and proceeded to hammer the six inch nail into the blade of the bat. I cried out in alarm. "Dad, what are you doing?"

"We have to make sure the oil soaks well in," he explained, banging the nail in for the second time.

"But surely, Dad..."

"Just stand back and watch, Sajit..."

In all, he banged the six inch nail into the blade a dozen times. I counted as he went along, praying that each one would be the last. Every blow emphasised his ignorance, but how could I tell Dad that? Then he solved what was, to me, the biggest mystery of all: the purpose of the umbrella stand. He stood it on the bench and then placed the bat in the metal container designed to collect drips from umbrel-las. He marked the container just below the level of the bat's splice. "Never oil the splice," he said, getting at least one thing right. Next, he opened the gallon can of oil and poured it into the container up to his Plimsoll line. Then he stood the bat in it. "Right. Now we leave it."

"How long for, Dad?"

"Until you go to Hillhead."

"But that's another three months..."

"Right... That should be long enough."

The worst part about my preparations for Hillhead was our visit to Knightbridge and Harrods. It was the clearest case I'd yet experienced of clandestine racism. Oddly, I'd never

Gran and Mr Muckey

minded racism so long as it was open and frank. I took our treatment as evacuees in my stride and being called an Indibum by my classmates never bothered me. However, what we encountered in Knightsbridge and Harrods was unnerving. It was malicious. It amounted to snide glances, with eyes flashing between Mum and myself, voicing the query, 'What's that white woman doing with that young wog? Surely she's not his mother?' Everywhere we went the crowds drew back with distaste. Massed ranks of advancing pedestrians kept parting miraculously, in much the same way as the Red Sea must have parted for Moses.

It obviously wasn't a new experience to Mum and I soon realised it was the reason why she hated going to the posher parts of London. She dreaded Harrods most of all, and with good reason. During Christmas 1933 she'd taken Brother Nothing to see Harrods's famous Santa Claus Grotto. The crowds were shoulder to shoulder and as Mum led the way through the various departments they happened to come across Bathroom Fitments. Mum was so over-whelmed by the splendour of it all that she couldn't resist lingering, wandering around as though in a dream as she examined the displays of baths, wash basins, and toilets, all with glittering gold-plated handles and taps. When she eventually tore herself away, she couldn't find Brother Nothing anywhere. She was just on the verge of panicking when she caught a glimpse of him through a pack of top-nob people bristling with mink coats and bowler hats and festooned with gift-wrapped parcels. He was sitting on her favourite avocado-shade toilet.

"Charles, get off that toilet at once," she called out, making heads turn to follow her gaze towards Brother Nothing.

"Just a minute, Mum..."

"Never mind just a minute. Do as you're told. Now!"

"I can't, Mum. I haven't finished yet."

*****

John Hollands

With that humiliating experience still fresh in her mind, Mum scurried through Harrods to the Schools Clothing Department as though we were criminals. When we got to the Hillhead Bay it took us ages to get served and the final ignominy came when Mum ran out of clothing coupons. She even had to spend Gran's, a thing she'd sworn never to do. However, that was Mum's worry. Several days later I had something far more important to worry about. The time had come for me to withdraw my cricket bat from the umbrella stand so that Mum could pack it in the ocean-going trunk she'd bought me. Not surprisingly, the bat dripped linseed oil all over the place. In the shed that didn't matter. The only trouble was that after I'd wiped it down several times it went on dripping. No matter what I did, it oozed linseed oil. I peered into the umbrella stand and was alarmed to see that it was three-quarters empty, way below Dad's Plimsoll line. Assuming linseed oil didn't evaporate, my bat now contained three-quarters of a gallon of linseed oil. I examined it more carefully and there was no doubt that it was much broader and thicker than when laid to rest. It was also three or four times heavier.

I had no idea what to do. I couldn't give it to Mum in its present, dripping, state, yet there was no way I could leave it at home. In the end I hung it from one of the rafters in the shed and told Mum it needed a little more soaking.

When I returned the following morning, there was a large puddle beneath the bat, but nowhere near three-quarters of a gallon — a mere two or three fluid ounces, perhaps. I had no alternative but to wrap it up in old newspapers and persuade Mum to pack it last thing of all. Amazingly, she agreed to this and when she finally slammed the lid down I thought I was home and dry.

20

*Hillhead Prep School – A new philosophy – My trunk
arrives the worse for wear – My first beating – Exploring
Exmoor on horseback – School reports with a difference –
Dad gives his approval.*

My days at Hillhead were among the happiest of my
life. Tragically, the school no longer exists. It was
an educational holiday camp rather than a school.
Everyone was expected to enjoy themselves and the staff
went out of their way to make sure they did. There were
three abiding passions at Hillhead: cricket, rugby, and
horse riding, and such was the expertise with which these
were taught that there were very few pupils who failed to
become proficient in all three.

The school was ideally situated in an old country house
nestling into the hills right on the edge of Exmoor, in the
village of East Anstey. Apart from a Norman Church and the
highest railways station in England (until Dr Beeching got
his axe out), the village was no more than a scattering of
thatched cottages. Yet within a stone's throw, to the north,
beyond Anstey Barrow, the full majesty of the moor
stretched before us, apparently endless, shrouded in
legends and myths, wildlife abounding: red deer were king,
Exmoor ponies the main supporting cast. Kestrels glided
silently among the air currents, watching all with an eagle-

eye. The moor lacked the grandeur and soaring peaks of the Alps, but as the wind swept across the gentle-sloping hills, and whispered and hissed around the wooded valleys, it was easy to understand why R.D.Blackmore had used it as the setting for his masterpiece, Lorna Doone.

Once on Anstey Common a deep purple sheen of heather covered the hills and although, at times, this looked like an endless carpet, the character and topography of the moor changed with dramatic suddenness. Within a mile or two of the school one dropped down into wooded combs and one could explore Dale's Brook, the historic Tarr Steps, which dated back to before Stone Henge, and further to the north the magnificent river courses of the Barle and the Exe.

I remember the summers best. They seemed to be nothing but endless days of sunshine. Although the area was notorious for rain, I only recall banks of nimbus clouds dominating the western horizon like a gathering of indulgent Gods who conspired never to reach us, leaving us to wallow and gambol under blue skies. In autumn and winter my enduring memory is of going down to the stables early in the morning, the dew on the lawns surrounding the house as thick as puddles, the air raw, burning our lungs. Having saddled the horses we clip-clopped down the stone drive to the moor, expectations high, alert to everything, my personal ambition being to find a new hidden valley comparable to that of the Doones. To a young boy there is always such hope.

Mr Steele, the headmaster, was an extraordinary man; the type of free-thinker who in life struggles under a cloud of suspicion but who, when safely dead, is declared to have been light-years ahead of his time. He was an imposing figure, a man in his mid-fifties, over six feet tall and with broad shoulders. He chain smoked and wheezed unhealthily, belying an otherwise sporting image. He ran the school on the principle that life should, as far as possible, be lived outdoors throughout all seasons. If, during lessons, the sun broke through, classes were abandoned. Teachers and pupils alike were so familiar with this dictate that as soon as there was enough blue in the sky to make a petticoat, there was a stampede for the wide open spaces. We never had to wait for permission, or a bell to toll, or a message to be sent round. Desk tops flew open, books were tossed inside, desk tops crashed down again, and it was abandon ship, every boy for himself, the first to the nets pads up.

Naturally, it took me time to adjust to this strange environment. Indeed, for the first two days I was only conscious of the dread of what would be exposed when my trunk was opened. My fellow pupils did their best to make me feel at home and the headboy, Calder, appointed two boys (Hegg and Bullock) to make sure I got to know and understand the school routine and foibles. I was sitting in the common room with my new friends, modelling with Plasticine, when I was called to Mr Steele's study.

It was my idea of a perfect headmaster's study: no learned tomes, no unmarked exercise books, everything devoted to sporting memorabilia. Stumps used in Test Matches were in glass cases, the walls were smothered by team photographs, bats used by famous players were scattered around on special stands, and there were rugby balls which had featured in Calcutta Cup games.

In the middle of it all was my trunk. The lid was open. It was a grisly sight. Everything inside was a bilious yellow. It seemed to be steaming, the way compost heaps steam, and it was exuding a powerful aroma of early season cricket pavilions. My Montague Odd had been removed. It was propped up against Mr Steele's desk. It was so large and ugly it looked more like a bludgeon than a cricket bat. I debated whether or not to tell Mr Steele that a puddle of linseed oil had already formed on his Chinese carpet (which had once adorned W.G. Grace's front parlour). I opted for silence. I was in enough trouble already.

John Hollands

"I suppose you realise the seriousness of your offence?" Mr Steele began.

"Yes, sir."

"Then why did you do it?"

"Don't know, sir."

"Of course you know. Don't be silly. Boys at Hillhead are expected to give sensible answers. Do you understand that?"

"Yes, sir."

"Good. Then give me a sensible explanation. I can't ever recall a boy at Hillhead committing an offence as serious as yours. So why did you do it?"

"Well, sir. I couldn't leave my bat at home. And I thought that if I wrapped it up well in newspapers the oil wouldn't seep through on to my clothes." I was on the verge of tears. All those wasted coupons! Mum would kill me. "I really am sorry I've ruined all my clothes, sir. I didn't mean to."

"Clothes? Never mind your clothes. A pint of bleach and plenty of hot water and Bucket* will soon have them back to normal. I'm talking about your cricket bat. Montague Odd makes the finest bats in the world and you've vandalised yours. You've banged a nail into it 12 times... Haven't you?"

"No, sir. Not me, sir. My Dad did that."

The relief of knowing that my clothes would recover gave me sufficient courage to explain to Mr Steele exactly what had happened and how Dad's actions had nearly broken my heart, how I'd pleaded with him but to no avail. Mr Steele's attitude softened. He'd obviously met some stupid parents in his time, but evidently none to compare with Dad. Eventually, he asked: "Does your father play cricket?"

"No, sir. When he was a boy he was in India. He never got a chance. He was an Untouchable..."

"Yes, well... Hardly surprising... Anyhow, be that as it may... I've a good mind to expel you, Contractor. Even

*Bucket was the matron. It was a nickname with no handle and which everyone, including the boys, used. She was a marvellous little woman with a solution for everything. She'd been at Hillhead for years and was totally devoted to the pupils, a feeling that was fully reciprocated.

though you've only just got here. I see little hope for any boy whose father bangs nails into cricket bats. And did he select your bat?"

"Yes, sir."

"But this is a Frank Woolley edition. Especially made for tall adult players to combat yorkers. Frank Woolley is well over six feet tall...."

"Six feet five and a half inches, sir."

"How do you know that?"

"From my cigarette cards, sir."

"And your father has driven nails into it," repeated Mr Steele, still unable to come to terms with such a crime. "And not just a Gunn and Moore, or a Slazenger, or even a Wisden... Damn it, that bat was a Montague Odd!"

"I did my best to stop him, sir."

"Well good. But understand this from now on, Contractor. Damaging cricket equipment is punishable by expulsion at Hillhead. However, since it wasn't your fault I'll let you off with a warning. But always remember... At Hillhead your cricket bat is your best friend, and it will remain your best friend until you get in the army..."

"Why not then, sir?"

My interruption threw Mr Steele off balance. He looked at me blankly, as though trying to decide whether I was an idiot or whether, in my innocence, I hadn't shattered one of life's basic truths, unmasked a flaw in human philosophy. Eventually he returned to the matter in hand, as though the question of a soldier's best friend was a matter he'd have to take up with the War Office at a later date. "I'll tell you what I'm going to do. I'm going to throw away your damaged bat and get Mr Odd to send down a size six for you."

"Thank you very much, sir."

"Well before you get too thankful, bear in mind that I will be putting it on your bill, together with the postage. We'll see what your father has to say about that."

"Right, sir. Then you're not going to beat me?"

"Beat you? Certainly not. Why should I beat you? This is a school, not borstal. There are only three reasons for beating boys at Hillhead. One is for cowardice on the rugby field. Another is for swearing and using bad language... You don't use bad language do you, Contractor?"

"Oh no, sir. Never."

"Good. I'm glad to hear it." Mr Steele paused to light a new cigarette from the embers of his old one. I was about to ask him if he had any spare cigarette cards, or at least some decent swaps, when he added: "Sit down, Contractor. You're obviously a keen young cricketer. And I understand that after some minor difficulties at home your... doctor... advised that you should come here to be taught how to play the game properly?"

"Something like that, sir."

"And excellent advice. Cricket has all the essential ingredients for a successful, happy and fulfilled life. If everyone played cricket there wouldn't be any aggression in the world. No wars, or bad manners. No swearing or foul language... What are you, a batsman?"

"No, sir. Bowler. A leg-spinner."

"Excellent. And how much do you know about leg-spin?"

"Oh, lots, sir. Tiger O'Reilly is my favourite."

"Indeed. And what do you know about O'Reilly?"

What did I know about Tiger? I nearly burst out laughing. What didn't I know about Tiger. "I've actually seen Tiger O'Reilly bowl, sir. Both at Lord's and the Oval."

"And what did you think of him?"

"Gosh, sir. Marvellous! He's a really cunning bastard."

So I got beaten after all.

It didn't hurt much and I regarded it as penance for spoiling my clothes. Beatings at Hillhead were fairly common but I soon discovered that there was never any desire to inflict pain. They were a matter of principle. That will no doubt be beyond the comprehension of modern educationalists, but to those of us at Hillhead it was perfectly clear and fair and acceptable.

So too was the third reason for beating boys: it was when you were made a monitor. You had to know how to accept the ultimate deterrent before you were considered fit to mete out even the most trivial of punishments. Once again, wholly acceptable.

Hillhead's dedication to sport, and the way we beat allcomers, including the junior colts sides of local public schools, gave rise to a good deal of jealousy among our rivals. They often expressed surprise that Hillhead wasn't investigated by the Ministry of Education, and since it was well known that we did virtually no scholastic work everyone was even more mystified as to how we managed to maintain our 100% success rate in passing the Common Entrance Exam into public schools.

The Ministry of Education probably knew nothing about Hillhead. In those days anyone could (and very often did) set up a school and there were certainly no qualifications demanded of those who taught. The best teacher at Hillhead had no professional qualifications. He was Ginger Warbutt. He was built like a bull but with the disposition of a lamb. He lived with his wife in a country house some miles away, over towards Dulverton, and every day he rode over to Hillhead on his chestnut mare, Clarisa. The story was that he wasn't actually employed by Hillhead but did everything – from coaching cricket and rugby to running the stables – on a voluntary basis. He was so rich he didn't need the money and by refusing payment he retained his independence, an attribute he always impressed upon us.

This independence also solved the problem of Hillhead boys passing the Common Entrance Exam. It enabled Mr Steele to appoint Ginger as our invigilator. Each year about a dozen boys took the exam and there were always one or two who had sufficient natural intelligence to pass it with ease. This gave rise to what Ginger called 'the knock-on effect'. In plain English, cribbing.

The exam was held with boys sitting around a large, pine table and Ginger had no objection to papers being freely circulated, rather in the style of side dishes at a Chinese restaurant. Those in need of assistance simply helped themselves, making the whole thing what these days would be termed a 'group project'. Ginger was dead against sly, over-the-shoulder cribbing. He said it led to inaccuracies. Also, it gave rise to the likelihood of individual papers alternating between high intelligence and utter balderdash, all within a line or two.

There was no danger of outside suspicions being aroused. None of the boys involved was going to say anything and the papers were sent to a wide variety of public schools which never had occasion to compare notes. Nor was Ginger's conscience ever troubled. He believed that the ends justified the means. He felt passionately that to stigmatise dim boys with failure at such an early stage was a shameful waste of talent. He always cited his own case, together with that of Winston Churchill. He would quote great chunks out of *My Early Life* in which Churchill describes how he bamboozled the Harrow examiners with the aid of a senior boy in the sixth form.

As for Ginger, he was one of Hillhead's original pupils and after cribbing his way into Sherborne he enjoyed a brilliant and varied career. At Oxford he won blues at cricket and rugby and, like many varsity sportsmen, did no work at all on the assurance from his tutor that since he (the tutor) set the exam papers, his students would be informed of the questions two weeks in advance, thus giving them ample time to research the answers and gain a good degree. After Oxford, Ginger made a quick fortune on the stock exchange through insider trading (quite legal in those days). His great regret was that due to a spinal injury sustained while playing for the Harlequins, none of the armed forces would avail themselves of his services, hence his presence at Hillhead.

At the start of every term he explained the Hillhead philosophy to new boys. He told us to ignore all previous schools we'd been to and open our minds to a completely new approach. He stressed that prep school education should resist the urge to knock useless knowledge into young minds. Its priority was to open minds, not close them; to awaken each boy to the joy of living; to fill pupils with zest, and make them value and practice consideration and good manners towards others; to embrace personal discipline and to realise that team spirit was the essential foundation of all successful enterprises.

Ginger Warbutt and Mr Steele worked in perfect harmony. Ginger took the more active part in coaching, with Mr Steele standing on the sidelines, making occasional comments, supervising generally, and selecting the teams. Ginger's major contribution, and greatest interest, was organising the riding. He accompanied every expedition on to the moor, but he never took the lead. He liked to hang back on Clarisa and let the bolder riders among us set the pace. It was up to us to seek out new and exciting valleys, streams, and river beds, to lay bare the secrets and mysteries of the moor. When boys fell off, which happened fairly regularly (but never with serious consequences), Ginger refused to get involved. He left it to the other boys to retrieve the loose horse and get their friend remounted.

I came off twice.

The first time was when we were going down a river bed with a canopy of trees overhead and I was so busy talking to my neighbour that a low branch caught me under the chin and nearly took my head off. On the second occasion a deer suddenly darted out in front of my mount, which caused him to dig his forelegs in, skid to a halt, and pitch me over his head into some gorse bushes: very painful.

Other than those incidents I was always among the first to chase after riderless horses and my greatest thrill came from riding down steep embankments towards a river or stream, with my feet thrust hard against the stirrups, braced out ahead of me.

Perhaps a couple of times each term, summer and winter, Mr Steele designated days for 'exploration'. The school was split into small groups and supplied with pack lunches. Then, starting at dawn, groups would be released on to the moor at intervals, heading in different directions, our only orders being to return by dusk. We entered so wholeheartedly into the spirit of things that there was great rivalry as everyone did their best to look the most like Dr Livingstone, right down to baggy khaki shorts, knee-length stockings, safari-style jackets, pith helmets, haversacks, water bottles, military map cases, a good supply of cleft sticks, and cromacks which we had selected, cut and carved ourselves.

Once on the moor, some assumed the mantle of Speke and Burton rather than Livingstone and went in search of the source of either the Barle or the Exe. Local residents at Withypool, Winsford, Exford, and Simonsbath, became accustomed to bedraggled groups of young explorers looking for additional refreshments, and there were even one or two publicans who welcomed us into their premises and treated us to lemonade and home-made meat pies.

Hegg, Bullock and I always went together and one term we caused great excitement. Instead of heading for the hinterland beyond the Barle, we got on to the Exford road and thumbed a lift in an army truck. This took us all the way to County Gate near Malmsmead and from there we followed in the steps of John Ridd, delving into Badgworthy Water, taking in Cloven Rocks and Black Barrow Down. At the end of Badgworthy Water – which we mistook for the Doone Valley – we even came across the remains of an ancient settlement which we were convinced was all that remained of the notorious Doone outlaws.

*****

Gran and Mr Muckey

Ginger Warbutt had been a huntsman from early boyhood and there was hardly a thing he didn't know and understand about the moor and he impressed on us that there was no better method of exploring it than on horseback. That way, other creatures would be far more tolerant towards us, even allow us to intrude upon their territory without taking fright, an advantage never extended to humans on foot. He also taught us how horses thought, behaved and felt, emphasising that they were very individual, especially when it came to a sense of humour. He explained that they could smell fear and how they lost respect for those who were nervous of them. Consequently, we stood no nonsense from them and made them realise that we were leaders in whom they could have complete confidence.

Ginger's favourite tip was to treat our mounts like women: he advised us to talk to them, flatter them, whisper sweet nothings in their ears, stroke them, and – as a final confidence builder – breathe gently up their nostrils. This led to the only occasion when Ginger lost his cool. A boy asked him: "Sir, do you really breathe up your wife's nostrils?"

Whilst every boy loved the school's lifestyle and supported it, we knew this was not always the case with parents. Sometimes, an overzealous father, or an over-anxious mother, would write to Mr Steele to ask why their son still couldn't spell properly, or why young Jimmy's letters home weren't in joined-up writing. We also knew that whatever the complaint, and no matter how reasonable it was, Mr Steele silenced his critics with withering scorn. He would inform the parents concerned that their son had been working flat out and had just completed his 500 runs in May, so they should be overjoyed, not moaning and nit-picking.

A way in which Mr Steele retained the confidence of parents was by taking sole charge of all end-of-term reports. He commented personally on every subject of every pupil. His brevity was masterly and with a string of single words

he allayed all concerns without promising anything specific.
I still have copies of my reports. The one for my second
summer term read:

Geography:	Adequate.
History:	Progressing.
Maths:	Steady.
Science:	Developing.
Latin:	Coping.
Greek:	Promising.
French:	Improving.
Art:	Interested.

Each term Mr Steele simply changed these words
around. At the end of the following year my report read:

Geography:	Steady.
History:	Coping.
Maths:	Adequate.
Science:	Interested.
Latin:	Developing.
Greek:	Improving.
French:	Promising.
Art:	Progressing.

The headmaster's report, traditionally a survey of a boy's
general progress and behaviour, often left parents confused
since the emphasis was always on sport. Once, Mr Steele
wrote of me:

'Last year I wrote that Sajit is the most promising pupil
we've had in years and his 6 wickets for 22 runs against the
Downside Junior Colts, and his 5 wickets for 12 runs
against the Blundell's Junior Colts, fully justifies this opinion.'

Every now and then Mr Steele sprang a surprise and
made scholastic awards which were presented on Speech
Day. The prizes were always cricket books. I won the
Geography Prize in 1943 for knowing the whereabouts of
Old Deer Park, Grace Road, Bramall Lane, Murrayfield,
Broadhalfpenny Down, and Fenners. Amid fervent applause

from the parents, most of whom were convinced that with
an eye for such detail I was destined to become a Fellow of
the Royal Geographical Society, I was presented with 'Ranji'
by Roland Wilde: another thing I still have.

Like all other Hillhead boys I regretted the end of term and
looked forward to the start of the next, yet I also loved the
holidays. It was great to be back at Silver Coombe. Dad
always gave me a wonderful reception. He'd fling his arms
open wide and shout:
    "Din, Din Din!
    Where the bloody hell yer bin?"
and whilst he and I roared with laughter and hugged each
other, Mum rebuked him for using bad and insulting
language. There was something especially comforting and
secure about the whole family sitting around the dining
table for our formal Sunday lunches, with Dad presiding,
Gran using her fingers and her chapatti to shovel Vindaloo
into her mouth, and Lucky at my feet, waiting for a few
titbits which he knew I would drop accidentally on purpose.
    Dad got Muckey to kill a couple of ducks for those
occasions and after the meal he and I retired to his study so
that he could up-date me on the war situation. Whilst he
enjoyed one of his rare cigars, he gave me his latest theories
on how things would develop. He repeated all the gossip
from Lomond Grove: how the bombing was going, which of
his workers had caught a packet and been rehoused, and
how they'd completely rebuilt the formation shop and the
lead reclamation plants. Also, how he helped his men and
their families by taking up eggs and chickens and rabbits to
supplement their meagre rations in exchange for a few
delicacies such as oranges which Old Percy got through a
relative who worked in the Albert Docks. Personal things
too: how Charlie's Mum was still as drunk as a skunk and
how Old Percy and others were continually asking as to
when young Gunga Din would put in another appearance.
    Dad wanted to know all about Hillhead, of course. To
start with I was careful what I said, but eventually he asked:

"But are you enjoying yourself, Sajit?"

"Yes, Dad. Tremendously."

"Good. And are you making plenty of new friends?"

"Yes, Dad. Really good friends."

"Because that's the most important thing."

"We don't do much work, though..."

"Sajit, when will you understand that working hard is not the only way of learning things? Learn through pleasure. And in this life it's who you know, every bit as much as what you know."

Dad was a perfect parent for Hillhead, so I told him all about the marvellous fun we had playing cricket and the thrill of galloping across Exmoor: cavalry charges, eight abreast, just like we'd done in Switzerland, except that this was so much more real; this was in the face of a westerly wind and plunging into wild, untamed country, not trotting along well-defined tourist tracks. I told how – before I'd finished at Hillhead – I was determined to know every nook and cranny of the moor.

Mum didn't change, of course. She would open my trunk and inspect everything in minute detail, holding each item up to the window to search for stains; but in Bucket she'd met her match, and having failed to find anything to criticise she would assert her authority by taking me through her new rules. These threw an interesting light on what had been going on. Bows and arrows had been banned on account of a chimney pot being broken off when Brother Nothing tried to shoot a crow that had perched on one. A piece of the pot had fallen down the chimney, scattered hot coals, and burnt holes in Mum's new Wilton carpet. Also, the use of chemicals was banned. This had to be explained in detail. In order to encourage James's continuing brilliance at school, Dad had once again courted disaster, this time buying him a senior undergraduates chemistry set from Gamages; and during his experiments James had not only produced several loud reports and pungent smells, but also a pestle full of a copper sulphate. Unfortunately, our newly acquired ginger kitten had jumped on to James's bench during the night and sampled the bright blue concoction. The result had been a very unpleasant death. Hence no more chemicals.

James was so upset by the kitten's death that he didn't mention it in his periodic letters to me. Instead he always asked what they'd taught us at science. I didn't dare to tell him that about the nearest we'd got to anything scientific was how to sharpen our sheath knives, although we often visited the local blacksmith to watch the horses being reshod.

Naturally enough, Brother Nothing never wrote to me, and when we met again he was more belligerent than ever. He claimed to be in the Caterham School boxing team: flyweight champion, if you please! He said he'd knocked out six opponents in school matches and that if I made a nuisance of myself during the hols, he'd knock me out as well. I told him to give it a try and he'd soon get a bunch of fives right on the end of his rebuilt Mary Rose.

My greatest joy came from being out and about again with Gran and Muckey. Their friendship was now so well established that even Mum was content to leave them in peace most of the time. Their courtship remained as unconventional as ever. It was as though the meeting of two alien cultures left a no-man's-land that could only be bridged spiritually, never physically. They never went out on dates. They never went for walks. They were never seen hand-in-hand, and they certainly never went near that bastion of most courting couples, the cinema – the back rows at the Electric Cinema, East Grinstead, being the favourite rendezvous of South Godstone and Blindley Heath fumblers and gropers. They didn't even go out for meals. The nearest they got to that was vindaloo in the potting shed.

Come five-thirty every evening, Muckey stamped his boots free of mud, put his top coat on, locked up his potting shed, and shuffled off home. What he did during the

---

evenings and at weekends was a mystery. Somehow, we couldn't imagine him reading or listening to the radio, and he certainly never extended an invitation to Gran to visit him. Mum was of the opinion that he lived in a pigsty and she was always urging Dad to pay a visit to the only pub in South Godstone to see just how many of his beloved Friary's Best Brown he sank every night. Dad always ignored her.

Of course, we never expected Muckey to flaunt passion, or even betray any affection, but his total lack of any social initiative was puzzling, even to me. Furthermore, it set such rigid constraints on their courtship that there seemed little prospect of a satisfactory conclusion. After all, one could court in a cabbage patch, and one could propose in a cabbage patch. At a pinch, one could even consummate a relationship in a cabbage patch, but one certainly couldn't get married in a cabbage patch.

About the only crumb of comfort, and cause for optimism, was Muckey's new tolerance. Originally, he had all but refused to speak to women. He merely cursed them and told them with a singular lack of ambiguity to "Bugger off!" or "Stop spearing around the bloody place." Now, although he still only spoke to Mum grudgingly, he did at least call her 'Mrs Contractor' and he had conceded that she was within her rights to wander the garden at will.

When we gathered around the dining room table with Gran present, Mum's attitude towards the romance fluctuated wildly. Sometimes she would be full of encouragement but then she would suddenly come out with snide remarks, such as, "When I was a young lady we did our courting at the weekends. We used to go out with our young gentlemen every Saturday and Sunday."

Then, one evening, when Mum made this observation with what was becoming sickening regularity, Gran astounded us all by announcing that she had an appointment to go out with Mr Muckey the following Sunday. She volunteered no further details which left us all agog with curiosity. Where would they go? What would they do? Would

Gran and Mr Muckey

Muckey come to collect her? What would he look like in his Sunday Best? Would he still be wearing his gum boots? Would he bother to shave?

At breakfast on Sunday there was no sign of Gran. We assumed she'd slipped off early to meet Muckey at Anglefield Corner, but as Mum pointed out, eight o'clock on a Sunday morning was a very odd time for a date, especially since neither the buses nor the Green Line were yet running. It was only when Dad went out to start the engine of the generator that he discovered what was going on. He came back from the generating shed full of smiles and told us that Gran and Muckey were hard at work in the vegetable garden, pulling up carrots for feeding to the rabbits. My brothers and I dashed upstairs to watch from one of the bedrooms. As I went, I heard Mum say to Dad: "Don't you dare pay that old Grampus overtime... He does his courting at his own expense, not ours..."

Gran's date with Muckey was a great success. They repeated it every Sunday and then it became all-day Saturdays as well. Indeed, they were soon spending so much time together that speculation rose in direct proportion. Mum referred to it as 'The Problem'. One evening I heard her discussing 'The Problem' with Dad. I was in the study with the door ajar and they were in the lounge, Mum knitting away at twenty to the dozen and Dad reading his *Daily Express.*

"I just don't see where it will all end," declared Mum. "Can't you tell your mother that they must get out and about like normal people?"

I heard Dad turn some pages, no doubt heading for the sports section. "And why are they so secretive? Perhaps he daren't show her off. Perhaps he's got relatives who will object..."

Dad still made no comment.

"I mean to say... What's his background? And who and where *are* his people?"

"Dead as dodos," muttered Dad.

"Perhaps he hasn't got any means..."

The Daily Express was thrown to the floor. "Good God, what other objections are you going to drag up? A white man fraternising with an Untouchable? Or perhaps my mother mixing with a working class gardener? Or perhaps you think Muckey has a string of other women in tow?"

There was a long silence, apart from Mum's needles clashing furiously, reflecting her displeasure. "All I'm saying is that I think you should ask Muckey what his intentions are."

"Don't be bloody silly."

Dad picked up his paper again, ending the discussion.

21

*The war goes well – A visit to the Works – Old Percy's
tragedy – The sporting spirit at Hillhead – Coded
messages on the sportsfield – A new friend and a fresh
atmosphere at Silver Coombe.*

S o life went on: term-time, holidays; Silver Coombe,
Exmoor. The war situation continued to improve.
First Hitler was stopped short of Moscow and then
the Japanese bombed Pearl Harbor, and when I got back for
my Christmas holidays Dad was full of smiles as we tucked
into our Duck a l'Orange. "Adolf's goose is well and truly
cooked, Sajit," he said. "Now he's declared war on America
it's only a matter of time... Maybe quite a time... But time
only."

He was right. From thereon the arrows on our war maps
thrust forward, sparked off by El Alamein and Stalingrad. In
contrast, the old excitement centred around the activities of
the Home Guard simply petered out. The possibility of a
German invasion had disappeared and instead we were
invaded by Americans and more Canadians in a long build-
up to the second front.

Dad only once took me back to the Works. The bomb
damage had been cleared up but in and around Lomond
Grove gaps in the streets were everywhere and a common
sight was baths and wash basins hanging by their pipes

from shorn-off bathrooms. Everywhere I went people were pleased to see me but they had no hesitation in telling me that I was becoming a right little toff and it was time I spent more time with real people. Old Percy showed me around the works very proudly. Battery production and tyre re-treading was at its highest level ever and the new formation and lead reclamation shops were real showpieces. In the latter, I couldn't help staring down at the spot where I imagined Charlie had died.

"In the other corner," said Old Percy. "You mustn't brood on it, Nipper. There's tragedies in everyone's life."

I thought about it for a time and realised I'd already had a few tragedies. The four Jews at Edgware, Eddie, and now Charlie. "Do all people have lots of tragedies?" I asked.

"Betcha life, Nipper," chuckled Old Percy. "Most, anyhow. But you always get over them. Except for poor buggers like me. We have tragedies that go on and bloody on, all our bloody lives, don't we?"

"Really, Percy? What happened to you?"

"I got married, my old mate, didn't I?"

Back at Hillhead life was a long succession of sporting triumphs. Mr Steele's secret of success was to recruit his pupils from fathers who were known to be excellent sportsmen. It was a good way of securing talent and it meant that the fathers concerned seldom worried about their son's academic progress. That wasn't usually the case with mothers, but Mr Steele ignored them. Even mothers who took the trouble to visit the school regularly to support their son's teams were merely tolerated. Mr Steele had a code of conduct for them which he expected them to abide by or cease their visits. Once on the touch line, or settled in a deck chair a suitable distance from the pavilion, they had to remain silent. Mr Steele had no objection to them being decorative (indeed he clearly had an eye for a well-turned leg and was once heard to remark that one mother had 'flanks like a thoroughbred'), but if ever a female shriek of 'Come on, Hillhead!' was heard, Mr Steele cringed and despatched Bucket to issue a firm reprimand.

Such restrictions were justified. At Hillhead boys were terribly sensitive about their mother's behaviour and were highly embarrassed by anything out of the norm; and whilst Hillhead mothers rarely offended, mothers attached to other schools frequently disgraced themselves. One overwrought mother stormed the pavilion at West Buckland and assaulted the lad who had just run out her son for the third week in succession. Even worse, one neurotic mother actually ran on to the rugby field at Barnstaple screaming hysterically when her son was injured, and although he had sustained nothing more serious than a fractured skull, she insisted that he be carried off on a stretcher and that an ambulance be called.

Undoubtedly the greatest value I got out of Hillhead was a host of new friends. There were two boys in particular with whom friendship has lasted a lifetime.

The first was Ray Hegg. He was captain of everything, even trivial pursuits such as table tennis, draughts, billiards and snooker. He was small in stature but even as a boy he had a pocket-Hercules physique. He was by no means the best player at any given game, but he had two supreme qualities. He was the finest schoolboy fielder I've ever known and a vicious tackler on the rugby field. He also had a touch of fanaticism. He couldn't bear to lose and in fact he never did, yet he was able to temper this single-mindedness with sportsmanship of the highest order. With Ray Hegg in control, Mr Steele could rely on impeccable behaviour by Hillhead teams. For example at cricket, when a Hillhead boy knew he was out, he walked immediately and without question. If he was given out incorrectly, he still walked immediately and without question. Our bowlers never appealed against a batsman unless they were certain he was out, and even then they did it discreetly and politely, never in triumph.

John Hollands

When in the field, Hegg made sure every incoming batsman was applauded from the time he reached the edge of the square until he took guard, and when he was out – even if it was first ball, as was often the case – he was applauded back to the edge of the square. If he reached double figures before he was out he was applauded all the way back to the pavilion. Had anyone ever scored a fifty against us, Hegg would no doubt have led us in three cheers.

Hegg always fielded at silly midoff. This enabled him to pass a suitable word of sympathy every time a wicket fell. Even to the most useless batsman, Hegg always remarked: "I say, what rotten luck." If the batsman clearly had no idea of what had happened when facing our star fast bowler, Henry Bullock, Hegg would say: "Are you sure you were ready?" Bullock was so fast and dangerous that they were always quite certain they were ready.

As captain, Hegg was fortunate to have some superb games players under his command. Heading these was the aforementioned Henry Bullock, another boy I still count as a close friend. He was such a fast bowler that he often dismissed sides for single-figure scores. In the end, it became an unwritten rule with all our opponents that Hillhead batted first, otherwise Bullock – urged on by Hegg – simply ruined games. Once, a game started at 2.30 pm and was all over by 3.14 pm. Even so, it never occurred to Hegg to take Bullock off or give him a rest, or let someone else have a try in order to make a game of it. Furthermore, he resented every run that was scored against us. In a game at Minehead, Bullock had reduced the opposition to seven wickets down for 0 runs when a lad came in and by sheer luck slogged him for four.

Hegg wasn't having that. "Bullock," he yelled. "What are you doing? Any more loose stuff like that and Y.O."

'Y.O.' meant 'You're off!' and it was no idle threat. All of us bowlers lived in dread of that cry. Most of Hegg's other orders were given by way of initials. He claimed that it saved

Gran and Mr Muckey

time. An abbreviation which was music to my ears when shouted in my direction was 'N.O.P.E.'. This meant 'Next over pavilion end'. 'B.U.P.' meant 'Back up properly' and running between wickets was fertile ground for abbreviations. 'W.O.' meant 'Wait on'; 'T.O.T.P.' meant, 'Two or three probably'; 'G.B.Q.' meant, 'Get back quickly'; 'Y.H.T.H.' meant, 'You'll have to hurry!'; and 'O.G.S' meant, 'Oh gosh. Sorry!'.

At rugby, in which I was fly-half to Hegg's scrum-half, we had abbreviations to meet all situations, but things did occasionally go wrong when we tried to invent new ones. Bullock, who was my inside centre, once yelled to his fellow centre: "T.C.", meaning 'Try scissors', and this proved disastrous since his partner, who also couldn't spell, thought he meant, 'Try kicking'.

My other great friend at Hillhead was very different. He was a non-sporting boy who, to start with, was a complete misfit at Hillhead. As far as I know he was the only other boy who'd been sent there because he was judged to be soft in the head. It would have been much more fitting if they'd sent him to a school specialising in physical disabilities, an establishment where he could have been taught to co-ordinate his limbs. The poor fellow couldn't even catch a cricket ball, although he refused to give up trying. He even insisted on taking part in the catching practices Mr Steele held every evening during the summer. More often than not, he would miss the ball with his outstretched hands and be hit on the top of his head. This made an alarming, echoing sound, and although it excited lots of rude remarks about empty vessels making the most noise, it never seemed to do him any harm. Indeed, since he was assumed to be soft in the head when he arrived at Hillhead, and he ended his medical career as the top brain surgeon at Westminster Hospital, it could well have done him a power of good.

This new boy gained my respect right from the start. Although only eight years old, his parents – despite his suspect intelligence – had sent him on an unaccompanied journey to Hillhead of approximately 10,000 miles, starting from the South Pacific. With war raging around the globe, and the Japanese closing in on his homeland at a rate of knots, it was an epic if foolhardy adventure more suited to the likes of Phileas Fogg. It entailed sixteen different types of transport, 43 connections of one type or another, and got him dive-bombed and machine-gunned on two occasions. The journey started in a dugout war canoe and finished with him riding up the school drive at the crack of dawn on the back of Farmer Dawson's horse-drawn milk float.

The name of this young fellow was Gilbert Gilbert and he came from the Gilbert and Ellice Islands. We got on so well that I took him home with me to Silver Coombe in the holidays, it being impossible for him to keep returning to the Gilbert and Ellice Islands. Ignoring that the Gilbert side of the equation was now in Japanese hands, even if he'd gone straight there and then come straight back he would still have been late for the next term, so late that it would be time for him to go home again, thus condemning him to around five years of perpetual travel, deprived of home and education.

Gilbert was a big hit with everyone at Silver Coombe. He was the most well-adjusted and resilient person I've ever known and for a boy of his age his confidence and self-assurance was staggering. He conversed like an adult and because of this formed a very close friendship with James. When I introduced him to Gran, he raised his hands in admiration and astonishment.

"Well, well," he declared. "So here we have it. The foundation stone of the family. I've heard so much about you, Madam..."

"And Sajit has written to me about you as well..."

"Really? Excellent. Then since we apparently know each other so well, may I suggest, with your permission, that I call you Mother India?"

"That would be truly lovely," agreed Gran.

Gran and Mr Muckey

When I took Gilbert around to the potting shed to meet my friend Muckey, he said: "Ah, Mr Muckey. Heard a lot about you, sir. And especially about your prize marrows. And rather keen on Mother India, I gather?"

"Gran," I explained.

Muckey never said a word, just doffed his cap. He knew top breeding when he saw it.

Mum's reaction was more guarded. At first she viewed him with suspicion, as though he was too good to be true, but eventually, after Gilbert had followed in Corp's footsteps with some outrageous flattery, he won her over.

Dad had such a high opinion of Gilbert that every Saturday after dinner he would usher him, James, and myself into the study, leaving the others to listen to the artificial entertainment of 'In Town Tonight', 'Into Battle', and 'ITMA', our usual family routine. Dad would lay down a Havana smoke screen and then, as we lounged back in the leather arm chairs with tumblers of weak shandy in our hands, we talked and talked and talked. We enjoyed a degree of intimacy I had never known before and have seldom experienced since.

Gilbert told us how they clubbed sharks on their snouts in the shallow lagoons near his home, and of the snakes that hung from trees, ready to kill with a single strike; then he progressed on to the bizarre native customs and some of the equally odd twists of colonial administration and justice. In response, Dad opened up for the first time with fascinating stories of his childhood in India. Some were comic, how he'd roamed around in nothing but a loincloth and turban, and others were horrific, as when he was forced to beg in Calcutta near the site of the old Black Hole; and some would probably have been best left unmentioned, as when he was so desperate with hunger that he stole fruit off market stalls in Old Delhi.

When it came to my turn to chip in, I embarked upon my usual exaggerations. Dad never corrected me. He even nodded in agreement as I described incidents we both knew perfectly well had never happened. To him, it was all part of the entertainment, a refinement in the art of conversation, the very thing he was trying to instil in us.

Once, we were still going strong well after midnight. Eventually, Mum poked her head around the door and, in a manner she would never have adopted if Gilbert hadn't been there, said: "I'm sorry to interrupt, but it's well past the bedtime of you young gentlemen."

As Gilbert and I mounted the creaking stairs, he said: "Saj, I wish I could talk with my Pa like that."

22

Gilbert starts the riding bug – Mum comes a cropper –
Muckey the champion – Biking around Exmoor –
Hitler's secret weapon – A nasty shock.

James had become a weekly-boarder at Caterham and since I was a full-time boarder at Hillhead, it meant that we three brothers had long separations. It did everyone a power of good.

Gilbert continued to go back home with me during the holidays. He had plenty of offers to go elsewhere, but I was delighted when he rejected them in favour of returning to Silver Coombe. It was obvious to all of us that his presence had a unifying influence. He balanced the numbers so that there was never an odd man out. To Mum's delight I never resumed my bowling on the tennis court and, as though in appreciation of this, she took far greater interest in our activities. Every day at breakfast she would look around and say: "And what do you have planned for today?"

My brothers and I often stared back blankly but Gilbert always had positive ideas.

His best suggestion was to get properly organised with our bicycles. To enjoy ourselves, he argued, we had to be mobile. We had to get out and about, ride to places where things were happening. He took the bus to Godstone, bought himself a Raleigh (he had plenty of money), and rode it back, and in the evening he persuaded Dad that it was high time he updated our bicycles. Dad not only agreed but he got a new one for himself, preferring an upright model to his previous racer. He even bought a Hercules for Mum.

"Me bide a ricyle?" she exclaimed with delight as she was given her present. "I've never ridden one in my life."

Brother Nothing appointed himself riding instructor and taught her in the lane. He held the saddle at the rear and then ran along behind her as she pedalled. He must have done the equivalent to a marathon over the few days it took her to learn because she would never permit him to let go.

Eventually he did, without her knowing, and she went sailing up the lane in fine style, all the time shouting: "Don't let go." By sheer bad luck one of Lake's tractors suddenly appeared, coming in the opposite direction, taking up most of the lane. Mum half-turned for help and on seeing no one there, she panicked and plunged straight into the ditch. There she lay, trapped under her bicycle, her legs akimbo, giving the tractor driver (as she later put it), "A right bloody eyeful."

However, we convinced her that she'd ridden at least a hundred yards unaided and from thereon she never looked back. With the exception of Gran, who preferred to carry on helping Muckey, we became a mobile family.

On Saturday afternoons Dad headed a convoy to Redhill where we watched the local football team's home fixtures, and on Sunday afternoons we rode to such places as Horley, Copthorne and Lingfield, all of which boasted teahouses where we gorged ourselves on our favourite dish of baked beans on toast. On weekdays we were more ambitious and went across to Sam Marsh's Riding Stables near Edenbridge and hired out horses for the day. It was never as exciting as Exmoor, but we enjoyed the horsy atmosphere so much that we went to all the local gymkhanas and agricultural shows. Being full of devilment, Gilbert and I took back to Muckey the most exaggerated stories about how much bigger the marrows were in Kent and Sussex, but he was never impressed.

"Clear off you young buggers," he'd mutter. "Them bleeders could never bloody beat me."

During an Easter holiday Gilbert became fascinated by Dad's old racing bike. He oiled it up and then raced it up and down the lane. One day he took me aside.

"Saj, has it never occurred to you that we could make a smashing speedway track around the grounds of Silver Coombe?" He then walked me around the perimeter footpath. "Being loose gravel it'll make an ideal track. Great for skidding around the corners."

After a trial ride, I was convinced. I brought Brother Nothing and James in on it and they were just as enthusiastic. So we stripped Dad's old bike down to basics and took it in turns to hare round our new track. The corners were fantastic. We put the bike into a sideways drift, stuck a leg out in the manner of speedway riders, and fairly streaked round them, sending a great shower of loose gravel into the air.

Trouble struck when Brother Nothing went hurtling along the back fence. When he got to the corner and put the bike into a slide, Muckey happened to walk out of his potting shed and was showered by gravel. He cursed and swore in his usual way, but Nothing sped on, recording the fastest time yet. James went next, only to find that Muckey had acted with corresponding speed. Just around the corner of the potting shed he'd erected a barrier of three planks.

For the rest of the day there was an impasse. Gilbert had a word with Gran that night and together they hatched up a plan of action. The following morning Gilbert and I went round to apologise to Muckey for not having consulted him first. Then Gilbert played his trump card. "Now look, Mr Muckey, let's be perfectly honest about this, old chap...

Mother India says you're against our track because you're too old to do it yourself."

This provoked a sustained spell of swearing which was pretty extreme even for Muckey. However, the upshot of it was that he accepted a challenge to ride around the course. Getting him on the bike was a major problem. Every time he tried to cock his leg over, his foot never got higher than the pedals – about the same height as Lucky cocking his gammy leg against a tree. In fact, Muckey's efforts to mount were so reminiscent of Lucky leaving his visiting card that we dissolved into laughter. Eventually, while Gilbert, my brothers, and I, lifted Muckey bodily, Gran slipped the bike in beneath him. Once he'd acclimatised himself, we lined him up with Magog for the start.

To be fair, Muckey had obviously ridden a bike many times before and the old saying is true: once you've learnt to ride one, you never forget. It was only on the corners that he looked likely to come off. As he came into the finishing stretch, we called out: "Come on, Muckey. Come on. You'll break the record."

He responded well, pedalling like mad. When he reached Magog, Brother Nothing grabbed the bike and James caught hold of him so that he didn't fall off. Gilbert and I rushed up to congratulate him. "You did it, Muckey. The fastest by two seconds."

As Muckey shuffled off towards the potting shed, with Gran at his side, clutching him firmly as though he was seeking his land-legs after an Atlantic crossing, we heard him say: "Bloody young buggers. As though I couldn't ride a bleeding bike."

When we told Dad about Muckey's record he wanted to get in on the act. Amazingly, he took Muckey's record seriously and first thing on Saturday morning he had a go at beating it. Of course, we pretended that he was miles off. Not that he minded. In fact, he enjoyed it so much that he reeled off a host of ideas as to how we could improve the track and for the rest of that marvellous holiday speedway racing held sway over everything else.

We knew Dad was up to something special when he told Gilbert and me to take our bikes along to South Godstone station at the same time as our trunks and make sure they were properly labelled up for Hillhead. When we told him that no one had bikes at Hillhead, he smiled and said: "They will when you take yours there, won't they?"

On arrival at Hillhead for the summer term we discovered that the local farmer and handyman was finishing off a new bike shed and inside were six brand new bikes. We knew Dad had donated them because they were white, identical to our own. In Mr Steele's opening address to the school, in which he welcomed new boys and outlined the fixtures he had lined up for us, he also mentioned that because it was increasingly difficult to fit everyone into a full programme of riding on the moor, cycling would now be introduced, thanks to the generosity of a parent who wished to remain anonymous.

The bikes were never as popular as the horses, of course, but they did enable us to see Exmoor from a different angle.

That summer term should have been superlative. Quite apart from our adventures on the moor, we had the best cricket team the school had ever known. Henry Bullock was more devastating then ever and I had a very successful time with my leg-breaks and googlies. What pleased Ginger and Mr Steele was that whilst Bullock could wipe out other prep schools, I was able to winkle out the more mature batsmen in the junior colts sides of the public schools.

We were, I suppose, living in a fool's paradise. Having previously been so interested and involved in the war, I should have known better, but I'm ashamed to say that I scarcely took any notice of all the momentous things that were happening. On June 6th the second front was launched and then, only a few weeks later, Hitler sent over the first of his new secret weapon, the doodlebugs or flying bombs, vicious things which droned noisily across the sky and then, once their engines had cut out, glided silently towards their destination. It meant one could anticipate the area where they would land and this bred a new style of anxiety and Silver Coombe was once again in the thick of things.

A main route for the doodlebugs was over East Grinstead, Blindley Heath, South Godstone, and Caterham, and then on to Croydon and central London. At first, their threat seemed insurmountable. There was even talk of the mass evacuation of London; but then the panic calmed down, people got used to them, and stories began to emerge which placed them in their true perspective. Some of them behaved in a most eccentric manner. For no apparent reason they would suddenly turn around and retrace their steps, with the populace waving farewell to them as they headed back towards the continent to give (everyone hoped) Hitler and his friends an very unpleasant surprise. Another story to delight us was that an Australian pilot had pioneered a technique of tipping their wings and diverting them into open spaces. We had visions of squadrons of Spits meeting them in the channel and sending them off to the Atlantic or the North Sea.

It was a gloriously sunny afternoon, the type that proclaimed the west country to be one of the best spots on earth. The only sound was the much-eulogised beat of leather on willow. We were having what Ginger called an open practice and I was bursting with pride, having just taken my first hat-trick. Then, unnoticed by most, a boy came running down from the school and handed Mr Steele a slip of paper. He read it, returned it to the boy, and sent him back to the school. A few minutes later he called me over. He was strangely uncommunicative. He didn't even mention my hat-trick. He merely told me to report to Bucket.

Gran and Mr Muckey

She was waiting in her surgery. Her normal smile and composure were conspicuously absent. She was nervous and agitated. "Sajit, my dear Sajit... I'm afraid I have some bad news for you... Things haven't been easy for your people at home, Sajit...Please sit down, Sajit..."

I sat on the edge of her surgery chair. I was alarmed by the way she kept using my first name. She moved round behind me and placed her hands gently on my shoulders. I felt them tremble.

"As I say, things haven't been easy, Sajit. And you've heard all about this wicked new weapon of Hitler's...The doodlebugs... The flying bombs... Well, I'm afraid one has landed near your home. Not on your house, but near it... On somewhere called Lake's field..."

Without looking round I knew tears were trickling from her eyes. "Sajit, I'm terribly sorry to have to tell you this, but your grandmother has been killed."

I was too stunned to say anything. Gran killed! That was the last thing I had expected. I stared straight ahead. I knew what Bucket had said. I understood her perfectly, but I couldn't absorb it. Gran, an Indian, an old lady, an Untouchable: killed by Hitler. It was preposterous, so futile. I tried to speak, to protest, to query, but no words came. My mouth opened and shut, but I couldn't utter a sound. My tongue was stuck to the roof of my mouth.

For what seemed an eternity Bucket talked on, trying to comfort me, urging me to be brave. Eventually I turned to face her. She was dabbing her cheeks with a handkerchief. In her other hand was a telegram.

"Your dog also, Sajit," she whispered. "You have a dog, don't you? Muckey?"

I went as cold as ice. Goose pimples spread over my entire body. I stretched out a hand and took the telegram from her. It read:

"Tell Sajit kindest possible Gran fatally injured
Doodlebug edge of Lake's field Muckey also killed Stop
Mrs Contractor."

I managed to gulp. My voice returned, a barely audible croak:

"Oh no! Not Gran **and** Mr Muckey."

THE EXPOSED

"I found The Exposed moving and extremely convincing. George was a wonderful character, brilliantly real and fresh, and the Japanese heroine (Katsumi) tremendously likable and convincing. The evocation of the era and the eye for the details of that time were most impressive."

Maeve Haran, author of *Having it All.*

"A wonderful story, superbly told, just crying out to be made into a film."

Guy Bellamy, Author of *The Secret Lemonade Drinker.*

"Marvellous characters. It's a superb piece of work."

John Pawsey, Literary Agent.

"Katsumi (the heroine) is just amazing."

David Grossman, Literary Agent.

"Katsumi is, of course, wonderful ... The whole thing is first class!"

David Bolt, author of *Author's Handbook.*

"The development of the relationship between George and Katsumi is delicately and beautifully handled. As a love story it works superbly, with all the right ingredients."

Bernard Boucher, author of *Opalesque.*

"Quite brilliant. Plot, setting, characterisation, all superb and most perceptive of human nature."

P Brooke Smith, Retired English Literature Tutor.

"A fascinating read. The love story is touchingly told: very funny and ultimately very moving. At times it takes one to the depths of despair but, in the end, its profoundly inspiring message is dramatically and effectively revealed ... A very fine piece of work ..."

John Hogston, author of *Hawker's War.*

"John Hollands has written the most superb novel ... His easy style and well-drawn characters will make it a sure-fire

A selection of titles available from
EDWARD GASKELL *publishers* and Lazarus Press

1-898546-31-2   *The Way of a Transgressor* Negley Farson   £23.00 h/b
First published in 1936, this enthralling autobiography was heralded by
The New York Times as 'a truly enchanting book ...' This new edition
contains many previously unseen photographs and a comprehensive index.

1-898546-37-1   *Journal of a North Devon Nature Lover*
                                Stewart Beer   £7.99 p/b
The author's observations of flora and fauna in this beautifully written and
elegantly illustrated Journal form a month by month, season by season,
pilgrimage through the miracles of nature.

1-898546-25-8   *Slaves of Rapparee*   Pat Barrow   £9.99 p/b
In 1796 *The London* was wrecked off Ilfracombe, North Devon. Chained
below decks were more than one hundred black prisoners. This book tells
the story of Pat Barrow's quest to unravel the intriguing and controversial
story behind the wreck and its human cargo, and make the truth known.

1-898546-40-1   *Knights of Raleigh Manor* Pat Barrow   £14.99 h/b
The chance discovery of a site at Littabourne Park, Pilton led to a five year
excavation which yielded many exciting medieval finds. The artefacts
supported the author's theory that the site was used as a camp and that
jousting took place there. This is the fascinating story of his discovery.

1-898546-39-8   *The Dawn Stand-to*   Christopher Hiscox
                                            £17.99 h/b
The biography of IVB (Peter) Mills. At 18, Peter left home in search of
adventure in Kenya. He joined the Kenya Police and was posted to the
Northern Frontier District. Promotions followed and, as a high-ranking
officer, Peter played a crucial role in the war against the Mau-Mau.

1-898546-34-7   *One Man's Boer War – The 1900 Diary of John Edward
                    Pine-Coffin*, Edited by Susan Pine-Coffin. £19.00 h/b
The diary begins on 16th February 1900 as John Edward Pine-Coffin set
off with his regiment from Pembroke Camp. Illustrated with rare
photographs, this diary tells the story of the Boer war more poignantly than
any history book could.

All titles are available post free from:
Lazarus Press, Unit 7 Caddsdown Business Park, Bideford,
Devon EX39 3DX • Tel: 01237 421195 • Fax: 01237 425520 •
email: lazaruspress@aol.com • www.lazaruspress.com
A catalogue of all our publications is available upon request.